CROSS MY HEART

Maureen McCarthy

Puffin Books

Puffin Books
Penguin Books Australia Ltd
487 Maroondah Highway, PO Box 257
Ringwood, Victoria 3134, Australia
Penguin Books Ltd
Harmondsworth, Middlesex, England
Viking Penguin, A Division of Penguin Books USA Inc.
375 Hudson Street, New York, New York 10014, USA
Penguin Books Canada Limited
10 Alcorn Avenue, Toronto, Ontario, Canada M4V 3B2
Penguin Books (N.Z.) Ltd
182–190 Wairau Road, Auckland 10, New Zealand

First published by Penguin Books Australia, 1993
3 5 7 9 10 8 6 4

Typeset in Malaysia by Longman Malaysia
Made and printed in Australia by Australian Print Group, Maryborough, Victoria

National Library of Australia
Cataloguing-in-Publication data:

McCarthy, Maureen, 1953–
Cross my heart.

ISBN 0 14 C36350 5.

I. Title.

A823.3

CROSS MY HEART

Maureen McCarthy was born in Melbourne in 1953. She has worked as a teacher in Victorian secondary schools and has written scripts for television and educational films including the SBS mini-series *In Between*, which was adapted to four novels. Her previous novel *Ganglands* was published in 1992.

Maureen lives in Melbourne with her husband and three children.

'I'm interested in the emerging adult from sixteen to the early twenties – the wild time when relationships are shifting, sexual identity is fiercely sought and life is imbued with conflicting desires and emotions.'

Maureen McCarthy

Cross My Heart was shortlisted for the 1993 NSW Premier's Literary Award (children's books).

For my parents, Edna and Jack,
with love

I would like to thank Bernie Geary, the
director of the Brosnan Centre Youth Service
in Brunswick. Thanks also to some of
the ex-offenders there, who spoke so willingly
about their lives when I was
researching this novel.

1

Michelle had a feeling something would happen the night of the party. A vague slippery sensation at the back of her brain told her things were building up but she couldn't work out *to what* exactly. The feeling would catch her unawares every now and again and leave her wondering. What could possibly happen now? More than ever before, everything had truly wound up. There was the engagement party next week for starters and then the wedding in a month. She'd thought it all through and couldn't see that anything else *could* happen.

The morning of the engagement party Michelle got up early as usual. She went to the toilet and threw up as she'd done every morning for the last six weeks, then had a shower and got dressed in the jeans she'd worn the day before – a bit floppy now because of her weight loss – and a checked shirt and worn windcheater. She ran her fingers through her thick dark hair and tried to avoid looking at herself in the mirror. Anyone would look like a dog in the light that bounced off these poky pale-green walls.

'Hey. Ya got more coffee?' It was her father's voice bawling out from the kitchen at her mother.

Michelle squeezed past the step-chair out into the passage way and then into her bedroom. She'd have to have something to eat soon or she'd faint. If only her father would get out of the kitchen so she could go and have a cup of tea and a bit of toast in peace. It was her favourite part of the day but only if she was left alone. Him sitting there, huffing and grunting around in his seat as he read the paper, smoking those foul cigarettes and slurping his tea, ruined everything. The thought of his fat red fingers on each side of the crackling newspaper made a familiar coil of nausea start up again in the pit of her stomach.

Stop it, she snapped silently to herself. *Just stop it!*

He usually left the house by eight to be at work at ten past. She stared into her own eyes in the dressing-table mirror, chilled suddenly by the depths of blueness there. They were like a couple of small bottomless lakes, heavy with promise and secrets. Her mouth spread into a tight little smile as she continued to stare. 'Michelle Brown,' she whispered to herself. 'Seventeen years old and full of unfathomable secrets.'

Well, one big one anyway. Her mouth twisted wryly. But not a secret any longer. There hadn't been much point trying to hide what would become so very obvious in a few months. She remembered the suppressed glee on the faces of her so-called friends when they'd heard the news. Bitches, all of them. Michelle watched herself lightly run one pointed finger over her nose and down to the very pale skin of her throat. Porcelain. White and hard as the old basin in the bathroom. She pulled back and looked away, listening. There was some movement out there in the kitchen. Cupboard doors banging and then the kettle being filled. Damn it. He was going to be there for some time yet.

When Michelle eventually did walk out into the bright little orange and tan kitchen at the back of the house he was sitting exactly as she'd imagined: at the table, face obscured by the newspaper, a curl of white smoke twisting up into the air from the cigarette in his left hand. A small heavy man, dressed in sombre greys and browns: perfectly pressed grey trousers and a thin mottled jumper stretched across a heavy gut. Michelle made herself speak.

'Morning.'

The paper rustled and shifted aside. His eyes met hers briefly. The large, freshly shaven face, grey, with an un-healthy pink spot on each cheek, nodded passively then immediately disappeared again. Michelle walked over to the kettle, relieved to find it almost full and already hot. The oily sweet smell of his slicked back thinning grey hair was already hitting her nostrils. She lit the gas and held her hands over the blue flame for a minute before settling the kettle on to it. It was cold outside again today. She knew, without having been outdoors or even looking out the window. An odd autumn. Rain every morning for the past week, followed by bitter winds for the rest of the day. It didn't seem to matter what she put on, Michelle couldn't get warm. The coldness went right through into her bones. Those piercing winds, throwing up leaves and debris into the air, stinging eyes and biting people's faces. The last few weeks she'd lain awake each night listening to it batter the walls of her parents' small, weatherboard home, half-believing it was trying to get at her. Never before had the house felt so flimsy, nor had everything about her life seemed so lightweight.

'Well, big night tonight, eh?'

Michelle jumped at the sound of his voice, almost spilling the boiling water over her hand instead of into the waiting pot. Making conversation. This was a turn-up.

'Yeah . . .'

'That young bloke of yours gonna be playing tomorrow?'

'Yeah . . . I think so.'

They both knew he would be playing, so what was this about?

She turned the teapot around three times and then poured herself a cup. It was easier to put up with his usual grumpy bad humour. What did he want her to say? She had a sudden desire to ask him if he wanted to have a cup of tea but stopped herself in time. They weren't that kind of family.

'I might get him to help me with the keg for the party . . .?'

Was he asking her if Kev would do that?

'Yeah, well, he'll help . . .' she mumbled.

'Okay,' her father grunted, as though everything was sweet between them. Michelle sat down, suddenly dizzy. She didn't even know Kev well enough to say if he was the sort of guy who would help out or not. She supposed he would. How could he refuse? After all it was his party too.

Before all this happened she'd been about to give him the flick but now it looked like she was going to marry him. The shock of it knocked her flat every morning. She'd wander around, like Rocky staggering around the ring from a punch to the head. It was hard even to see straight.

Better get this tea into me somehow and make some toast. But suddenly the bread seemed a long way away. She closed her eyes and prayed her father would get up soon and leave the room. But he continued to sit there, solid as a rock. Michelle took a few sips of the scalding tea and stumbled to the back door. She could see her mother pruning back the roses, the prickly debris lying in tidy vicious heaps around each bush. Would it be worth trying to get past and out on to the street without drawing attention to herself?

Feeling the few notes in her pocket reminded her of the new cafe that had opened last week in the centre of town. She could walk down there and eat something before the prying crowds came out to shop. Her mother looked up and gave a tight smile. Michelle turned away, making out she didn't see. *Smiles now, is it? And chirpy conversations instead of the wall of hush. They must have discussed a thing or two before I got up.*

The Commodore purred along the town's main street towards the pub. In the front, both her parents sat immobile, staring ahead, impassive as statues. They might have been going to a funeral. Michelle felt like a ten-year-old again as she hunched into the corner of the back seat, angry in her short tight black skirt, studded leather jacket and boots, staring out the window, wishing again that it was all over. Not just the party, but the wedding, the honeymoon and the kid. Everything. Just thinking about all she still had to go through made her jittery.

Friday night and the centre of the town's wide main street was desolate, gleaming like thick wet paint in the soft rain. A few cafes were open but there were no people about except at the video store. There'd be a heap of people at the pub already though; she'd bet on that with anyone. The word about the free booze would have gone around the town like a bushfire.

Hey, Alan Brown's turning on a keg for his daughter!
For who?
Ya know! Little Shelly Brown. Up the duff to Kevin Buckley.
Yeah?
Yeah.
They haven't been goin' together long, have they?
Nah. Few months. Ya comin'?
Too right! I'll be there.

They'd all be there, dressed up and getting stuck into it. Priming themselves for the jokes when she and Kevin arrived. He was the town's star centre-half-forward so everyone knew him. Would he be there yet? She pulled her skirt down as far as she could and plucked at the few tiny white balls of fluff that had appeared on her tights after the last wash. He'd really starred the week before. Kicked three goals in the last quarter just when everyone thought they were done. Her father had come home red-faced, smacking one fist into the other open palm, unable to contain his simmering excitement. Michelle had made the mistake of going out to the garage with the old newspapers exactly as he'd arrived home in the car. Bad timing.

'That little Kevin's got guts,' he spat at her, unable to stop himself.

'Oh, yeah . . .'

'That kid can tackle . . .'

Michelle wavered, unsure how to respond. Should she pretend to be surprised or pleased or . . .? Anyway it was embarrassing. She had no interest in football. *A kid? I'm marrying a kid, am I?*

'You need any cigarettes?' her father asked his wife.

'Yeah. Better get a carton . . .'

'Well, hurry then. Don't want to be late . . .'

He veered the car over to the lighted milk bar and her mother got out, slamming the door. Michelle stared after the tight bunch of new blonde-tipped curls on the bustling head, and prayed that she would hurry back and that her father wouldn't try to talk to her.

It wasn't a bad town as country towns went. It was the same as it had always been: close and friendly or dreary and confining, depending on your point of view. Michelle used to think it was okay. It was where she'd been born, where she went to school, where she'd probably end up too. So what? One place was as good as anywhere else. It all depended on your attitude; if you wanted to whinge all day about how boring everything was then that's how your life would turn out, boring. That was the way she'd been brought up to think: the accepted local way of looking at things. *But is that really the way I think about it?* A deep shiver went right through her. Somehow the standard line was wearing thin, rotting away at the seams like a bit of tattered curtain. Saying that kind of stuff over and over to herself as she'd been doing lately made her go numb inside.

'Your brothers coming tonight?' He spoke gruffly to show he didn't care one way or the other. How would she know! Why didn't he use their names? *Why can't he just ask if Darren and Wayne are going to the party?*

'I dunno.'

He shrugged and grunted, pretending it was nothing to him. He cared desperately about both the boys, Michelle knew that. His eyes would go all soft when they were mentioned but Michelle tried not to see. It was too awful knowing it and then hearing them fight whenever they were together. The old man just couldn't help himself. He cared so much that it made him lash out when he was with them, berating them about jobs and bad friends and saving money; about all the mistakes they were making. They both hated him or said they did. Lately though she'd noticed that whenever she saw Wayne or Darren they kept bringing the conversation back to their father, like dogs digging up an old bone they thought they'd finished with ages ago.

Her mother was taking a long time in the shop and the silence between herself and her father was thickening. That would be one good thing about marrying Kev. *I won't have to sit like this with my father ever again.* He'd not said one unnecessary word to her for the past six weeks. Not one. What did he have to be so hoity-toity about? A tiny coal of fury immediately began to flare as it always did in his presence. She'd found out from her mother a few months ago that they'd had to get married themselves when they were twenty. Just the same as was happening to her and Kev now. It was just the same. Next time he had a go at her she'd throw that one up in his face.

It was a relief to notice a couple of kids walking along the footpath laughing and sharing a can of drink. She strained forward. One of them looked like he had a bomb under his arm. *A bomb exploding in the main street is just what this place needs.* As they ambled closer she recognised Ben and Joe Carruthers – twin brothers who'd been in her class last year. They were carrying a couple of videos. She sighed and thought longingly of lying alone in front of the television watching something. Anything. The twins' father was a popular local cop and the boys were both good-humoured smart-alecs who did anything for a laugh. Tonight, Michelle kept her head low. She'd have to pretend she didn't know them unless they recognised her. School was finished now. Along with everything else.

'Well, here they are!'

A rough hand grabbed her elbow and another one slapped her father's back. Michelle gulped self-consciously and hid behind her mother as she entered the warm noisy pub and felt, rather than saw, a sea of faces turning towards her.

'Here she is.'

'Little Shelly Brown.'

'G'day, love!'

'Er ... g'day, Mr Johnson.'

The room started to rock slightly as she looked around and tried to smile. There were a lot of her cousins over in one corner and the kids she worked with in K-Mart on Saturdays sitting by the fire, then people from church and Jim and Margaret Handley with their three bashful teenage sons. She could see the daughter Marie, who was her age, holding back, looking embarrassed. They'd sat together in history earlier that year. All through February poring over the same book and taking notes from the board. Marie had copied the last paragraph of Michelle's first essay and got caught. Now, two months later, it was hard to believe.

Everyone was here. *And everything about this is wrong.* All the guys from the footy club, Kevin included, were standing by the bar with their assorted girlfriends and wives sitting in a ring of chairs around them. All of them turning towards her and her parents.

'On ya, Alan!' the men almost shouted, pumping her father's arm.

'Good on you, love. Congratulations!'

Margaret Handley's plump face pressed against her own.

'Mum said you weren't feeling too well, love ...'

The woman's firm hands held Michelle a few centimetres away from her for a second or two as though she was a doll, breathing into her face and expecting Michelle to say something.

'It'll pass, you know ... in a few weeks ...'

'I'm okay. Thanks, Margaret.' Michelle tried not to mumble but she wished the woman would let her go. Her breath smelt strong and Michelle noticed all the little hairs growing around the moles on her face.

There was more kissing; people lined up and took their turns. None of the men could look her in the face for more than a second. Eventually, when most of the greetings were over, Kevin came over with a glass of beer and gave her a wet kiss on the cheek.

'G'day, babe.'

'G'day ...' As neutral as she could make it. 'How are you?'

'Hey, Kev! Cut it out!' A few guffaws behind them which were thankfully drowned in the wash of general conversation starting up again. Kevin's short fair hair, sitting up in spikes, was still a little wet. He smelt clean, very clean, and washed and young – like somebody's kid brother. *This is all wrong.* He was holding her hand and swinging it a little, smiling sheepishly. With the other he held out the glass.

'Want a drink?'

Michelle shook her head, still smiling nervously.

'How come you always ask that? I don't drink beer.'

It was meant to be jokey but came out wrong. He immediately bristled and put the beer down.

'Sorry I asked ...'

She panicked to see him so readily take offence.

'I didn't mean ... that ...'

God, did this mean she had to apologise? *Is this seriously happening? I have to live with him?*

Someone handed her an orange juice and she looked around, aware of Kevin standing sulkily beside her still

9

holding her hand but looking away. She didn't even know what he ate for breakfast or if he was interested in anything ... apart from football. Did he even like kids? A strange kid that would be his – and hers. *God, this is unreal.*

'I've come to ask Michelle to marry me ...' Kevin had blurted out in her parents' lounge room as soon as he arrived. It was about a week after she'd told him she was pregnant. Apart from one cursory phone call she hadn't heard from him at all and was so surprised to see him looking subdued and serious on her front doorstep that she didn't even ask him in.

'What do you want?' she'd snarled instead.

He shrugged, not looking at her.

'Your parents home?'

'Yeah.'

'Can I come in?'

She'd shrugged sourly and held the door open. Neither her mother or father had waited to see what she had to say. They didn't even look at her. Both of their puffed-up worried faces flew open and her mother started to cry.

'Oh, Kev ... I knew you were a good sort of kid.'

Her father grabbed his hand, shaking it wildly and Michelle looked on dumbfounded. *Would I have said yes if they'd asked me?*

Later, when he'd gone, they went through his credentials with her as if they couldn't believe her good fortune.

'Well, he's a plucky little bloke to come in like that.'

'Owns his own car ... Mazda, isn't it?'

'Yeah,' Michelle said. She wasn't sure if he owned it but it made a nice change to have them pleased about something.

'How old did he say?'

'Twenty-two ...'

'Good job at Steigers Garage too ... more than you could say about a lot of young blokes around here.' Her mother was unpacking the groceries, talking to no one in particular.

'We can have the wedding in May.'

'Comes from a decent enough family too,' her father slipped in.

Her mother stopped and sniffed a little as she remembered Kevin's mother.

'I've never liked his mother much, but never mind that.'

Michelle stifled a laugh. That sniff meant her mother was suspicious of Kevin's mother. Probably because Joan was so friendly and easy-going; a big woman with loud opinions who always gave the impression that life was too short to be bothered saying anything she didn't mean. *So unlike her sulky self-centred son.*

Conversation amongst the guests dipped and flowed around her, the voices buzzing along steadily, cracking up every now and again into giggles and little squeals of laughter. *At me? Are they laughing at me?* The room was now divided into men and women. The latter were sitting around the tables holding glasses of moselle and picking every now and again at plates of nuts and chips and club sandwiches; talking intimately and seriously to each other. *What about?* Michelle looked around wonderingly as she sat next to Kevin by the fire. It was hot sitting there, listening to those guys all prattling on about the football. Every now and again a couple of girls tried to engage her in conversation about the wedding, what she was going to wear and how many people were coming, and she answered as best she could but knew she fell way short of the accepted gossipy tone. She just couldn't concentrate. *Darren and Wayne aren't here.*

She looked over to where her mother and a few other older women were laughing and joking as they hovered around another large table, setting down plates of chicken, bowls of salad and cutlery. A proper supper would be served soon. Kevin and his mates' conversation was boring.

So what? She knew she only had to go and plonk herself next to someone at the other end of the room and they'd let her join in. But who? Everyone seemed so taken up and busy. *My brothers haven't come . . . why not?*

Most of the men still stood at the bar. Some of them were only a year older than her. Nineteen-year-olds she'd been at school with only twelve months ago, most of them only one class ahead of her, now standing like grown-up men with glasses in their hands and shaven faces and intense looks. They spoke slowly, watching each other as they drank, grinning sheepishly every now and again as they traded jokes and jibes about football and marriage, babies and work. She could tell they were wondering when she was going to get up and go and talk with the other women.

She did get up but not to talk to anyone. The heat from the fire was making her feel faint. She needed to go to the toilet, to get out of this room and wash her face. *If my brothers don't care about me, who does?*

Both of them had been very quiet when she'd gone out to the little run-down farmhouse they were renting with another unemployed farm labourer about two kilometres out on the other side of town. She told them the news and they both just grunted and went on with what they were doing. Darren was trying to fix a hole in the kitchen roof that had flooded the room the night before and Wayne was cleaning out his shotgun in the grubby little lounge room, listening to loud hard music.

They both looked sombre when Michelle finished speaking, but said nothing. Michelle wished that they'd tell her they were disappointed or angry. Anything rather than no reaction. Eventually, when the album finished, Wayne got up and asked her if she wanted him to go and bash up Kevin. When she said that she didn't see much point in doing that, there didn't seem to be anything left to say. *Maybe I imagined I was close to them.*

As she left for home she only just stopped short of apologising, for disappointing them. She knew they used to be proud of the way she was good at school.

'Ask Shell. She'll know how to work that out . . .'

'What's that word mean, Shelly?'

Michelle had cried all the way home. *Stuff 'em all! It's my life, isn't it? My life that's getting messed up. Why should I have to apologise?*

Michelle headed for the Ladies'. When she got inside she bent over the basin and splashed cold water on her face. Too bad about the make-up she'd applied earlier. Anyway, if she thought about it, there wasn't one person out there that she wanted to impress. Wiping her face with a paper towel, she entered one of the lavatory cubicles and slumped on to a seat, staring in front of her. *Something is eating me. Something is eating away at me.*

She thought of the tiny life growing inside her and closed her eyes. Never had she ever had any desire for a child. No feelings of wanting to love and protect. And she knew that wouldn't change over the next months. Kids and babies had never been part of her scene. Just another way she knew she was different to the other girls at school and the ones she worked with at K-Mart. They actually liked babies, liked the whole idea of being married and settling down to look after kids. It had never entered her mind. In fact she had often thought that it would be something she most definitely didn't want to do. And here she was, with the whole thing escalating into a bigger unmanageable mess by the minute. *I've got to make something happen. Something has got to give.*

The day before Kevin came around to propose marriage she'd been sitting at the table eating dinner with her father.

'So you say it's only a few weeks late?' her father said.

Michelle nodded sourly and pushed the vegetables around on her plate.

'Well,' he went on, 'Mum reckons ... that you could be seen to, without too much trouble ...'

Michelle started suddenly. *Do they really think I haven't considered this?* She stared over at her mother who was crimson-faced and averting her eyes as usual, handing out the food and acting as though none of this had anything to do with her.

'You mean an abortion?' Michelle enjoyed saying the word and watching them flinch. Her mother snapped back angrily.

'No! Not that. You could have a curette at this stage, I'm sure.'

Michelle didn't know why she felt so angry. Couldn't understand it at all. *Hell!* She wanted to smash the woman's head into her bowl of soup and hold her down by the back of the neck and drown her in it.

'Oh, yeah,' she said. Her own voice felt like paint stripper in her mouth.

'Like getting an annulment instead of a divorce ...?'

Her father stood up and slapped her across the face twice, hard both times, on both cheeks with his flat heavy open hand.

'You little tramp! Don't you get smart with your mother like that!'

Michelle gasped and reeled backwards with the impact. The shock of the hot stinging pain on her face brought tears to her eyes. She jumped up from the table but her father stood up too and made a grab for her. Michelle was too quick.

'Leave me alone! You old bastard!' she screamed at him and ran from the room.

'Come here and sit down! Finish your dinner!' His voice thundered after her but Michelle was out the door. He would have to kill her before she'd go back to that table. Once in her room she quickly pulled the small bookcase over the doorway and then piled a couple of chairs on top of it. If he wanted to get at her again, he'd have to fight his way in. She stood in the middle of the room, shaking with rage and trying to think. *If only Veronica was alive. She'd know what I should do.* Finally she threw herself face down on the bed and simply cried.

The door into the toilets creaked open and bodies shuffled through. Michelle sat up stiffly and listened.

'So you'll have them all off your hands soon . . .' An older woman was speaking. But the other one was her mother. Michelle could tell by the little sigh she gave as an answer before going on in her own best voice.

'Ah, yes. I think this might be just what Michelle needs.'

Michelle's fists clenched and she had a wild impulse to pull off the silver toilet-roll holder and throw it over the top of the cubicle at her.

The other woman grunted in agreement. *Who is she? The interfering old bitch.*

'I think you're right, Bev. Settle her down a bit. She's never been an easy girl for you, has she?'

'No. Never easy. And she's given me hell the last couple of years.'

'Ah, well, she'll settle down now . . .'

'She'll have to!' It was said bitterly with an acid little laugh.

'With a baby . . . she'll have to settle down.'

The other woman sniggered and pulled paper from the container. Michelle could hear her pulling it out, crushing it up and getting more out. *How much toilet paper does one person need, for God's sake?*

'Do her good to have to think of someone else for a change.'

'I couldn't agree more . . . she'll grow up. You just watch.'

Michelle got up as quietly as she could and went back to the party.

It went on for a couple of hours. Supper, speeches and a bit of dancing. But it didn't get any better. She watched everyone getting drunk around her and felt increasingly cold and sleepy. The music thumped around inside her head. Each song was like the one before and she didn't recognise any of them. She just sat quietly by Kevin most of the time, unable to make herself leave his side. Eventually even he noticed it.

'Hey, babe, you don't seem too good,' he whispered at one stage. He'd been having a grand time joking and boozing along with his mates and had forgotten her.

'I'm okay . . .'

She looked up at him and was surprised to see real concern in his eyes.

'Listen, Michelle. If you want to go home, I'll take you.'

She wavered. It would be good to go home. To be in bed away from everything.

'Well, I do feel a bit . . .'

He got up straight away.

'I'll take you back.' And then more gently than she'd ever heard him speak, 'Everyone reckons the sickness only lasts a little while . . .'

She smiled and took his hand, suddenly remembering the first time she'd held it like this. After the film that neither of them had liked much, he'd reached for her hand quite naturally. Although she'd half admired the assertive way he'd told her that they'd go and have a coffee and then head on to a party out the other side of town, she knew then that she didn't really want to go. But how do you go about telling someone that what they've planned for you isn't what you wanted at all? She smiled grimly, remembering herself wondering that at the time.

On their way out the pub door they ran into Michelle's parents putting on their coats. Her mother smiled at them both.

'You off now, too?'

'Michelle doesn't feel too good.'

Her father didn't even look at her directly as he spoke.

'Well, we were just going. You want us to run her home, Kev?'

Michelle looked up and saw the momentary look of relief on Kevin's face. She shuddered, pulled the coat tightly around herself and tried to shut down her brain.

'Well, that's probably not a bad idea ...' Kevin looked down at her, wanting her to say that it would be okay. She only hesitated briefly.

'Yeah. I'll go with them. You go back to the party.' She gave him a weak smile. He must have been feeling guilty because he saw her out to the car, gave her a kiss, opened the door and helped her get in.

'I'll ring tomorrow, eh? And see how you're feeling. Neil is throwing a turn for Anne's birthday tomorrow night if you're feeling up to it.'

'Okay,' she said, as carefully as she could. Another boozy party with people she didn't like. This was like walking on eggshells. If she allowed herself anything more than this bleak flat voice then she might break open: rant, rave, scream. Burst out all over the car.

He slammed the door and smiled at her parents in the front seat.

'Okay. Take care now.'

They both nearly fell over each other to reply; as jovial as a couple of old dogs.

'You too now, Kev! See ya soon, son.'

'Yeah, see ya!'

Her mother wound the window down a little.

'Now mind, Kev. No driving home tonight if you've had too much.' Her voice chided him playfully. Kevin grinned conspiratorially. There was this cutesy code people used when they were talking about drinking alcohol that gave Michelle the creeps. *Why don't they all just drink themselves into oblivion and be done with it?*

'Don't worry about that one, Mrs Brown.'

'Oh, call me Bev, will you! Makes me feel too old!'

He grinned and then leant over and tapped Michelle's window.

'See you tomorrow then, Michelle.'

She nodded and turned away. Her father started up the engine and the car slid off. Michelle sat hugging herself in the back seat, wondering what was happening. She felt as though something *had* burst inside her. All her insides now seemed liquefied, like putrid soup – mushy and old. How could it be that she, Michelle Brown, could feel so lost and so afraid? A couple of years ago she was the captain of the basketball team, the one everyone in class counted on to speak up if something was wrong or unfair. She was the one the old music teacher Sister Veronica had loved, and the only girl in the class who didn't want to get married. Everyone around town knew that Shelly Brown had guts. Even the real dead-heads had to admit that much.

At home the 'good nights' were said matter-of-factly. Michelle went to her room. It was well after midnight, so her parents followed quickly. She could hear them muttering to each other as they undressed and put clothes away and then eventually the creak of the bed as they climbed in and clicked off the light.

She sat in the dark in her old flannelette nightie, no longer sleepy at all, and stared out the window into the cold night. The clouds had cleared away and the stars were as bright as ever. It was comforting to think that they knew nothing of her, that she could throw herself under a truck on the highway and the stars would still be up there, blazing away. She was getting colder and colder but still she sat there, not getting under the blankets or even putting a rug around her shoulders. It simply didn't matter. She didn't care if she froze into a piece of ice. A vivid scene from a film floated its way into her consciousness, playing itself slowly back and forth in front of her eyes.

What was it called? Where had it come from? But she could remember nothing, except the man, the hero, proving his love for a woman by putting his hand down on to the burning hot-plate of a stove. He'd pushed it down there and screamed with pain. For how many seconds? How long had he left it there? Long enough to leave great raw blisters and red welts across the palm of his hand and to prove his point. Someone had rushed in from another room because of the smell. Barbecued human meat. In the next scene the hand was swollen up to twice its size and he couldn't use it at all. All for love. *Who do I love? Kevin? No. Kevin is someone I simply ... don't hate. I can say that in all honesty. I don't hate him and I don't love him. He is ... nothing to me. Have I ever loved anyone?*

Michelle had loved Sister Veronica, but she was dead.

As she sat there, freezing on top of her bed at two o'clock in the morning, the idea came to her. It just popped into her brain as though it had been waiting on the sidelines all along and only now dared to take a chance in the main arena.

I don't have to go through with this.

So simple that it took her breath away. She chuckled and said it to herself again. This time aloud, just to test the strength of the words. To make sure they were real.

I don't have to do it.

She got off the bed and quickly put on the warmest clothes she had. She would have to move *now*, this instant, before it all became impossible. Thick denims, flannel shirt and two jumpers. And then her waterproof coat over everything. Breathing heavily with excitement she pulled down a case from on top of her wardrobe and stood considering it for a few moments. Too big and bulky. What about that nifty little soft one her mother had bought recently. Could she? Dare she?

Michelle straightened her shoulders and biting her lip nervously, tiptoed out into the hall and pulled it out of the

19

cupboard. It would be the only thing she'd pinch. That and a bit of food. She wouldn't be asking for anything else from them for a long time. The case wouldn't hold that much but it would be easy to carry around and it looked good. So what would she need? *Doesn't that depend on where I'm going?*

A few pairs of undies. More jeans. Better bring that old loose skirt for when ... and that long sloppy jumper and the two big shirts and the sleeping-bag. She hesitated over her leather jacket. It was her favourite bit of clothing. She'd saved up for ages to buy it. But there wasn't much room left in the case and she still had to fit in shampoo and toothpaste and her diary. Also that leather jacket was heavy. It made much more sense to wear the light water-proof and use the extra room to carry stuff she really needed. They could sell it when she'd gone, and replace the case. *I don't know where I'm going and I don't care as long as I don't stay here.*

Tiptoeing out into the kitchen, Michelle was tempted by the bit of paper and pencil lying by the phone on the side-board. She felt she should write something. Even if it was 'Goodbye and don't come looking for me' but the more she tried to work out exactly what she should write the more confusing it became. Better to leave no clues at all about her state of mind. You never knew what they'd think of doing. Maybe they'd get a detective or the police after her. She shivered, grabbed a few apples from the dish in the middle of the table, then a packet of dry biscuits, and some cheese and celery from the fridge, picked up her bag and, as quietly as she could, let herself out the back door. She would just extricate herself from their lives without a bump or a murmur. She wanted them to forget she'd ever existed.

Once out of the house, and walking swiftly down the badly lit street towards the highway, the enormity of what she was doing hit Michelle with the rush of freezing cold air. *It'll be okay. Okay for sure.* The heels of her comfortable flat boots hit the pavement with sharp short clicks that gave her confidence although she wished she'd remembered the gloves her mother had given her last winter. *I've got these two legs and they're taking me somewhere. They're taking me away . . . away, away, away.*

Their steady rhythmic sound sprang out wild against the dead silence of the sleeping town. Down to the railway line, through the underpass and up to the main street. Bubbles of excitement started to explode inside her chest as she breathed in the icy air. Past the banks and the shops, all so closed up and bricked in and . . . finished. She turned the corner and saw the streaky coloured lights of the busy highway, now only about a kilometre further down the hill. It wouldn't take long to get away.

Once down on the highway, Michelle stood on the road outside the big cafe which was open every night. She wasn't sure where to stand so that she'd be seen by drivers but be able to hide if she was recognised. A couple of huge semi-trailers thundered past and Michelle felt herself almost dragged along in the slipstream behind them. *What if someone I know sees me? It'll be around the town like wildfire.* The party, *my party*, at the pub would be finishing up now. What if a carload arrived to get coffees and hamburgers? She'd done the same thing herself only a couple of months ago.

There was nothing for it but to take the risk, and hope that she'd get a ride before anyone saw her. She walked past with her head down, facing the traffic coming up behind her, and held out her thumb. It had been a long time since she'd hitch-hiked and then only with someone else and in broad daylight. She began to stamp her feet to keep the circulation going, thankful that the rain had stopped for a while. Cars whizzed past, most with only one driver in them. *Damn them all.* Couldn't they see she was just a girl after a ride and not likely to attack or harm them?

21

Her anger flared as one car came very close, causing a puddle to splash up on to her boots. *Bastard!* She'd have to go back a bit towards the cafe where she could see the ground more clearly.

'Hey, girlie. You want a lift?'

Michelle looked over to a man of about forty who was returning the fuel nozzle to its place on the pump, having just filled up his enormous semi-trailer.

'I'm not going as far as the city but ...' His voice was nice, sort of airy as though he couldn't care less. She missed his face because he'd already shambled off to pay without waiting for her reply. Michelle came back into the light of the cafe and stared at the giant silver engine. She hadn't really thought about hitching a ride in a truck before. *But why not?* She touched the engine gingerly as she waited for him to get back. Would someone be less or more safe sitting up in one of these things? When the man got back, he was stuffing money into his wallet and grinning at her.

'Well, what d'ya reckon, love? She pass the test?'

Michelle took her hand away and saw that his face, although tired and lined, was genuinely friendly. She smiled back tentatively.

'How far are you going?'

'Just to Warragul. Only a couple of hours from town.'

'Okay then ...'

He pulled a can of Coke and a Mars Bar from the pocket of his jacket and began walking around to the driver's side.

'Okay, then. Just jump up there, love, and I'll open the door for you.'

Once safely in the cabin with both doors closed, Michelle began to relax. The distance between herself and the driver was considerable and the height gave a terrific view. She could see all around: cars racing past on the highway and a few people sitting at tables in the cafe. No one in that town could touch her now.

'Okay then, off we go.' The man was talking to himself as he started the engine and pulled out on the road. Michelle watched the sure way his large calloused fingers handled the steering wheel and gearstick and tried to think of something to say. For sure he'd be asking her questions soon and she'd better have something ready for him. But every idea that came just whirled off into another until her brain felt like a puffy sponge. She couldn't think of one simple coherent explanation of herself at this moment – seventeen years old and hitching a ride at three in the morning on this cold Friday night, to God knew where. Not one that was halfway believable anyhow. The man manoeuvred the cumbersome vehicle expertly out on to the main road and Michelle suddenly knew that he wasn't going to ask her any questions at all and that it was she who wanted to ask *him* things. *What's in the back of the truck?* she wanted to know. *And where are you taking it?* But his face was very still, staring impassively at the road, caught up in his own world. Light from the dashboard made his chin and forehead burn red every now and again before the flashing white from the passing traffic wiped it clean again. An ordinary looking bloke who had his own worries that had nothing to do with her.

Once they got past the edge of town he put his foot down hard and though initially a little scared to be going so fast, Michelle soon found the powerful shuddering engine beneath her comforting. Safe and lucky. That's how she felt. Every kilometre took her further away from where she didn't want to be.

The minutes stretched by and still no word had passed between them. Michelle settled into a corner of the cabin and stared out into the darkness. It would take roughly three hours, Michelle figured, before they got to Warragul and from there only another couple to the city. *God knows what I'll do there.* The truck thundered through one small highway town and then another: Stratford, Sale, Rosedale,

Traralgon, Morwell. She knew their names by heart; the Princes was her highway. She was doing the right thing. She knew that much for sure.

When the driver did eventually turn around to ask if she liked Elvis because he was going to start singing to keep himself awake, Michelle was already asleep, curled up on the seat, her head under one arm like a little bird. *Poor kid*, he thought, as he launched into a low lazy rendition of 'Wooden Heart'. *I wonder who the hell she is and what she's running away from.*

2

That same day was quite a momentous one for me too, although I never could have guessed then how neatly it would tie up with hers. The screw called me as we were all heading out in line after breakfast.

'Doyle, you're to make yourself ready to see the governor at ten.'

'Yes, sir,' I answered.

I knew it was coming and yet now that it had, I was surprised in a way. I felt as though I'd just arrived and I didn't know what to do.

The other guys cheered immediately.

'On ya, Doyle!'

'This is it, mate!'

A couple of the guys grabbed me by the hand and others slapped me on the shoulders.

'Don't forget us, mate, eh?'

'No worries...' I joked back, acting pleased. And of course I *was* pleased but a strange chill was blowing through me nevertheless. I had been waiting for this day and imagining what it would feel like for almost three years.

Mick Doyle's the name. *Ex*-crim now. Just over six foot. Pretty strong build with a couple of tatts on both shoulders. Blue eyes like Mum's and freckles everywhere. Not a bad head, except for the nose which is too flat and wide. I won't go into how that came about now! Enough to say I've never worried too much about my looks. Too much else going on to think about, if you get my drift. I'm nearly twenty-two and I've just done almost three years inside for armed robbery. The fact that it was my mate who was holding the gun and me the crowbar (to be used to bust open a safe I might add – not someone's head) didn't matter to the judge we got. Bunged us both in for five years with a three-year non-parole period. Nice one! First off the old geezer gave us this rave about being a menace to society and making the streets unsafe for ordinary citizens and I thought, *Oh, here goes, he's going to give us the lecture and then let us off.* Both the dim-witted lawyers strung us along too, telling us we'd get off for sure because we were so young and had no serious prior convictions. But no such luck. After standing there listening to him, as polite as could be for nearly fifteen minutes, trying not to slouch or give in to the temptation to scratch myself in my prickly new Brotherhood of St Laurence suit, he decides to hand out a stiff one. Five years hard labour, he says, and then slams down the hammer. I'll never forget that moment. It sort of crashes down on you like a heap of tumbling bricks. Five friggin' years! And I was only nineteen. Do you know the thing that really worried me most, the one stupid thing that kept going round and round my head as the cops moved in and the handcuffs locked on again? It was this: that I was going to turn twenty-one in jail and I wouldn't be able to have a party. None of that sort of stuff means anything to me now. But at nineteen that was what got to me. In jail at twenty-one and no party.

Anyway to make a long story short, I did my time in there. Time I never want to have to think about, at least in detail, ever again. I'll tell you straight, I was headed for nowhere. Right down the gurgler if you want to get specific. There were a couple of good people who helped me in there. Funny that they were actually great mates with each other as well and yet they couldn't have been more different. One was Charlie Morris, a fifty-five-year-old crim who was just finishing up his time for man-slaughter when I arrived, and the other was Brian Walsh, the Catholic prison chaplain. They both took me under their wings a bit and gradually I got sorted out.

So there I was. I'd had the call to go and see the governor and I was standing in the middle of the yard sort of in shock, thinking about it.

'When you're ready, Doyle,' the warder whined sarcastically. 'You want to stay here or something?'

Some of them weren't so bad but I hated this little mongrel and he knew it. I'd only been there for a couple of weeks and I'd seen him bash another young bloke who was handcuffed. The poor kid was choking on his own teeth before that bastard let up.

'Yes, sir,' I said, not wanting to antagonise him. The petty ones loved picking up last-minute infringements that could delay your release.

'Permission requested to visit K cells, sir, to see Pino.'

He looked at his watch pointedly and grumbled.

'Okay. You've got five minutes.'

Prisoners in our division were allowed a certain amount of personal freedom. For example there was a bit of free time between breakfast and work. We could go back to our cells, or into the bog, clean teeth or whatever. Most of the guys just stayed out in the yard, chucked a ball around a bit or had a smoke. I knew where Pino would be.

'I'm going today.' I could barely keep the excitement out of my voice as I walked into Pino's cell but I tried to flatten it. He was lying on his cot, smoking as usual, one arm twisted back behind his head and concentrating on the perfect smoke rings that were slowly wafting up in front of his face. It was one of his favourite pastimes, so I waited before saying anything else because I knew Pino liked to concentrate on one thing at a time. He smiled at me sadly with those great big droopy eyes of his and we both watched the last ring almost touch the ceiling before it dissolved.

'Is that so?'

'Yeah.'

'I thought it was going to be tomorrow?'

'Yeah that's what they said last week, but . . .'

'Good for you, mate.'

I sat down on the end of his bed and looked at the floor. There wasn't a lot to say. I knew Pino's time would be a lot harder without me there but neither of us wanted to talk about that. Before we'd become mates he used to get walloped by someone every day. It's hard to describe Pino without giving the wrong idea. I mean he's not retarded or simple, nor is he a dwarf or at heart such a bad bastard, and yet sometimes he seems all of these. I can't really say why I took to him. In fact if I was honest I'd have to say he was a surly, ugly, squat little Italian guy with bad skin and a tight foul mouth. He was in for murder and had another five years of non-parole to go. Not that I could imagine him ever getting parole. He was always in trouble. If there was a fight on you could be sure Pino'd be in the thick of it. But that gives the wrong idea about him too. I've never actually seen him pick a fight. Ever. But he just never seems to know how or when to walk away from trouble.

'You got everything ready, then?'

I grinned.

'Oh, yeah. I've got all me classy suits packed in grandma's trunk . . .'

He laughed and coughed as he got up off the bed. The poor bastard would probably die of lung cancer before he got out of that hole.

'I've got something here for you.'

He started scratching around inside the steel side-cabinet, looking for something, and I took the opportunity to take a last look around his cell. Every other guy I knew did something with their cell – a poster on the wall or a photograph of someone, even just a plastic mug on the basin or a dirty joke written in pencil on the wall. But Pino's cell had nothing. He'd been inside for nearly four years and there was still no indication he lived there. Just the high barred window, the bare lino, empty steel bookcase, cabinet and the narrow bed.

'I can't find the bloody thing,' he mumbled, still shoving things around in the drawer. Once we got to know each other a bit we would often talk; about families, places we liked and things we wanted to do. He was older than me. Twenty-six he said but he looked older. He had a few scores to settle when he got out, but he never went into that much, whereas my score, the thing I was going to do eventually when I got out, was something we both talked about a lot. Pino always surprised me the way he understood stuff. Anything you told him he'd take seriously, no matter how wild or crazy, and he'd think before giving his opinion, which was more than you could say for most of the guys.

'Mate, I gotta go . . .' I said hoarsely. I was scared of that mongrel warder outside. He'd said five minutes. He'd be just the sort to push it into something big if I went much over.

'Got it!'

He turned around suddenly, a broad grin of triumph spreading across his big, lop-sided face. I took the small white package that he handed me but I felt very awkward. We'd never given anything to each other before. I mean, we were just mates. And I suppose I didn't want to think about not seeing him again.

'Thanks, mate. I wish you were coming too . . .'

'Yeah.'

Inside the white tissue paper was a thick gold cross on a chain. I fingered it stupidly, not knowing what to say. I certainly didn't want the bloody thing. I mean who except wogs or religious freaks wears this kind of stuff?

'Oh, thanks . . .' I mumbled.

He nodded, his face as grave as an undertaker's.

'My mother gave it to me when I was fourteen at my confirmation.'

'Yeah? Well, it's nice . . .'

He took the cross out of my fingers and popped it into the cavity he'd made in the heel of his shoe then closed it over and looked at me with another of his slow smiles. I laughed outright.

'What do you reckon?'

'Not bad. But don't you want it? I mean your mother gave it to you. I don't want to keep something she . . .'

He butted in before I could finish.

'Nah . . . you have it. Wear it around your neck like this . . .'

He pushed me around so my back was facing him and slipped the chain around it. His hands at the back of my neck felt strange; I don't think we'd ever touched each other before. He then spun me around again roughly so he could have a look at it from the front, nodded in satisfaction, and pushed me towards the door.

'Yeah. That's good.' His voice had gone into a funny deep tone. 'See you around, mate. Good luck.'

I almost went when he pushed me but I'm glad now that I turned back and grabbed his hand. We kept shaking each other's hands for much longer than it normally takes. Neither of us wanted to be first to let go. But what could I say? I watched two big tears slide down his pitted, olive cheeks and splash on to the front of his shirt and my own face jammed up. Two more came rolling down and he swiped at them roughly with his fist, then smiled a bit. I wanted to say something to Pino. Something important and comforting but you know I couldn't think of a single thing. For a few moments there I wished it was him getting out. I know that sounds like bullshit but it was true. I wished he could have taken my place. More than a friend he was the brother I never had.

'I'll see you, mate,' I growled.

I left then because I knew he didn't want me to see him crying.

'Michael James Doyle, you have served two years ten months of the five-year sentence you received in June 1989 . . .'

Mick stood up straight and quite still as he listened to the old man read from the plastic-covered piece of paper in front of him. These guys always had to play everything straight by the book. If the rules said all this bullshit had to be read out, then they'd read it out. Though why they couldn't just say 'piss off now while the going's good' beat him. Anyway what did it matter? It felt good.

'Owing to advice received concerning your positive behaviour and attitude, I deem it appropriate for you to be a beneficiary of the early-release scheme . . . We wish you well and hope . . .' Here the stooped white-haired man in the old-fashioned navy suit looked up from his paper with a smile, a wry gentle smile that made Mick turn away sharply.

'. . . hope we don't see you again.'

Mick took the large dry hand that was offered across the desk, shook it and tried to smile.

The formalities over, the governor relaxed a little and came around to the other side of the desk putting his hand briefly on Mick's shoulder.

'Now, Michael, will there be anyone to meet you today?' A stab of shame hit Mick before he'd had a chance to ward it off. He picked up the small canvas bag that contained almost everything he owned in the world and settled the strap across his shoulder.

'Er . . . I'm not sure, sir.'

'Well, do say so because there is an extra fifty dollars to pay for a train fare if you need it. Only a matter of filling out a form. Remember you may need what money you have for accommodation tonight, you know.'

Mick turned away from the older man's questioning look, and shook his head. Another form to fill out? No way. He had a hundred bucks in his pocket. That would do. Accommodation. He'd slept in the open before and it hadn't killed him. Besides it was so close now, he didn't want any hold-ups. Forms. He'd filled in so many damned forms in his life and where had it got him? Fair and square in the slammer, that's where. Let them keep their forms and their money.

'No thanks, sir. I think my mate'll be there,' he lied. 'He'll give me a lift.'

'Very well then, if you're sure.'

It was rotten enough having to admit to yourself that you had no one without whingeing on about it.

Mick walked with the governor out into the corridor along the strip of blue carpet; a part of the jail the crims never saw until their last day. The walls were clean and white and there were even a few pictures on the walls. Mick recognised one depicting a kid lost in the bush as a favourite from his stint in the boys' home a few years back. A couple of policemen walked towards them from outside, guns slung easily on their hips. They nodded politely at the governor and stood back for him and Mick to pass through a doorway. Their eyes slid over Mick for an instant but gave no sign of recognition.

Now through the front entrance of the building and out into the watery sunshine of the yard. It had rained during the night and a few big puddles remained in the potholes near the fence. The governor gave an abrupt wave to the guard on duty at the gate. They both watched the man nod and shift slowly off his behind, sauntering over to the small iron gate alongside the big one, jangling his keys.

Once again the governor shook Mick's hand.

'Good luck, Michael,' he said quietly.

'Yeah. Thanks.'

Mick's throat suddenly clammed up. For an instant he felt utterly bereft. Sad to be leaving. Rotten as the place was, it was somewhere. Somewhere to be. You knew people.

You could talk and fight, make friends, plan, dream and scheme together. But within a couple of moments he'd managed to shrug that feeling off before it could take hold. It was important to do that. The guys used to talk a lot about that feeling. It could drag you under if you let it.

The governor smiled again, in a kindly distracted way, turned around and walked back towards the entrance of the jail. Mick took a couple of steps towards the gate and then stopped, hesitating for a moment. Looking at the place now, front on, with no one else around made it hard to remember that the place was actually filled with living men – warders and prisoners – shouting, talking, working, cleaning their teeth and fighting. Standing very still like this Mick could hear only a very faint hum of human voices. It was eleven o'clock now so most of them would be in the workshops getting on with things. He swore again under his breath, the way he'd sworn every night for the last year that he would never come back, that they would never get him back inside this joint again.

'You planning on staying, Doyle?' the voice jeered from the gate. Mick started, turned and walked slowly towards the uniformed figure with the big ring of keys jangling in his right hand. Mick reached the gate, bending slightly to get through.

'See ya then, Doyle,' the guard scoffed nastily. 'Maybe next year, eh?'

Mick didn't even grunt to indicate he'd heard. None of those little runts could touch him now.

3

Around six the following morning, Mick drove his motor bike into the service station for petrol, noticing the hunched-up figure of a girl standing in the doorway to the restaurant. He wondered what the hell he'd do if the place was shut. He'd been running on empty now for more than half an hour, so he'd have to wait. But for how long? He wanted to buy a paper, and look through the job section and hopefully tee up some kind of job for the next week. A long shot, he knew, but it was important to try. Then he'd go and see Brian, and check out any ideas the priest might have about where he could stay.

'This joint open?' he called out, as he parked the bike near one of the petrol pumps. It obviously wasn't, so what was she doing there?

'No, I don't think so,' she mumbled gruffly and turned away. Mick switched the engine off, slipped the key into his pocket and walked past her over to where the 'Open for business' hours were written on the door. Half-past six. Only a few minutes away. On the way back to his bike he took a swift look at the girl but couldn't catch much of her face. The waif-like frame wrapped in the sleeping-bag made him twinge with sympathy though. Last night had been cold. Spending it in a doorway would have been terrible. Mick blew on his own hands and started jumping around to thaw out the blood in his feet. He was practically numb with cold himself and he'd only been on the road for a couple of hours. If only he still had his leathers. Then again, he'd been very lucky to get his bike back at all.

It was all still a bit unreal. He hadn't been out of jail for twenty-four hours and yet here he was, acting like a normal person, waiting to buy petrol. The simplest things gave such pleasure. He stared across the road to the closed shops. The rising sun was creeping slowly up over the roofs, pouring pink and gold light over everything, making all the ordinary things suddenly seem brilliant, coloured in with some kind of magic brush. Even the shiny surfaces of the petrol pumps were glowing, and all along the flat concrete paving where he was standing there were puddles of pale wet colour – oil and water congealed in the chilly morning air. Crazy, but he was even enjoying being cold.

A rush of memories hit, giving him a feeling of physical heaviness in his limbs and a kind of longing inside that was hard to get a hold on. As young kids they'd got up early; there had always been work to do before school. He and his sister Jill used to clean out the pigpens and feed the calves before breakfast.

After getting out of jail Mick had walked the eight kilometres to the centre of the nearest town of Yarram and got himself a feed in the local cafe. The whole time he was ordering the food, eating and walking he felt unreal, as though he was on some drug. A buzz went through him, from his toes to the tips of his fingers, right into his bones. He had to keep reminding himself who he was and what he wanted to do. Cars, all different colours, waited like toys by the side of the roads. And the trees, shedding their gold and red leaves haphazardly over the grass and pavement seemed like careless giants, wider and higher than he ever remembered. All the people too, walking about slowly and freely. Especially the women, with their bums wobbling under their skirts, the soft skin on their faces and hands, grumpy looks and smiles, and voices that breathed out words that sounded as though they'd been written by someone a long time ago.

The feeling wore off gradually but wafted back every now and again like ether, imbuing him at first with intoxicating pleasure and then fading into a vague sense of disquiet.

It had taken him six hours to hitch-hike the thirty kilometres along the South Gippsland Highway to Welshpool where his bike was stored. It had been frustrating having to just wait for rides especially when he had no idea if the bike would be there. Why was he coming all this way, wasting time, when he should be heading straight for the city to find work? What made him think it hadn't been knocked off by now? No one answered his phone calls, he'd lost contact with his friend and so had no information to go on. It was only when he actually laid eyes on the black dusty Norton Commando that he admitted to himself just how much he'd counted on getting that machine back.

The old bloke, an uncle of his mate Frank, had been surprisingly friendly considering he knew Mick was just out of jail. He lived alone in a run-down little house just out of the town, but he'd given Mick a cup of tea and a sandwich and offered his old couch in the back room for the night. Mick accepted gratefully. When he told the man he'd probably leave around four in the morning, the old-timer chuckled disbelievingly.

'I've never seen a young bloke today get up early yet...'

But Mick woke on the dot of four, wrote a note of thanks and left the house immediately on the bike. It was all a bit of a long shot but he was determined to give himself the chance of being in the city early so he could get a paper and look for some kind of job. He had to find a few days' work so he would have the money for petrol to go north.

He turned to look at the girl again. She was huddled over slightly and looked cold and pretty miserable. Slowly she folded up the sleeping-bag and moved out towards the highway. Hitch-hiking at this hour! A couple of cars whizzed

36

past and then there was nothing for some time. Just cold stillness. Mick watched her stamping her feet and rubbing her arms and shoulders. She looked too young to be by herself. Young enough to be at school or laughing with her friends in some cafe somewhere. The glass door behind him rattled. Mick turned to see a grey-haired man in overalls struggling with the lock. Great. The place was opening. He'd hardly been held up at all. It was just a matter of filling up now and he'd be in town in an hour. The man nodded at Mick and set about slowly unlocking the pump with stiff fingers.

'Chilly enough for you?'

'Yeah ... it is,' Mick replied awkwardly. He didn't know what to say or even if he should say anything else.

'How much do you want?'

'Fill her up, thanks.'

A large olive-green Mercedes in tip-top condition suddenly pulled into the station, gliding softly up to a nearby pump as Mick was pulling out his money. A young guy immediately jumped out and, ignoring the proprietor's friendly nod, tried to grab the nozzle, swearing when it wouldn't budge.

'Hey, man! You selling petrol, or what?' The sharp words were flung out into the air like steel filings. They caught Mick in the face and he looked over at the guy in surprise.

'I haven't unlocked that one yet,' the older man returned mildly.

'Well, c'mon. We're in a hurry.'

'Won't be a minute. I'll just finish here.'

The young man sniffed and stood waiting edgily by his car, thumping his fingers on the hood, obviously irritated at the time it was taking to screw on Mick's cap. Mick noticed the beautifully cut leather jacket and sighed with envy as he handed over his money. His own had been rather like that although a little longer and less flashy.

Suddenly the newcomer noticed the figure of the girl standing on the road. A sneer slid across his mouth. Then he tapped the windscreen of the Mercedes, waking his mate who was slumped forward inside the car.

'What's going on?'

Leather-jacket jabbed in the general direction of the road with his thumb and leered.

'Give her a ride, eh?'

The guy inside the car strained forward but couldn't see properly. Slowly he opened the car door and got out, resting his elbows on top, one foot still inside. He was muscular and tall and looked half asleep with about three days thick growth on his face. Eventually he grinned languidly at his companion.

'Yeah,' he said softly, 'I think we could manage that.'

They both laughed and he belted out a few loud thumps on the car's roof to get her attention.

'Hey, chickie, you going to town?'

As though deciding to disengage himself from the whole scene, the proprietor shrugged and without meeting Mick's eye, felt in his pocket for change, handed it to Mick, then walked over to fill the Merc. The four men – Mick and the proprietor and the other two – watched the girl slowly turn around and walk back towards them. Mick saw her face properly for the first time and noticed something stubborn there in spite of the apprehension in her voice.

'Yeah, I'd like a ride but . . . ' The voice was husky. Mick could see she was being careful, checking the guys out as quickly as she could before committing herself.

'Well . . . we're going all the way to Melbourne,' leather-jacket replied casually, his voice suddenly flat and careless as he mucked around with his wallet, flipping it from one hand to the other. A sudden tiny chill went through Mick. Was there something else in that voice or not? He had his change now and knew he should get on the bike but he held back.

'Where are you heading?' She was still playing for time. Taking in the shiny old car and still trying to assess the men.

'We're going right through the city to the coast but we can let you off anywhere.'

Something in Mick wanted to warn her. These guys were tough. He knew those gestures: the tone of speech, the repressed violence in the way the unshaven one was tapping his hand on the roof. He'd learnt all those signs at close range when he was inside. She was troubled too, he could tell, looking shyly from one to the other trying to work out whether to risk it or not. The unshaven one heaved himself carelessly back into the front seat, slammed the door and stared through the window at her.

'You'll be lucky to get a ride now, love. Not much traffic around ...' He smiled and continued in a more cajoling tone. 'You been out there for a while, have you?'

She nodded and smiled weakly. She was very tired, anyone could tell that. Mick watched. She didn't want to but she was going to take the risk. He almost *felt* her teetering on the point of moving over to open the back door. In spite of the insistent voice inside that told him not to be a complete jerk, to just stay away from other people's troubles and to get back on his bike, he took a step towards her.

'I'm going to the city. It might be safer on the back of my bike,' he said carelessly.

Leather-jacket, who was handing money to the man and smiling at the girl, spun around abruptly, staring with light cold eyes.

'What the ... who ...?'

But Mick didn't even glance at him long enough to see the hostility in his expression. He looked directly at the girl instead who was momentarily bewildered by the sudden increase of options.

'What's with you, bikie?' The unshaven guy jumped out of the car quickly.

Anger added pitch to his previously dull-toned drawl.

'Nothing. I'm offering a lift.' Mick shrugged. He knew he was very good at this kind of thing. He'd had tons of practice that these jerks wouldn't know anything about.

The first very important rule was never to get into a fight unless you wanted to. Very important. He most definitely didn't want a fight at this moment. The two guys didn't take long to size him up. His powerful build made them shrink back instinctively, even with both of them on to him they might not win. Besides it would all be too much of a gamble. Mick almost laughed as he watched the information click through their heads. It took about four seconds. Too much trouble, that's the conclusion they'd both reached simultaneously. Still they'd slam him with a bit of verbal to make themselves feel better.

'Why would she want to ride on that shit-heap, bikie?'

'Mind your own business, petrol-head . . .'

Mick didn't even twitch. Now that he'd given her the option he was actually hoping she'd turn him down and choose to go with those shit-kickers. He wanted to get going. He had things to do. Someone else would only hold him up. The small smile on her mouth surprised him.

'Thanks,' she said looking straight at him. 'You're right, it would be safer, except I haven't got a helmet.'

Mick sighed. The same thought had just occurred to him too.

'Well, it's only a couple of hours. You want to take a chance . . .?'

Inside he groaned at himself. Typical. Out for less than twenty-four hours and already putting himself on the wrong side of the law. The other two guys moved in unison. Doors slammed and the engine revved.

'See ya, slut!'

'Have fun with the bikie, moll . . .'

The Merc lurched off before she'd had a chance to change her mind.

The ugly words hung in the air between them for a few moments along with the foul-smelling fumes from the old car's exhaust. The proprietor shook his head and sauntered off to his workshop leaving Mick and the girl standing looking at each other.

'Well, I'll take a chance if you don't mind.' She was tense as a cat. He could see that he was now under scrutiny and it annoyed him. Let her do what she liked but he was going to buy a packet of chewies now and then leave, with or without her.

'Okay. I'll have to drop you off before we hit the city though. We'd get picked up there for sure. How about Dandenong?'

She nodded. 'As long as I get away from here. I've been waiting here for about three hours . . .'

He turned away and walked into the restaurant. A few truckies had stopped for an early breakfast. The coffee smells and eggs and bacon made him feel suddenly wild with hunger. One meal a day, he reminded himself. That's all I can afford until I get up north. The woman behind the counter had a soft face. She smiled encouragingly when he hesitated over a packet of chips. It would have been nice to sit down and tuck into a real feed.

When he got outside she was standing near the bike, her bag next to her. 'I've never ridden on a bike before . . . is there anything I should know?'

Mick shrugged impatiently but didn't answer. Fitting the bag down with octopus straps and leaving enough room for her was a job enough. He was so mad at himself for getting involved that his tone became short.

'Well, is that so?'

He looked up, surprised to see her eyes narrowing at his brusque answer.

'Perhaps I'd better forget it.' There was a tentative note in her voice that he didn't want to have to think about.

'Nah. Get on. It's all right.' He showed her where to sit and how to hang on. Her arms were as thin as a kid's. He turned around and grinned as a kind of apology for his earlier sharp tone.

41

'Not much of you, is there?'

She nodded, but didn't smile and avoided his eyes. He thought at first that she was being huffy and then understood she was nervous.

'Don't worry. It'll be all right. I'm a good rider.'

He kick-started the motor and began to edge slowly up on to the highway. Her arms tightened around his waist as he began to build up speed but when he asked if she was okay she didn't answer.

Mick tried not to worry. With a bit of luck they wouldn't meet any cops and the trip to Dandenong would only take an hour.

Just before picking up speed he thought he ought to call out.

'If you want to stop or anything, you'll have to yell out.'

He could feel her face pressed hard into the rough twill of the old second-hand jacket he'd picked up in the op-shop the day before, and it made him think of his young sister Beth who used to ride behind him on the horse, back when they were kids. She had been small and fierce too in those days and scared to be going so fast, not that she'd ever let on.

'I won't want to stop,' the girl shouted back. This time there was a determination in her voice that surprised rather than annoyed him. Funny kid with those big blue eyes and peaky-white skin. She didn't look like a toughie and yet, there was hardness there . . . in the voice and the way she looked at you. It made him wonder a bit.

4

Out of town Mick stepped on the gas, forgetting every-thing except his own enjoyment as his mind slowly went limp. There was nothing like being back on the road again with the old Norton fully opened out and thundering away underneath him, the highway stretching out forever ahead. An empty stomach and a full tank of petrol. It would have been perfect except for the wind. It raced straight through him, bitter and sharp leaving him chilled through within minutes. A lump of ice in the shape of a man glued to the roaring bike, that's how he felt. But it wasn't long before he got used to it. He knew now that he could get used to most things. *Endure. Just endure*, Pino used to say in those early days inside when Mick would start getting edgy, talking about trying to escape or knocking someone off, or even once about hanging himself to get the whole mess over with once and for all. He had become good at enduring. It was one of the things you either picked up quickly in jail or you didn't. If you didn't, then your life would be twenty times, maybe a hundred times worse. Mick didn't even have to think about it any more. But now his mind simply took over and adjusted. The bike was handling okay and that's all that counted.

Hills, fences, cars and tiny towns flew past. He concentrated on the road ahead and the feeling of his own freedom. He had nothing, but neither did he owe anybody anything, and that was enough to make him smile.

As they got nearer to the outskirts of the city the traffic started to build up and Mick remembered the girl sitting silently behind him. How could he get rid of her? It was all coming back to him; he knew these streets but they were different somehow. He remembered all those dreams he'd had in jail, about being in familiar places that he somehow couldn't recognise any more.

Slowing down at a red light, he looked around apprehensively for any sign of coppers. He'd have to put her off soon or he'd be pulled up for sure. But the thought just knocked around the outside of his brain – it was hard to make it penetratc. All round him the busy suburban shopping centre was frothing with Saturday morning life. People dressed in cheery clothes, matching scarves and footwear, getting in and out of cars, shops, calling to each other, laughing and frowning. Hurrying along and looking serious as they waved goodbye. He felt like he'd just been plonked in the middle of a toyland village; everything was too colourful and cute to be real.

There were shops on both sides of the road; camping gear, outdoor furniture, jeans-shops and pizza takeaways. Bright and inviting, full of things he'd forgotten existed. Looking down at his own thick unfashionable jeans, cowboy boots and horrible brown wool zipper jacket, Mick suddenly felt keenly his own position in the face of this casually displayed wealth and frivolity. Money hadn't really mattered in jail, except on a very small scale. He'd been considered a good enough sort of bloke, young, good-looking and straight talking. He'd had status and been accepted. But here at the lights as he watched people crossing in their fancy clothes with their kids and dogs he felt himself to be a member of a different species altogether. It scared him a bit. His rough bravado meant nothing against all this.

Mick's stomach growled angrily and he was aware of a sudden wild urge to eat. Anything. He had to fill that hollow space inside. It ceased to matter that he couldn't afford to eat, he had to. He remembered the girl and groaned to himself. He'd have to get rid of her before he stopped. He couldn't afford to feed her too.

At the next traffic lights he leant back.

'Whereabouts do you want to be let off?'

He saw her hesitate and realised without a doubt that she didn't have anywhere to go. Jerking his head back to the front again, furious with himself, he revved the bike and tried to work out what to do. Just his luck to get caught with some little drifter. Well, too bad! He would drive her to the next petrol station and let her off there. But before he had a chance to speak, she answered him plainly as though she had guessed his thoughts.

'Just let me off at the nearest cafe, will you ... I want to get something to eat.'

He nodded, surprised. So she must have some money. He was ashamed suddenly. Would it have hurt to buy her something? He'd always prided himself on not being mean, yet here he'd been looking out for a way to save a few stingy bucks.

'Okay, then. I'm going to get something myself so we may as well eat together ...'

She didn't answer and he hoped she didn't think he wanted to eat with her particularly. In fact he'd rather have been by himself but it didn't make sense to look for separate places.

A takeaway food sign loomed up in the next block and Mick pulled the bike over and stopped outside it. Hamburgers, pies, fish and chips. The lettering on the window was a bit faded but the message was clear. Just the sort of low-key little joint Mick was after. He tossed up whether to ask the girl if the place looked all right to her but decided against it. If she didn't like it she could go to the American-style outfit up the road. He got off the bike and without waiting for her, skipped around a bit on his toes on his way

45

into the shop, trying to get some feeling back into his feet and legs that were stiff from the cold ride.

She followed him into the shabby little place and they sat down awkwardly at a slightly greasy laminex table. The residual smell of food made him feel irritable, more crazy than ever with hunger. He was tempted to pick up the bowl of sugar and pour its contents straight down his throat. He glanced briefly at his companion but she was staring passively out the window, eyes mostly hidden by a fringe of thick curly hair that had come loose from the two childish bobby-pin clips on each side of her head. Mick thought he might as well ask her name seeing that they were going to be eating together, but he didn't get a chance. A worried looking Greek woman bustled out.

'So sorry, I not hear you come.'

Mick nodded and took the menu she was offering. It irked him for some reason to see the girl wave away the one offered to her.

'I want two steak sandwiches with the lot . . . and coffee, please.' Her voice was nice, deep, not unfriendly but not friendly either. More interesting anyway than the ordinary little peaked face and thin body. Mick smiled in spite of himself.

'Hungry, are you?'

She merely nodded and turned away again. He ran his eyes down the menu and tried to find a better choice than the one she'd made. But it was hard. Steak sandwiches definitely made sense.

'Same, thanks,' he said gruffly and handed the menu back to the woman. 'Except I'd like tea . . .'

The woman nodded and then rolled off into the kitchen on her fat bare legs.

The girl didn't seem to notice what he'd ordered. Mick gave up any notion of talking to her and rubbed his hands together enjoying the warmth of the place. It would be good to see Brian, the chaplain, again at that ex-crim centre. But how would he feel if there wasn't any work around? Everybody reckoned that things were pretty stiff. What would he do? He had to get up north. It was his chance, up there with Chas, to find a job and a way of life that he understood. Hanging around the city with no job, no money, he knew that sooner or later he'd just fall back into the old stuff. It was what everyone did. It was frightening to feel so vulnerable suddenly. In jail it had been easy deciding what would happen. Quite a different thing once you got outside.

'Where are you headed?' Her voice startled him, making his head jerk up. She was looking straight at him now as though she'd only just discovered him there opposite her.

'I'm going north. Gotta job to go to.' It felt good saying it aloud. Made it seem real, as though it was definitely going to happen.

'Where's north?'

'Up past Broken Hill.'

'Where's that?'

Mick repressed a sigh of exasperation. It really bugged him how ignorant people were about the country.

'Mid-west New South Wales.'

'Ah. Not near Sydney then?'

'No. Nowhere near Sydney.'

The woman arrived with the coffee and tea. They both reached for the sugar at the same time. Mick pulled away with a frown, strangely embarrassed.

'After you.'

The girl actually smiled at him then as she poured two heaped teaspoons into her cup and pushed the bowl his way.

'What sort of job?'

'Fencing, a bit of shearing maybe.' He felt put out suddenly by the questions and turned away, sipping the hot tea.

'You've done it before?'

'Yeah.'

'Whereabouts?'

'South Australia.'

'You come from around there?'

'No.'

He saw with relief that the food was coming. As soon as the Greek lady put it down he grabbed one of the thick sandwiches, undid the paper and took a huge bite. It was great; he couldn't remember anything ever tasting better. He took another bite, swallowed it quickly and then another before he looked at her. She was going at it slower but he could tell she was hungry too.

They both got through the first sandwhich without saying a word. Two bites into his second and with one cup of tea gone, Mick felt a lot better. The food was settling his nerves down as he knew it would. Looking at her now he could see she was just a kid. And nice enough too. Why had he got so paranoid before? He was about to ask where she'd come from but she beat him to it.

'So where do you come from?' Her mouth still full of food made her voice muffled and young.

'Gippsland,' he said shortly.

'Working?'

'Not really . . .' He took another bite and cursed himself.

How come with all his planning hadn't he thought about what he was going to tell people he'd been doing for the last few years? Bad oversight. It actually felt more awkward than he could have imagined.

'So what were you doing?' she continued conversationally.

He looked at her and couldn't help a small smile. She was interrogating him but he liked the flat business-like tone and her straight look all the same.

'Er, just doing odd jobs.'

He could have told her easily. Why would he bother hiding anything from some little girl he wasn't ever going to see again? But then what would have been the point? It would have started up a big conversation about jail. She would ask all the standard questions and he would have to try to answer them. And in the end she'd never understand. No one could understand unless they'd been there, felt the slam of the iron door and heard the turn of the key. And all the rest. Being locked away every night like an animal was by no means all of it. He didn't even feel like thinking about it. One day he might want to talk about what he'd been through in there, but not now.

'Can I come with you?'

Mick nearly choked on his mouthful of steak sandwich.

'Er, what?'

'Can I come with you up north? I want to get a job too. I promise I won't be a hassle to you. If I am, just piss me off . . .'

'Sorry, but I don't think so . . .' he said. 'I actually have to earn a few hundred bucks to get up there. Have to work in the city for a few weeks to get the money . . .'

She pretended not to notice the hard, dismissive look on Mick's face and continued a little breathlessly.

'As I said, I won't be any trouble. Soon as I'm a hassle, just get rid of me . . . I really want to get away. I don't like the city. I'd have more chance in the country. I know country people better.'

So she wasn't a city girl. Funny he'd thought when he first saw her that she was some little street kid but now looking at that face and the blue eyes, there was something about her that didn't quite fit that bill. Poor but not desperate. Maybe it was the voice and the plainness of her expression. He was curious suddenly and wanted to ask what it was exactly that she was wanting to get away from but she broke in again.

'I'm quiet. Won't be yakking on all day at you. I can look after myself too . . .'

He was keenly aware that she was intent on maintaining her dignity and liked her for it. Everything about the way she held her head, the direct way she was looking at him, even the way she placed her hands together on the table as

49

she spoke told him she wasn't begging, just asking, and it made him shift uncomfortably in his seat. He didn't want to be mean but there was no way he could afford to lumber himself with anyone else.

'I've got money. I'll help pay for the petrol.'

Mick looked away for a few moments, silent. He let the words roll around in the air for a while, before breathing them in. Then he looked up and met her eyes directly, seriously considering her request for the first time. She smiled, knowing this shot had hit home. His voice came out harder and meaner than he intended. Even so he didn't care. This was serious. It was a decision that could affect the rest of his life.

'How much money?' A crazy shaft of hope was starting to pulsate in his chest.

'A few hundred. In the bank,' she said defensively.

'You're pretty young to have money,' he countered coldly. This was no time to be nice. If this worked out it would mean he could head north straight away instead of looking for a job in the city. He saw her face twist angrily as she fumbled around in her bag. Pulling out a small yellow passbook she threw it disdainfully on to the table and looked away.

'See for yourself. I'm seventeen and I've been working every Saturday in K-Mart for the last year.'

Mick realised that his coldness had hurt but decided not to care. He picked up the book and read the final figures. Seven hundred and fifty dollars. His heart soared. He would have sixty dollars left after paying for this meal. A hundred and twenty, perhaps a hundred and forty would get him up to where he was going. He could pay her back when he got work. But what about her? Would she be able to find work in Broken Hill? He was going a long way past there and didn't want to take her. What if she insisted on coming? He didn't want to use her. If she wanted to go further he'd have to take her. Jumbled thoughts and rough calculations roared around his head. It was too good an opportunity to pass up.

Now that it had suddenly become possible, he allowed himself to admit that the next time he saw Brian he wanted to have money in his pocket and a job to talk about. He didn't want to be just another young ex-crim with his hand out. Next time he saw Brian he wanted to be a success.

'Would you want to go as far as Broken Hill . . .?'

'Maybe.' She was fiddling with her cup now, turning it round and round on its saucer.

'Maybe I'd want to go further . . . it depends.'

'On what?'

'What do you think! Work, of course!' she snapped angrily.

'Okay, okay,' he mumbled, a little put out. He tried a tentative smile, but she'd turned her head away towards the window. Leaning forward, he deliberately softened his tone.

'Well, it's okay with me, then. If you agree to split the price of the petrol down the middle. I've only got sixty bucks. I reckon we'll get to the Hill for a hundred. From there we'll have to decide what to do . . .'

She butted in curtly.

'But no strings attached. Understand. I'm not after you. I don't want a boyfriend. I want a ride and I'll pay my share. You understand that?'

Mick nodded and sat back dumbfounded. What did this smart-arsed little moll think? That he was desperate or something? He found his voice after a couple of moments and went on calmly enough although the former hardness had returned.

'Well, good. Because a girlfriend is about the last thing I need right now.'

'Well, that's understood then, isn't it?' Her flat tone really annoyed him.

'Okay. Then that suits me.' Mick tried to keep the anger out of his voice. He picked up the docket.

'This one is straight down the middle too.' He stood up and fumbled in his pocket for money. She followed suit and they paid separately at the counter.

51

Once they were out of the cafe she turned to Mick, her tone quite friendly again.

'What's your name?'

'Mick,' he said gruffly. 'Mick Doyle.'

She gave him a funny lopsided smile and held out her hand.

'Pleased to meet you, Mick.'

Mick shook hands with her, a little awkward with the formal gesture.

'So what's your name?'

She looked uncomfortable, as though she'd forgotten that she would have to declare herself.

'Michelle.'

Mick shrugged, aware that her hand inside his own had felt as small and delicate, as easy to break, as a child's.

'We're going to have to get you a helmet.'

She nodded.

'Do you mind stopping at the bank? I'll get some money out with my card.'

Mick looked at his watch and pretended to care that they would be held up for a few minutes. He was actually buzzing inside with excitement. To think he was going to skip the city! It was too good to be true. He just couldn't wait to get out into the bush. To meet up with Chas again. Fate was dealing him a lucky stroke. He could feel it. The chance meeting with this girl was making what he really wanted possible.

'That's okay. I might as well fill up the bike too while we're at it.'

But when they went to fill up the bike at the petrol station across the road, the proprietor, noticing Michelle's bare head, offered to sell them a helmet out of the blue for twenty dollars. Michelle was delighted. She put it on and turned to Mick with a grin.

'What do you reckon?'

Mick tapped it a couple of times, checked it over carefully, inside and out, then handed it back with a small smile.

'Nothing wrong with it.'

Michelle pulled a twenty-dollar note from her purse and handed it to the man.

'Thanks a lot. Just what I was after.'

He took the money and smiled before turning away to his next customer. A wave of well-being suddenly flooded Mick again. For a couple of seconds he felt as though the watery sunshine had somehow got inside him, rolling down from his head through his arms and legs like golden honey.

'Hey, I reckon this was meant to happen.' He grinned at Michelle and climbed back on to the bike.

'What do you reckon?'

Her face closed down immediately and she glowered from under the helmet.

'I don't believe in that sort of shit.' The girl's words fell like a pile of stones between them as she slid on to the bike, as though she'd been doing it all her life.

'Nor do I,' he sniffed lamely and started up the engine. On the way out he swore he'd win the next round.

5

They headed north, out along the Calder Highway, past
the airport and through undulating hills that were lush in
clover and weak autumn sunlight. The sort of countryside
that just about everybody likes. *Reasonable* countryside
with houses and fences in the right places and animals
crowding together in neat flocks, shorn sheep sheltering
under trees, lambs bleating and dairy cows stumbling out
of sheds after their milking, feeding contentedly. It was
pretty, Mick could see that. He could understand that it
was something. Wasn't he out of the city now and roaring
through fresh air with grass and trees on both sides of him?
Compared to jail this was a hundred per cent on something!
Even so, he couldn't wait to get back to his own country.
Every mile that flew by deepened his longing, made him
woozy with memories of the flat scrubby secret country of
his childhood. Northern NSW, central Queensland and the
west. The whole family was always moving about, working
like dogs on other people's properties. Something in him
needed to know if all that space and light and heat was
really still there. In jail he'd often woken, dazed and
disorientated, to hear the guys next to him, sometimes on
both sides, spluttering, coughing and clearing their throats.
But Mick's dreams had been full of dry hot blue days and
unremitting flatness. He and his sister Beth on the horses,
on the motor bikes, feeding animals in the morning or out
shooting kangaroos and rabbits at night with the other

workers' kids. The long days with his old man, mustering sheep. His older sisters laying bait for foxes under a blazing still sky, branding calves, often with nothing better to do than to watch eagles soaring, searching for something to kill. Watching them drop in an instant, like lead. And it used to make him shiver to hear the far-off squeals of a baby bush rat or rabbit, or to watch a writhing snake or stumpy-tailed lizard being carried off, further and further into the blue. You knew that whatever it was would be torn apart, limb from limb, within seconds. So much for things being bad at home, he used to reckon to himself. Seeing the eagles always made him thank his lucky stars.

Towards night up there the sun painted everything over and over again in those harsh wild reds, thick purples and golds. The colour slowly saturating everything until you'd swear it wasn't real, that you were seeing things. You could look around, out across the land and hear the day sighing its last, hear the final shuffles and whimpers of the light just dying away after its long battle through the day. Then the quiet steady breathing of the night would start up and the black sky above would prick open everywhere with stars. You knew then everything would be okay.

Behind him the girl was still and quiet through most of the day. If they stopped it was only because one of them wanted a leak or a drink of water at a town park. The couple of times he tried to engage her in conversation she answered in monosyllables.

By Ouyen Mick had forgotten her name. He was waiting for her opposite the park in front of an estate agent's window after using the nearby toilets. He could see her walking around the park, taking her time but not straying too far from the bike. She had no idea he was watching her and it made him feel sly, but she interested him in a way. Such a thin little piece and tough too. The look of her walking slowly around the trees, pushing her feet through the leaves and looking up into the branches as though she was really enjoying herself. It made him smile. A couple of locals walked past Mick on the footpath. He saw their heads turn curiously in his direction and then note the figure of the girl he was watching in the park. This, followed by a couple of quizzical country frowns. Mick wanted to laugh and hold out his hand. *Hey, it's only me, Mick Doyle,* he wanted to say. *Only me and I'm one of youse . . . up from around Brewarrina way originally. The old man worked on a station up there called 'Two Chain Creek' for close on four year, I reckon, till . . . But then I'm not really, am I? I'm a crim. An ex-crim just passing through. You're probably right to keep your eye out for me.* The thought pulled him up quickly. He headed straight back to the bike, trying to make himself angry with her for keeping him waiting.

'Hey!' he called, realising he'd forgotten her name. Was it Sharon? Suzie? No. Something else. Some pretty name that didn't fit right with her at all. She had her back to him, not hearing.

'Hey . . . er. Ready to go now?' Much louder this time. She turned around, nodded and started walking back swiftly. Not a flicker of a smile or any wave of recognition, nor, damn it, any note of apology in her walk. Just straight back to the bike and on with the helmet.

'Sorry. I forgot. Your name . . .' Mick mumbled, hating having to ask her, but the rest of the trip would be impossible if he spent it trying to remember a name.

'Michelle,' she said tersely.

'Oh, yeah . . . right,' Mick grunted begrudgingly. That was a nice name. It didn't suit her at all. He turned away and put the key into the bike.

'But most people call me Shell . . .' He looked around, surprised to hear her speak one word above what she was formally obliged to for politeness sake. Damn it, she was smiling at him! Mick looked away. *The less I have to do with this moody little bitch the better.*

'Is that so?'

'Yeah. Or Shelly. My brothers used to call me that.' The smile had already disappeared by the time she'd finished the sentence. She was frowning now, looking worried, as though somehow she'd let her guard down and revealed something she shouldn't have. So, she had brothers and that meant, presumably, parents. Where were they all? And what was she doing running off like this? Mick only just managed to dampen his curiosity. No way was he about to risk being made to feel a dork again. If she wanted to talk then he'd listen. He wouldn't ask any more damn questions and be handed one of those surly, mind-your-own-business replies. He started up the engine.

'Let's get going. We'll probably have to stay in Mildura overnight. I'm pretty stuffed.'

For most of the way to Mildura the sky was a thick milky grey, but changing all the time. The clouds, stringing out into transparent lines, occasionally let through patches of faint blue that got Mick's hopes up. But just when he thought it was going to even out and clear, he'd look up and they would have clotted up again into a big steamy grey mass. This sort of a sky belonged to the southern states, to jail. He was free now and going north. In some crazy way he needed the sky's validation of what he was doing. But the clouds continued to swirl and race across the sky, as mixed up and volatile as the connections inside his own head. One minute he'd have it all worked out. Everything sorted. Then he'd have to remind himself who he was exactly and what he was actually planning on doing. Panic surfaced, jabbing through his skin, making his heart pound and his hands numb with fear. *What if Chas isn't there? What if he's dead?* He was in his fifties. It wasn't as though the old bastard had ever looked after himself. Maybe Mick had imagined that they were mates. How could you trust the word of a guy who'd killed someone? Chas had a mad streak in him. Mick knew that. So why was he spending his last hundred bucks in the world going up to see this old guy now, relying on a vague promise of work made six months ago? *Well, what else is there to do?* There was the letter, Mick reminded himself. He must stop panicking. There was a letter. Mick knew exactly where it was; inside the back pocket of his jeans, still in the cheap little worn envelope addressed in Chas's scratchy fountain pen and he knew the words off by heart. Even so, if he hadn't been driving the bike, he would have taken it out, read it again.

Come on up when you get out, boy. I'm on a station called Wilyarna about three hours north-west of Wilcannia. I'll be there for at least a few more months yet. They'll be shearing here some time in the winter. But before that there's a bit of fencing, cattle work etc. Things are tough now. They're not employing many but I reckon I'll be able to wangle something for you at one of the stations around. Pay's all right. Free tucker. Board is pretty rough but okay. All the best, son. Keep your chin up. Stay away from the vermin. Chas.

It had come out of the blue about six months before when everything was starting to look hopeless, and his release date too far away to matter. Chas had done five years before Mick met him and was released soon after Mick had done two. Mick had missed the old-timer a lot during his last year in prison. Pino had been a good mate but Chas was something else.

Mick grinned as he remembered the way the older man had recognised him as a fellow countryman right from the start and not part of the 'vermin class' in prison. Most of the other young crims were messed up with drugs in one way or another and old Chas wouldn't have a bar of any of them. 'Pack of little runts,' he'd say. 'Kill their own mother for a hit.' And it was true in a way. The ones who were seriously on drugs had no compunction about anything much. They stole from each other. They lied and slagged on their best mates. Cunning as foxes, they had no sense of right or wrong or at least if they did it was well hidden. Mick's height and build spoke of hard physical work and his burnt freckled skin of the outdoors. He stood out as a tough country boy right from the word go and the rapport between him and Chas had been instant. They understood each other. They'd talked a lot about the bush: jobs, people, horses, even farm machinery. Having Chas's friendship had helped Mick make the early months of prison life bearable. The old boy was well respected by fellow crims and warders alike. He was one of those types who never wasted words, so when he did speak, everyone listened.

Travelling along now it was easy for Mick to remember the weather-beaten face and slow raspy voice, the slightly stiff, lean and wiry figure of Chas. 'Don't worry, son. Keep ya head down and you'll be right. I promise ya.' The first friendly words spoken to him in a long time. He'd been shoved into a two-bunk cell at noon on his first day at the country jail and been left there to 'cool out' all afternoon. He hadn't seen or spoken to anyone for about six hours when Chas arrived back from a stint of forest work.

'Well, g'day there. Chas is the name . . .'

'G'day . . . I'm Mick,' he barely mumbled as he held out his hand.

'You had something to eat?'

Mick's head shook. His hands were clammy, his brain was aching and he felt sick with fear. Recent events were tumbling around in front of his eyes, spooking him badly. *This is it. I've hit the real thing. Big jail. Jail for big boys. Not a kid any longer. Why am I here? Five years. I'm finished.* Snatches from the past few weeks were floating around his head: the court room, the nasal voice of the judge, the bust, and those three young cops kicking him in the guts in the back room, but making sure the telephone book was there first so there would be no tell-tale bruises – the break-in . . . the wailing sound of the police car. Everything was flying around the cell in front of him. Mick could feel his mind cutting loose from reality and it was terrifying. The old guy's concerned face looking at him was barely visible. Instead he could see himself standing up there in the dock in that prickly suit waiting for the words. Guilty. Guilty. Guilty. The one word resounding again and again and then fading away like a dream. *Well, of course I'm guilty. I admit that but I've gotta get you to understand I didn't mean no harm. I want a chance . . . You gotta give me a chance . . . shit, I'm only nineteen . . . I want to . . . want to . . . want to . . .*

Then it got worse. A lot worse. His father was there, right in front of him, watching from a great height as Mick, just ten years old that day, was trying to get up from the ground. All over his legs, bum and back a criss-cross of hot electric pain. The old man had stopped belting into him with the horse whip but the sniggering had continued. 'That should teach you something . . .!' The words cut into his brain like barbed wire. Were the cops kicking him or was it his father? His father or the cops? And his mother was on the ground too. Moaning. 'No, Les! No!' she'd been screaming before, trying to catch hold of his father's arm but then he'd hit her too. Two big ones across the face with the horse whip and a punch in the side of her head that had sent her flying. Now there was blood coming out of her ear and her face was white . . .

He felt a hand, dry and heavy on his shoulder. His own body was making it shudder and twitch. Who was it? Then a voice friendly as before, raspy as an old nail-brush.

'What you worryin' about, son?'

A sudden rush of hot tears. Shit! Mick couldn't remember the last time he'd cried. It was the hand on his shoulder. It had some kind of heat in it and the heat was spreading through him like booze.

'My mother.' Bawling like a baby now but too far gone to care.

'She alive?'

'No.'

A sympathetic breath. Out first and then in.

'How old are ya?'

'Eighteen.'

'You scared?'

'Yeah.'

'Don't you worry, son. Keep your head down. You'll be right, I swear.'

Mick didn't know if the girl was still behind him or not. He couldn't feel her at all. Could she have fallen off? He didn't care very much either way. If she wanted to ride let her hang on. He had enough stuff to worry about.

6

I'd have to say this guy is all right. He doesn't ask too many questions and most of the time he keeps to himself as though he's preoccupied with something. Suits me fine.

We've been through so many towns I never knew existed. All of them more or less the same. Kilometre after kilometre and the country getting flatter and flatter. I don't know if I like it or not. I like the feeling of getting further away though. As far as I know I haven't any relatives in Broken Hill. None up this way at all. I'd be surprised if my parents even knew that Australia went up this far. I'm not kidding. They go to Melbourne about once a year and that's a real big deal, something they talk about for the next six months.

About midday I bought a few sandwiches at one of these little joints and he waited for me. When I started to eat I suddenly had a feeling he was hungry, that he was kind of watching me eat, but when I offered him something he got huffy and went off for a walk.

We got to Mildura at about six, stopped, bought some fish and chips and sat in a big leafy park and ate them. I didn't expect it to be so cold. The idea of spending the night outdoors was something I didn't want to think about until I'd had something to eat. He sure was hungry. Just sat down at one of those wooden picnic tables and wolfed down those chips like he was starving. I tried to say a couple of reasonably friendly things, thinking that it was time to get to know him a bit but he seemed moody as though he didn't want to talk, almost as though I was pissing him off. Of course *that* pissed *me* off and so by the time we'd finished the chips we were both pretty snappy with each other. Finally I said, 'You going to go any further tonight?' He turned around then to face me properly. It was the first time that I'd had a really good look at his face. A nice face, sort of honest and to the point. I appreciate anyone who can look at me straight. But I could tell he was really whacked. Anyone could by the way his eyes were blinking. His shoulders drooped and he couldn't stop yawning. He could see me taking all this in and, as though it was something to be ashamed of, he turned away and sat up straight.

'I'll drive you down to the town if you want to sleep somewhere . . . I'm going to sleep out. I'm used to it . . .'

By this stage it had got really chilly. I knew he was proud so I tried to make it easy.

'Too expensive. But I'd like to get a caravan. You're welcome to share it if you want. Out of season they're cheap to hire and they have blankets and a bar heater which would be all right . . .' I waved in the general direction of the gathering cold and gave a weak little smile. I knew I was running off at the mouth but I suddenly felt as though I wanted to be friendly. I reckoned this guy was okay. Safe anyway.

He turned around and looked at me quizzically as though he didn't know what I was talking about.

'This joint will have caravan parks for sure,' I found myself explaining again. 'You can just hire a van for the night. They're all set up. A stove, fridge, kettle. They have beds . . . at each end . . .'

I felt embarrassed saying that. But I didn't want to risk him thinking I was suggesting anything or even more importantly that he could try anything. Much better to lay everything out straight right from the start. He hedged around a bit but I could tell the idea of sleeping under some kind of roof was tempting him a lot. The dark was starting to close in around us now and I could feel the cold night air creeping around my neck and into the toes inside my wet boots. The sky too was thick and grey. It looked like it could open up any moment. I couldn't remember if I'd put in my sneakers or not but I sure hoped so. It was hard to remember back to the morning of that very same day. Seemed like an eternity away. Funny that I hadn't once thought of Kevin or hardly of home either.

I could see he was thinking.

'How much is not much?'

'About twenty-five . . .'

He stiffened.

'I mean, if you were on your own, would you . . . er, hire this caravan?'

'Yeah. Of course.' I tried to think of a joke to brighten him up a bit but nothing came. What a stupid question. If I was on my own I wouldn't be here, would I? Seeing as I don't drive. I sensed that for some reason he needed a bit more encouragement.

'Hey, it's a fair deal. You've been driving and everything. It's your bike that's getting worn out . . .'

He sighed and nodded.

'Okay, then.'

'Good.'

I smiled at him but he pretended not to see. Standing up abruptly he walked over to the bin with his rubbish. I crunched up my chip paper and stood up too. A small shiver of fear went down my spine as I checked him out. He was a big guy, lean and very strong too. Compared to him I was a joke – physically that is. He was over six foot and I reckoned if my assessment of him happened to turn out wrong, there was no way I'd stand a chance.

We hired a caravan in a park right on the Murray, from this sour old biddy who took my money as though there was something wrong with it.

'Hope you've got your own linen,' she snapped at me, not wanting to do herself out of a bit of business during the slack time but not wanting me to get away without knowing she thought I was a little tramp either. Two can play that game. I pulled myself up, and stared straight back at her as I took the key. I can make my eyes flash really spookily when I want to. They held hers until she got flustered, not able to work out what was going on. Then I put on my very best toffy voice, the one that Sister Veronica had taught me to use in nasty situations.

'Oh yes,' I breathed out. 'We've both got sleeping-bags, haven't we, Michael?'

I turned around. He was behind me, staring at a map on the wall. With the sound of my new voice he looked up suddenly, at her first and then me, as though he couldn't work out who was speaking. I went on, enjoying myself.

'I think we'll be fine, just for one night. We normally stay at the Hilton but I've been looking around this . . . this little town and you don't seem to have one . . .'

The old girl knew then that I was mocking her but I had the key now, secure in the pocket of my jacket. She wouldn't try and grab it back. Old ducks like her are big on maintaining dignity and she'd reckon, by the look of the bike and our old clothes, that we'd probably give her a couple of knocks rather than give it back quietly if she asked. I turned quickly and nodded to Mick, who to my satisfaction was looking rather stunned and we both walked out of the office.

Once outside and heading for the van I allowed myself a grin and sneaked a quick look at Mick. I was proud of myself and I suppose I was waiting for him to acknowledge what a smart-alec I was. He caught my eye with a shy smile then looked away abruptly. I felt confused by that. Maybe I'd embarrassed him? I tried to swallow the feeling as I trudged on through the mud to the right van and he went back for the bike. I unlocked the door and went in.

Almost at the exact moment he shut the door behind him and put down our things it began to pour outside. A real racket on the tin roof of the van. I shivered.

'Listen to that, eh?'

We both looked at each other and risked a smile as we went to opposite ends of the van and sat down. I can tell you I felt as lucky as I've ever felt, just to have that roof over me that night. I know he did too.

'Well, I reckon that was good timing, Michelle ...' he said softly.

'Yeah, I reckon. What would you say to a cup of tea?'

He nodded and gave another small grin.

'Couldn't think of anything better right now.'

He lay on one of the bunk-beds with his hands behind his head and shut his eyes for a minute. I pulled the carton of milk I'd bought that day out of my bag, then started to look around in the cupboards for what I needed. Everything was there – tea in a caddy, matches to light the gas, water to fill the kettle, plates, cups and knives. It was all clean, neat and small. But how come I was hungry again after having eaten those fish and chips less than an hour ago? Then I remembered the apples, dry biscuits, cheese and sharp knife I'd stuffed into my bag that morning on my way out of the house. They'd be just the thing. I dug them out of my bag and banged them on the table.

The blustering wind was actually shaking the van a bit and the rain was getting heavier. I lit the flame and felt proud suddenly to have got this far in one day.

'Hey, what d'ya reckon?' I said, grinning a bit, suddenly not caring if he answered me or not.

'Is this a good set-up or what?'

'It's great.' Once again, he spoke softly. A flat, quite gentle voice for someone that big. Funny that I hadn't noticed it before.

When the tea was made he slowly got off the bed and came to sit at the little table opposite me. I pushed the

66

biscuits towards him and he took a couple, then a big gulp of tea.

'That's good! God, am I whacked!'

'Yeah. So am I. Have some cheese.'

He hesitated and not looking at me, doodled with a knife.

'You sure . . .'

'Of course.'

I could see he wanted to ask me something but then he stopped himself by stuffing a biscuit into his mouth. I had probably been a bit surly with him before so maybe he reckoned I'd snub him again if he spoke. I can't remember why I was like that earlier in the day. I suppose I was feeling pretty freaked out. Every hour that went by made me feel a little easier with what I was doing. I decided to open the conversation up and see if I could warm things up between us.

'So whereabouts did you come from today?'

He went on crunching, his face flat and passive. I thought that he mustn't have heard me, he took so long to reply. I was just about to have another go at him when he spoke.

'Jail,' he said simply, without looking at me and taking another biscuit.

'I've been in jail for nearly three years . . .'

I tried to hide my surprise. I didn't say anything for a while, just kept munching my biscuits and cutting off more cheese. Eventually I couldn't contain my curiosity.

'So when did you get out?'

'Yesterday.'

I laughed out loud.

'Yeah?'

'Yeah,' he said bashfully. But he was proud and I understood that.

'So what's it like being free?'

It was his turn to laugh.

'A damn sight better, I can tell you that much!'

We said nothing after that for quite a while. Just kept eating and drinking more tea. But it was an easy silence, the steady thudding of the rain on the roof helping to make not talking seem quite natural. When he'd finished his third cup of tea he got up and put the dishes in the sink.

'I'm going to have to hit the sack, Michelle.'

'Yeah. Me too.'

He pulled a toothbrush out of his bag, a bar of soap and a thin towel.

'You reckon that was the shower-block we passed on the way in?'

'Yeah. Don't forget the key.'

He took the key and was halfway out the door when he turned back.

'Aren't you gonna ask me what I was in for . . .?'

I shrugged, then indicated that he should shut the door because the rain was getting in.

'Nah. I can tell,' I said, dampening down a sudden urge to smile. 'You murdered three cops. Right?'

His face broke open into a laugh making him look completely different, sort of fun-loving and easy like any young bloke, then he headed out into the rain to the toilet block.

By the time he got back, I'd pulled the table down into a bed and changed into my one thick flannelette nightie, thankful that I'd brought it and not the prettier, lighter one. On an impulse I picked the knife up off the table and popped it under my pillow. There were no sheets but plenty of blankets. I spread one out underneath and heaped a few more on top of my sleeping-bag and climbed in. Cosy as a burrow. I turned away as he got undressed down the other end, hoping I'd left him enough blankets. I felt good. Happier than I'd been for a long time. For a start I didn't feel sick at all and so hadn't had to think about being pregnant for hours. All that rain outside made me feel warm and safe. When I heard the creaking of him getting into his bed I turned around on to my back.

'I leave you enough blankets?'

'Sure. Yeah. Fine.'

'Well, goodnight, Mick.'

'Yeah. Good night, Michelle.'

We lay there in silence for a while. I could feel myself drifting off but every now and again I'd try and drag myself back from sleep, just to go over the day again. The most momentous day in my life. It had gone okay, all things considered.

'Big trip to the Hill tomorrow.' His voice was slurred with tiredness.

'Yeah. How long will it take?'

'Five or six hours, I reckon.'

'You've been there before, haven't you?' Had he told me that?

'Oh, yeah. Lots of times. I used to live around there.'

'You're going home, then?' I was curious now.

'Not really.'

There was a pause.

'Michelle. You mind me asking something . . .'

'Go ahead.'

'You running away?'

'Kind of. Yeah, I s'pose you could say I am.'

'Family?'

'Yeah, sort of. And a boyfriend. Mainly family though.'

He grunted as though he understood and rolled over, facing the other way.

'Well, good night, Michelle.'

'Yeah. Good night, Mick.'

I felt under the pillow for the knife, my small hand fitting perfectly around the handle. I could leave it there comfortably all night if I wanted to. This knife had belonged to my brother Wayne; he used to take it fishing when he was younger. The blade was sharp and slightly curved like

69

a dagger and the handle was some kind of white bone. I remembered him being proud of it, keeping it in a leather holder on his belt. I was glad I'd taken that knife that morning and not another one.

'So, Mick,' I said suddenly. 'What were you in for?'

'Armed robbery,' he replied sleepily.

'Right.'

My hand tightened around the knife but I didn't say anything else.

I started drifting off to sleep again, my thoughts turning to my old teacher, Veronica. I found myself praying for her. Well *to* her really. If anyone ever got to heaven she'd be there for sure. I mean who knows what God looks like? On the other hand I can often almost see Veronica watching over me.

So what do you reckon? Was it the right decision to just head off into nowhere with this bikie stranger? Or will I pay for it later? Tomorrow? Anything can happen. Just when you think you've got these quiet types all sewn up, they'll sometimes explode and go crazy. Like my brothers. They're both quiet but every now and again they'll go off the deep end, and there's no telling what they'll do. Once Wayne threw a shovel at the old man's head. And I mean blade first. It only missed him by a couple of centimetres. It's okay if it's your brother and you know them inside out, all the little things that are likely to set them off. In that situation you sort of work out when and how to stay out of the way. But with a stranger I reckon you can't be too careful.

I can tell Veronica doesn't exactly approve of my knife. *'If only people would think of some other way, Michelle.'* She gave up a musical career to be a nun, to teach little nerds like me who didn't even have a piano at home to practise on. I hope she's getting a fair deal up there, that she gets to play all her old favourites as often as she wants to. And I mean the complicated, classy church music that went out of style by the time I came on the scene. I hope, I mean I *really* hope that lots of the others up there – the angels or souls or whatever you call them – want to listen to her music too, that she gets to play for them on one of those grand shiny pianos and that she gets real big audiences.

7

Michelle woke feeling like she was about ten again. It was blissful just lying there snug in her cocoon watching the grey morning light drift in through the fake lace orange curtain above the tiny sink. If only she could stay like this forever. There were no sharp rattling noises, no voices in the kitchen snapping at each other. No calls for her to get up or sighs or grumbling or doors slamming.

She woke slowly, enjoying it all, then looked at her watch and panicked. Nine o'clock! She sat up with a start and looked over at the other bed. He wasn't there. Nothing except the messed-up blankets of where he'd been. No bag or shoes or clothes. A sharp spike of anxiety hit her below the ribs. She was completely unprepared. Had he tried to wake her and given up? Why would he leave without saying anything? How come she hadn't woken when he'd opened the door? The bastard. Most of her clothes were tumbling out of her bag, strewn over the floor. She hadn't left them like that, had she? She felt under her pillow for her wallet and breathed a sigh of relief as her fingers found the worn leather. That's what he would have been looking for. There wasn't much else of any value to pinch, unless he wanted girls' underpants, toothpaste or a couple of jumpers or a pair of jeans.

Michelle pushed off the warm blankets and set both feet down firmly on the hard cold lino of the van's floor and stretched. She'd have to get going now: wash quickly, make a hot drink and move out on to the road and try and hitch a ride. She didn't want to be stuck in this hole for one extra minute. She'd drifted off to sleep last night thinking that the crim was all right. Nice enough anyway. Someone she could at least trust in a basic way for the next couple of days.

She pushed the orange curtain aside and peered out the window just to make sure. But there was no bike. Just the tyre marks where he'd skidded into place the day before. She was on her own again. But the icy coil of fear was starting to creep up and around inside her. This feeling had nothing to do with being alone. She'd always prided herself on being able to suss people out quickly. Him leaving like this meant that if she was going to continue on this trip, she'd have to take more care. No one could be trusted.

Michelle walked towards the stove. A cup of tea would calm her down a bit. She could hear birds outside and remembered the van was under a big gum. Later she would go out and look. Then there was the roar of a car outside. Pulling up right outside the van. For one crazy instant she thought of Kev and her father. She could almost see their satisfied faces as they dragged her back to where she belonged, kicking and screaming. She prayed that it wouldn't be them. Being alone and afraid in a strange place was far better than going back there. *I don't want to see that town until the kid has been born and I've given it away. Until I'm ready and sure about how I want to start again. If ever. Do I ever want to see any of them again?* She pushed the question away for later. At the moment she was too raw and cold and sick to even think about it. Waves of nausea rolled through her. She'd have to have something to eat soon or she'd vomit. A couple of knocks at the door made her cringe and her heart beat wildly. Then the terse muffled voice.

'You right, Michelle? Can I come in?'

73

Relief flooded through her even as she tried valiantly to quell it. She felt weak, dizzy with it. It was the crim, his voice. Ex-crim, that is. Mick. He'd come back. She had to sit down; her legs were shaking.

'Yeah. Sure.' She tried to keep her own voice flat but it wavered, thin with anxiety. She hadn't realised how jumpy and nervous she'd become. He walked in carrying his small bag and smiled at her.

'Hey there! You have a good sleep?'

She nodded vigorously, tongue-tied. He put the bag on his bed and pulled out a few items: eggs, bacon, bread and a small container of butter then looked at her shyly.

'Feel like breakfast? I hope you like this stuff. It's, er ... cheaper this way. I thought seeing as we had the stove and everything it might be a good idea to cook.'

Michelle nodded. She could tell he was nervous too, hoping she'd approve of what he'd bought. As if she wouldn't? As if she'd care what he came back with!

'Sure,' she managed at last. 'A good idea.'

Her eyes fell on the carton of eggs and she felt suddenly famished, as though she could eat a dozen. These sudden wild urges to eat had been happening since she first became pregnant; a ravenous feeling that would come on out of the blue and completely overtake her. It was vaguely shocking in a way. More than anything else these hungers made her realise she wasn't just Michelle any more. She was Michelle and someone else. There was someone else inside her fighting to live too.

'I'll be off for a shower for a few minutes ... you start on all that. I'll be back.'

Michelle grinned at him but he didn't see. He was already bent down searching in the cupboard for a pan.

'Okay. When you come back it'll be ready for ya!'

'Okay.'

Michelle needed a pee badly. And a wash. She put on her socks and boots, wrapped her coat around her, picked up her wash bag and clothes and bounced out of the caravan. Outside was wonderful. A clear blue sky above as she hurried through the slush and puddles towards the shower block. Everything would work out. And there was no point thinking about tomorrow.

She soaped herself all over and let the hot powerful stream of water pummel her face and back. It was good, facing up into the water keeping her eyes shut. The slightly swollen belly and enlarged breasts dominated the rest of her body when she was naked like this and she didn't want to have to look. They made her know it was real, the whole thing, not just a strange idea. *A baby! I'd better start thinking all this through.* But she kept her eyes closed and gave herself up to the warmth that went deeper and deeper by the second.

Michelle returned to find Mick dishing out fried eggs on to two plates covered in slices of toast. Another pan on the stove was sizzling with bacon. Michelle smiled.

'It smells all right.'

'Yeah. It does, doesn't it.'

She sat on the plastic-covered seat on one side of the table and waited like a little kid. Bacon and eggs. Her father was always cooking up big dishes of eggs and bacon, tomatoes and chips and sausages. It was all he ever seemed to want to eat in spite of having an ulcer and the doctor telling him it was the worst thing for him. Now here she was salivating at the smell that only yesterday would have made her sick.

When Mick handed her the full plate she began to eat immediately. Hungrily. She'd never eaten three eggs before at one sitting. The toast was hot and buttery and the bacon just a touch burnt around the edges. Crispy and delicious.

Mick sat down opposite her. He offered her the pepper and salt first but she refused. Slowly he began to shake them on to his own meal, then he picked up his own knife and fork. Neither of them spoke for some time.

'You've got a good appetite for a small person.'

Startled, Michelle looked up, immediately embarrassed.

She'd nearly finished what he'd given her already. But when she met his eyes, blue and friendly, staring straight back at her, she smiled back.

'Yeah.'

'You've always been like that?'

'Nah ... not really.' There was no way she was going to tell him about being pregnant.

'Just the fresh air, I suppose?'

'Yeah. It must be the air,' she agreed and immediately felt an anxious spasm spread across her stomach. If only it was bloody air! If only she had air to worry about. She felt hot suddenly and a little dizzy and stopped eating, leant back against the rubber padding of the seat and pushed her plate away. Suddenly all this food didn't seem such a great idea.

'So jail, eh?'

As soon as she said it she wished she hadn't. He might think she was having a go at him when she'd only meant to be friendly and to take the focus off herself. But there was no need to worry. She watched relieved as he nodded and then methodically consumed his food, mopping up the leftover egg with a piece of crust. Finished at last, he put down his knife and fork with a satisfied sigh, pushed his plate away and looked up at her.

'Yeah, jail. Another cup?'

She nodded and he reached across to the teapot, pouring out for both of them. Steam rose in front of their faces as they picked up the cups and brought them to their mouths. Suddenly he grinned and held his cup out towards her.

'Here's to it, Michelle.'

'Er, what?' Her puzzled expression only opened up his grin wider.

'To jail, the can, the slammer . . .'

Michelle smiled tentatively, and touched his cup with her own. She wasn't quite sure what she was drinking to but it seemed appropriate to join in somehow. He looked buoyant. She took a couple of hot sips then ventured shyly, 'Is it as bad as they say?'

'Worse . . . but better in a way too. Hard to explain.'

Still smiling a little, Mick took a sip, put his cup down and shut his eyes for a few moments. Michelle felt excluded as though he'd forgotten about her even being there. He was lost in his own thoughts, probably back there behind the high wall, the bars, hearing all the noises, smelling the smells, reliving it all and enjoying *not* being there. She used the opportunity to have a good look at his hands. Big and bony, both now encircling the cup, holding on tight for some reason. When he eventually spoke his voice was soft and another pulse of dull sadness ran through her and was gone before she even had time to work out what it was about.

'I never got used to it. Thank God. Some of the blokes do, you know.'

'How do you mean?'

'If you spend enough time inside, then there's nothing for you when you get out. Your mates are inside and . . . everything that you know about is there too.'

Michelle nodded. That sounded depressing. It wasn't something she wanted to think about.

'So you're going to look for work?'

'I've got an old mate. He wrote and said he'd help me get a job on a station up there. But what about you? You looking for anything in particular?'

Michelle shrugged and tried not to feel scared. Him asking her plainly like that made her feel as light and inconsequential as a feather. A bit of a breeze and she wouldn't even be in the same spot.

'Anything I can find . . .' She looked away, towards the window and shifted in her seat angrily. That sounded *pathetic. Anything I can find! I must be out of my mind doing this! Sitting in this joint with a bloody stranger eating bacon and eggs! What the hell am I doing here? I've always hated bacon and eggs.*

'Your boyfriend know?'

Michelle turned back to Mick and defensively picked up her cup again.

'Well, I reckon he will now.'

Mick chuckled.

'What about your parents? You gonna contact them?'

'Oh, yeah. I guess I will. Eventually.' Michelle sighed and wondered if she would, and when.

'What did they do that was so bad?' he asked quietly.

Michelle looked down at the orange laminex table. Exactly the same colour as at home. *How do you put that kind of stuff into words – years of shitty stuff into words?* She ended up blurting out the first thing that came into her head.

'They wanted me to marry this jerk. I just couldn't. I just couldn't bear the idea of doing it! Even if it means I'm gonna mess me whole life up!'

She looked up and saw that he was looking at her with great interest. It was a free look, not furtive or sly.

'So why didn't you just say "no I don't want to"? I mean why did you have to run away?'

Michelle felt herself go hot again. And prickly. She started to rub the back of her neck and then scratch her chest and scalp. It was as though someone had placed nettles inside her clothes and in her hair. Why? Why had she run? Why hadn't she faced them all with what she wanted to do? They couldn't have forced her, could they?

'Country towns,' she murmured in a voice that sounded unconvincing, even to herself. 'Friends and family you know. I'd . . . I've had a gutful of everything.'

To her surprise he simply nodded as though what she said made perfect sense. And then chuckled.

'You're a tough little squirt, aren't ya?'

She smiled.

'I dunno.'

Michelle struggled around for something to say. It was time to ask him something. She didn't trust herself to shut up, sitting like this so comfortably, drinking tea and having him look at her as though . . . well, as though they were old friends.

'Have you got parents?'

Mick shook his head, then looked away frowning.

'An old man, somewhere,' he said slowly, then rose quickly as though he was sick of the conversation and had something better, more important to do.

'I'll find him though.' This last part was flung out at her defensively as he made his way towards his end of the van.

Michelle waited. She almost asked what for, but stopped herself in time. His face, now staring out the back window and only moments before soft with an easy grin and light-filled warm eyes, had hardened. The mouth had turned into a straight line and the eyes had gone small and angry under the furrowed brows. She would have to say something, or this . . . whatever it was that was happening inside him, might escalate.

'That sounds like a threat.'

But Mick didn't answer. He turned abruptly to the table, picked up the two plates and pitched them into the sink. Then the cups and knives and forks. A hell of a racket. Crash. Michelle winced at the noise. She hated people throwing things around. Both her parents had been experts at it. Everything boiling up inside, unable to say what was eating them and so chucking things around to make every-one else miserable. She knew she should shut up, that he didn't want to talk about it, but suddenly curiosity was eating her alive. After all, today would be the last day she'd spend with this guy. It might be her only chance.

'What are you going to see him for? I mean if you haven't heard from him for a long time . . .' Her voice came out normally. Very matter-of-fact, and that pleased her.

Mick was kneeling with his back to her, stuffing belongings back into his bag.

'I gotta few big debts to pay back to that old bastard . . . a few teeth to smash and a few bones to break . . .' His voice had gone taut.

Michelle stared for a while at the broad back, at the way his shoulder bones showed through the worn shabby jumper, the sandy hair cut short around his ears and neck. His words hadn't made her feel afraid at all. There was too much pain in the way they'd come out. She knew instinctively that the old man, whoever he was, wasn't the victim.

'You sound mean, Mick,' she said suddenly. 'Real mean when you say stuff like that.'

A couple of moments hesitation and he turned around, something odd pulling at the corners of his mouth. Was he going to cry?

'I *am* mean, Michelle. Damned mean!'

His mouth opened out into another grin and she laughed in relief. He kept looking at her, then started to laugh too. She was glad she'd taken the risk and had a go at him. Called his bluff. He was okay this guy. He could take a joke.

'You wanna come to Broken Hill or you want to stay and ask more dumb questions?'

Michelle laughed again. She still felt very light but it was different somehow. Not so bad. She knew she could hack it. She could manage the rest of the trip up there to Broken Hill, no worries.

'Yeah,' she said, getting up. 'I reckon we'd better shift ourselves.'

By late afternoon the wide main streets of Broken Hill were soaking up the last heat of the day. Mick rolled the dusty Norton through the main shopping drag with its ornate low-slung verandahs. They were going so slowly that Michelle could hold her arms out for a moment as she looked around and give her hands a shake. It would be great to get off the bike and have a proper stretch.

The last few hours had been hard, the endless kilometres of flat road, saltbush and the occasional scrubby tree the only things to see. Michelle had found it absurd; unbelievably, stunningly monotonous. No people, apart from the occasional passing car, no houses, no animals. Just flat land as far as she could see in any direction, an enormous blue sky and dusty, faded blue saltbush. And then more saltbush. She'd heard about this sort of land at school, but seeing it was something else.

'Does this God-forsaken country go on forever or what?' she yelled at Mick's back as they roared along.

She could see one side of his face, grinning with pleasure.

'Why? Don't you like it?'

She gestured helplessly with both hands.

'It's just that there's . . . nothing.'

He laughed then.

'This is the best country, Michelle. The best. Look!'

He slowed the bike down and Michelle looked over to a small gnarled tree not far from the road. Five huge dark birds sat there impassively, staring. The tree seemed ready to collapse under the weight of them, their hooked beaks menacing even in the bright sunlight. They were close enough for her to see the enormous sharp talons clutching the faded grey bark, and the glinting, unflinching, dead-alive eyes and she felt a shudder go through her.

'Wedge-tails,' Mick stated matter-of-factly. 'Mean-looking bastards up close, aren't they?' He added the last bit almost joyfully, as though he got a real kick out of seeing them there. It confused Michelle. There was something spooky about those birds sitting there like that. Waiting. Like a bad omen, a sign of worse things to come. If you were superstitious you could think they were waiting there for you to break down, get lost, get sick, lie down and die. Then they'd be at you, claws, beaks, the works. She watched, relieved, as they all suddenly flew off, at exactly the same moment, their enormous wings slowly stretching out, up high and then into the distant blue, like kings, dipping and soaring for their own pleasure.

There didn't seem to be much to say after that until they reached Broken Hill. Michelle shut her eyes and tried to think of the poem Veronica used to quote to her sometimes, but could only remember a couple of lines.

'I have seen the Bird of Paradise. She has spread herself before me, and I will never be the same again ...'

The bike roared on and Michelle wondered what came next. *The Bird of Paradise.* She could hear Veronica's clear soft voice plodding her way through the words. Michelle wondered how it would sound if she transplanted 'eagle' in place of 'bird'.

'I have seen the wedge-tailed eagle. He has flown like a king before my eyes. And I will never be the same again.'

When they first neared the city Mick slowed down and pointed to the enormous slagheaps and shining steel machinery that lay ahead of them like the huge leftover toys from another, grander age.

'Used to be a few mining companies up here – North Broken Hill, CRA – now there's only one, Pasminco ...' he said. 'The others joined forces a few years back. Be hard to get a job now. So much of it's done with machines ...'

Michelle nodded, awed at what she was seeing and curious too.

'What do they ... er, dig up?' she asked tentatively. Mick smiled but didn't turn around.

'Zinc, lead and silver. Just about everyone depends on mining in one way or another up here. Or used to.'

This pleasant ordinary metropolis with pubs on every corner and familiar shops like Sportsgirl and Portmans scattered throughout the city centre seemed strangely dreamlike after the arduous drive through nothingness. Crossing one intersection, Michelle could see the great slagheaps sticking up like giant black pimples. There were no corners or hills for the machinery to hide behind. It rose up against the horizon and above the town in shining odd shapes that made her think of space capsules and lost cities. The people too looked different, like part of a film or a dream that had lazily come to life. She supposed she was simply disorientated and would get her bearings soon. After all they were just ordinary people on a Sunday afternoon, lolling around on seats, eating, drinking milkshakes and cans, ambling slowly towards parked cars, calling out and smiling. Old ladies with grey perms, kids in strollers, young men in blue singlets and girls in light halter-topped dresses and bright lipstick. Maybe it was the warmth and clear light that made it all seem so strange – this town, city rather, silver and shining, buzzing with life amidst the dry barrenness of the outback.

By the time they'd walked around a bit, got something to eat and had a wash in the public washrooms it was well into the afternoon. Mick sat on the park bench trying to fix the zipper on his sleeping-bag and Michelle lay on the grass next to the bike, her eyes closed, enjoying the sun on her face.

'So what do you plan to do, Michelle?'

Michelle opened her eyes and sat up a bit. He was genuinely interested. She could tell by his eyes. Concerned. And so blue in that broad serious face.

She shook her head and tried to shake off the feeling. She'd known the guy for about forty-eight hours and she was going to miss him.

'I dunno. Hang around here until tomorrow. Then register with the CES I guess. Ask around, in the pubs and cafes, you know ... I'll do anything.'

Michelle turned away, her attention caught by a crowd of teenagers her own age on the other side of the road. About eight of them, rambling along noisily in T-shirts, light pants and shorts, most of them with brown skins and shiny well-cut hair. They were all dressed to go somewhere, their clothing, although casual, was well-pressed and clean, chosen with care in spite of being worn so carelessly. One of them was out in front showing off, throwing and catching something in the air. Someone's jacket, or was it a bag? The others yelled out and jumped around trying to catch the thing he was throwing. She couldn't hear what they were saying but every now and again there would be a burst of loud laughter, then squeals as someone else got hold of whatever it was. She longed to be among them suddenly, to be part of that easy careless joking world of gym boots and boyfriends, school and future plans, and more than anything, the feeling that life was in front of you, that it was simply there for the taking. The longing left as quickly as it had arrived. She didn't have time to start feeling sorry for herself. It would be better by far to get this over with quickly.

'You'd better get going, Mick ... if you're going to get out to that place by night-time. Reckon you could give me a ride down to the main street again? I've got to ... get some more money out and find somewhere to stay.'

She didn't look at him but was still with the group careering around the corner now and out of sight.

'Where do you think you might stay?'

'Maybe I'll get another van.'

'I can take you to one ... if you like.'

'If you've got enough time I'd appreciate that ...'

Here it was again. This feeling that she wanted to howl her eyes out. It was probably the exhaustion – the emotional exhaustion catching up with her. It wasn't so much that she was feeling sorry for herself. Okay she was in a fix but nothing that a job and a decent place to stay wouldn't cure – at least for the next few months – but no, it was the kindness in his rough voice making her feel inexplicably, unbearably sad. It made her think of her brothers, the way they used to be when they were all still living at home. The way they would become tender sometimes, in spite of everything.

'Anyone want a cup of cocoa?' That would be Darren. He was always making sweet drinks and offering them around.

'I'll lift that for you, Mum. It's too heavy.' She could just about hear them.

Darren and Wayne were always quick to forgive, whereas Michelle could forget nothing. Every mean snipe and ugly bad-tempered slap was scorched on to Michelle's brain. Every stupid comment fuelled the bitterness she'd felt from the time she was ten. Seven years of it. So many things to remember. At night she would lie in bed and go over the latest outrage and match it up with what had happened a year before, or maybe two years before that, in a sort of bizarre counting game, the scoreboard all the time growing bigger and heavier inside her own head. Sometimes it got so heavy she was afraid to go off to sleep; the weight of it might crash right down and snuff her out altogether.

When the boys lived at home sometimes the three of them would sit for hours playing cards on the kitchen table. After tea, with the washing up done they'd go right on into the night if the game turned out to be interesting. The aching in their sides as they tried to stifle their laughter so their parents wouldn't come in and interrupt. Big waves of it used to hit them all, usually over some stupid thing Darren had said. They'd hold their bellies, cover their mouths with their hands, gulp, splutter and turn red with it. At such times Michelle used to feel as though she were on a little boat with them both, out on the wide green sea with nothing else around for miles. The love rocked between them, to and fro, as refreshing and wonderful as a nippy sea breeze on a hot day. The dark curly hair falling into Wayne's eyes – the thin open mouth, always moving, talking, smiling, grimacing, and opening wide to laugh. Michelle used to love watching his blue eyes fill with tears when he was really cracking up.

85

Shoulders shaking. Both boys were always great suckers for each other's jokes. Those eyes would well up and gleam, and then spill over. And seeing him do that always made them all laugh even more.

Michelle hardly ever cried. Yet here she was, remembering everything, her brothers, the table they played cards on, even the slightly sour smell of the floor polish in the kitchen, having to fight to stop her face crumpling up. She looked up and to her dismay saw that Mick had been watching her. She turned away sharply, angry with him and herself. There was no way she wanted sympathy from anyone.

'Okay, let's go and find you a van,' he said, a little awkwardly. Good. He was going to pretend he hadn't noticed.

She nodded, and without looking at him stood up and got on the bike. Mick climbed on in front and started it up. She was glad that her face was looking directly into his back. The new bubble of sweaty feeling was freaking her. *I'm not someone who cries ... I'm tough. Always have been.*

By the time they'd found a caravan park, paid for it and settled Michelle in, it was after four. Michelle wondered why he didn't get going but said nothing.

'Why don't we have a cup of tea?' He smiled as he plonked himself down at the table. He seemed in no hurry at all now and it made her wonder.

Pleased, Michelle nodded, filled the kettle and began searching around for the matches.

'Damn. No matches. Have to go and ask at the office.'

She was on her way out when he reached into his canvas bag, drew out a box and threw it at her with a grin.

'Here.'

'Oh thanks ...' She fumbled as she took one out, lit the gas and tried not to think about staying in this van at night all alone.

'I'm not just an ugly face ...'

She tried to think of something smart and cheeky to snap back, but nothing came.

'Michelle ...' He spoke hesitantly as though he wasn't quite sure what he wanted to say.

'Would you mind if I stayed again tonight?' He was nervous. She could tell by the formal way he was sitting there with his hands still.

'Say no if you'd rather I didn't but ... well, I've never been out to this place before ... It's apparently three hours out. I'd rather set out early tomorrow, so that if there's nothing going, I'll be able to get on to somewhere else in the light ... if it's okay with you?'

'Sure.' Very matter-of-fact. She was trying very hard not to sound happy.

'That's no worries at all.'

'Thanks. Thanks a lot.'

The water boiled. Michelle made the tea and Mick got up and stood at the caravan doorway, staring out into the softening light.

'They sometimes have work for women on these stations ... you want to come out with me and try your luck?'

'What sort of jobs?'

He shrugged and turned back towards her, leaning his back against the flimsy caravan.

'I dunno. Looking after kids. Housework ...'

'I hate housework ... and kids,' she snapped straight back at him.

He grinned. But she looked away sulkily and wouldn't meet his eyes. What did she mean she hated kids and housework? She'd never done much housework in her life and she didn't know any kids.

'Well, I guess that puts the kibosh on that, then. I don't know that there'd be much else.' He was still grinning a bit ruefully – and she was still embarrassed.

'Then again I don't much like serving in a shop either ... or working in a pub,' she mumbled.

This time he laughed aloud. Threw his head back as though she'd just said something really funny. Michelle looked away, biting her thumb. It was really nice the way his face opened up when he laughed. But why was he laughing at her?

'So, what sort of work you gonna do, Michelle?'

'I thought I might go looking for gold or something like that . . .'

For a moment he thought she was serious. His mouth dropped open and then he noticed the dry playful twinge around her mouth. He rose and got out a couple of mugs from above the sink and poured the tea that she'd forgotten about.

'I'll think it over tonight . . .'

'What?' He'd forgotten already. Michelle felt the knot in her belly do another somersault. Perhaps he hadn't meant it at all.

'Whether I'll go out to the farm with you . . .'

'Sure. You think it over. It might not be such a great idea actually. If there's nothing out there for you it'll be hard getting back.'

'Yeah, that's just what I was thinking,' Michelle said thoughtfully.

They sat opposite each other and sipped their tea. After a few minutes silence Mick looked at his watch.

'What do you say we go into town and get a few hamburgers for tea?'

Michelle's face brightened.

'Yeah. Good idea.'

8

She decided to come. I thought she might. And in the end I was glad she did too. We were getting along pretty well by this stage so I just let her decide. Sometimes I have the feeling that things happen or they don't and that there isn't much any of us can do about it. That's different to saying things are *meant to be*, if you get my drift. In my position I have to believe I can make things happen. But sometimes you've got to chuck your dice up in the air and see which number comes up.

It turned into a great day for me. Only my fourth one out of jail and the sky, the ground, the smells – everything was just as I remembered. I just kept feeling better and better about being up around those parts, away from the city, back in my old stamping ground.

We'd gone into town last night and had some hamburgers. That was all right, sitting in the warm lighted cafe listening to the jukebox down the other end. The hamburgers were good and the coffee just how I liked it, hot and strong. By chance we must have hit on the groovy place to be in Broken Hill. There were a lot of young people hanging around together near the music, yelling out, laughing, scraping their chairs and acting up. The proprietor would glare at them every now and again and occasionally yell for them to behave but he knew he couldn't do too much, they were buying stuff after all. It was funny to watch them, getting up to order their hot chips and drinks, flouncing around for each other, pretending they weren't. Showing off. It made me feel old and sort of like an outsider, which I suppose I was. Some of them were talking about leaving for the movies or the pub. Places I haven't seen or even thought about much for years. The girls were young and all tarted up and the guys were pretty flashy too although they didn't make it as obvious. Most of them looked to be around eighteen or twenty, still at school I reckoned, or at college or wherever people go these days. Anyway not that much younger than me. Michelle was sitting opposite me and must have been thinking along the same lines because she just blurted out, in that gruff little voice of hers, 'You ever feel like a freak?'

What a question! I laughed. I mean if you wanted to take a question like that the wrong way . . . But I knew she didn't mean it like that.

'I know what you mean,' was all I said and finished off my drink. I wanted to get out of that joint quickly after that. It sort of made me feel down, her putting it into words.

As a kid still at school I was never part of any gang or group, especially after Mum died. It wasn't that I didn't want it. I did, a lot. It was just that it never worked out for me. I was fourteen when she died and I think I kind of went troppo for a couple of years. Just around and around into myself, and then deeper and deeper into it all until when I finally did manage to come up and look around I didn't recognise where I was any more. Everything was unfamiliar. I mean what gang wants to know about that kind of stuff?

That first year, I could hardly even talk. I let the old man belt me around for the slightest thing whereas before, me, and the girls for that matter, used to be pretty good at sticking up for ourselves, or at least getting out of his way. Once, he knocked me down in the cow-yard and started smashing the back of my head against the concrete floor, because I'd forgotten to wash out a couple of buckets. I can still smell all that hay and cow shit that I was lying in, hear the dull clunking sound of my own head against the stone

90

too, and see the spasms of pink streaks shooting up something crazy in front of my eyes each time my head struck. He was sitting on my legs and going to kill me I reckon – no worries – he had the mad look in his eyes real bad that day. It was just lucky for me that the manager of the property came along at the right time or I reckon he would have done me. There was a lot of blood and I had to have stitches and everything but the most puzzling thing about it was that I'd completely lost my guts. I didn't seem to have any energy to protect myself. I hadn't shouted much or tried to kick him either. It was like I didn't really care.

At school I'd hang around the sidelines and look at the other kids, the way they joked and kicked around; the loose gangs that formed, the split friendships and the quiet bonds that grew tighter as the months passed. All separate from me. Looking back now, I reckon I would have given my right arm to be part of it all. I actually liked school. I wanted to listen, do the work and play the games outside but the rest of my life made it all more or less impossible.

After that attack in the cow-yard I was taken away from home and put with people I didn't know for a while. I had to go to another school and because it was in town there was nothing to do at night except watch TV. I guess the station manager must have reported him or something. I can't remember much about the foster family they put me with except that the house was tiny and neat, like a doll's house. I'd never seen anything like it. A heap of pink and white towels lined up in the bathroom like candy. All the corners neatly folded. I couldn't remember ever seeing a towel folded at home, much less anything soft like this, and so clean. Everything was clean. They weren't bad people. The old guy – I think he worked in the local bank – tried to get me interested in Aussie Rules football. That was all right. We had a kick around the backyard a few times and I pretended to listen to what he was telling me. But nothing much got through. Inside I was churned up, worrying about

Beth being back there with the old man on her own. How would she manage without me to stick up for her?

It wasn't until I'd been sent back home months later that I found out she'd also been taken away and put with another family.

The day she came home was the best day I can remember, ever. Even better than the day I got out of the jug. I thought I wasn't going to see her again. The old man wouldn't tell me where she was. No one would. I don't know if they all thought I was going to kidnap her or something. Fat chance, I was only fourteen. It wasn't as though I could do much. My older sisters had left for good by then, fixed up with jobs in the city, and I thought that Beth would end up with them for sure, in spite of her age.

Anyway she just arrived back one day, wearing a new dress. It had a white top and blue trimmings on the collar and cuffs. And new shoes. She had these shoes with brass buckles on them. I knew how much they'd mean to Beth and I felt this incredible buzz of happiness for her. I mean we never got new shoes, none of us. God, the picture of her walking up the path towards me is so sharp. Wherever she'd been they'd fattened her up a bit. All her fair hair tied back in a pony-tail and she was grinning like a bloody cat, happy as hell to be coming back to that terrible house with the old man and me. I remember thinking that she looked like a beautiful bird. Something delicate and graceful like a swan or ibis, gliding towards me. I ran out on to the verandah whooping like a maniac and reached her midway on the dirt track leading to our front door. I was about to pick her up and whizz her around like I used to but something stopped me doing that. She'd changed somehow. I don't know, developed. She seemed older anyway. So we just looked at each other for a few moments and then hugged quickly. On the way back into the house we were both choked up, crying a bit.

We didn't talk hardly at all. She just went in and changed out of her good clothes. I still had all these jobs I had to get through before the old man got back; the pigs had to be fed and the sheds cleaned, a wheel had to be changed on the old truck, then the trees around the house watered. I remember everything we did on that afternoon. The way she followed me around, helping where she could, hardly saying anything.

I hung on for two years after Mum's death. Going to school, working the farm at night, putting up with him. Being taken out to stay in different places when things got really rough. Beth was only twelve and I really wanted to stick it out for her sake. She needed protection. Well, I suppose I did too for that matter but I loved Beth. We got on, I didn't want to leave her with him. But after a year or two it became a question of survival. After one really bad time I just thought: I've had enough. If I want to go on living I'll have to go. I tried to talk her into going with me. She was tempted, hating him as much as I did but she was all right at school. She had her friends – one girl in particular she used to stay over with a lot. I felt bad about leaving. Even now it makes me feel bad. I mean he probably wouldn't have actually killed me – his bark was always worse than his bite – but I suppose I'd just had a gutful, so I took off.

As I say, I was just a kid then and I was mad and optimistic and young enough to think that if I ran away I could maybe just head off and pick myself up the kind of life I wanted, but it didn't turn out to be that easy.

Michelle and I left quickly after we'd finished the hamburgers and headed straight back to the bike. I was looking forward to a good hot shower and an early night. I was nervous about the next day too. Couldn't stop hoping that things would work out, that I'd land some kind of a job. If I didn't, then what would I do? I tried to think of some options but nothing much came to mind. In the end I knew that at least until they were dashed, I was pinning my hopes on Chas.

We talked a bit more that night, lying in our sleeping-bags, up opposite ends of the caravan. It was good in a way, not being able to see each other, just talking and listening with the dark space between us. It felt a lot more comfortable than being in the cafe. I mean we were still cagey with each other but were both gradually opening up. She told me a bit about her old music teacher and I started telling her about Pino.

'Well, he's real short and he's got this rotten skin. Sort of little holes in it, you know ...?'

'Pockmarks?'

'Yeah.'

'He sounds pretty ... well, ugly.' She started laughing and it set me off. I'm not sure why.

'Yeah, well, I suppose you could say that ...'

Pino used to describe himself as ugly. Often. It was one of the few things he accepted very easily about himself.

'My horrible looks are the least of me worries, mate,' he'd say and we'd both grin. So I didn't feel like I was being two-faced.

'You ever seen those pictures of Snow White and her little men ...'

'You mean the dwarfs ... the seven dwarfs?' She was starting to really giggle again.

'Yeah. That's right ... shut up! Stop laughing.'

But she couldn't stop laughing and she'd got me going again too.

'Which one was he?' she spluttered. 'Pino, I mean ...'

'Well, I dunno ... What're their names again?'

It's weird. I can't explain what was so funny about trying to remember the seven dwarfs' names but both of us could hardly speak we were packing up so badly.

'Well, there's Sleepy ... and Dopey ...!'

'And Stumpy ...'

'Lumpy!'

'No! What about Hungry . . .'

'No . . . there's no Hungry. You just made that up!'

'Well, Horny, then!' she blurted out and we both busted up again. I could tell by her voice and the laughter that she'd got the devil in her. She reminded me of Beth! Exactly the same way of cracking up. The van was starting to shake we were both laughing so much.

'What about Grumpy . . .'

'And Dumpy?'

'That's me. I'm dumpy and grumpy most of the time,' she shouted loudly, then cracked up again.

'God, stop it. My belly's aching!' It was too. The muscles across my guts were really hurting.

'You haven't told me which one your friend is.'

'Well, it depends on what day you catch him . . .'

And so it went on. It was great having a laugh. When it was over I felt warm towards her. I mean she was just a bit of a kid but it was nice having her there. Much better than being on my own. I wanted to tell her that I liked her, that I appreciated her company but I thought she might think I was trying something on so I shut up. We were both drifting off to sleep when she said sleepily as though she was dreaming, 'You written to that guy yet?'

'What guy?'

'Your friend in jail? Pino or whatever his name is.'

'Nah, I've only been out a few days!'

'I reckon if I was in there it'd be good to get a lot of mail.'

'Yeah. You'd be right there.'

I woke up a little after that, thinking. Remembering how hard it was at first doing without letters. It was bad in those first few months when every other bastard's name seemed to be called out except mine. Had I ever really got used to it? Knowing that there was no one much on the outside who gave a stuff? Well, yeah, I suppose I did get used to it. What scares me now is thinking I might slip back into that frame of mind where I can't take stuff like that. That kind of pain makes you incapable of doing ... anything much. I don't even want to remember what that was like.

I got one postcard in the first year. Just one. From an Aboriginal kid I used to knock around with when I was about eight or nine when we lived on a property about a hundred miles out of Bourke. Tough little Buster. I remember being real glad to know he was still alive. But how in hell had he found out I was in the slammer? I hadn't seen him for years. Over the rest of my time inside, I only had about three other letters from my sisters in Western Australia. Yeah. I reckon it was only three.

We got out to the property about midday after a four-hour drive straight through that bleak country that I loved so much. The flat, airy, hard nothingness made my head spin. For the first time in a long while I wished she wasn't there because I knew she couldn't see it the way I did. Like most people from the south and the edges she was only seeing the surface, and if you look at this country like that then it *is* boring. But for me it was like coming back to the thing I loved most. That red dirt and those scraggy wilgas and cypress pines made me want to start singing and shouting out. Hundreds of kilometres without a car, a house or a person in sight. The dome of clear blue above and the occasional group of roos startling off into the scrub. Then emus, bolting off in a mad panic on the other side. I was finding something that had been lost inside me and I wanted to weave in and out on that straight white ribbon of road for the joy of having found it again.

Eventually, after a few hours and a couple of wrong turn-offs we saw the name on the white gate – 'Wilyarna'. It was Michelle who spotted it first.

'There it is,' she said.

I stopped the bike and found myself just looking at the word and feeling that earlier sense of being carefree just sort of steam out of me, like air from a hole in a balloon. Without the roar of the bike the quietness out there just sort of closed around us, deep and serious. I found myself panicking, wondering if I'd be able to hack it. I don't know whether she noticed my change of mood but she gave me a funny look.

'Well, looks like we're here then, Mick . . .'

'Yeah.'

I kept staring at the name. There it was, the same word that I'd read over and over again in Chas's letter. '*I'm working on a station called "Wilyarna", north-west of Wilcannia . . .*' What if Chas wasn't there any more? Worse, what if he didn't want to know me? Did I really want to see *him*? I mean we'd been mates in the clanger but things would be different outside. Perhaps he was just a nobody and I'd imagined all his good points. Perhaps he'd treat *me* like a nobody . . .?

Things were pretty bad in the bush, I knew that much. The bum had fallen out of wool and the Yanks had pinched our overseas meat and grain markets in the Middle East. Even so this place looked all right. The fencing looked good and the nearby cattle pit was wide. I wondered about the size of the place, how many head of cattle and how many sheep. They were employing people, so it would have to be at least a hundred thousand acres. At the very least. With a bit of luck at this time of the year they'd still have the shearing to go. There was no homestead in sight but that wasn't unusual. Sometimes you had to go a further ten or twenty kilometres in from the road to find the house.

The woman who answered us at the front door of the old white wooden homestead looked nervy. She'd probably been good-looking a few years back, but now, probably hitting her forties and with a few kids under her belt, she'd faded. She stared at us for a good three seconds before actually speaking. I nodded politely, and stood well away from the door in the country manner, waiting for her to speak first.

97

'Yes. Can I help you?' She frowned as she spoke.

'Hello. Yes. We're looking for a bloke by the name of Charlie Morris. I believe he's working on this property.'

She frowned again and sighed impatiently as she stared out past us to the bike outside the front fence.

'You come on that?'

'Yes.'

'Both of you?' Her eyes slid over Michelle again. Curious suddenly.

'Yes.'

'Well, he could be working here. I don't exactly have anything to do with who's employed or not . . .' She broke off and shrugged then as though reminding herself that we were complete strangers. I blurted out the next bit because she looked like she was about to shut the door.

'Well, I'm . . . er, we're after work too, you see. Chas wrote to me and said there might be something going up here.'

I hated the way it was all spilling out. What was the point in telling her all this? She said herself that she had nothing to do with who was employed or not. We could hear kids running and yelling excitedly in the yard. Within seconds they were there standing next to their mother and staring at us, open-mouthed and suspicious. I grinned. You couldn't hold it against them. These kids most likely hadn't seen a new face for at least a month.

There was a boy about ten, a girl of maybe six, then a couple of twins probably no more than four. This place was too far out for them to be able to go to school. It would be school-of-the-air for the eldest two for sure. I nodded at the boy and he nodded back seriously. The woman sighed and held the door open.

'You'd better come in and have a drink. My husband won't be back for a few hours.'

'Thanks. Thanks a lot.'

I stood back for Michelle and we entered the cool wide

hallway of the old house but couldn't see anything at first while our eyes adjusted. Dark wood panelling lined the walls up to perhaps a foot above the heavy doors. There was a musty, dusty smell as we walked down past closed doors to the kitchen at the other end of the house.

'The shearing starts soon . . . shearing early this year, but I did hear him tell Bert . . . that's the old fellow that's been with us for ages, that the contractor he works through is all fixed up for men . . . that they don't need anyone else.'

I tried not to let my hopes fall as we entered the kitchen and looked around. It was huge and quite a bit hotter than outside. A real old-fashioned farmhouse kitchen with a big black wood-fire cooking range in the corner, complete with blackened kettles and pots on top. One of the pots was bubbling away, and a soupy smell mixed with the bread and cake smells and the heat that came from the oven made the atmosphere thick and intoxicating. The last couple of properties I'd worked on had all the mod cons including microwaves and dishwashers. Seeing these cupboards covering one entire wall up to the ceiling, the huge old dresser and the stained white washing-up sink that was more like a bath, was like taking a step back into the past.

A memory hit me suddenly, something I hadn't thought about for years. I couldn't have been more than three or four and I was standing next to my mother as she stood at a sink, exactly like this one, washing up. She was humming to herself and smiling. Then suddenly she picked me up and sat me next to her on the sink and let me play for a minute in the sudsy dirty washing-up water. I remembered the feeling of my hand passing through the little bubbles and the delight of pulling it away and seeing the suds still clinging to my fingers. Fragile and translucent as fairy lights, holding them up for my mother to see. Her laughter and gentle voice burrowing into my neck.

'See! Little castles right there in your hands.'

The things you remember, eh?

This joint didn't look as though anyone had whacked any new paint around for about fifty years. It was clean but very shabby. The yellow-cream paintwork and worn-out lino made me think of all the people who must have come trooping through here, people we'd never see or know. I could almost smell them: the women, men and kids who would have cooked, eaten, washed up, cried and argued here over the years. The woman, now filling the kettle at the sink, must have been reading my thoughts.

'This part of the house is well over a hundred years old . . . built by my husband's grandfather . . . they were Germans.'

I nodded, not knowing what to say. She didn't seem to want a conversation, just to tell us things.

By the enormous covered table in the centre of the room a very pregnant Aboriginal girl stood stringing beans. She turned around when we came in and gave us a shy smile before going straight back to her work. I nodded back, surprised. I hadn't seen a real black Aboriginal person in years. There were quite a few guys in the clanger with a bit of blood in them, but you could hardly tell. Their skins only looked nicely tanned. Sort of coppery. Of course you always *could* tell, the nose and the mouth were different.

'This is Sharon. She won't be working here for much longer . . .' the woman said, then walked brusquely past the girl and repositioned the kettle on the stove.

'A cup of tea? Or coffee?'

'Tea thanks,' I said.

'Me too.'

I glanced at Michelle briefly to see how all this was affecting her, but she was looking away, a bit uneasily, towards the window. She'd probably never seen a real old-time joint like this.

'Won't you sit down?' The woman indicated the opposite end of the table to where Sharon was working, then got the tea caddie down from the mantelpiece. The kids stood motionless in the doorway, still staring at us. Maybe that was what was making Michelle feel uncomfortable. I leaned forward, about to tell her that the kids were only looking because they would hardly ever see strangers, when the woman spoke.

'You can wait till my husband gets back if you like.'

We murmured our thanks. She was being nice, probably in the best way she knew how. All the same, there was a sharpness to her voice that set me on edge. The telephone suddenly rang up the other end of the house. The woman jumped nervously and immediately put down the caddie.

'Sharon, perhaps you could make this tea,' she ordered.

'Yes . . . sure.' The Aboriginal girl took the order easily.

'And there's some biscuits too,' she added and then pushed past the children and disappeared.

The children continued to watch. I got up and headed over to where Sharon was struggling to lift the heavy kettle.

'I'll do that.'

She smiled and moved away.

'Thanks . . . things are getting a bit hard for me now.' She had a nice smooth voice. Gentle and easy. As she spoke she looked over at Michelle with a smile that said girls-understand-this-kind-of-thing but got no response.

Michelle only shrugged as though she hadn't any idea what the girl was referring to and sourly turned away to the window.

I brought the full teapot over to the table while Sharon got cups and saucers out from the ancient kitchen dresser.

'You people look like you've been travelling a way,' she said.

'Yeah,' I said. 'We've been going a while, haven't we, Michelle?'

Michelle grunted and kept staring out the window. Suddenly the woman was back. Without saying anything she took over from where Sharon was pouring the tea. Sharon put down the tea-towel that was lying across one arm and said mildly, 'Think I'll go and do the lounge room, Nina.'

'All right, Sharon. Don't forget I want the bookcase sorted out. Would you like a cup of tea first?'

'No, I'll get on with it, I think.'

'Okay, then.'

The woman turned to us brightly.

'I've just had an idea.'

We both looked at her, waiting. *She's a strange one*, I found myself thinking. *Don't know if I'd want to spend too much time with her.*

The light-brown eyes had now settled on Michelle.

'You're looking for work too, I assume?' she breathed excitedly.

Michelle nodded.

'Well, Sharon, as you can both see, won't be with me much longer. I'm really quite desperate about how I'm going to manage the shearing. They have their own cook but ... things being what they are these days, I have to provide morning and afternoon teas for the men. I've got the children and everything. I need someone in the house to help look after the children while they're doing their school work ... they do their lessons with school-of-the-air ... and, well, shearing is a very busy time. I'd have to bring the food up to them in the truck.' She was blurting all this out very quickly. I couldn't work out if she was nervous or angry. Suddenly she stood up and moved to the other side of Michelle, staring at her as though she was a cow she was thinking about buying.

'But could you manage it? What experience have you had? Have you got any references?'

Michelle stared straight back at the woman so hard that the older woman's eyes dropped first.

'You're talking about looking after kids ... general household stuff?' Michelle growled slowly, her voice as tough and scratchy as an old nail scraping along a tin roof. 'I reckon I could manage that. You don't want me to cook, do you? I've never had any experience with that.'

'No. I'd do the cooking. Mainly the housework and the children.'

'That would be okay. But I, er ... left my references at home. I've worked in shops ...'

'How old are you?' the woman snapped.

'Seventeen.'

I sighed. I should have told Michelle to up her age. The pay for a seventeen-year-old in this kind of job would be pitiful.

The woman was looking cagey again.

'I'll try you for a week. If you don't work out then I've still got a few days to get someone else from town.'

'Okay.' Michelle was hesitating. She didn't like the woman or the job, I could tell that. But like me she wasn't in any position to say no.

'You'd have to sleep in the same room as my eldest daughter ...' She gave me a strange look. 'You're not married or anything, are you?'

'No.' I smiled at Michelle and she smiled back drily.

'Just friends.'

The woman looked relieved, then turned her attention back to me.

'Trouble is, I don't think there'll be anything for you ...'

'I realise that ...'

The woman got up and smoothed her faded dress.

'I have work to do.' She indicated the children in the doorway.

'Their lessons have to be supervised.' She looked at Michelle. 'I'll ask Sharon to show you around. Say in half an hour. Give her time to finish what she's doing. How do you feel about starting at the end of next week? The shearing starts the following Monday. It will give you time to ... er, settle in.'

'That's fine,' Michelle said.

The woman walked out, dragging the kids with her. Michelle and I were left looking at each other at the kitchen table. Suddenly she smiled a little.

'Well!'

I grinned back.

'Well!'

'I dunno, Mick. Shit, I imagined working in a pub or a milk bar, not out here in the sticks with ... with one woman bossing me around.'

'Well, you can always nick off ... Give it a try first though.'

'Yeah. You're right. I can leave if it's too ...'

'Too what?' I smiled.

Michelle shrugged and smiled back a little self-consciously. She motioned towards the window, through to all that expansive flatness. For a moment I saw it through her eyes and I understood that she was afraid of the desolation.

'Let's go and have a look outside while we wait for Sharon,' I said.

We stood together out on the verandah. She was fidgeting, and didn't look too happy.

'You'll get used to it,' I said.

'Will I?' She seemed preoccupied and didn't even try to smile back.

'What will you do if there isn't any work for you?' she suddenly burst out.

I shrugged.

'Nothing for it but to keep moving on.'

I made myself sound easier than I felt. Anyway, it would probably be the case, whether I liked it or not. The woman had said as much. There probably weren't any jobs going and I'd have my marching orders pretty soon after the men got back that afternoon. Then it would be off to God knows where. Still, if Chas was working here he might have a few ideas about where I could go. Funny how I suddenly didn't care. It was Michelle I was thinking about. I would miss her.

'Thanks for everything, Michelle ... all the best and everything. I've really enjoyed talking to you.' I smiled at her trying to keep it light. 'It's gonna be hard going off without you . . . you've been a great mate . . . over these last few days.'

It was the truth but I hadn't intended getting so heavy. By the time I'd finished she'd turned her face away. I watched her fingers peeling the paint off the wooden house post as the silence settled in between us. Picking and scratching with her short little dirty fingers. A twinge of longing hit me suddenly. Those hands brought up a flood of half-forgotten stuff that I didn't understand. I felt like telling her everything suddenly. Every single thing that had happened to me. What was the point of keeping it buried? She'd listen, I knew that now. Now that it was too late. I wanted to bury my face in her shoulder and blurt out a lot of stuff – about how I liked her blue eyes, the way they sometimes got icy, and the way she looked at me, always so direct. And that voice. I wanted to tell her how much I appreciated her saying exactly what was on her mind and that I'd never quite known a girl like her. I was going to miss her quirky toughness. Her surly attitude. The way she never giggled in that annoying way girls sometimes have and the way she would sometimes laugh, quick and spontaneous. Her rough, straight way of seeing things. But I had probably embarrassed her enough already so I shut up.

I waited there awkwardly, the silence deepening between us. There was only the rustling sound of the breeze in a nearby tree. I looked around the garden. A few straggly gums down one corner, a kids' swing set up between them and some other quite well-grown European poplars and maples. All pretty untidy, overgrown. I liked it. I wondered about the water supply. There must be a bore nearby. It would take a lot of water to keep this garden alive through the summer. The summers out here would be blistering, day after day after day.

I can't tell you what I felt when I heard the first sniff. Well, the truth was I thought I'd heard wrong until there was another one. Unmistakable. Louder this time. I looked back to her quickly but her face was still hidden from me. When I saw her put her face in her hands and her shoulders shake a little I knew she was crying. I put my hand out to touch her shoulder but stopped at the last moment.

'What's up, Michelle?' I said at last. I was at a complete loss. The only thing I actually wanted to do was to turn her around and hug her, but I knew that was exactly what I couldn't do. She didn't answer. Just went on shaking and sniffing. I knew she was trying to restrain herself but it wasn't working. It made me smile a bit, remembering how Beth used to be like that. She'd be hiding under the bed after a belting, sobbing her heart out, and trying like mad to stop. I'd creep into her room after a while and sit and wait for her on the bed, wondering what to do. If she went on for a long time I'd risk climbing under the bed with her – if I was caught I'd get a belting – and hold her under there for ages, my arms tight around her and her face pressed hard against my chest. I'd tell her anything that came into my head. Anything to comfort her. I knew she just needed to listen to a voice, any voice, talking to her. I'd tell her she was terrific, the best kid in the world, that when she grew up she'd most probably marry a prince and end up the queen of the whole country. When she was going through her actress craze I'd tell her that she'd be spotted by a talent scout soon and be taken to Hollywood to live. There'd be swimming-pools and great big shiny cars, and houses as big as castles. The tears would eventually peter out.

Eventually I took Michelle by the elbow, still keeping a distance between us and led her to the edge of the verandah. I indicated that we should sit down there together. She did this willingly, and once seated there with her feet next to mine on the concrete footpath, she put one small nail-bitten hand on my knee and pressed very hard.

'I'm sorry, Mick . . . I just feel. It's hard to explain . . .'

106

Very apprehensively I put one arm around her shoulder and gave her a hug, waiting for the fresh lot of tears to ebb.

'You don't have to explain anything to me, mate,' I said at last. I could feel her still shuddering and trembling near me. I was eaten up with curiosity but quite determined not to ask her a single question. When and if she wanted to talk would be soon enough. She suddenly leant in next to me, putting both arms around my middle, holding me tightly.

'You're all right, Mick,' she said between sniffs. 'You're all right.'

I laughed, I think a little awkwardly, but I was pleased and I think she could tell. I then put my other arm around her. We stayed there together on the verandah for what seemed like ages, in silence, arms around each other and holding on tightly, both thinking our own thoughts.

Slowly we let go of each other and looked into each other's eyes. Calmly and seriously. Michelle and me just looking at each other and not touching. I think we both knew then that things had somehow changed between us. Another wall had broken down. I stood up.

'Why don't we have a look around?'

'Are we allowed?' she said, a little nervously. I laughed, and held out my hand to help her up.

'Of course we are. We won't do any harm.'

I could see the big shearing shed in the distance, about half a kilometre away.

We walked off towards it. I can't tell you how I felt when she casually took my hand without saying anything or even looking at me. Just slipped her own small one into mine. It felt so good. My face probably gave nothing away. I'm good at not letting on, but inside, I tell you, I was humming.

9

Mick and Michelle returned from their short walk around the shearing shed on that first afternoon and were heading back to the house when they heard a dry cough some way over to the right of them. Mick had seen the two work vehicles pull up near the fence but it wasn't until they'd almost reached the house and heard the cough that he realised they were being scrutinised by someone.

'The wife tells me you're after a job.' The gruff voice startled them both, making them drop each other's hands guiltily and wait. A tall lean man in work clothes, about fifty, emerged from a shed and came slowly towards them. His hair was grey and thinning and his eyes cold and light. Mick nodded and stepped forward, away from Michelle.

'That's right . . .'

The man returned the nod tersely. He was watching them both very carefully as though waiting for them to speak. Michelle looked away, wishing Mick would explain who they were and what they wanted, but he stayed silent. Mick remembered what these kinds of blokes were like. Working most of their lives in isolation on this kind of land made them wary. There was nothing they hated more than someone who talked.

'You look fit enough,' the man said at last, letting his eyes skim over Mick while at the same time giving the impression that they'd never left his face.

'Yeah. I'm used to work.'

The man gave no indication at all that he'd heard.

'The wife says you were looking for someone here?'

'That's right. Bloke by the name of Charlie Morris.'

The man gave the slightest of nods but the features on his face didn't move for even a fraction. Nevertheless Mick could feel the the air between them change.

'Old Chas, eh? What's your name?'

'Mick Doyle.'

For the first time the man's granite face moved. You could hardly call it a smile, just a slight loosening around the mouth. The eyes stayed as clear and hard as ever.

'He left instructions about you.'

Mick swallowed the urge to grin.

'Yeah? He still working here?'

'He's had a couple of weeks off and is coming back for the shearing . . . says he's gone and bought himself a house in town. Menindee, you know?'

Mick nodded. It was the nearest town. They'd passed through it on their way out from Broken Hill. Tiny place on the Darling River with maybe a couple of hundred people. The man continued coldly.

'Must be a dump I reckon. No decent houses in that joint to buy. Too many blacks living around there.' The steel eyes sought out Mick's for confirmation of what he meant.

Mick nodded again, not showing a moment's hesitation.

'Funny thing to buy your first house in your fifties. He used to always stay in the pubs around about when he had his days off.'

He was still staring at Mick keenly, assessing him. It irritated Michelle no end. There was something going on underneath the words that she didn't understand. When would this drawn-out process end? She hated the feeling of being stood over.

'Old Chas was put away for a few years. Some business up in Tibooburra . . .' the man continued slowly, 'with a woman . . .'

The air between them changed again. In the warmth of the sunlight, shards of meaning stuck out all over the place like tacks.

Mick stared straight back into the man's eyes. If he shifted for even a moment he knew he wouldn't have a chance.

'I don't like criminals . . . if you get my drift?'

Mick nodded.

That understood, the man went on more conversationally. 'But I went to school with Chas Morris, or my brother did. He's a bit older than me . . . and he's a good worker. Everyone knows him around these parts.'

'Yeah,' Mick said at last. 'He's a good bloke.'

The man looked away suddenly, sighed, and relaxed.

'I would have taken you on if you'd been here last week. I've got two blokes out fencing for me at the moment. Wouldn't mind doing a good turn for old Chas. It's bad luck you weren't here.'

Mick's heart did a dive inside his chest but he stayed absolutely calm, still meeting the old codger's eye.

'Nothing going with the shearing?' He only just managed to keep the pleading note out of his voice. 'I can rouse, pick up, muster. Anything, really.'

'Nah. The shearing is all contracted out now, son. That'll be your best bet though. To get in with a local contractor.'

'Right.' Mick turned away a bit, thinking. 'I'll do that.'

'But I'd go and find old Chas first.' The man actually smiled at this point. 'He might have something up his sleeve. You never know.'

'Yeah. Thanks. I will.'

'Sorry I can't help you.' The man suddenly waved both arms awkwardly about him in a desperate bird-like motion, indicating the hard red dirt around them.

'It's this damned drought. We'll all be out of work if it doesn't break soon.'

Mick nodded and started to walk over to the bike.

'Be seeing you then . . .'

The man waved goodbye before turning to Michelle for the first time.

'You want to sign up now or next week?'

Michelle shrugged.

'I guess now. Yeah. I'll sign up now.'

After Michelle had signed up for work, Sharon showed her around the place – where she would sleep, the kids' school room. She explained where everything was kept and how the house was organised, in a friendly way but distant too. Michelle tried to question her about her employers but the girl would not be drawn.

'Fine,' was all she'd say, an enigmatic smile teasing around the dark pretty mouth. 'They're okay.'

When they came back out into the strong sunlight Michelle turned to her.

'See you next week, then.'

'Sure. Next week.'

Michelle headed over to where Mick was waiting on the bike.

On her way indoors, the black girl hesitated before running back down to the bike.

'If you want to find old Charlie,' she said breathlessly, 'the house he bought is in town, opposite the pub and right next to the old bakery.'

Mick smiled at her. 'Thanks. Thanks a lot.'

Michelle tried again to draw her out a little.

'So you're not exactly sorry to be leaving, eh?'

Sharon smiled her assent gently and Michelle stiffened. She knew that look, that secret smile that pregnant women had. It drove her crazy. A few of the girls she'd worked with in K-Mart used to call back to say hello, with the ring on their fingers and that stupid dumb-cow look on their faces.

'I'll be glad to leave,' she said suddenly.

Michelle looked directly at her for the first time that afternoon and motioned back to the house with one hand.

'What's *she* really like to work for?'

Sharon looked up, surprised by the sharp tone. 'If you've got energy you'll be okay. But there's a lot of work and the hours are long. You won't finish at night until the kids are in bed.'

Michelle nodded and tried to smile. She hadn't meant to sound like such a bully. It upset her now to see the girl shrink back inside herself, edging away as though she didn't feel right standing there with them.

'Well . . . thanks for that. I'll know what to expect . . .'

'Sharon! Shar-on!' The woman's voice could be heard calling from the house. The girl seemed relieved.

'I've gotta go.'

'Sure,' said Michelle. 'Thanks, Sharon.'

10

They found the single-fronted, sun-blistered weatherboard next to the bakery but it was locked up and didn't look as though anyone had lived there for some time. Mick was puzzled as he noted the rubbish nestling into the wire fence of the overgrown front garden. He unclipped the squeaky gate and walked up the front path to the verandah. A few of the boards had rotted away and a grubby torn blind stopped him seeing anything through the front window. The place was in serious need of repair and it somehow didn't fit with his idea of Chas. He looked back at Michelle who was standing by the bike chewing her nails and staring around the wide empty main street. Down one end a couple of Aboriginal women and a few kids were sauntering away from the one milk bar, arms laden with white plastic shopping bags, voices babbling good-naturedly to each other in the light dry air. Outside the bluestone pub opposite there were a couple of older men – probably local landowners – standing about talking next to their dusty vehicles. But that was about it.

'I can't imagine Chas living in a place like this.' Mick knocked again just in case. 'He must have cleared out and gone back to Broken Hill for his few days off.'

Again no answer, but just as Mick was walking back to Michelle, the door of the bakery next door opened and a pleasant-looking man of about forty approached them with a smile.

'Hello there. After old Charlie, are you?'

Mick was surprised. The man had a city look about him. Neatly dressed and softly spoken he might have just stepped off a plane or a bus. It was odd to see him in this dry flat run-down joint.

'Yeah, that's right . . .'

The man smiled and pointed to the pub.

'He's probably over there having his lunch.'

Mick's face brightened.

'Yeah?'

The man was genuinely pleased to have helped.

'Yes. He often has his meals over there. Hasn't moved in properly yet.'

They found him sitting next to a small potted tree at a wooden table in the central square courtyard of the old pub, reading the paper and sipping a beer. Mick called out at him across the empty tables and stood waiting.

'Hey, Chas! G'day, mate!'

The tone of Mick's voice was enough to make Michelle step backwards into the shade of the verandah. She wished she'd waited out by the bike, or gone up to the milk bar for something to eat.

The old bloke looked up quizzically like a lizard, squinting a bit over his glass before recognising Mick. When at last he stood, a grin spreading out lazily across his mouth and up to his eyes, his gnarled old face suddenly broke open, alive and surprisingly youthful. He walked towards them on thin tightly-encased moleskinned legs, arms outstretched. He reminded Michelle of the emu they'd almost hit on the road that morning.

'Mick! Good to see you, boy!'

Michelle had never seen a man like Chas. He was like someone she'd dreamed about as a little girl or some character out of an old television programme. He was dressed cowboy-style like some hot shooter from the American mid-west: skin-tight, cream moleskins, shiny black cowboy

114

boots, and a black silk shirt with two lines of white tassels running in a deep V from his shoulders to his waist. Michelle watched dumbstruck as Mick shook the gnarled brown hand, tossing up whether to go and wait outside before they noticed her. Nothing of what Mick had said about Chas made her expect this. The only thing missing seemed to be a ten gallon hat and a couple of silver guns slung in holsters at his hips.

'Didn't you get my letter?' said Chas.

'I got it ... sure I did.'

'Didn't know when you were going to turn up ...'

They held each other at arms' distance, both laughing but awkward too with the surprising depth of feeling that had burst into their lives. Then Mick noticed Chas's clothing and was as stunned as Michelle.

'Shit! You're all spruced up!'

'Holiday time ...'

Mick laughed and lightly flicked a few of the tassels on Chas's shirt as though he couldn't quite believe them.

'Yeah? This shirt is something, Chas. I didn't expect ...'

Mick broke away, suddenly remembering Michelle.

'This is Michelle, Chas. She, er ... we travelled up together.'

Chas's blue eyes lit on her. Michelle found herself unfolding, coming to life under their warmth, and holding out her hand.

'G'day, Michelle.'

'Hello ... Chas.'

Her hand disappeared inside his huge rough one. It felt as dry and comfortable as old bark. Then he let her go and stepped back looking at them both, from one to the other, smiling with those bright eyes, finally settling back to Mick with a twinkle.

'Looks like you didn't waste any time. Found yourself a girl ...'

Mick looked away, trying to stem the heat that was

threatening his face and neck – awkward on her behalf as much as his own. He remembered suddenly the way she'd said to him on that first day. 'I don't want a boy-friend ...' and the way he'd agreed; they'd both been so adamant.

'Michelle and me ... we're just friends.' After saying that, Mick felt he could afford to risk a quick glance in her direction and was pleased to see she didn't seem overly put out. In fact she was smiling a small guarded smile right back into Chas's inquisitive face.

'Yeah. Mick gave me a ride up here ...'

Chas made a po-face as though he didn't believe a word of what either of them were saying.

'Ah, come and sit down both of ya! Let me buy you a feed.' He winked broadly. 'Later we'll go across the road and check over the new family estate.'

Michelle and Mick sat down at the small wooden table and watched Chas giving instructions to the bartender, who seemed to know him well.

'Give us your best steak, will ya, Ted? Chips, vegetables, salad, bread, everything you've got, eh? And don't be skimpy or I'll jump the bar and give ya one! For three. All that for three.'

The man nodded laconically, smiling to himself.

Mick and Michelle looked at each other and laughed. Mick wished he could have reached out and taken Michelle's hand and held it just for a moment. He wanted her to know that as far as he was concerned she was part of this, that it was better because she was there. Chas called out to them suddenly remembering his manners.

'Hey, you both *like* steak, don't ya?'

'Sure we do,' Mick grinned back.

'What about you ... er, Michelle?'

'Yeah, it'll do me ... thanks.'

Chas gave a fake sigh of relief, slapping his leg as he laughed again.

'That's good. Because I don't think they've got anything else!'

The bartender, pouring beers into glasses, looked up.

'Don't take any notice of him, love,' he said lazily. 'We've got snags, fish, chops ...' The foam on the beers spread out over the top of the glass and down the sides. Chas picked them up and returned from the bar beaming.

'Last time I ordered fish here old Ted had to go out the back and catch the bloody thing in the river ... I waited about three hours for a mingy little carp. All bones!'

'Bullshit!' Ted pretended he wasn't laughing.

Chas and Mick finished the first beer quickly between much laughter and easy shorthand talk. Much of what they said was superficial, almost meaningless. The weather, the ride up, the countryside, times and temperatures, but it was the flow happening underneath the words that counted. It didn't take Michelle long to catch on to it either. Mick stood up to get the next round and she sat quietly listening to Chas describe the horse he'd had as a kid.

'An old draughthorse. Fat as butter. Four of us used to ride her six miles to school back in the forties ... Mum never worried. I was handling a pulling team of six bullocks by the time I was eight. Now I bet ya find that hard to believe? Never actually went to school much, come to think of it. Too much work to do ...'

Michelle never knew that an old man could be like this. He'd have to be older than her father, yet he was so ... so easy. Just when you thought you had him pinned down, he up and changed again. He'd seem good-looking one minute, in a rough weather-beaten kind of way, a rugged old timer with good bone structure and the kind of liveliness that made him younger than his years. And the next he'd look exactly like an old turtle, with that scraggy sunburnt neck sticking out of the ridiculous shirt, and the funny croaky laugh that revealed the line of stubby, yellow teeth. Every feature on his face seemed to be jostling for position.

The small bright eyes filled with humour when he heard about the job she'd landed.

'Oh, that's great! That's what you need! Any trouble with the German and I'll sort him out for you. He's not such a bad bastard. Went to school with the lot of them ... watch your pay though ... mean as cat's dirt.'

He turned to Mick then.

'Now, we'll have to get you in with a few contractors around. There's Hardy's in Wilcannia but we'll probably have to go back into Broken Hill to get you signed up with the others.' The old face closed over in a worried frown as he looked away. 'Mick. Things are bad. Real bad. You know that, don't ya?'

'How bad?' The sudden seriousness in the old man's voice jolted him.

'It keeps gettin' worse. Even over the last six months. This bloody drought for a start. If rain doesn't come in the next eight weeks then there'll be no summer feed. The cockies are closing ranks, hardly employing anyone. Some of the poor bastards are walking off their stations. It's that tough. They can't pay their bills.'

Mick nodded and tried to swallow his panic.

'But, Chas, they still have to shear ...'

Chas was smiling again.

'That's right. They still have to shear. So we just gotta get you on a team.'

'You lose touch ... with everything in jail.'

Chas flashed him a broad smile.

'That's for sure, mate ... but don't get down. We haven't even started yet.'

The food came and they all ate hungrily. Salty fresh chips and meat, salad and bread. It all tasted fantastic. Michelle had a glass of light beer, then stopped, thinking that it must have been that making her feel so light, as though she didn't have a care in the world. But with a full stomach and now sipping lemon squash, she still felt airy. Was this called happiness? Nothing that had happened up to this point in her life seemed to matter. In spite of the baby growing inside her, there was suddenly everything to look forward to.

By the time they'd finished their meal, the courtyard had filled with maybe a dozen others. Local station owners and working men mainly until a family arrived, obviously passing through on to somewhere else. Dad, with flecks of grey running through his handsome head, and the woman, slim as a whippet and coolly anxious with a mixture of dull gold and silver streaking through hers. The three kids were as perfect as thoroughbred pups. The lot of them stood out like sore toes in their designer casual gear and polite questions about what kind of fish was being served that day. No one minded them though. After all their money was just as good as anyone else's.

The pub was nearly a hundred and fifty years old, blue-stone painted over in white, built in a square around a central courtyard. Three of the low walls had guest rooms all opening out into the centre and the fourth was the bar, wooden chairs and tables dotted here and there amid the dusty, half-dead potted plants and faded green lawn.

Out through a back door on his way to the toilets, Mick stopped and looked. A few metres down a slope and there was the river, the gleaming Darling, low now because of the drought but flowing away swiftly under the willows, as alive and perfect as a huge brown snake, waiting for what was coming in the sun. Even as they ate and drank inside the courtyard, then picked up and drove off wherever they were all heading, it flowed on. It made Mick think of Buster and the stories he used to tell. He smiled and took a moment to watch it before going back to where Chas and Michelle were sitting, finishing their food. Buster and the Darling. They belonged together somehow. What would Buster be up to now? He could think of no way to find out.

Who knew what happened to anyone?

When Mick returned, Chas spoke.

'Now, got anywhere to stay tonight?'

Mick and Michelle looked at each other uncomfortably. Neither of them had dared think past this day and *that* seemed suddenly ridiculous. Had they decided to hang out together until Michelle's job started at the end of the week? Nothing had been said and they didn't know what to say.

'Well, ya have now!' Chas thumped the table and laughed. 'You can help me fix it up a bit.'

Mick looked at Michelle.

'What do you reckon?'

'Yeah ... well, if that's ...' She wanted very much to say yes to Chas's offer but she didn't know if it was her place to do so.

Chas got up and paid at the counter.

'Come over now and take a geezer. I've been working all week on the bloody joint.'

Chas unlocked the door, pushed the rusty iron doorknob and stood back for them to enter. At once they were hit with the strong smell of turps and paint, plaster and new wood. Michelle felt herself gag as she followed Mick inside.

'What do you reckon?'

Mick and Michelle looked around. The whole interior had been gutted. It was just one large room, newly plastered with white undercoat over half of it. Down one end was a stove, an old fridge and an ancient pitted wooden table with a few chairs, all covered in paint-spotted newspaper. Further up, near the middle of the room, was a fireplace filled with half-burnt stumps and a few dead coals. Two long thin windows on either side of the fireplace looked on to the red brick bakery next door, the dividing fence covered in wild jasmine and bougainvillea. A heap of Chas's used plates and cups was stacked haphazardly on the sink.

Chas couldn't keep the pleasure off his face as he watched them take it all in. He threw off his hat and began hopping about a bit on the brand-new, untreated floor boards.

'Put in this floor last week. Bastard of a job. Restumped the whole place too,' he added proudly and picked up a few of the more offensive dirty cups scattered around the room and clattered them into the sink with the rest.

'It's gonna be great, Chas,' Mick said, bending down to feel the smooth wood. 'You've done a good job.'

'Next I gotta polish these up, or put on lino. What do you reckon?'

Mick shrugged and chuckled.

'I dunno. Not exactly an expert on that kind of stuff.'

They both laughed, a secret kind of understanding between them that made Michelle feel excluded. *What was funny about that?* She walked over to the window and unlatched the frame.

'Mind if I open this up a little bit, Chas?'

He waved at her kindly, impatiently, as though she shouldn't even have asked.

'Go for your life, love . . . the smell a bit much, is it?'

'Yeah a bit . . .' Michelle pulled up the window and breathed in the outside air deeply as she stared out at the purple plant draped over the bakery wall.

'How come you bought it, Chas? I mean you reckoned that you never needed a house before,' Mick asked curiously.

Chas caught Michelle's eye and winked.

'Ah, I thought it was time I put down roots,' Chas replied and then burst out laughing.

'Don't worry, Mick, old son. I'm as surprised as anyone.'

They all laughed then.

Somehow after Chas said that, the house took on a kind of warmth and sheen for both Mick and Michelle because it had been bought on the spur of the moment and was obviously giving him such pleasure.

121

'You've done a lot already,' Mick said, moving a few things off one of the chairs and sitting down. 'How long have you been on it?'

'Couple of weeks. I had young Nat Longry to help me for three days. Not a bad kid. Family live up the road. Mother says she doesn't know what to do with him. Half-bloods, you know. But I couldn't find fault with him.'

Chas moved over to the stove and began to fill the kettle.

'You can stay here, you know, until your job starts, Michelle. Both of you, stay as long as you want.'

Mick nodded and looked at Michelle.

'What do you reckon, Michelle?'

'Yeah. I reckon. . . If we won't be in the way.'

'In the bloody way!' Chas sniffed, feigning impatience.

'You won't be in the way, especially if you give me a hand.'

'We haven't got much money . . . least I haven't . . .'

'Don't want your bloody money, boy. Just a hand.'

Mick grinned and shook his head.

'All right.'

'It'll be a bit rough for you on the floor. I've got extra blankets but no mattresses.'

'We got our sleeping-bags . . . I don't mind it hard,' Mick said.

'Just one other thing. Can't have any . . . funny business, you know. Not while I'm here anyway. You see, there aren't any walls and I'd feel bloody rotten listening to you. I'm a bad sleeper . . .'

Mick laughed uncomfortably but didn't dare look at Michelle. The old boy's eyes were twinkling.

'Now if I go away . . . that's a different story . . . you can go for your bloody lives for all . . .'

'We're friends, Chas,' Mick cut in drily. 'Just friends. No need to worry about that.'

11

The next couple of days were the happiest Michelle could remember in a long while. She worked with Mick and Chas on the little house: sanding, building and painting as though her life depended on getting her part of it – one wall and undercoating the skirting boards – finished before her position on the station began at the end of the following week. The physical work relaxed her brain. She found that she rarely thought of her former life at all. If it wasn't for the baby growing inside her she reckoned she could have easily forgotten that she'd spent seventeen years in that dreary dump in Gippsland.

At night they crawled into their sleeping-bags quite early, arms aching and exhausted from all the hard work, but in good spirits from the meal they'd had and the talk they'd shared with Chas around the fire. Chas insisted on buying all the food.

'I reckon you're earning ya keep,' was all he said when Michelle offered to pay for one of their meals at the pub. 'You'll need every cent you've got, girl, if the job don't work out.'

It was lucky they were both so tired because Chas's loud snoring, starting up almost as soon as he hit the mattress up the other end of the room, would have been terrible if either of them had been a light sleeper.

Each day, Mick, usually accompanied by Chas, would head out early looking for work. Sometimes they'd only be responding to a rumour heard in the pub or to some hunch someone they'd met had about what was going in another town or on a station a few hours out. They'd arrive back mid-morning or sometimes after lunch, their faces flat and non-committal, always with the same story. The station owners were pressed to the boards, not employing anyone until the drought ended. Some of them were only there by the good grace of a bank or pastoral company, hanging on by the seat of old pants, living on credit, relying on the profits they hoped to make if the rain came. Everyone was waiting for rain. If the rain didn't come soon then more of the smaller farmers would have to walk off their properties and go to the city for work. Although they knew things were just as desperate there. Even those who had enough money to hang on, had little to spare to pay someone to fix their broken fences or kill the rabbits and wild pigs that were wrecking the land, the sort of work Mick was looking for. Just about everyone they spoke to said they were just trying to get by, until the rain came.

There was the shearing. Although the price of wool was low it was the only chance the station owners had to pay something off their debts. But the jobs were tied up. Every contractor Mick went to see said there were plenty of reliable shearers around already. Good men who could shear over two hundred sheep a day, who travelled around in teams from South Australia to Queensland to New South Wales. Teams that were more or less fixed. The contractors all had lists as long as their arms of guys wanting to sign on for work. There was nothing for Mick to do except add his name to their lists and hope.

By the end of the week Michelle could see Mick's spirits starting to slide. He still laughed at the daggy way she mixed her paint in the old fruit cans instead of in the big tins Chas had bought especially, and smiled too when he handed over the cups of tea and sweet buns from the bakery but she could tell that he was starting to lose something.

The buoyancy was slipping away. As the days passed he gradually got harder to reach.

After about ten days – close to the day she and Chas were due to start out on the station – Mick's dislocation seemed particularly marked. His hopes had been well up that morning because the day before he'd travelled a long way out to a big station north of White Cliffs, having heard on the grapevine that the contractor there was minus one man in the yards. The expert (the man in charge of the shed) had seemed pleased with Mick and had taken down his particulars, telling him to ring the next day to confirm the position for the following week. Chas didn't have a phone so Mick was up early and down to the post office the next morning on the dot of eight only to be told by the station owner's wife that the job had gone. Some local grazier's son had beaten him to it.

All day he'd only spoken when he had to and then guardedly. Michelle saw the panic surface in his eyes while he was standing by the door, waiting for Chas to nail in the last board and looking out on to the street. She wondered if it was just the lack of work that had him so scared. Times were tough but he could go on the dole for a while and there was Chas to fall back on if things didn't look up eventually. Only the night before she'd overheard their terse conversation on the verandah when she'd been inside getting a drink.

'Nothing much going, Chas. Looks like I'd better move on up north . . .'

'Things are no better up there. You know that.'

'Well, perhaps I'd better give it a try.'

'Nah. You're better off here.'

'Can't live on you forever.'

'You're not. I need this house done up. You're doing a good job. You and young Michelle.'

'And after that's finished?'

'Then we'll see.'

'Shit. What if nothing turns up?'

'It will, son. No worries. This country's not finished yet.'

'You reckon?'

'I know it.'

She figured there was maybe something deeper freaking him. Was it the father he wouldn't talk about? Or the time in jail? She'd watched him often after that, fixing something, painting maybe or sawing a piece of wood, alone in the world. His face would tense with concentration, the eyes flicking wide every now and again in a kind of mute fear, like someone drowning. Occasionally a rush of whatever it was would rip through Michelle too, throwing her back into that terrible light, only-half-there state, and she'd have a flash of knowing what it was like being Mick.

Michelle and Chas would occasionally catch each other's looks behind Mick's back. She knew Chas was worried too but he didn't say much, just went on doggedly checking out any work rumours and handing the information over to Mick.

'Something's sure to come up soon,' he'd say, every day. But nothing did.

'Pass that little brush, will ya, Squirt ... I'm gonna attack this window-sill now.'

Michelle found it impossible to take offence. Chas's careless warmth over the last couple of days was like sunshine. She could feel herself being renewed and sustained by it. Mick would occasionally call her 'Squirt' too without thinking. Although the first time he did stop and ask if it was all right by her. She shrugged and smiled, unsure somehow. It was such a dumb name.

'It's just that it suits you in a way,' Mick mumbled clumsily. 'I mean you're little ... tough and ... I dunno, funny.'

Michelle gave a wry look and threw the old smelly paint rag she was holding straight at him. He ducked, but not fast enough.

'What d'ya mean, funny?'

'In a good way. I meant it in a good way.'

They shared a quick smile and turned away back to their work.

'So how do you feel about tomorrow?' Mick's voice whispered across the space between them. It would be their last night together before Chas and Michelle headed out to the station. Some coals were still burning in the grate and the shadow of her profile loomed up sharply across the wall opposite Mick. She was on her back and looking towards the window. They'd both been in their sleeping-bags for over half an hour but he could sense she was just as wide awake as he was. Chas's heavy snores resounded throughout the room, loud and discordant but strangely comforting too. Nothing much could go wrong with old Chas over there, dead to the world.

'I'm okay,' came her unsure reply. 'Bit jumpy. How about you?'

'Yeah. Pretty good.'

'You haven't seemed too good lately,' she said tentatively. She hadn't dared broach the subject of how he was feeling before, sensing his fierce need for privacy.

'No ...'

Michelle shifted on her side and tried to feel tired. She should sleep. It was arranged that she would leave early with Chas in the morning and that Mick would stay on in the little house until he found work. She should be tired but all she could feel was kind of undone, about leaving Mick here by himself, of thinking that she mightn't see him again.

'You homesick at all?' His voice, soft in the dark, eased the knot in her stomach.

'Nope.'

Mick laughed.

'That's what I like about you, you don't say stuff you don't mean.'

Michelle smiled to herself in the dark. The warmth of his voice never failed to disarm her. But this night it made her feel as though she had to fight to keep her head above water. It would be easy to drift out on to his pool of kindness then find it got deep suddenly – and scary. Tomorrow it would be all over.

'Couldn't ever see the point in doing that,' she countered, making herself sound drier and tougher than she actually felt.

'No. I guess you're right.'

There was silence for a while after that.

'I can see the stars,' Michelle murmured, staring out through the window, keeping her voice calm. Mick turned himself around to face the same way.

'Yeah. I think that's the cross up there . . . Good, isn't it?'

'Yeah.'

'What was Chas like in jail? I can't imagine him . . .' She didn't want the quiet intimacy between them to end.

'Just the same,' Mick chuckled. 'None of the warders could touch him. He was his own man in there . . . just like now, if you know what I mean.'

Michelle yawned and stretched. 'I haven't felt as good as this for such a long time . . .'

The words caught Mick by the throat. He was suddenly inexplicably scared. *Hey, watch out, man. This is a little girl you've known for two weeks She's got nothing to do with you. Remember.* He said the first thing that came into his head.

'I never thought we'd be here, did you . . . together? I mean, it's over two weeks now.'

Michelle laughed.

'No way! I never thought. Funny, isn't it?'

Mick's heart began to pound. Sick with indecision he could feel his blood roaring around like a truck inside his head. Now or never. Could he risk it? He could see one of her hands, rolled in a little fist outside her sleeping-bag and he wanted desperately to reach out and take it, not to do

128

much else but hold it for a while. If he could do that then the mad rumbling cloud of fear that had been building up all this last week might blow off somewhere else and leave him alone. But what if she didn't feel like that about him? If it all came out wrong she might get put off completely and they wouldn't even stay mates. The moments ticked by and still he hesitated. Gradually the throbbing intensity of the feeling subsided. He was left feeling furious with himself, but also, at the same time thoroughly relieved that he hadn't acted.

'Tell me more about that teacher you had ...' he growled suddenly. A dead, disappointed feeling was threatening to overtake him now. Anything. Say anything to stay talking. To his relief Michelle seemed pleased at his suggestion.

'Well, she wasn't what you'd really call good-looking ...' she began slowly. 'Sort of a round face. Kind more than anything. I can't really say how old she was. Maybe forty, forty-five, I dunno. She died of cancer anyway. Too young. She had these big hands, really strong hands for such a thin woman. The fingers were long and white. I used to look at them a lot when she was talking. I went to see her in the chapel when she was dead. And her hands still looked good. They had ... someone had arranged them really nicely, folded easy-like across her chest, holding her rosary beads and the bit of rolled-up paper.'

'What paper?' Mick was fascinated in spite of himself.

'Some kind of certificate. I think it was her religious vows or something ... I couldn't tell. You ever seen anyone dead?'

'Nah ... Well, I saw my mother but she wasn't all laid out like that. I just found her ... in the house ...'

'Your mother?' she said wonderingly. The image of her own mother's face came to her suddenly. The small bright eyes and plump cheeks. It was shocking to think that she could die.

'Yeah.'

'Didn't you ever see her laid out in her coffin?'

'No. I never even went to her funeral.'

'Why not?'

Mick tried to think, tried to remember those terrible days after his mother's death. Had he even wanted to go to the funeral? He'd been a kid then, only fourteen. He couldn't remember if he even knew what a funeral was. All he could remember was the misery that had banked up inside him like a double-brick wall, the anger and disbelief that it was actually *his* mother!

'It's hard. Can't really remember ...' Mick paused uncomfortably.

'How come this nun took to you like?' he asked, trying to fend off the flood of jumbled memories and feelings. Sometimes it felt as though he had a river of them inside and that the banks holding them in were on the verge of collapse.

'I mean, I get the feeling you were special to her in some way ...?'

'Well, I used to learn music ...'

'Yeah? Were you really good at it or something?'

'Yeah ... well, no, not really,' Michelle said slowly.

'You don't sound too sure!' he laughed.

They were quiet for a while and a slight uneasiness began to grow without anything being said. Michelle hadn't joined in his laughter. Had he said anything? What had they even been talking about? Finally her voice broke the silence, the words drawn out thinly, strung across the dark between them.

'Something happened to me when I was about ten. She ... helped ... me. She was the only one who would ... help me.'

Michelle felt rather than heard her own words slip past her mouth and into the air. She imagined she could hear them hit Mick's ear-drums. Smack. Smack. *The only one ...*

who would help me. How come she'd had no idea at all that she would say this? She had never spoken of Veronica in this way. And there was no sense of the release that she might have expected. None at all. Instead her skin felt prickly and hot, heat crackled around her legs and feet. She shifted position on the hard floor and suddenly felt her breath go shallow. The air was getting lighter and lighter. Was there any air left in this room? She couldn't catch her breath. It was just like those asthma attacks she used to have years ago, except then she had her little puffer by her side to help. The little puffer of ventolin that could get her through the attack and help her calm down. She sat up suddenly, gasping wildly.

'Mick. Mick!' her voice rasped out. 'Help me!'

'What! What's the matter?'

He sprang out of the bag in his T-shirt and underpants and was at her side.

'What? What is it, Michelle?' He couldn't see much in the dark but he could hear her gasping.

'I can't breathe!'

'Shit! What can I do? You got any stuff for it?'

Michelle shook her head. He could see her face now. It had gone very white in the moonlight but her eyes were wild with panic. Without thinking, Mick picked her up, the bottom half of her still in the sleeping-bag, and walking straight past the snoring Chas, opened the front door.

Outside the clear dark night was very cold, but lit up with an almost round, flat yellow moon and a million stars. Nothing moved in the little town as Mick gently tipped Michelle up on to her feet. Standing behind her, he put his arms loosely around her for warmth and his face down near the side of her face.

'It'll be all right,' he said slowly and calmly into her ear. 'You just breathe in what you can. In ... and ... out. Like this. Not too slow. Not too fast.'

'But I can't!' Her strangled cry tore at him, made him

start to panic too. She was gasping, her hands clawing the air in front of her, struggling with some unseen enemy. Perhaps she really wouldn't be able to. Should he look for a doctor, or anyone that he could find. At the back of his mind he tried frantically to remember if the town had a chemist. If he just knew for sure, he could rush down and wake him. Beat the door down until he came with the drug.

'In and out. That's right. Good. In and out, Michelle,' he made himself continue calmly.

'I was thinking about what happened and it just set me . . .' She gasped and then whimpered like a little kid.

'No. No. Don't talk about that. Take another breath.' He spoke as quietly and confidently as he could. What *had* she been talking about? He couldn't even remember.

'That's right, Michelle. Take a breath. You're doing well.'

It seemed like ages – probably only a few minutes – and it started to work. He could hear her breathing getting deeper and more even.

'In and out. That's right. In and out. You're doing well, Squirt. You're gonna be okay.'

Eventually her breathing returned to normal and she turned around to face him, still with his arms lightly around her. They shared a tentative smile.

'You feeling better now?' he asked shyly. It felt so good to be holding her. He knew it would end any second now but he was waiting for her to move first.

'Yeah. I feel better. I dunno what happened . . . I . . .' She wasn't moving away, but coming closer. In closer for warmth. She put her arms around his waist. They were locked together in the moonlight, listening to each other's breathing, his face pressed against her neck. He could feel the life pulse there, thudding away. It felt like his own blood, pumping strongly.

'Thanks, Mick . . . I was so scared.' Her small voice was hoarse, and it seemed to come from way down inside her chest. He could feel the skin on her arms, contracted into icy goose-bumps. She felt as hard and cold and breakable as a little doll. They were both shivering. Mick ran his hands over her shoulders and down her arms, then drew up her hands into his own, rubbing them.

'You panicked, that's all,' he said softly.

'Yeah. I did.'

He smiled down at her, still rubbing her hands.

'Hey, you're freezing . . .'

She smiled, and then quickly, impulsively, withdrew her hands and put them around his neck. Standing on her toes she pulled his face down to meet her own and then she kissed him firmly on the mouth. A matter-of-fact sort of kiss that said . . . what? It lingered on his mouth like a burn and he wished it could have gone on and on. For a moment he felt suicidal, as though he wanted to throw himself into the heat and burn to death.

'So are you . . .'

But it was good to see her smile, her spirits revived into the old dry perkiness.

'Yeah.'

Mick bent down and picked up her sleeping-bag that lay to one side of their feet. They walked back into the house again and settled their bags side by side this time, near the fire.

Michelle turned on her side to face Mick, one arm propping up her head.

'Can I tell you about it, Mick?'

'What?'

'What I started to say before . . . about Veronica?'

'Yeah. If you feel all right about it . . . I . . .'

She smiled and slipped her other hand out of the sleeping-bag, reaching for his.

'Don't worry. I don't think I'll chuck another one.'

He caught her hand, and held it in in his own, caressing it gently and laughing a little, mostly with happiness, but with nerves too. There was a kind of springy lightness inside him that he didn't trust.

'That's good, Michelle, because it's damned cold out there.'

They pushed their pillows together and lay looking at each other in the light that was still spilling in from the moon outside.

Mick still held her hand lightly, only occasionally caressing it with his thumb.

'Fire away,' he said simply. 'I'm all ears.'

'He was Mum's brother,' Michelle began quickly. 'Our favourite uncle. Popular with everyone. My brothers and me, we all loved him. He was handsome, had a good-looking wife – my auntie Carmel – and kids of his own. Mum used to work on Saturday afternoons and she would bring me around to their place while my father and brothers went to the football. The first couple of times were good. There were all my cousins to play with and my auntie Carmel too, who was always good to me. It's hard to remember when it started but I think it was the time when they all had to go somewhere and I was left alone with him for the last hour or something. It began gradually, you know, joking, and kissing. I remember really enjoying it at first, even hoping that it might happen again. That's the worst thing about it all. I thought it was a bit naughty, but fun you know, because everyone liked him so much so I was kind of flattered to have his attention.

'He'd be watching TV and he'd grab me and tell me that we were the film-stars, you know. He'd kiss me and pinch my bum and poke me here and there. After a few times I knew there was something wrong with it all. Every time I'd be left there the others had to go off to different places and he always found an excuse for me not going with them. I felt bad about that. Sort of sneaky and odd. I thought they were all in on the secret about me, that they knew what he wanted me for. Anyway, up till the last time, he never hurt me much. Just used to lie on me and feel me up. You know, rub himself on me until he ... you know. I used to be so glad when it was over and life could get normal again. After he'd finished with me he'd let me get on with what I wanted to do. I was just ten. I was into drawing pictures and dreaming about pop-stars and I didn't know anything ...'

Mick stayed absolutely still as she spoke.

'This is probably boring for you? You want me to go on?'

'Of course ...'

'But why? I've just thought it's probably pretty stupid telling you. I mean it's got nothing to do with you ...'

'I'm listening.'

'Well, I've told you most of it. Except the worst bit and that was when I told my wonderful mother.'

'What did she do?' Mick asked as calmly as he could. The bitterness and fury in her tone frightened him. He put his arm around her. Her shoulders were shaking and although she wasn't making any noise, when he pressed his face next to hers, it was wet.

'Come on. Get it out, mate ...' he said softly, both arms encircling her now.

'You sure you want to hear?'

'Yeah. You want to tell ... I want to hear.'

'Well, she hit me when I told her ... slapped me on the face ... told my father I was making up lies to make her brother look bad ...'

'What did your dad say?'

'He believed her, of course. Well, he pretended he did anyway. Sometimes he'd get this funny look on his face while he was watching me ... and I'd think, *he knows* I'm not lying. But it was a horrible look ... of disgust for me. When he'd look like that I'd feel bad ... so bad. And he never said anything.'

Michelle moved away from him then, sitting up quietly. There was nothing he could do but wait.

135

'Mick. I don't know why I'm telling you all this! I *never* cry normally . . .' She shuddered as the words spluttered out. 'Maybe it's because I think we mightn't see each other again.'

Mick smiled.

'We'll see each other.'

'You reckon? What if you get something a million miles away. I mean . . . I . . .'

A bubble of happiness crashed about drunkenly inside him as he fished a big hanky out of his bag and handed it to her.

'I'll come back sometimes. We can write to each other.'

Michelle blew her nose loudly and moved back closer to him.

'Did you have to go back there . . . after you told them?'

'No. That's the funny thing. Nothing was ever said but I never went back there. *That's* what used to make me think that they *did* believe me, but they just wouldn't tell me that they did.'

Michelle looked up angrily, in control again in spite of her puffy tear-stained face.

'I was the one who was punished for what he did.'

'Yeah,' Mick agreed slowly. 'And did anyone ever get on to him?'

Michelle looked away towards the moonlit window, a hint of a smile as she remembered.

'Yeah. Veronica did . . . she did what she could anyway.'

Mick watched the smile fade as she continued.

'I was a cot-case, Mick, before I told her. I was really in a mess. You might think that's impossible for someone only ten. But I tell you I was seriously thinking of knocking myself off. I was living in this house with these people, who were *my family*. And I felt so completely alone . . . my parents, both of them, treated me like shit . . .'

'What about your brothers?'

'For some crazy reason I was too ashamed to tell them. I

knew they liked my uncle so much and ... it was the whole business of it. You know ... I was too embarrassed.'

'But the Sister ... the nun, got it out of you?'

'Yeah. She did. Bit by bit. She heard the whole story and wanted to go and talk to my parents about it but I wouldn't let her. I'd told her their reaction, so you know she went and had it out with him.'

'What did she say?'

Michelle began to chuckle as she remembered.

'Oh, it was fantastic. She was fantastic. He denied it of course. But then she threatened him. You should have seen her! This old bird with her walking stick – she had something wrong with her leg – advancing on him, poking him in the chest and him stepping backwards with his arms up as though she was gonna shoot him! Said she was gonna call the cops. Made up stuff that wasn't true about how she had all this evidence. Photos and stuff. I loved her for that because she ... I knew she hated lying. And he eventually broke down and admitted it.' Michelle stopped talking and shook her head, as though even after all these years she couldn't quite believe it had happened.

'It would have been pretty hairy for you? Listening to him apologise,' Mick said quietly.

'Yeah. It was. But I didn't feel anything about him by that stage. It was all too late. And anyway it was ... is, my parents who I hate more. I hate them a lot more than I hate him.'

They talked on into the night, holding hands. By the time Mick had heard the whole story they were both tired.

'You haven't said much, Mick.'

'I'm thinkin'.'

'I've never told anyone this before. Except Veronica.'

'It's safe with me, Shell.'

'Thanks.'

They both yawned.

'I've got something else to tell you too, Mick.'

137

Mick's voice was groggy with tiredness. They were cuddled up together on the floor, both in their separate sleeping-bags but hanging on to each other too.

'Yeah?'

'I'm pregnant.'

'What!'

'I'm having a kid.'

Silence.

'A kid?'

'Yeah. A kid.'

12

The next morning they were all up at five. Michelle didn't look at Mick as she prepared to leave. Her bag was packed; all she had to do was eat something, put on her coat, and go. Chas was due out there for a muster at eight and she was getting a ride to the Wilyarna homestead with him.

Mick was standing by the car waiting to say goodbye.

'Well, all the best then, Shell. Hope it turns out okay.'

Michelle found it impossible to fend off the surly mood that was hanging around her head, making her shoulders hunch and her mouth tight. He knew a lot about her now, probably more than anyone else in the world, except Veronica – and she was dead. So what did that mean? How come she'd blurted out all that stuff? Had they really gone to sleep like two little kids, with their arms around each other?

'I'll be all right.'

Mick grinned.

'I know you'll be all right. I just hope the job turns out okay.'

He opened the door of the ute for her and she slipped in beside Chas. She had been tossing up whether to hug him goodbye but now somehow the decision had been made for her and she couldn't work out if she was relieved or not.

'You still want to write to me?' Her voice was husky.

'Sure I do.' He seemed surprised that she'd asked, then smiled.

'So who'll go first?' he said softly. 'No point the letters crossing...'

'Me,' she said. 'I'll go first. But make sure you write back.'

'No worries.'

Chas started the engine and waved to Mick as he backed the ute out on to the road.

'Look after yourself! I'll be keeping my ears open.'

'Thanks, Chas. See ya!'

Chas suddenly roared forward, leant across Michelle and wound the window down, looking hard at Mick.

'Now there's money there, Mick, in the tin above the stove. A couple of hundred bucks. If nothing comes up soon, go to Broken Hill and get yourself on the dole for a while until something does, okay? And eat all the food or it'll go bad.'

Mick's face hardened. 'Yeah. Okay, Chas.'

'I mean it.'

'Sure.'

Mick stood for a while watching the ute slowly submerge into a faint dot on the horizon. Then he walked inside and flopped down on to his sleeping-bag, thinking. *Something's gotta happen soon*, he found himself saying aloud. *I'm nearly twenty-two. I've got a right. Something's got to happen real soon.* After a while he got up and started mixing a fresh lot of yellow paint. It would only take a few days to finish off Chas's little joint properly. And yet part of him was dreading the day. What would there be for him after that?

A month passed before Mick received his first letter from Michelle. He'd wondered about her every day but had got past the stage of hoping any more. His life was a mixture of anxiety, chasing up jobs mainly, as well as helping out different people around the town with their cars and other bits and pieces of broken machinery. And long periods of boredom. So, when it did arrive, it was like a burst of sweet rain on the thirsty red earth around him. He opened it at the gate and sat down to read it on the verandah, furious because his hands were trembling. She had written as she'd promised. That meant he existed. He was real. The last few weeks had flown past. They'd capsized and jumbled, each day more or less indistinguishable from the last.

As soon as he saw the date he realised that she'd actually written the letter two weeks after getting there. He'd forgotten that the mail usually only went out from those stations once a week. Remembering that made him feel a whole lot better.

Dear Mick,

I'm doing okay, how are you?

Letter writing is a funny business, I reckon. I used to enjoy it when I was a kid. But I don't know now. It's strange writing to you. Shit, I don't know if I really know you or not! Then again, I think I do. Do you mind if I just ramble on a bit, tell you about what's been happening? Hope I don't bore you out of your brain!

At the beginning I thought I'd never fit in but it's funny the way things change. I'm getting used to the job here and although I can't exactly say I'm enjoying it, then at least I'm managing. (As you told me, the pay is terrible!) What can I tell you? There are the four kids that you probably remember from the day we went out there together. I don't really go for kids that much. But these ones are real little wackers. Henry is nine years old. Very serious. Interested in everything. He pesters me to tell him anything I know about other boys around his age. What are schools like? What games do they play? You see, they never even see another kid from one week to the other. When I first got here I thought it would make them weird but it hasn't. They're just a bit lonely, that's all. Henry will listen to any story at all about kids. All the detail about how they talk and what they eat! I find myself dredging up every last thing I can remember about my brothers at that age. You know, boats they made, the wars they had with two older boys down the street, Wayne's broken arm, the football they played. You name it! Everything. I have learnt to make up the bits that I can't remember. 'And then what happened, Michelle?' he'll say when I've finished. 'What did he say then? What did they do after that?' Shit!

Heidi is eight and she's more fun than her brother. Bubbly and outgoing if you know what I mean. Always talking and fast on the uptake if any kind of argument breaks out. But she'll sulk for hours if she gets into a mood. I know I was like that too as a kid. It's really interesting in a way seeing that kind of thing from the other side!

The four-year-old twins sort of live in their own world and they're not so dependent on me. Most of the time they're there simply to be washed and fed and helped along. They seem quite happy so I don't interfere with them too much.

Their mother is a bit of a weirdo, quiet and tense but all right. She's kind enough but in an offhand, bored way. Often it seems the kids are almost like little strangers that don't really have that much to do with her. Then again that's not quite fair ... she's a nice woman but kind of preoccupied most of the time.

She wakes me every morning at six-thirty. I'm sometimes hard to wake but she does it quietly because I'm in with Heidi.

'Michelle,' she'll whisper shaking my shoulder. 'It's time to get up now ...'

'Okay, okay. I'm awake,' I groan. I wish she didn't have to touch me, if you know what I mean. We keep our distance during the day. On the first morning I'd gone back to sleep after saying a knock on the door would do, so I don't want to repeat that again! Jeez the reception was chilly when I finally made it down to the kitchen and all the washing up had been done. I'm raving on. Is any of this interesting for you? I'm kind of enjoying myself. I'm hoping you want to know this stuff about me. Maybe I'm wrong but I've been thinking about you a lot. Wondering how you're going. Hoping something has come up for you, work-wise.

After washing and dressing myself I have to prepare the kids.

Get them dressed and fed. Then there's the washing up to do, the chooks to feed, the eggs to collect and the school lessons to supervise. It really is one thing after another, a stream of things to do through most of the day. Hardly ever finishes! Except I don't mind. I don't really want to sit around. That'd mean I'd have to start thinking! Anyway, it's not too dreary if I've got the kids with me, which I do most of the time. Sharon is still here but we don't have much to do with each other. She's leaving any day now.

I'm quite proud of myself actually. Yesterday I cut the head off a chook. As you can imagine the kids were hanging around loving every minute of it. All the blood spurting out. Isn't it funny the way kids love blood? In just two weeks at the station I've learnt how to milk the cow too and cook cakes – something I never thought I'd be able to do – not to mention entertaining kids. Plus a lot more. So what d'you reckon, Mick? Bet you never thought it possible, eh?

Nina and Karl are both moody bastards. Every day is different. I never quite know how they're going to be. When you're actually living with people you have to work out how to calculate their moods, answer questions without actually answering them if you know what I mean. The hardest part, well, the part I find hardest, is filling in time when there isn't much to do.

I hate this country, Mick! It's so friggin' dismal. Every morning I get up and look out at all that flat boring land and my insides heave. I'm not kidding! I know there's a drought on. (No one around here talks about anything else!) So maybe things will look different after the rain comes. But I'm not holding my breath. I don't think I'll ever get to like it the way you do. (Also I don't think the rains will ever come either.) There's a big blue sky out here every day. I can't imagine anything else.

Sometimes the nights are okay though. With the light gone you don't see how boring everything is. When the kids are in bed, I often sneak back down into the garden. The moon will be out, and the stars ... Yeah, the stars are really something. Some nights I go for a bit of a walk through the side gate, past the dog kennels and woodheap, a couple of hundred yards away to the windmill. If there's any kind of a breeze it'll be spinning around, squeaking and shuddering. Kind of mysterious. I look up at those circling tin blades and wonder what's happening to me, if I'm learning anything at all worth knowing.

I think about my brothers too, if they've found work or girlfriends, if they miss me at all or even wonder where I am. I think about this kid I'm carrying and I tell myself (yet again!) to get to a doctor somehow soon to check everything is all right. It's one of those things I keep putting off.

I wonder about the people who will have it next year – everyone says there are queues of people waiting to adopt babies. I wonder about the ones who'll take mine.

And I often think of you, Mick, of the way we met and that last night we were together. In a few weeks I get a couple of days off. Anyway I'm going to see if I can get a ride into Menindee with one of the shearers (maybe Chas?). I know you can't say if you'll be around. It will depend on work. But if you are, what about meeting up with me?

I see Chas every now and again but he's always real busy. He was out mustering the stock in the first week and now the shearing's started he's in the shed. Might see a bit more of him now. Although there isn't too much mixing between us in the house and the shearers up in the quarters. There's all these little rules that no one really tells you about and I've been a bit dumb picking them up. Like the other day when I was taking the station kids down to the river I suggested to Nina that the couple of shearers' kids who were hanging around could come too. She got this look on her face and I knew then that it was 'no go'. Didn't say so but, you know, I got the message. My kids don't mix with shearers' kids! And the kids know it too, although they find their own ways of getting around all that stuff. I lost Henry the other day. When I found him eventually he was up at the shearers' quarters playing swords with one of the kids there. I nearly told him off and then I thought, Ah, stuff it! I'm not his mother and

144

besides what's so wrong with shearers' kids? You probably know all about that kind of thing. Got to go. See you soon, Mick. Again, I hope everything is okay with you. I'm looking forward to hearing from you.

Love,
Shell

By the end of the letter, Mick's hands had stopped trembling. He read it through a couple more times then stood up on the verandah, facing out across the sleepy street towards the river. An Aboriginal woman with a few kids sauntered by on her way down to the post office. She lived at the back of Chas's place and Mick often heard her in the morning getting the kids ready for school. The grumbling and swearing, the shouts and the laughing would fly up into the cool clear morning air. Their dog was always barking too. She grinned at Mick and cuffed her four-year-old who was trying to climb the fence.

'G'day, Mick. How's it goin'?'

'Not too bad, Dawn. How are you?'

She shrugged and smiled again, without stopping. One of the kids hung back staring at Mick curiously. Mick made a face and pretended to chase him off and the kid ran off after his mother, laughing.

The late afternoon light was already seeping away as Mick turned back to the house. He smiled to himself as he carefully folded the letter, put it in his pocket and pushed the door open. If there had been anyone around to see he would have done a few cartwheels right there and then in front of the house in the main street of Menindee.

13

After the first week, when Michelle realised that Sharon would soon be gone, she knew she'd miss her quiet, dependable presence in the house and went out of her way to be friendly. But Sharon kept a polite distance, right up to the last day.

That day, Michelle did the kitchen chores as usual, made sure the twins were happy playing out the front then rounded up the older kids and took them to the school room at the back of the house. After settling them in front of the radio she decided to sneak out. Sharon was leaving at midday and Michelle had a sudden urge to have a few words with her alone, at the very least to thank her for helping her settle into the job. Michelle ran around to the small bungalow at the back of the house but found she wasn't there. She ran quickly to all the obvious places, not wanting to be away too long. It was expected that she stay with the children all the time when they were doing their lessons and she knew she would be reprimanded if she was found absent. After calling out a couple of times she eventually found Sharon down one side of the house, slowly sweeping the concrete path that led out to the chook pen.

'Oh, hello. Why are you doing that? Thought you'd be packing your stuff.' Michelle was strangely shy now that she was face to face with the girl, with no better excuse for seeking her out than the wish to say goodbye.

Sharon smiled and continued sweeping.

'Nah. I've already done that last night.'

'Is someone giving you a ride into town?'

Sharon looked up at her quickly, a little surprised.

'My husband's coming for me about twelve . . .'

'Oh.' Michelle stiffened. Strange that she'd assumed, in spite of Sharon's advanced pregnancy, that she would be alone, that she'd be going back to her mother maybe or to live with aunts or friends.

'Does your husband work around here?'

Sharon stopped sweeping and began slowly shuffling back towards the back verandah. Michelle followed, trying not to see the way the girl's heaviness made even walking difficult.

'He used to work on properties about, but now he works in town. Well, in town and everywhere really, all over the place.' Sharon slipped off the old sandshoes and edged her narrow feet into rubber thongs, one hand on the verandah post to steady herself.

'What's he do?' Michelle asked curiously. She wanted to know what their life would be like together. Was he Aboriginal too? What did Sharon hope for? How would *their* future pan out?

'He's involved in land rights,' she said, eyes averted.

'Got a position in the organisation,' she added proudly as an afterthought.

'What's that mean? Land rights? I've heard about it but . . .' Michelle stopped. Sharon was looking at her and smiling, and she suddenly felt really dumb.

'You never heard of land rights for Aboriginal people?' she asked gently. The white smile was spread right across her face. For the first time Michelle thought that she was pretty, that there was something really pretty about that wide white smile set right in the middle of the velvet-smooth dark skin.

'No. I mean yeah. I've heard of it. I don't know what it means though.'

147

'It's just Aboriginal people trying to get back some of the land that was pinched from them years ago.' The girl spoke seriously now as though she wanted Michelle to understand. 'For a lot of the tribal people the land is everything...'

Michelle nodded, pushed the cat off the old wicker chair and sat down.

'Fair enough.'

Neither of them knew quite what to say for a few moments after that. Sharon stood side on to Michelle, leaning against the post, her head turned away, looking out into the distance. Michelle took the opportunity to check out the enormous round belly under the simple cotton sleeveless shift. Panic puffed up like smoke inside her. *How am I going to manage, getting around like that? Why didn't I get rid of it? What would a dead nun know about any of this?*

'So when exactly is your baby due?' She tried to speak brightly, not wanting Sharon to walk away yet.

'In about three weeks.' The Aboriginal girl's voice was dreamy and soft. She was still staring out into the flatness and Michelle couldn't see her face.

'You going to have the baby in hospital?'

Sharon turned around to Michelle, smiling again.

'Yeah. Of course. In Broken Hill. We're going in there tomorrow to my aunt's place to wait...'

Michelle nodded and sighed. She felt left out, stupid and boring. Everybody had things worked out except herself.

'How about yours?'

Michelle looked up, startled. She hadn't heard right. Couldn't have. It wasn't obvious yet, was it? She could still fit into her loose jeans if she tied them around the top with string, and she wore her two, wide, long-sleeved shirts every day in spite of the heat. In the bath she had to see the round belly expanding every week but no one else could. She was sure of it. Sharon was looking at her, waiting for an answer. Michelle was wondering whether to pretend she hadn't heard but then found herself saying, 'What do you mean?' aggressively. It was a stupid thing to say and she immediately regretted it, but the panic had returned. It threatened to engulf her, drown her in a tide of confusion.

'Your baby,' Sharon said simply. 'When is it due?'

'I'm not sure ... exactly,' Michelle mumbled, looking away.

'Have you been to a doctor?' Sharon asked mildly.

Michelle shrugged angrily. She'd come out here to say good-bye and here she was being made to answer questions about something she wasn't ready to think about. She got up, trying to stay cool, on top of the situation. Without looking directly at Sharon she smiled weakly.

'I just wanted to say thanks for everything. Showing me around and that. It would have been a lot harder getting used to things with just her ...' Michelle made a swift ironical gesture with her thumb in the direction of the house.

'And all the best with your ... kid. Hope it goes okay.'

Michelle didn't wait for a reply. She headed off towards the school room, her mind buzzing. Was it really obvious? What did that mean for her future employment? *Did I really expect that it wouldn't be obvious? After all I'm probably near enough to four months.*

'Michelle?' It was Sharon's voice behind her. Michelle slowed down but didn't turn around or stop. She could hear the footsteps coming along behind her on the gravel.

'Michelle, wait!'

Michelle stopped.

'Yeah. What?'

'Why'd you run off like that?' the soft voice puffed.

They stood looking at each other. Michelle's head was spinning. She couldn't trust herself to speak at all. If only she had somewhere to go. Somewhere to hide until it was all over.

'I'm not going to tell anyone. I ... know you want it to be a secret.'

Michelle sighed. Relief spread through her but she didn't know why.

'Yeah. Okay. I'd appreciate that,' she grunted ungraciously.

'But look, it's going to be obvious soon . . .'

'I know.'

'So why don't you come into the clinic.'

'Clinic?' Michelle repeated stupidly. 'What clinic?'

'Every Thursday there's a clinic in Menindee. You could go there and see a doctor. Where were you thinking of having the baby?'

Michelle shrugged. She felt as though she was about six, caught somewhere she wasn't meant to be.

'I dunno . . .'

Sharon suddenly reached out and took Michelle by both shoulders.

'You're all right, Michelle. I've . . . I've been watching you these last weeks . . . out at the windmill. That used to be my favourite place too.'

Michelle shook herself a little, surprised that she didn't care at all that the girl had been watching her when she'd been sitting out there thinking she was alone.

'Yeah?' Michelle smiled.

'Yeah.'

Sharon smiled warmly. Her eyes were huge, shining and dark. Michelle couldn't do anything but look straight back into them.

'Is that guy . . . who I met that day, is he your man?'

Michelle shook her head miserably.

'No. No, he's not,' she breathed, one hand moving instinctively to her belly. 'He's not the father.'

Sharon shook her gently again.

'Doesn't matter. *He* likes you.'

'Who?'

'Mick. The guy I met.' Sharon was still looking right into her face. Michelle couldn't help it. Her spirits rose just hearing the words.

'You reckon?'

'Anyone can see it. He'll help you.'

They smiled at each other, then Michelle thought she should make herself clear.

'Actually I won't really need any help ... I'm not keeping it.'

Sharon was genuinely confused.

'How do you mean ... you're not keeping it?' she asked softly.

'I'm going to get it adopted.'

Sharon's face became tense with a kind of bewilderment.

'You're going to give your baby away?' she said slowly, as though unable to believe what she was putting into words.

Michelle looked away uncomfortably.

'Yeah.'

'Who to?'

'I dunno.'

The young man that followed Henry down the wide hallway into the kitchen after lunch that day was tall, lean and very black. He was dressed casually in old jeans, sandshoes and a black T-shirt. The words 'We Have Survived' stood out in white against the gold, black and red ribbon which was tied casually around his wiry hair. Michelle, who was sitting at the table with Nina and the children eating Sharon's specially baked farewell cake, saw Karl wince as he stood and held out his hand, eyes everywhere but on the younger man's dark face.

'Well, if it isn't Vincent.' The light sarcasm in Karl's tone was only just there. Someone who didn't know him might have thought he was just being friendly.

The black man hesitated before taking the outstretched hand.

'Mr Schultz.' He spoke very quietly, without even a small smile.

'So how about some cake, Vincent.' Once again the cold

light sarcasm that was hard to pinpoint. Michelle could almost feel the bristles rising between the men. The white man with his tense jerky movements and the black, solid and unflinching in his hostility. And she wasn't the only one. Sharon turned around from where she'd been rinsing a glass at the sink with a tight, slightly forced smile on her face.

'Meet Michelle . . . she's taking over my job.'

One of the twins began to cry for no apparent reason. The black man turned around to face Michelle. He looked straight at her for a couple of seconds, not so much a cold look as simply an appraisal, ending in a terse nod. He held out his hand.

'G'day. Pleased to meet you.' Once again the surprisingly soft voice.

Michelle felt her hand disappear into his smooth black one and mumbled something in return. She was confused. This man was so completely different to what she'd expected. He looked wild and smart and . . . completely sure of himself. *Why had I expected anything else?*

'Would you like some tea and cake?' Nina had come back into the room, and, having sensed the hostility between the men, was trying to smooth things over.

'No. Thank you.' He looked at Sharon. 'I think we'd better be going.'

Sharon nodded. She looked at the kids then and held out her arms, tears welling up in her eyes.

'Well, you kids . . . this is it.'

They ran towards her, the twins nearly knocking her over with their kisses and hugs.

'Bye, Sharon!'

'Come back, won't you!'

'Don't forget us.'

'I won't. I won't.'

Sharon, Vincent and the kids walked out into the sunshine where the old ute was waiting, and Michelle, Karl and Nina

152

followed some distance behind. It surprised Michelle to see the husband and wife holding hands as they said their last goodbyes to Sharon.

'Take care of yourself now.'

'Don't forget to tell us when bubby arrives.'

Michelle and Vincent were both on the periphery momentarily as the children and their parents played out the last rites. Sharon now had her things in the back of the ute and was awkwardly climbing in amid the excited cries and final well-wishing of the kids.

'Come back!'

'Bring the baby!'

Michelle watched him as he stood on the other side of the ute, staring out across the land as though he wasn't part of what was happening at all. Was he arrogant or rude ... or shy? Suddenly he turned back and caught her eye. She smiled at him tentatively, surprising herself. Her first instinct had been to turn away but in that split second had thought, what have I got to lose? Her impetuosity was rewarded with a warm grin before he quickly opened the door and leapt into the ute. A crazy spurt of energy inside her coincided with the loud spluttering revs from the engine.

The ute began to back out from the fence and Sharon suddenly stuck her slim black arm out the window and beckoned to Michelle.

'Hey, Michelle!' she called.

Surprised, Michelle ran over. Sharon caught Michelle's small nail-bitten hand in her own narrow-fingered dark one.

'Yeah?'

'See ya, girl.' The dark eyes gleamed back at her, laughing and warm.

Michelle grinned, really pleased. They slapped hands playfully as the car started to edge off slowly down the track. Michelle had to run a couple of feet to keep up.

'Yeah. See ya too!' she yelled back.

'Good luck!'
'You too.'

Two weeks after Sharon had left, Nina handed Michelle a letter as she was getting lunch for the children. She stuck it in the pocket of her trousers, deciding to wait for a quiet moment before opening it. By half-past two the twins were resting and the older ones were busy with their schoolwork. Michelle sat on the cement step in the warm sunshine, outside the school-room door and tore open the envelope.

Dear Michelle,

Thanks for your letter. Didn't arrive until today. I thought you'd forgotten me!

Things are all right, I suppose. Ah, why say that? Think I'll take a leaf out of your book and not say anything I don't mean. It's been pretty shithouse since you and Chas left. No talk around of jobs. At least nothing real.

Last week I went into Broken Hill and signed up for the dole. Hated doing it but I guess it's either do that or rob a bank. (Joke! You know how fond I am of eating!) Should come through soon. When you get that day off, if I've got the money, I'll come and pick you up on the bike.

Yesterday I got a letter from Pino. (That mate of mine in jail.) He's given this address here to a couple of guys just out. Would you mind asking Chas if they can stay here a night or two? They're on their way to Broken Hill. I don't know what they think they're going to find there but Pino has specifically asked me, so tell Chas, will you? They arrived in the slammer long after he'd left, so he won't know them. Pino told me the names but I can hardly place them myself.

Michelle, I don't know what to say. This hanging around is getting me down. If I knew there was something at the end of it then it would be easier. I'll do anything. I was talking to a few guys over in the pub yesterday and they reckon some of the stations

154

around are killing their sheep. There's nothing to feed them with and they're not even worth shearing. Something is badly wrong, I reckon.

I don't really see anybody much. The Greek at the cafe is all right. Remember him? Nick. Doleful bugger, but when his old mother isn't around he sparks up a bit. Sometimes I go down there for a few dim sims and chips. I do a bit of car work too and fixing machinery for people around. Not paid work though, of course. Just helping out. Every day I head over to the pub to find out if Ted has heard anything about work. He's good, always asking around for me in case anything turns up. It's a real meeting place, that joint. A lot of people passing through. Every day he hands on a few tips to me but nothing comes to anything much. Although I did get a day last week, at the garage in Wilcannia. Just greasing and oiling trucks mainly, nothing too hard and seventy bucks in my hand which was all right. Every day Ted offers me a drink but I say no. I reckon if I started drinking in the mood I'm in these days then I'd never stop. So I guess you could say I'm not at rock bottom yet!

I'm glad your job is working out. The pay is bad but at least, stuck out there, you have no way of spending it! You'll have a nice little pile by the time you leave.

I'm in the wrong place at the wrong time, Shell. Reckon I'll be off soon. Up north or over to the west. I'll wait for the dole, then once I get the money for petrol I'll be off. If I could get a few more days anywhere I'd be off sooner. There's no point hanging around here. Thinking about it I wonder why I've stayed so long.

I do think about you though, often. And I miss you too. All that stuff you said in your letter about your kid, thinking where it will end up, I'm not ignoring it or anything. I'm glad you wrote to me about it. But I don't know what to say. It's hard for me to understand if you know what I mean. I can't remember the last time I even saw a baby. I wouldn't know what to think if it was me.

Don't forget about that day off. I really want to see you before I go.

Your friend always,
Mick

Michelle cried a bit when she'd finished Mick's letter but she didn't care, there were only the kids around to see. So he was going. Up north. The west. There wasn't anything for him here. His plain words had brought back her own precarious situation, something she usually managed to avoid thinking about as she went about the daily work on the station. She felt bereft already and chilly with loneliness in the warm sunshine.

After Mick's letter she began sleeping with the knife under her pillow again, unsure why, just knowing she needed to feel that small white handle in her own hand every now and again, especially if she woke in the middle of the night. It wasn't as though she was afraid of anyone, more that it gave her back her sense of purpose. She'd take it out sometimes and run her finger against the sharp edge and think of home. She was aware of the baby growing inside her most of the time now. But it was like all those kicks and tiny twinges. The tender breasts and expanding waist were happening to another Michelle, the one back there in Gippsland who hung about with Kevin, left school in a huff and gave her mother hell. Besides it didn't really belong to her, this kid. She was just carrying it for someone else.

As the weeks rolled by she began to get used to the flat country surrounding the house on the station. There was a certain continuity about the blueness each day and the sweet, scent-filled air which took up the excited shouts and cries of the children, that gave her something. She was waiting it out, just as she'd planned, putting in the time before her life could change. That country had her thinking about things in a wider way than she'd never done before. Veronica had been right after all – there was more to life than what you could see. It was just a matter of letting your head open up.

14

Mick was awakened one night by loud banging on the front door. Half asleep, he stumbled out thinking it might be someone who'd run out of petrol on the road or a local wanting help with his car. He pushed off the warm blankets, grumbling. He'd only been living in Menindee for about two months and already he had a reputation as someone good with his hands. Trouble was, some of the locals thought they had a right to call on him day and night for anything.

'Yeah, okay, okay! I'm coming,' he shouted as he slipped on his jeans and jumper.

Outside were two strangers, both rugged up against the cold. For some reason he was immediately on guard. There was something vaguely threatening about the way they stood there. Mick only just managed to check the rush of adrenalin that pulsed through him before speaking.

'Er . . . Hello.'

'G'day, Mick.' It was the taller one who spoke. When he saw that Mick was having trouble placing him, he pulled off the slouch hat that was half-covering his eyes and grinned, combing his thin fair hair away from his face with grimy fingers.

'Don't say you've forgotten us already, mate!' The voice was friendly, with just a fine edge of hardness to it.

At once Mick recognised him – Steven Dolby from jail. He'd spent time inside with him but hadn't known him well. Mick made himself smile.

'Oh. G'day, Steve. Yeah, Pino wrote . . .'

'Good. This here is me mate Gully. Gully Hamilton.'

'Good to meet ya, Gully,' Mick said and held out his hand. The short guy shook it without looking at him. Dolby moved forward and Mick stepped aside apologetically, holding the door open.

'Sorry. Come on in. Sorry I didn't recognise you. I was asleep.'

'Bit early to be asleep, isn't it?'

They followed him in and Mick switched on the light. It was around midnight and Mick could see now that they both looked tired and cold.

'When did you guys get out?' He turned the old heater on and poked the fire around a bit before heaving on a fresh log.

'Last week . . . came up as far as Mildura by train.'

Gully still hadn't spoken a word. He slumped into a chair near the fire and watched Steve move slowly around Chas's little house, touching and picking up whatever he could as though he was looking for something.

'So who owns this little dump?'

Mick tried to suppress his irritation. Chas's house was now painted, bright and cheerful, and he'd done most of it himself. He hated this guy snooping around.

'Er . . . Chas Morris. Before your time I think. You want something to eat?'

Mick was doing his best to get the conversation rolling in a more ordinary way. Dolby was making his nerves jangle.

'Nah, thanks. We've just had hamburgers. What 'bout you, Gully? You right?'

Gully looked up and Mick saw how young he was. Barely twenty, he'd bet, with close mean eyes and a tough straight little mouth. Mick wondered what the kid had seen to give him a mouth like that.

'You got anything to drink?' Voice was flat, almost disinterested and very young.

'Coffee, tea … water … milk.' Mick smiled. The kid cut in gruffly, ignoring the smile.

'I mean something to *drink!*'

Dolby grinned, pulled a flask from his pocket and went to the sink for glasses.

'Don't think there's any grog here, Gully. Have to use up some of our own supplies.' The light sarcasm hit its mark and Mick shifted uncomfortably. Dolby poured the drinks and handed them out, a Vegemite glass full of some strong smelling stuff in his hands. Mick sighed and wondered how long they'd want to stay.

'So, Mick, what've ya been up to?'

'Nothing much. Unfortunately.'

Dolby held up his own glass pointedly before taking a sip.

'Well, here's to it, gentlemen. The future.'

Mick took a sip and shuddered as the rough bite flowed down his throat. He smiled grimly and raised his glass.

'Yeah. To the future.'

'Been working?'

'Nah. Looking. But nothing happening on that front.'

Dolby shrugged, disinterestedly, and then sat down suddenly.

He took a gulp from his glass, slid his chair over near to Mick under the hanging light, and looked straight into his eyes for a couple of seconds before speaking.

'Actually, Mick. We've got something going. In Broken Hill. Need a third partner to pull it off. You interested?'

A strange combination of excitement and relief flooded through Mick. Of course! He'd forgotten. Forgotten where all this edginess and tension came from. It had been so long. He'd been misreading the situation – they weren't hostile or threatening at all. They were planning a job. Everyone was nervous and edgy before pulling something off.

'So what've you got planned?' He was curious in spite of himself. Dolby indicated Gully and spoke intensely.

159

'There's a soccer match on Sunday. Gully comes from the Hill. Knows all about it. Big crowd. Gully's brother is playing. Isn't he, Gull?'

'Yeah,' the kid whispered, staring back at Dolby. His face had that pinched look, as though he'd never had quite enough food when he was growing.

'Knows the club rooms, the safe system, when the van comes to pick up, the guys in charge of the proceeds.'

Mick's mouth went dry as he listened. He couldn't help it. The tense excitement in Dolby's voice was intoxicating, rubbing off on the desperate longing he had to be part of something real again. Even as he knew he mustn't, couldn't, wouldn't be part of it . . .

'It's all sweet. Everything's planned.' Dolby's voice droned on, slower now, more sure, encouraged by Mick's rapt expression. 'We're going up there tomorrow. Have a couple of days to really suss things out. And the beauty of it, mate, is we've got Gully's brother! Not that he knows it . . .'

Dolby started to laugh as he went on, looking at Gully every now and again. Gully stared back at him, dully, unreadable. No one would know by looking at him if he was comfortable with the situation or not.

'Gully's brother is the star player and he'll be showing us around, through the club rooms etc . . . give us the grand tour so we'll be familiar with everything for Sunday. That part is all teed up.' Dolby choked a little on his drink, still laughing. 'It's just what we need. We have to be absolutely sure of the details.'

Mick's brain lurched back down into a lower gear. What he dreaded so much was happening and he wasn't doing anything about it. Chas's words come to him through the fog of Dolby's rambling drone.

'Stay away from the vermin, boy, and you'll be okay in the long run . . .' But where was Chas now? *Where the bloody hell was anyone?* Chas had said there'd be a job for him and he'd been here for two months and still nothing had turned up.

'We need you in the car, Mick. It'll be sweet. All worked out. We'll be out of there inside five minutes. With at least two hundred thousand bucks to cut between us. Cash, mate. At least two hundred thousand ... A great start for something else ...'

One part of Mick was listening very intently, taking in all the details, assessing the two in front of him coldly, wondering if they had the brains, if they could be trusted to get a job right. Another side was spinning off in a dreamy way, remembering bits and pieces from here and there, splicing them together, weighing them up ... wondering. Suddenly, it was like he could hear Norman's soft menacing voice again, right in his ear. Norman, his partner. Over three years since they'd been together but now suddenly very close again.

'Work with the right people, Mick. And there'll be no stopping us.'

Norman and him had been partners all right. It had begun the night of their first job, the night they'd rolled the little pop singer outside the concert hall and very nearly got caught. After that they'd gone on to bigger things and had seemed more or less invincible for quite some time. Unbeatable, they told each other constantly – until the one that stuffed them both up. Norman used to say that if you sensed your luck was on the way out then it would be better to lay off for a while, to lie low and take it easy.

They'd planned it, simply, from the beginning, innocent in a way of what could go wrong. Thinking of it later, once it was over, and they'd come out on top, they'd rolled around the floor laughing, amazed by their own audacity. Imagine picking someone who was well known, who had a name. It was madness! Against all the rules.

They'd followed her from the the back door after the concert. Watched her part from her trendy little hangers on, kiss another one, and say goodbye. Heard her giggle and fling her arms around when one of the guys had called

161

out that he'd see her at eleven the following morning. Then she'd walked, with only a couple of guys around her, the short distance over to a parked BMW. Pretty little thing with long dark shiny hair, wearing a full-length fur coat, jewellery and carrying a large soft leather bag. Mick ran up behind, punched out her two companions then shoved her up against the car, holding his hand across her mouth and making her put both arms on the roof. Norman had moved in then with his knife scaring off the guys, giving Mick time. Off with the coat, then the jewellery. Whimpering, she'd handed over the bag without being asked. So far, so easy. All and all it had taken about two minutes. Two mind-numbing, mind-blowing minutes, when the blood had pounded in his head and he thought his heart might give out under the pressure. And her face – he would always remember her face, so near his own – that fearful pleading look that made him want to run without taking anything, to finish it all much sooner.

Then a five-minute sprint. Straight for the back streets and into the close darkness of the railway yard. He'd ordered her to get in her car, not to make a noise and simply drive off, leaving the guys. And so the surprise when he'd heard the scream and the shouts only thirty seconds after leaving her. Outrage really. Part of him wanted to go straight back, knock those guys out again and clamp his hand over that little posh face once more, kick the legs out from under her, really make her shut up this time. But Norman had the brains to keep him focused. Just run, Mick. Run. Faster, over the railway line, dipping under the wire fence and on to a street they didn't know. Dead end. Shit. They were down by the river now. Only thing was to jump through a backyard then come out near that stinking drain. The sound of the police siren, sounding at the back of their panicking brains. Norman and him, huddled together in a concrete drain, clutching the coat and the bag. Thumping footsteps, the searchers nearby, the swearing and waiting for the torch to find them. Waiting for it all to end with police batons and handcuffs. But it didn't. Within half an hour the searchers had left. Norman and he had crawled out and shaken off the dirt clinging to their clothes. On the way back to Norman's flat they'd celebrated by buying a couple of hot roast chickens to eat and a bottle of crappy sherry that Norman liked.

The next day they read about themselves in the paper and rolled around Norman's grimy floor, laughing their heads off. They sold the earrings for eighty dollars and split the two hundred bucks they found in the purse and the fur coat. Not much really, but food for another week. And experience. It was a start, Norman kept saying. And you had to start somewhere.

Dolby was at the sink pouring another drink. Mick sensed that they were waiting for him to speak, but he hadn't been concentrating. It was very strange remembering Norman so vividly after all this time.

'So what do you say, Mick? You want to be in it?' The question startled him, coming from the kid, Gully, in that hard, young voice.

He shrugged. This was the moment he'd been dreading. The moment of decision. So many things to consider, so many things to weigh up.

'I don't know. Let me sleep on it, will ya?'

They were both studies of disappointment and surprise.

'Aw ... come on! What you going to do here? Hangin' around in this little hick joint with no money! Give yourself a break, man!'

'I'll tell you in the morning.'

'If you're in, tell us now. We're leaving in the morning!' Dolby cut in loudly, hard as dry ice.

Mick shrugged and stared straight back at him. These jerks needed him. He knew that much now. They needed someone with experience who could be relied upon. But he knew what this was about. The tough act was about Dolby making his play to be leader. If Mick was going to team up with these two then he'd better make it damn plain from the start that he didn't intend being pushed around.

'In the morning,' he repeated slowly not shifting his eyes from Dolby's face.

Of course, he didn't sleep. He tossed and turned, on his back, on his side, trying to weigh up the consequences of both going and staying, telling himself lies about doing only one more job – just to get some money behind him. But even as he told himself that, he knew it was bullshit. It never worked like that and he knew it.

By the morning, he lay feeling slightly nauseous, hands behind his head in his sleeping-bag on Chas's bed, waiting for the others to wake up, thinking that he would probably go along with them because he was fed up and there wasn't anything much else going on in his life. Realising he was that weak was enough to make him want to vomit.

Dolby and Gully were still asleep when Mick heard the whistle. Early today for some reason. He put down the cup of tea, got up from the table and sauntered outside into the freezing air, thinking that the dole cheque might have arrived and if that was the case then it might make him think again about what was possible.

'G'day, Michael. Nippy, eh?'

'Yeah. Mornin', Barry.'

He felt a real twinge as he watched the man roll off slowly on his bike to the next house, his fat bum encased in blue shorts, whistling some dotty old tune to himself. Going with those guys today would mean goodbye to the likes of Barry. And Ted in the pub, the ordinary friendly people around here who'd accepted him because he was a mate of Chas's. Then again they had jobs, didn't they? Something to look forward to. Something going on in their lives. He picked the letter out of the box and saw at once it was from Michelle.

Dear Mick,

Thanks for your letters. I got the next one only two days after the first. Don't put yourself down. You're a good letter writer. I really enjoyed reading both of them. By the way, I told Chas about the message from Pino. He wasn't too keen but said to leave it up to you. That you would know what to do with them.

Listen, the mail is going out in about an hour so I won't rave on too much. I've got all day Sunday and Monday off! Chas is going to drive me into Menindee on Sunday morning, should get there about ten, I reckon, if we set off at six like Chas says he wants to. Then I don't have to be back till the next day. Chas has got to go out for a while to see about some other jobs after this shed has finished. Reckons there might be something for you there too, although I'm not supposed to say that in case it doesn't work out.

Mick, I'm looking forward to seeing you. Badly. Hope you'll be around. Has your money come through yet? Don't piss off without saying goodbye, eh?

Love,
Michelle

Mick stuffed the letter in his pocket and grinned. There was no way he could let Michelle down. No way. What could he have been thinking of! He'd only been out a couple of months. He wasn't finished yet. Far from it.

He went inside after that, woke Dolby and Gully up and made them tea, then told them to piss off after they'd had something to eat. Their protests rolled off him like water from an oil slick. He didn't care what they thought. So, he was gutless and stupid, was he? Passing up the big chance of his life. All that crap only made Mick laugh. Crims were always talking big, making out everything was more important than it was. What did he owe them? Or anyone else for that matter? After that muddled night of

165

sleeplessness and worry it was great to simply feel clear-headed again.

Mick was down the back with a fern hook when they arrived the following Sunday, trying to tidy the mess of tangled weeds and bushes that were threatening to take over Chas's block. He'd been working without a break for two hours, obsessively, trying to quell the uneasiness he felt in anticipation of seeing her again. How would he seem to her now, after weeks out on the station? Why did he have this mad hope that something might actually *happen* that day which would somehow galvanise his resolve to either go north or stay? It was hard work because some kind of wild berry bush had grown over everything, the prickles catching in the soft flesh of his palms every now and again. He was considering going down to Nick's to see if he could buy some kind of spray poison when he heard Chas's voice.

'Hey! Give it a break. Day of rest, ya know!'

Mick started a bit, then grinned when he saw Chas behind him standing on the verandah, looking the same as ever, the big broad-brimmed hat in one hand, moleskins covering the skinny legs. And the weathered, worn and ancient face, smiling.

'G'day, Chas.'

Something in Mick's chest plummeted when he saw that his old friend was alone.

'Michelle not here?'

'She's here . . .'

Mick tried to suck a prickle from his thumb as he placed the fern hook against the wooden fence.

'That berry stuff is a bastard, Chas!'

He'd begun walking up to the house when Michelle appeared alongside Chas on the verandah. Mick was self-conscious suddenly. Here he was all sweaty and dirty, wearing jeans with holes in them. Why hadn't he left himself

166

enough time to have a shower? Seeing her now smiling tentatively at him, he felt too shy even to speak.

'Hi, Mick.' That funny low voice that he'd half forgotten. He looked up, eyes on her face for a few seconds and he saw that she looked well. Her hair was tied straight back from her face and she was wearing a loose, red-checked man's shirt, wide green trousers and boots. She looked fantastic actually. Not at all like the little scrap of a girl he'd waved goodbye to around eight weeks ago.

'G'day, Michelle.'

They were both very shy as they took a longer look at each other. She'd really filled out, her cheeks were rosy and he could see that there was a warm brown tone there too, over her arms and face. It jolted him to remember that she was pregnant and that was probably the reason why she looked so different.

Chas looked shrewdly from one to the other, sensing their awkwardness. He gave Mick a clumsy, warm slap on the shoulder before turning back to the house.

'You've done a good job on that door, mate.'

'Yeah, I reckon it's all right . . .'

'Too right it is. Now listen you both. I gotta go out to Tilbra straight away. So I'll see you tonight . . . want to have tea at the pub?'

Mick and Michelle followed Chas inside and watched him hunting around in the old trunk near his bed.

'Yeah. Sure. What ya goin' out there for, Chas?'

Chas turned around with a wry grin as he slipped on a fresh shirt.

'Gotta see a man about a dog. Gettin' too old for the shearing caper.'

Mick grinned disbelievingly as Chas continued.

'Too right. Very nice old dame in charge of a mail-run up there. Think I'll make known that I'm available . . .'

Chas winked at them as he headed for the door.

'Maybe we'll forget the pub. They tell me at the station that young Michelle here is a pretty hot hand with the cakes. She'll probably whip one up for you today, Mick.'

Laughing, Michelle picked up a cushion and hurled it at the closing door.

'Ah, shut up, Chas!'

They waited until they heard the rev of his ute starting up before daring to look at each other again.

'You're lookin' all right, Shell,' Mick said. He was standing by the stove watching as she moved around the room, like a little cat sniffing around, checking out familiar territory.

'Yeah. I feel okay.'

'How's the job?'

'It's not bad. S'pose.'

'Feel like a cuppa tea or coffee . . .?'

'Yeah. Tea, thanks.'

Mick filled the kettle. He settled it on the stove and turned around again. She'd moved in, standing there, only a few feet away, watching him, a brazen smile slipping across her mouth and into her eyes.

'You look all right yaself. You know that?'

He grinned as he felt the awkwardness falling away in billowing clouds, making the floor they were standing on springy and light.

'Oh, sure. I bet I smell something great.'

Only a moment and they were in each other's arms, laughing and gasping a bit with how good it felt. That low guttural laugh that he loved. As though he'd deeply amused her.

'I know. I know.'

Inside, Mick was trembling. The small strong body locked with his own brought out a tenderness in him that made him feel he could hardly stand up much less talk. Eventually he broke away, cupping her face in his hands, looking at her seriously.

'Hey, what do you want to do on your day off?'

She shrugged and smiled, and something deep in Mick did a quick breezy, double back-flip. That shrug said she didn't care, that it was enough that they were together. And that was exactly how he felt. It was more than he could have hoped for.

'I thought we might go down to the river. Take some food,' he garbled quickly. 'I bought some stuff, but you say. I mean if you just want to sit around ...' He trailed off helplessly. 'I dunno what you had in mind.'

'Sounds good,' she said quietly, raising both clenched fists to his face and lightly touching his cheeks with her knuckles. 'The river sounds real good to me.'

15

It was a very warm day. A huge bright blue sky – harbinger of the summer months to come. In another two or three months, the heat would have been welcomed. After a wet winter it would have meant the turning of the season, the necessary conclusion to what had been before. As it was, there was real despair in the voices of the people Mick and Michelle passed on their way by the old pub down to the river. The greetings were sour; like old chips crackling, dry with baked-in emotion.

'Look at that bloody sky!'

'Never lets up, eh?'

'Reckon we'll get anything this winter?'

'Who knows? Better be soon or we'll all be buggered.'

Mick and Michelle passed on, a little guilty to be secretly savouring the warmth, enjoying the feeling of the sun bearing down, and the look of the white light dappling through the blue, sweet-smelling leaves. They walked hand in hand along the river, under the shade of the enormous gums, the dry earth, old leaves and sticks crackling under their feet. They walked slowly, aware of the huge, two-hundred-year-old smooth white trunks all around them and exposed root systems twisting down into the dry earth like the clutching misshapen fingers of forgotten giants. And their counterparts, the branches, reaching the other way, up into the sky.

Mick carried a small tatty overnight bag of Chas's, full of the food he'd prepared for their meal. They walked away from the town along the river, for at least an hour, hardly even speaking, listening to the call of the birds and the shuffling sounds of small animals – a darting lizard there, a family of ducks on the river, the thudding of shy kangaroos retreating.

They stopped when they came to a secluded twist in the river. At some stage it had obviously been a swimming spot for kids. There was quite a long thin patch of fine white sand by the water out of the shade. To one side of the enclave a matted thick rope hung on one of the horizontal branches that leant out across the river.

'What do you reckon, Shell? Feel like a drink?'

'Yeah. Let's stop here a while.'

They smiled as though each had somehow known it was the place they'd been heading for. Mick shoved the bag of food in the shade then went to join her down at the river-side. Michelle had taken off her shoes and was dipping one foot gingerly into the water.

'Freezing,' she muttered, smiling at him. 'How come it's so full when there's a drought on?'

'It's regulated. They harness the water in the lakes and release as much as they need.' Mick was overtaken suddenly with a wild urge to be frozen – all over.

'I'm going for a swim.'

Michelle's face dropped open with surprise.

'Feel it first. It'll kill you!'

But Mick only laughed. Tearing off his shirt, shoes and jeans he stood for a moment white and strong; the blue tatts on each upper arm standing out like old brand names. He shivered a little in his underpants, staring out across the river, gathering up his strength for the plunge.

'Used to do this all the time when I was a kid ...' he shouted suddenly, and with a loud whoop he sprang forward and caught the rope. Howling with mock-dread he climbed up it a bit and then swaying back and forth, teetered for a second before letting himself fall deep into the river.

Michelle laughed as she watched his head surface a couple of metres from where he'd gone in, spluttering and half-screaming with the cold.

'What's it like?'

He was laughing and could hardly speak, his teeth were chattering so loudly.

'Fan-friggin'-tastic!'

She watched him swim out strongly for a few metres then turn around and swim back the other way. Quite terrified but also suddenly hopelessly in love with the idea, she began to take off her own trousers and shirt. Too shy to really strip off in front of him she left on her underwear and T-shirt. They would dry on her in the sun afterwards.

'Okay, here I come!'

He turned back, the wild joy in his face giving way to alarm.

'What about the bab . . . Do you think you should? Might be dangerous . . .'

'Shut up!'

She grinned at him and walked into the water, slowly, steadily, squealing all the way.

'I can't! Oh, this is terrible! This is freezing!'

Huffing and panting, Mick dog-paddled up to her, his face rigid with worry. For the first time he really under-stood that she had a baby in there. It was quite obvious. Without the loose man's shirt, her belly was only half hidden under the green top and it stood out as round and smooth as a small balloon.

'Then don't. Please, Shell, don't . . . the current is strong. It might . . .'

'Shut up!'

At last she was in, up to her chest, her neck and then swimming towards him determinedly. Still squawking out in short shrill yelps about how cold it was.

Mick watched her swim past and catch hold of the rope, dragging it back to the riverbank.

'I'm going to have a go, Mick.'

'Be careful.' He trod the icy water, and waited, the wild beating of his heart sending panic messages off in all directions.

'I will. Don't worry.'

Mick watched, as she took a running jump off the bank and swung out over the river, higher and higher. Time seemed to slow down for him as she got closer to the apogee. And there, at the highest point, she let go of the rope and started free-falling, eyes closed in a look of complete ecstasy, arms outspread, legs straight – like a crucifix, seemingly suspended against the clear blue sky. Falling ever so slowly, she hit the water with a resounding splash and disappeared, a plume of water shooting skywards and marking her point of entry like a tombstone. Mick knew then, without a doubt, that the image of her like that, hanging between the water and sky, would remain with him for the rest of his life. It would be something he could think about last thing before going to sleep at night or first thing in the morning, along with his mother's face and the single black swan he'd found on the Darling that day when he was ten, gliding like a queen in the watery pale light of dawn. The images he'd never forget.

'Michelle! Ah, shit! Shelly!' He half-sobbed, his freezing brain closing down, refusing to comprehend what he'd just witnessed. He swam swiftly towards the spot where she'd disappeared. She hadn't come up. There was just the water, the clear running river beneath him. Had she been caught by a snag, hit a rock? He called again, looking around for any clue to her whereabouts. He had been crazy to go in himself. Madness to give her the idea. Ultimate stupidity to let her take that risk.

'Hey, over here, ya dingbat!'

He looked and saw her emerging from the river a hundred yards downstream from the rope, dripping and shuddering, the wet green T-shirt clinging to her breasts and round

173

belly. She was completely packing up, hardly able to talk, laughing that hard.

'Did ya think you'd lost me?'

Mick grinned and started swimming towards her.

'Yeah!'

'Hey, let's eat, Mick. I'm hungry!'

Late in the afternoon, they slowly walked back along the river towards the town. Silent, both trying to shrug off the melancholy mood that had shifted in between them, wafting around like fly spray and threatening to settle on their remaining few hours together. Mick was trying hard to fight it. He kept telling himself to forget tomorrow. To forget that she would be gone soon and that his life would return to that limbo-land of no meaning. Now was enough, surely? They'd had a fantastic day: eating and sleeping in the sun, swimming and laughing by the beautiful river. The dark was closing in and they were nearly back in Menindee. He found himself hoping guiltily that Chas wouldn't be back yet and that he and Michelle would have an extra hour alone. Maybe they'd light the fire and cook something, get each other cups of steaming tea, make toast, spread jam, laugh and revive their spirits back into that drunken state of happiness which had been theirs for most of the afternoon.

He trudged on, holding her hand in the fading light, imagining the different things they might talk about.

'Hey, you know where Mick Doyle is?' Ted's booming voice broke into the surrounding quiet. Far off, but clear as a bell. Startled, Mick frowned and looked at Michelle. Had he heard right? She nodded, also puzzled. They quickened their pace and heard a few muffled men's voices calling out and then Ted again.

'Ah, shit! He's gotta be around. Have a look for him, will ya? I've got Schultz on the bloody phone.'

Mick looked at Michelle again, quizzically.

'Schultz?'

'That's the guy I work for. Remember?'

'Maybe he wants to get in contact with you?'

'Maybe. You go. I can't go much quicker.'

Mick dropped her hand and left her, running the last hundred yards, taking a short cut through the twisted half-dead fruit trees of the now disused orchard at the back of the pub. By the time he burst into the bar he could see Ted at the phone about to hang up.

'Hey, Ted! You want me?' Mick called loudly, panting.

Ted's face broke into a relieved grin as he motioned Mick over and began speaking rapidly into the phone again. Mick hurried across.

'Who is it?'

Ted placed a broad hand across the receiver, unable to keep his voice down or the delight off his florid features.

'It's the German. Schultz. Needs a rousie. Here you are. Talk to him.'

When Michelle entered the busy, smelly bar, Mick's face was hidden in shadow. She could see he was concentrating very carefully but couldn't work out why Ted was looking so alert, his eyes flicking over to Mick all the time.

'Who's Mick talking to, Ted?'

'Your boss, love.'

'What's he want with Mick?'

'You wait and see, eh?' He was teasing her but she didn't mind much. Something good was in the air.

When Mick put the phone down and turned around to her, his face was transformed. An exuberant smile spread right up from his mouth into his eyes.

'Hey, Shelly, I've got a job!'

Michelle ran towards him. 'You're kidding!'

'No! Out on the station where you are. Rousing. For the rest of the shearing. Then maybe some fencing next month. Young guy they had, busted his ankle this morning. Fell off his bike. I start tomorrow ...'

Ted and a few of the other local men who knew Mick by sight gathered around, thumping him on the back and raising their glasses.

'I reckon this is my shout, everyone,' Ted yelled across the din.

Mick grinned, accepting their drinks and good cheer gratefully but as soon as it was possible his eyes sought out Michelle, standing now a little to the side of the crowd, waiting. She met his look seriously, reaching out, gripping one of his upper arms with her hand.

'Good on you, Mick.'

'Thanks, Shell!'

'See,' she went on, teasing now, 'we told you something would happen, didn't we?'

Mick shook his head as though he might be dreaming. He gulped down another half glass of beer but couldn't calm down, couldn't keep the dopey smile from his mouth.

'I reckon this has been one great day, Shelly.'

'Yeah,' she said laughing quietly. 'It's been good all right.'

Dear Pino,

A lot has happened since I last wrote, mate, so, now that I've got an hour, I'll just try and barge ahead and tell it straight.

I got a job on that first station I told you about. I'm not shearing, just rousing. So I can move around the shed a lot and out into the yards, bringing the sheep in. It's not as hard on your back as shearing. Mostly though I'm picking up the fleeces as they fall from each shearer's comb – or the sheep's back, whichever way you want to think about it – picking off the dags and bundling it into the press. A lot of sweeping up and sorting too. This time of the year it's not real hot in the shed, which is something. It took a while to get used to the work. The first couple of weeks I had aches and pains in muscles I never knew I had. By the end of every day I was ready to drop. Now I'm getting used to it and my muscles have calmed down.

As you know I was getting pretty low, so you can imagine the great feeling it was getting that job. Just walking in the shed on the first morning, meeting the other blokes, smelling the greasy floorboards – you know that wool smell, strong and oily. Tangy. Full of air and dirt and sweat. Like nothing else. At first it was a bit mesmerising watching the gun shearers gliding their combs over the sheep, the big fleeces falling away like bloody clouds. I was like a little kid, with my mouth open. Culture shock, I suppose. Anyway it didn't take me long to get into it. Watching the sheep being set back upright on their legs after being shorn, the way they blink and sort of shudder a bit reminded me of how I felt when I first walked out of the slammer on that last day, a new life starting. I dunno. I'm raving on a bit here. Of course the best feeling of all was actually signing on for the job, a real job, mate, with decent money.

The worst part is having to live with the other guys, full on, all day and night too. Des and Jack are young guys, they're all right and so is old Lindsay. But the expert, the guy in charge, Grenfield is a real mongrel. One of those unpredictable bastards who'll be on your back all day for something really petty, then leave you completely alone the next. All depending on how he feels. He doesn't live in the shearers' quarters with us which is something, but stays nearby in this big caravan with his wife and kids. They travel around from shed to shed. Every night you hear him yelling at his wife. He hits the bottle pretty hard and I reckon that's probably his main problem.

Chas was only there for the first week. After that he was sent out mustering stock and was away for nearly a month. It's okay now but for a few weeks it was a pretty miserable existence after work. That was when I really missed all you guys back in the hole. Up here I was on the outer. Same as when you first arrive in the clink I suppose. They'd play cards with each other and drink. I was the odd man out. I suppose they would have accepted me sooner if I'd drunk more. But I'm determined to save money. So after tea I'll just wander around outside a bit (they think I'm nuts) watch the sun go down, breathe in the air and think.

Some nights, maybe once or twice a week, I'll walk up to the house and see this friend, Michelle. She's working for the station owner's wife. Housework and looking after kids, that kind of thing. Remember the girl I told you about that I met the first day I got out? We've been mates ever since. I don't know how to describe her. She's small and pretty tough looking. Nice eyes. Blue but much darker than mine. She's a little girl with real guts though, if you know what I mean. Only seventeen and she's got this voice. Sort of deep and raspy. She doesn't say nothing that she doesn't mean.

She's running away from her home town and family and some boyfriend that she won't talk about much. Anyway to cut a long story short she's pregnant but is going to get the kid adopted. The reason she didn't get rid of it at an earlier stage is an even longer story about something she had going with a dead nun. Don't put shit on me, mate! You said you wanted details!

I don't really know much else. She never wants to talk about it. Sometimes I think she's trying to pretend it's not happening. But what can I do about that? It's her business. We're making plans in a vague sort of way. When her kid gets born and farmed, I reckon we might . . . well, get together properly, go on down to Lightning Ridge. Have a go at the opals. Hard work and a bit of luck, mate, that's all I'm after. For all the stuff written about how bad things are I reckon I can make a go of it. I reckon this country has still got a lot going for it no matter what they say.

I've been asking around a bit about Beth. Chas has been on the lookout too. Asking about the old man mainly, but Beth too. He thinks if we find the old man then it will be easier to trace her. I guess we'll find out something soon. Chas knows most people on this side of the country. As you know it's Beth I want to find at this stage. The old man will keep until I'm ready for him. Might be years yet. But when it's time, I'll let him have it in just the way we always used to talk about, mate. Straight, and to the point. I'm in no hurry for him just at the moment. I'm too busy getting on with my life, in just the way I planned.

I've got to stop here, Pino. I'll write again when I get some news.
All the best, old mate,
Mick

16

'Why don't you come to the pub, Mick?' It was Des, the youngest shearer, sprucing himself up in front of the small square mirror in the shearers' quarters. The Friday night routine that Mick usually passed up.

'You want to come along some time, Mick, see what it's like, you know . . .'

Mick smiled, standing half out the doorway. The sun was setting and rich red and gold streaks of light were hitting the top of the homestead about half a kilometre away, making it look as though it was on fire.

'No thanks, mate. You know me. Want to save me dough.' He was thinking about the way Michelle had looked the day before. He'd seen her walking along the track with all the kids, laughing and playing with them. She probably didn't realise how much her stomach stuck out but he'd seen her side on, and well, no doubt about it, she looked pregnant. He'd stopped the bike expecting to have a chat but she'd simply grinned and walked on, then called back asking if he was going to be around the following night. 'Of course,' he'd answered. 'Well, I'll see you then,' she'd replied. 'I'll walk over.' Then she'd gone before he could say anything else.

Lindsay emerged from the shower wrapped only in a towel, the water still glistening over his round gut and through the mat of grey hair on his chest and head. He sniffed disapprovingly at Mick's last remark but grinned as he shook a plastic container of baby powder under both armpits and rubbed it in.

'Mate, since when has money spent on grog been money wasted?'

They all laughed. Mick sat in the doorway and continued to watch the sun. He'd had his shower and was looking forward to being alone for a while. After giving him a hard time for the first few weeks these guys he was sharing with had all turned out all right. When they saw he was a hard worker they'd slowly started to accept him. Now he felt quite easy with them.

This evening Mick felt particularly good. Grenfield had grudgingly offered him a place on the team. They had a 'run' of sheds for the next four months and so 'if he was interested', he could join up. He wanted to talk to Michelle about it, but of course he was interested. A few months concentrated work was just what he was after. With a bit of money behind him, maybe he and Michelle could meet up again in a few months and go on to Lightning Ridge together. The offer would have been perfect except for Grenfield himself, who seemed to be getting crazier as the weeks flew by.

In the nearby caravan the heavy bullying voice started up. Grenfield, as usual, was berating his family, his wife this time. The same thing happened most nights.

'Of course I don't know what time I'm coming back, ya useless bitch!'

Mick winced and tried to block out the snarling voice. Grenfield and his bullying was the only thing that marred the job. The woman's voice rose into a high-pitched yell and then there were banging sounds as though dishes were being chucked about. A door slammed, there were kids crying and Grenfield's voice still droned on above it all. Lindsay turned on the radio loudly near his bed, looking wryly at the others.

'Jeez, he's a lovely person, eh?'

'That poor bitch ought to piss off.'

Mick said nothing. It was something he didn't feel able to think about without freezing up inside. He'd seen the little kids playing outside a few times. Timid little blokes of about eight and ten, too scared to answer when he'd said hello and asked what they were doing. The wife was ultra-shy too. He'd passed her often on the way to and from the laundry and toilet but she always averted her face before he could get a good look at her and she never said anything.

Outside there was a roar of a four-wheel-drive then a loud cheery shout from the driver.

'Hey! You useless bastards ready yet?' It was Jack, the fourth shearer, showing off his new wheels.

Lindsay poked his head past Mick.

'Give us a minute, will ya?'

'Hurry. Don't want to miss the action!'

Inside the others grinned. It would take them at least two hours to get to the pub in Menindee and they all knew there wouldn't be anything even resembling 'action' there. But it was somewhere to get sloshed after a hard week.

'That prick isn't coming, is he?' Lindsay asked suddenly, jerking towards Grenfield's caravan. 'I think I can do with out him tonight.'

'Yeah. He's coming. Told me before,' Des growled despon-dently. 'Says he had a win at the races or something.'

They all groaned. Last week they'd taken Grenfield and he'd had two fights, got totally drunk, and passed out, after vomiting in the back of Jack's brand new ute.

'He says he's taking his own vehicle though.'

'Well, that's something,' Lindsay commented darkly. 'Let's hope he knocks himself off on the road coming home . . .'

'Is Chas coming?'

'Yeah. He said he'd be in there already . . .'

They left quickly after that, shouting goodbye and calling out good-naturedly that Mick was an idiot for refusing to come. Not long after, amid much angry slamming of doors Grenfield's vehicle also took off. Mick stayed inside until he heard the roar of the Falcon station wagon disappear completely, then he went outside to wait for Michelle.

As soon as the dust had cleared from the track Mick could make her out walking over in the semi-darkness. He smiled. She must have been waiting for them all to go. He watched her for a while then went out to meet her. It was unusual for her to get away so early from her chores.

'G'day, Shelly,' he said softly. She looked beautiful. Rosy and full, brimming with health. Every time he'd seen her lately she was looking better. Tonight her hair was still a little wet from being freshly washed, her clothes neatly pressed. All of her smelling clean and sweet.

'You just had a shower or something?' he joked, kissing her cheek.

She flushed a little. 'Yeah. So have you.'

'You wouldn't be able to get near me if I didn't after being in the shed all day. So what's the occasion for the royal visit?'

He was teasing her again about the fact that they hadn't seen much of each other lately in spite of living in such close proximity. Both of them worked very hard all day and Michelle wasn't free until after eight most nights and then she usually fell into bed with exhaustion. So their evening walks and chats at the halfway point between the house and the sheds had petered out. Of late it had become simply a few words here and there, or a wave when they passed each other and usually in front of the other shearers, or the kids, which made it hard.

Mick was shocked to see her face crumple up with his words and tears rush to her eyes.

'Shell! What's the matter ... what's up?' He put an arm around her shoulder.

Michelle swiped angrily at her face. Stopping the tears

182

and pushing him away, she continued to walk on steadily, towards the shearers' quarters.

'Oh, nothing much. Let's keep going.'

'Must be something. Come on, Shell. We tell each other stuff, don't we?'

She turned around and tried to smile at him.

'Yeah. Well, she knows about me being pregnant.'

Mick took both her hands in his. They were almost at the shearers' quarters now.

'That was only a matter of time, wasn't it?'

'Why?' she countered sulkily. 'It's not worrying me. I don't think about it. Why should she?'

Mick sighed.

'Shell, anyone can tell by having a good look at you.'

Michelle looked down and cupped her arms around her small bulging belly.

'I reckon I just look fat.'

Mick grinned. 'Maybe. Hey, come on, sit down and talk about it. What did she say?' Mick dragged a couple of chairs outside on to the verandah.

'Oh, she went crook. Both of them did. Said I should have told them before I took the job.'

'Then they wouldn't have given it to you.'

'That's what I said.' Michelle sniffed and sat down.

'Do they want you to go ... or what?'

'No. Not really. Said I could stay for as long as I felt comfortable. They're pleased with me ...' Michelle looked at Mick defiantly. 'I'm good with those kids and they know it.'

'Of course. So what's the problem?'

'No problem.'

'So why were you crying before?'

A tentative smile began to play around her mouth and stained cheeks but she looked away. Mick watched her closely.

'Come on, Shell. Spill it. You've got that sneaky look ...'

He laughed softly trying to cajole her. She sighed, got up and stood between his spread knees, placing two hands firmly on his shoulders.

'I'm sick of this, Mick.'

'Sick of what?'

'Of never getting ... together with you,' she continued, her face flushed with embarrassment and a kind of angry determination. 'Can't we go in there now? Into where you sleep? They won't be back, will they?'

Mick stared back into her face, mystified. Eventually he stood up and put both arms around her.

'You're right,' he said softly. 'They won't be back for ages.'

They walked in and sat down awkwardly on Mick's unmade bed. There wasn't much else in the room except the beds, four small chests of drawers along the far wall and a large ugly cupboard in the corner near the door. The warm red light of the sunset was still seeping in through the window, catching odd edges and planes of the furniture, but it too was slowly fading. Michelle grabbed Mick's hand impulsively.

'We should have done it that day at the river.'

'You mean ...?'

But she didn't let him finish, pulling his face down to her own, biting him lightly on the chin and then kissing his mouth passionately. Immediately aroused, Mick gasped a little. Both his arms went around her, cradling her tenderly as he sought out her mouth and eyes.

'Ah, Shell ... little Shell. I don't know that we should do this.'

Slowly they settled themselves, lying side by side, breathing heavily – both half terrified – facing each other. Mouths and fingers, teeth and skin. Both overcome with surprise as they felt the other discovering the secret half-forgotten places around their necks and ears and shoulders, the round knobs of bone running down their backs.

Surprised with the pleasure of the other's hands on their bodies.

Michelle reached around to undo her pants, then kicked them off. She slid her hand down Mick's chest and undid his jeans, helped to pull them down, freeing him. Mick moaned with pleasure as she guided him into her.

'But, Shell . . . I . . .'

Her eyes were closed as she felt herself close around him, but she smiled at the sound of his voice.

'Shut up.'

And Mick closed his eyes with pleasure too, unable to prevent little moans escaping as he felt his hips begin to move in rhythm against hers.

'Oh God, Michelle . . .' he moaned.

There was a lull between them suddenly. A stop in the gentle movements. Michelle opened her eyes as Mick pulled away abruptly, humping his body away from under her. Michelle sat up, in shock. She had been deep into that vague, half-dreamy state, inside her own pleasure and his withdrawal made it collapse around her, like a pile of dirty bricks.

'What are you doing?' Her scratchy voice came out more like a snarl than a whisper.

In the half-light, Mick's face looked drawn, tight with anguish.

'Getting out of you!'

'Why?'

'Because . . .'

'Because what?'

He had turned his face away towards the window. She could only see part of his profile in the darkness. The sudden change had brought back all her former feelings of confusion. Had she done the wrong thing pushing this? Misread the situation? What was the matter with him? She wanted to cry now and hit out at him for messing it up, for making her feel like a fool. But instead, as gently as she was able to make herself, she touched his chin, trying to get him to turn around so she could see his face again.

'Mick? Come on. What is it?'

But although he allowed her to shift his head back he refused to meet her eyes.

'Because I don't want to, you know ... hurt the baby inside you.'

Michelle hesitated for a moment, stunned, not quite believing her ears.

'What?'

He moved away, sat up, his feet on the floor now, facing the other way. Michelle suddenly started to chuckle, low at first and then louder, cheerfully vulgar.

'Oh shit, Mick! What? You think you're going to spear it in the head or something?'

Mick turned back, surprised by her laughter. Tentative now and smiling a bit ruefully himself.

'Well, I don't know, do I?'

Michelle held out both her arms and hugged him again. Still laughing, she gave him a pack of hard reassuring kisses on the cheek.

'Relax, Mick. There's no chance. I promise.'

'You sure? I thought you couldn't . . .'

'I'm sure . . .' Then very gently. 'Come on. Let's . . .'

And they moved in close again, making love this time, right to the end, laughing their way through it all.

When they'd finished, Michelle started laughing all over again, thinking about what he'd said, hugging him and kissing the top of his head which lay on her chest.

'What's so funny now?'

'I was thinking.'

'What?'

'One good thing about being pregnant . . .'

'What's that?'

'Don't have to worry about contraception.'

'Shit, Shell ... very funny.' They both knew it was a dumb kind of joke but neither of them could stop laughing.

They awoke a couple of hours later, still in each other's arms but cold, with only a sheet over them. Mick pulled up a blanket, but then heard the distinct hum of a vehicle approaching. He looked at the time over on Des's radio clock and shook Michelle gently. Headlight beams were cutting through the darkness outside, momentarily lighting up the inside of the hut as the vehicle made its way along the windy track towards the shearers' quarters.

'They're back, Shell. We'd better get up.'

She snuggled in closer to his body, not wanting to give up the warmth. Mick reached for her things, then rummaged around for his own.

'Better get dressed ... or ...'

Michelle was awake now and putting her clothes on grumpily in the dark.

'Or they'll give us hell, eh?' she mumbled sourly.

Mick pinched her bum jokingly as she stood up to put on her pants.

'Come on, Shell. They're not so bad.'

The car pulled up outside the shearers' hut. Male voices swearing and grumbling immediately filled the outside air. Dressed now, Michelle shrank back hoping to make her escape back to the homestead without having to put up with the lewd comments she knew would come if they found her.

Mick walked out of the hut to see that it was only Chas's ute that had arrived and that Chas himself was helping a very drunk and belligerent Grenfield out the passenger door. On the other side was Des, looking sheepish and a little drunk, leaning on the car and looking up at the brilliant night sky, packed full of blazing stars.

'G'day, Mick.' Chas gave Mick a bored wave as he struggled with Grenfield towards the caravan.

'Come on, Bob. Time for bed.'

'I'm all right. Leave me alone!' The man was vainly trying to walk by himself but every time Chas moved away, he fell over. So with Chas hovering by with a steadying arm, Grenfield eventually managed to stagger up to the caravan door, now held open by his sleepy and apprehensive-looking wife.

'Thanks for bringing him home, Chas.' The woman's face was in the direct line of the blazing headlights. Mick was surprised to see her actually smile at Chas. Suddenly she became a person. That smile made her someone, not just the poor dumb woman who was stuck with Grenfield. Mick watched as Grenfield disappeared into the van and Chas gave the wife a sympathetic little grimace as she was shutting the door.

'He'll sleep it off, Viv. No real harm done.'

'Thanks again.'

'You're right, love.'

Chas made his way over to the verandah where Mick was sitting. Michelle appeared and Chas gave a suggestive chortle.

'Well, I can see everyone hasn't wasted Saturday night.'

Mick ignored the gibe.

'What's up with happy Bob?'

Chas sat down wearily on one of the chairs next to Michelle.

'Ah, the usual. Too much grog and not enough brains. Reckons he got cheated at cards.'

Michelle stood up.

'I'd better go. The others will be back soon.' She smiled at Chas and gave him a quick hug.

'I don't want to be caught here.'

Chas laughed and pointed at Des who was still standing by the car, staring at the heavens.

'Get out before he sees ya or he'll tell the others and then both of your lives won't be worth living for the next month.'

Mick stood up.

'I'll walk back with ya, Shell.'

'No need,' she said.

Mick and Chas shared a smile.

'I know there's no need but I'll walk you back anyway.'

They all turned as the familiar rumbling in the caravan began – muffled shouting and banging noises.

Michelle shuddered. 'So, he's going to take it out on her because he lost at cards.'

Chas sighed as the noise showed no signs of abating.

'That's right . . . that's the way it goes, love.'

The caravan door burst open suddenly and one of the kids, the eldest boy, in pyjamas, flew out, thrown bodily on to the ground. Grenfield, stumbling and drunk, staggered close behind, undoing his belt. His face seemed contorted, twisted up in the strange half-light of the car's yellow headlight and the blazing stars. On the verandah, the three onlookers froze, struck dumb as they watched.

'I'll teach you to piss your bed, you little mongrel!'

The terrified boy got up, whimpering a little.

'Sorry . . . Dad, sorry . . .' He repeated the words over and over, holding out one hand like someone begging for food. The belt now free, his snarling father advanced drunkenly, knocking the boy down with a cuff to the side of his head.

'I'm going to teach you once and for bloody all!'

And doubling up his belt he began to lay into the kid. Legs, body, face. The whimpering boy cringed into the tightest smallest ball he could manage, vainly trying to protect himself.

Agitated, Michelle stood up. Clutching Chas's arm, she began to rock, backwards and forwards, half crying herself.

'Oh, no! He's really hurting him,' she screamed out suddenly, not knowing what to do, turning wildly to the others, then back to the boy on the ground, not wanting to look, unable to stop.

'Leave him alone! You damned bully,' she shouted.

But the sharp sound of the leather stinging the child's flesh continued. Smack! Smack! The man towered above the boy, grunting obscenely with each heavily executed downstroke.

'Take that! And ya might learn something. And that!'

Mick cleared his constricted throat. His hands were trembling, his mouth twitched. Michelle turned and saw that his face was transfixed in terror by the sight of the small boy on the ground being struck by his father. Tight and unreal, like a mask. She watched him get up and then get pushed firmly down again by Chas.

'Better not, Mick. The kid'll only cop more.' Chas's voice was harsh and it made Mick stand back, his mouth open as though he was gulping for air. At one point he yelled, 'Enough!' But the word came out croaky and meant nothing at all. Grenfield didn't even look up. Michelle was outraged.

'Chas, he's going to kill him!' she yelled, running over to catch the man's arm.

But Chas caught her before she was able to take hold. He shook his head sadly.

'No, love. He won't. He's got it down to a fine art.'

They watched as Grenfield continued to lay into the kid, screaming abuse.

'Too lazy to get up and have a piss, are ya? I'll show you how to get up!' He kicked the kid in the legs.

'Go on! Get up!'

Mick stiffened again, pulling away from Chas's restraining hand.

'Get up, I said! Get up!'

The boy stumbled to his knees and then froze, completely terrified. Chas stepped forward, placing one hand on Grenfield's arm, trying to make his voice light and reasonable.

'Righto, Bob. That's enough now. Kid's had enough. Okay?' Chas's mild intervention seemed to enrage Grenfield anew. A sly sneering smile spread across his face as he cuffed the boy hard on the other side of his head knocking him down again.

'When I tell *my* son to get up, I mean him to get up!'

It was that second punch to the side of the head that cracked Mick. With one leap he jumped over the verandah rail and sprinted towards the unsuspecting Grenfield, hitting him full tilt and knocking him bodily back against the caravan, winding him.

'You rotten bastard!' he screamed, at full pitch now, bringing Grenfield's wife to the door.

Mick straightened up a moment, looking at her, his face quite twisted in a fury of incomprehension and contempt.

'And you! You hopeless bitch! How can you let him . . .'

The woman stood staring back at him impassively, then opened the caravan door wider to allow her small, damaged son to crawl up inside. She then quickly shut the door – an action that said that whatever was happening out there had nothing to do with her.

Mick turned back and began attacking her husband again, very seriously and methodically this time. He punched the stunned Grenfield wherever he could find a place to lay a fist. In the face, on the body, in the crutch. Big, hard, heavy punches, one after the other, each one intended to cripple. Dull heavy thudding sounds, then a loud crack as Grenfield's nose broke; crunching, as a couple of teeth were dislodged. Grenfield slumped towards the ground, trying to defend himself, but Mick's fists just kept on flailing.

'Mick! Stop! Enough! Stop it, for God's sake.'

Chas, Michelle and Des were running forward, trying to haul Mick off. 'What are you doing! You'll kill him.'

Mick, completely out of control, pushed them away like flies and kept punching wildly.

Finally, together, they managed to haul Mick away from Grenfield who was slumped on the ground, battered, only

191

half-conscious and bleeding profusely. There were cuts above both eyes and around his mouth, two yellow broken teeth sat on his chest like buttons and a stream of blood poured from his broken nose. One of his hands seemed twisted in an odd, slightly deformed way. He lay there moaning, in great pain.

Panting, his fists still clenched, Mick stood staring down at Grenfield, then slowly around at the others who were watching him. There was a slightly surprised look on his face, as though he'd only just found Grenfield lying there and was deciding what he should do with him.

Shaking, Michelle reached up to touch Mick's shoulder but his body might have been a rock, it was that rigid. His face was a desperation mask, complete with an unseeing, cold kind of flickering in his eyes that made her feel she wasn't there. She shuddered and removed her hand, understanding at that moment that he was in the pit of some private hell, in some terrible place she hadn't been.

Chas knelt down trying to assess the damage to Grenfield, mopping up the blood on his face with a couple of hankies, trying to get a look at the hand which the man was attempting to shield.

'Get us that torch from inside, will ya, Des?'

'Sure ...' The dumbstruck Des strode off to the shearers' quarters to get the torch. When he returned, Chas was still kneeling, prodding here and there for broken bones.

'We'll have to get him to a doctor,' Chas said wearily after a while. 'I don't think he's that bad but the nose is broken and that hand doesn't look too good. He might be worse inside.'

He stood up and sighed.

'There was no need for that, Mick. No need. You haven't done the kid any good at all, you know ...'

'I know.' There was no emotion at all in Mick's voice. He might have been a robot.

'You'd better help me get him into the car ...'

'Okay.'

Grenfield woke up a bit after that. The cuts above his eyes had stopped bleeding and he seemed brighter all round. Chas hesitated, thinking of the long boring drive back into town.

'Hey, Bob,' he said kneeling down again. 'You think you need a doctor right away? Or can it wait till the morning?'

The man shrugged noncommittally, and sat himself up a bit.

'Nah, my hand's strained a bit, that's all. I'll go in tomorrow ... get it looked at.'

He then turned his whole body around painfully to face Mick who was still staring down at him, unseeing, both fists flexing and unflexing.

'You're finished, Doyle,' he said through the now fast-swelling split lips. 'Completely finished. I don't want to see you in my shed tomorrow, or any other day. You understand?'

Mick stared back. Michelle could see the same tense hatred as when he'd been bashing the man coiling around all his features like a snake. A strange, slightly drunken smile of disbelief suffused his features before he turned suddenly and walked away.

'Suits me.'

An hour later Mick was packing his things in the shearers' quarters, alone. Well, more or less. Des had flaked out on his bed and was snoring peacefully, oblivious of everything. Chas was up at the station homestead getting Grenfield fixed up with bandages and antiseptic. The others, Jack and Lindsay, were still not back from the pub but would be any time now, so Mick was moving quickly, hoping to have cleared out before they came. They were nice enough guys but he didn't want to have to say goodbye. Michelle seemed to have disappeared.

Mick folded up the sleeping-bag and stuffed it into his bag, his head still reeling. He was trying to comprehend, to make it really sink in that he'd just viciously attacked his boss and lost his job. After all it was a big enough event. He'd tried so hard, waited, ached for so long to get a decent job and now he'd blown it. Wasn't that something to think about? But there was nothing happening inside his head, just unimportant stuff like how he was going to get away before the guys got back and how he was going to fit the two extra shirts he'd bought into his bag.

He felt quite loose actually, unhinged and free from care. What did it matter that he was stuffing up his life? Didn't everybody?

Chas had tried to talk him into waiting until the next day. The cocky might stick up for him, make it hard for Grenfield to sack him. It was worth telling his side of the story, surely? Chas and Des were witnesses. Wouldn't it be worth putting up a bit of a fight? But Mick wasn't interested.

If he had to go then it might as well be straight away. Why wait until the morning? He'd been going to kill the guy. That much was fact. Had wanted badly to see him dead. If Chas and Des hadn't pulled him off he knew the man would now be gone. *Finito*. For ever. Mick shuddered inside his zip-up coat and made sure his wallet was in the inside pocket. Slightly different circumstances and the cops would be out by now, or at least looking for him; charging him with murder – maybe manslaughter if he was lucky – handcuffs, batons, court case, the lot. He had to get away now, from everyone he knew.

When Chas finally understood that Mick meant to go, he sighed as though he understood, and wished him well. Told him to stay in the Menindee house as long as he wanted and that he, Chas, would make damned sure that Grenfield paid Mick out to the last cent. Mick thanked him and said he'd see him soon. But a deeper part of Mick was wondering if he'd even stop in Menindee for one night. He felt like driving on forever, further north, away from everything.

Michelle's hot words were still smouldering around his brain and he hadn't begun to understand what her face meant when she'd confronted him later, after Grenfield had been taken away.

'What was the friggin' point, Mick!' she'd snarled, following him inside, trying to make him look at her. 'Why couldn't you just let up when you'd pulled him off?' He'd turned around wanting to explain. Wanting to tell her what had been going through his head when he'd let loose on Grenfield. But she looked so freaked out he hadn't been able to speak.

'I'll tell you now I'm not interested in hanging out with a human time-bomb! Understand? Someone I've gotta watch all the time in case he explodes. I've had enough of that sort of shit to last me a lifetime!'

In some important way he knew he'd let her down badly. But he'd work all that out tomorrow when he was on the bike and travelling north. Alone.

Everything ready now, Mick took a final look around the shearers' hut before switching off the light. There was nothing left for him here now. And every trace of him would be gone by the next day. He wondered who'd be next to sleep in his bed and whether that person would ever guess or imagine how he and Michelle had lain on it together earlier that night, made love, and drifted off to sleep in each other's arms. The sweetness of it filled his head suddenly, making him giddy with longing. It was followed immediately by an intense, raw pain in his chest, as if someone had dumped a plate of hot chillies down his gullet. It was over. Finished. Everything was finished.

Now that he was really going he felt like waking Des up and saying goodbye, but the young man, still fully dressed, was sleeping deeply. Mick went over and slipped off Des's shoes then covered him roughly with the blankets.

Des grunted a bit as he settled down into the warmth.

'Er, thanks, Mick,' he mumbled, then rolled over and went back to sleep.

'You're welcome, mate. See ya,' Mick said quietly and turning out the light, he picked up his bag.

Mick closed the door and stepped out onto the verandah. The brilliant star-filled night made it easy to see his bike waiting for him over by the implement shed. He would fill it up in Menindee then head on up to ... His thoughts were interrupted by a small movement. Turning, he was startled to see Michelle down at the far end of the verandah, sitting on one of the chairs. She looked like a painting, something unreal anyway, fixed in time in the middle of the night. Sitting there, looking out across the flat earth towards the house with her hands on her knees.

'Er, Shell?'

She got up slowly.

'Yeah. It's me.'

She picked up her bulging overnight bag and began to walk towards him wearing the coat they'd bought her in the op-shop in Broken Hill.

'Where're you going, Squirt?' he said wonderingly, looking at the bag.

He could see, now that she was getting closer, that her face was very grave. Not a flicker of a smile around her eyes, no twitch around her mouth either.

'Looks like someone's got to keep you out of trouble.'

'You mean ... What about your job and ...?'

'I'm coming with you.'

Mick held her serious look, trying not to smile, trying to hide the sudden surge of joy that threatened to swamp him.

'I haven't got anywhere to go, Shell. You know that.'

'Nor have I,' she said simply.

An impasse for a few moments.

'Okay?' she asked, still not smiling.

'Okay, then.'

*   *   *

The bike's single headlight, bouncing and shimmering, briefly illuminated the Menindee sign as they continued, slower now, on down the road past the pub towards Chas's place, the river gums looming stark and menacing in the long yellow beam of light.

Michelle's arms were frozen into place around his waist. She wondered if she would ever be able to get them warm again. When they pulled up outside the little house it was nearly 4 am and she was shuddering with the cold, relief and exhaustion, her arms still around him, unable to move.

'I thought you were going on, Mick,' she said quietly. The first words either of them had spoken since leaving the station.

He gently unlocked her hands and she lowered her arms.

'You need a rest first, Shell.'

Part of her wanted to reply immediately, argue that she'd been for real, that she'd go anywhere, any time, that she was as tough as anyone. But just the thought of being able to lie down somewhere was too enticing. She needed to sleep.

'Well, yeah . . . I appreciate that.'

They both got off the bike and began undoing the straps around their bags.

'We'll head off tomorrow, or the next day.'

'Yeah.'

'Won't make much difference.' His voice had taken on a bitter edge. 'It'll be the same difference wherever we go. There won't be much around.'

Once inside and with the fire going, their spirits picked up a bit.

'How much money did you make back there, Mick?'

'I've saved over a thousand, but I'm owed another week . . . Chas said he'd get it for me. How about you?'

'I've got about a thousand too ... for about three times the amount of time you worked,' she said flatly.

Mick smiled wearily as he flattened out the bed and threw their sleeping-bags over it.

'Not fair, eh?'

She didn't answer but turned around and started pulling off her clothes near the fire. Mick looked and saw her naked for a few seconds, before she slipped the heavy night-dress over her head. He saw her in profile and the roundness of her belly and the one breast he could see, stunned him. She seemed so totally other, it was hard to believe that only a few hours before he'd held and caressed her, entered that body with his own. Now he was awed by it, quite intimidated; it made him afraid of everything.

'Shell,' he managed to say at last. She looked up, her night-dress on now, face round in the warm glow from the fire.

'I think you were right back there. I don't know if it's a good idea, you hanging out with me ... I mean ...' He shrugged, and raised both arms in a hopeless gesture of defeat.

'I mean ... I'm probably rooted from now on ... might never get another job. Who knows? And I've got things in my head ... plans ... violent stuff. I don't even know how to explain it. You'd be better off with somebody else.'

Michelle nodded slowly, seeming to agree.

'Let's just go to sleep now, Mick, talk about it later.'

'I sort of ... want to warn you.'

She smiled as she headed for the bed.

'Okay. You've warned me.'

In the morning they were woken by loud pounding on the front door. Mick sat up first, instantly awake, but disorientated. Where was he? What had happened? He looked down at Michelle, still asleep beside him, and it all came flooding back. The pounding on the door started again, along with muffled shouting. Mick began to shake Michelle.

'Shell. Wake up. Someone's at the door.'

Michelle sat up, still half asleep.

'Who is it?'

The urgency in Mick's manner alarmed her.

'Dunno. Sounds like cops. Maybe Grenfield died,' he whispered, the tension bolting through his features like lightning. Michelle frowned and watched him jump from the bed and pull on his jeans and boots, not really comprehending what he was on about. He turned to her again and gestured pleadingly at the door.

'You go and see, will ya? Don't tell 'em I'm here.'

'What're you going to do?'

'I'll hide out the back. Just make up something. Give us some time to get away. Just go and answer the door, will ya?'

Unsettled, Michelle reluctantly got out of bed and stumbled to the front door and opened it. Outside stood Ted, from the hotel, obviously freezing in his dressing-gown and slippers and very fed up. A rush of cold air hit Michelle's face as she stared back at him, not comprehending.

'Ted.'

'Jeez you kids take a while, don't ya! Chas is on the phone. Says he's got to talk to Mick!'

'Okay. Thanks, Ted. I'll get him.'

Shirt-tails flapping behind him, Mick sprinted as fast as he could over to the pub, passing the dour Ted on his way.

'G'day, Ted.'

'I don't appreciate this one little bit, Mick.'

'I know. Sorry!'

Mick ran in through the open front door and into the empty bar, picking up the phone sitting on the counter.

'G'day, Chas. It's me.'

'Listen, Mick, you got your car licence?'

'Yeah, why?'

'Got something for ya.'

'What? I mean . . . where?'

There was a low chuckle from the other end.

'Out where blokes like Bob Grenfield won't give you any trouble.'

This was too much. Mick tried to breathe easily and stall for time.

'Chas, tell me. What is it?'

'General station hand. Fencing. Lot of rabbits need killing. Can you shoot?'

'Yeah. A bit.'

'You'll have to go out a few nights with him for pigs. But mainly checking the water-holes. That kind of thing. It's a very big place near Tibooburra. I told him you'd be all right as far as the size was concerned. He's sick of town kids. Reckons the last few he's had workin' for him were getting lost all the time. Spent all his time looking for them. Pay isn't fantastic. You interested?'

'Sure. I'm interested.'

Another chuckle.

'Thought you might be.'

'Hey, Chas?'

'Yeah?'

'You reckon Michelle could come too?'

'I don't see why not. You'll be spending most of your time out bush anyway, just in the four-wheel-drive. I don't reckon it would matter to him, long as the work gets done. I'll ask. Thought I'd come in tonight and give you the details. Gotta go now. Will I tell him you'll do it?'

'Yeah. Sure. I'll do it. And Chas . . . thanks a lot.'

'No worries. See you tonight.'

17

We didn't get to talk about that night with Grenfield until much later. Life sort of intervened. I think we both knew we had to hold tight to the job for a while or there wouldn't be any kind of future at all. Not that either of us ever spoke about it like that. We were so busy working on that station that we didn't talk about anything much at all.

We'd start work about seven. In the first month we did a lot of fencing, working together all day, driving out along these flat lonely tracks of red dirt until we came to the right place, then hopping out and getting started. Mick always seemed to know where we were. All that took me a lot longer. But I worked hard, especially in the first month before the heaviness really set in and I got too tired. The job mainly involved fixing up the fences that had been knocked down or damaged by the wild pigs and kangaroos. Sometimes we had to put in new wire but it was mainly picking up and repositioning the posts and tightening up the existing wire. After a while Mick and I got to be a good team. We worked for hours at a time, a few hundred yards apart, and hardly speaking. He did any heavy lifting and I got pretty nifty with the wire-strainers and light posts.

After that we'd tackle the rabbits which wasn't so pleasant. Took me quite a while to get used to that kind of work. Like most people, I thought rabbits were lovely little animals that didn't hurt anyone. It came as a bloody great shock to see the way they damaged the land. Whole acres of it ruined, made completely bare with mazes of burrows. Because of the drought there was hardly any feed, but in a good year, according to the station owner, the rabbits and kangaroos would have most of it eaten before the sheep could even get to it. Sometimes we worked with the owner of the station, using a kind of spiral ripper connected to the end of a tractor. That method consisted of slowly ploughing up the ground, wrecking the warrens and killing them that way. Other times we blasted them out with explosives. That was scary to watch the first time – the noise and all that dirt shooting up into the sky – like a bomb blast. Anyway both methods were pretty ugly. The end result was a lot of dead, or half-dead animals. Mick and I used to wander around after a blast and finish off the half-dead ones by wringing their necks. I got used to it. Even the blood all over my hands. It's amazing how you get used to things. Only a few weeks and I got to really hate rabbits.

That station was only paying Mick so he got a good deal with the two of us.

On that first day we got to the main house around four in the afternoon. The owner of the joint came out with his wife and sons. They stood in a line looking at us and the bike for a full minute I reckon before they moved over and shook hands. Both of the parents had white hair and creased faces but they looked fit enough. They worked the place with their two sons, both of whom had families of their own in different houses on the property. They invited us in and made us tea – all of them friendly enough, but shrewd too.

You could see them checking Mick over, probably wondering if he could do the job. When he told them that he was used to the bush, knew about animals, fencing and shooting, they kind of relaxed. They told us about the conditions, the rate of pay and everything. Instead of taking the normal one day off a week they said they'd prefer us to take a few days off every few weeks. It sounded all right.

Anyway, after travelling all that way we weren't in any kind of position to refuse. I could tell they didn't quite see where I fitted in, but I didn't care. We didn't tell them anything, except that I'd be going out on the job with Mick and that I knew how to look after myself.

After the first month it started getting really hot. I began to get tired and couldn't keep working the way I had been, although it took me a while to admit it. The station owner gave us both a couple of big broad-rimmed hats to keep the sun off our faces, but after a while that didn't make much difference.

We'd stay out usually for about three or four nights, either sleeping in the back of the station's four-wheel-drive or setting up camp. Then after the few days out bush we'd head back to the station for further supplies and instructions. Depending on the job, we'd try and set up camp near a creek or water-hole. It was always good at night. We'd cook something together, eat and then just sit in the dark watching the fire, talking a bit. Then we'd both fall into the tent and lie together in the dark.

By the end of September when we'd been working on the station for a couple of months, we decided to take a few days off for a rest. On our way back to see Chas at Menindee, Mick took a detour off the main road, back to the house he'd been brought up in as a kid. That day we talked about a few things and I think I started to understand more.

'Hey, Shell, you mind if we take this turn-off?'

'What for?'

'It's where I . . . I used to live out here. I want to see if the old place is still standing.'

'Sure.'

I didn't care. I was happy to be driving away from the daily grind of the station work. Because of my condition the station owner let us take the four-wheel-drive back to town. He was a funny, really shrewd old codger, not all that friendly. I could tell he thought he was absolutely the best guy in the world to be letting us have the truck, and I suppose it was good of him. But the other side was that he was getting two workers for one, fairly paltry, wage. Anyway, I was enjoying the comfortable air-conditioned drive.

Mick swung the vehicle left, up a narrow dirt road. I peered forward curiously and could only just make out some sort of building way up ahead of us. I was looking forward to seeing Chas so I hoped this detour wouldn't take too long. We had to drive quite a way up that bumpy dirt track before we got to it.

Eventually we came to a group of ramshackle and falling down sheds near a half-demolished wooden house, a broken creaking windmill standing guard over them all. There were two or three trees near the house but the rest of the garden was overgrown with weeds, completely dead. Mick didn't say anything, just stopped the four-wheel-drive and slowly walked towards one of the sheds. I got out too and began to walk towards the house, suddenly not sure about where I was or even if I should be there. There was a still, almost eerie feeling about that place.

The dilapidated buildings out in the middle of nowhere took on a sort of power for me that day. This was none of my business, yet I was moving forward, following Mick at a distance, listening. Apart from the breeze making the trees rustle about a bit, the old windmill's creaking, maybe a bird or two, there was nothing. But I was listening very hard. After a while I knew I was waiting for the people who'd lived here – Mick as a little kid, his sisters, mother and father – in the same way that I used to wait for the sound of Veronica around me after she'd died.

I walked in through the broken front door. There was sheep shit everywhere. Well, I suppose it was sheep's, could have been from kangaroos or some other animal. Torn wallpaper rolled away from the walls in dried-up curls. Dirt and grease hung all around where the stove must have been in the tiny kitchen. Two overturned broken chrome chairs lay scattered on either side of a scratched upside-down laminex table. Had there been a hasty get-away, a final show-down? Had someone lost everything before leaving this place? I could *almost* hear what I was listening for. Kids' voices playing and calling to each other, the scraping of the furniture as they scuffled and ran about. Under it all, a woman crying.

I walked from one small ripped-about room to another, trying to piece together what must have gone on here when Mick was a kid. A built-in cupboard with its doors hanging off in one room, in another the last remains of a narrow wooden bed complete with wrecked mattress, the stuffing spilling all over the rotting floorboards like dirty bits of white sponge-cake. I shivered again and the kid inside me began to kick frantically as though trying to get out. Usually it kicked at night when I was still. I put one hand on my stomach and felt the limb – I couldn't work out if it was a hand or a foot – gradually subside. And I was glad suddenly that I'd decided to give life to this – whatever or whoever it turned out to be. There was nothing peaceful about this old joint. There were voices everywhere, trying to make themselves heard, refusing to head off into oblivion without a last word.

Suddenly I wanted Mick to be in there with me, explaining what went on. What had this old tin can been used for? Where had he slept? Why wasn't there a bathroom? In which room had he found his mother dead that day? And a whole lot of small incidental things to help me understand. We'd been too careful over the the last couple of months, too careful of each other's feelings and respectful of the privacy of our different backgrounds. We'd been growing closer without really knowing much about each other. Suddenly I wanted to blow it all open – lay him, myself, everything on the line. I wanted to see the different sections of our lives explode up into the air like those bloody rabbits we'd been knocking off every day, the fur and severed guts, the lumps of dirt and blood all flying up and around, coming down hard. How would it all look in this bright spring sunlight? I needed to know everything about him.

On my way out I found a child's glove. It was bright red and dirty, woven with little yellow chickens dancing around the top edge. I picked it up and walked out into the sunlight. He was already over at the truck, sitting down on a nearby stump, slumped over, looking at his hands, waiting for me.

'Hey, Mick,' I yelled from the doorway. 'Come in here.'

'No, I don't think so,' he called back and then waved as though everything was all right, before turning back to his hands.

'Why not?' I called.

When he didn't answer or even look up, I made my way over to him.

'Hey, you haven't even had a look in the house yet . . .'

He looked up and I could see that his face was wet with tears. He didn't try to hide them or turn away.

I felt undone, completely. I'd never expected to see him crying. I forgot all about exposing each other and walked over and sat with him, feeling like a complete dork.

'Bad memories, eh?'

'Yeah. Well, actually I'm thinking of the Grenfield kid.'

'Who? Ah, yeah,' I remembered quickly, ashamed. How easy it was to forget when it didn't suit me to remember.

Mick started to talk then. A long rambling kind of talk. I'm not sure that he was actually talking to me so much as speaking to himself. Anyway I didn't interrupt. It was the longest I'd ever heard him speak. He used these short, sharp little sentences that tumbled together into lumps between the quiet spaces. Part of me wanted to hush him, tell him to slow down but I didn't. I'd got a strong feeling that talking like this was a first for him so it was important for him to be allowed to do it in his own way.

'Once I ran away from a foster family. I was fourteen and

I just wanted to go home. Even though Mum wasn't alive any more. Anyway I hitched a ride into town, found out that the old man was about. First place I looked was the pub. And that's where I found him. He didn't say "hello, Mick", or "what're you doing here, kid". He just grabbed my arm, got his belt off and started laying into me in the public bar. The funny thing was that a couple of men drinking there tried to stop him but they couldn't. He was always a tough old bastard. But one of them rang up the RSPCA. I'm not kidding! Not the police or the social welfare but the animal protection agency! The bastards wouldn't come. I can still hear that old codger's voice booming out over the heads of the men who'd stood watching me getting walloped. He was standing by the red phone in the corner of the bar, a cocky with an old oil-stained felt hat and heavy gut that was splitting his shirt open at the front. "Nup, they won't come. Said they're only interested in animals".'

Mick started to laugh and I joined in, I'm not sure why. I sure as hell didn't think what he was saying was funny. I hated imagining what he was saying but I couldn't help seeing it vividly. In that warm air, goose-bumps were rising all over my skin.

'I was lying on the floor, shaking, my teeth chattering uncontrollably. I watched them turn back to their drinks. I think the old man had just about finished with me at that stage but I was watching his boot, sure that he was going to kick it in my guts or groin pretty soon. That was the way he usually finished off hidings. Even with the girls, he'd kick them in the bum or the legs. Once when Beth was nine he punched her so hard in the stomach, winded her so badly, that her face went blue and we thought she was going to die. But this time he didn't kick. Must've been the other men watching that stopped him . . .'

Mick was quiet for a while then, just staring at the house. After a while he got up and walked over to the rusty gate leading into the garden.

'I remember coming back to this house after that belting in the pub, Shell. Can you believe it? I wanted to . . . in spite of everything, I wanted to come home. Can you understand that?'

'No.'

He grinned suddenly. 'Neither can I. But I remember slinking in through this gate and then around by the side of the house to the back. I dunno. I must have thought it was where I belonged . . .'

His face seemed stretched, as though he was wrung out in some way. I wondered if he would ever get over all that stuff he'd been talking about, if he'd ever beat it.

'I reckon I'm different to you, Mick. I don't think of myself belonging anywhere.'

'Don't you?'

'Nah. Not really.'

'Yeah, I reckon you are different then. Hey, let's go.'

When we were back in the four-wheel-drive I handed Mick the little glove I'd found.

'Hey. You recognise this?'

His face softened as he took it, putting two big fingers inside and feeling around, and smiling as though he could hardly believe what he was seeing.

'Yours?'

'No, my sister's . . .'

'Beth?'

'Yeah. Beth, I think.'

He threw the little glove on the dashboard and started the engine.

'Better move or we'll never get there.'

18

See how hard it is to stop once you start? I went back to that house on a crazy impulse and all it did was make my bad memories more real. I was doing all right in that job. It was doing its thing for me, calming me down. I reckon that I'd be better off trying to conserve my energy for the future. And she was probably thinking the same thing. Reliving stuff would take too much out of us both. Maybe one day we'd both get drunk and spill the beans properly. But when you think about it, what would be the point?

One evening in early October the station owner came out to see us. Michelle and I were camped by the river and he and I were going to go out in the truck later to shoot pigs. Michelle handed him a cup of tea and he came straight out with it.

'How far gone are you?'

Michelle didn't like it one bit. I nearly laughed. Could see she was on the point of saying 'mind your own business', but then thought better of it.

'It's due in November,' she said, then turned away as though she wanted to change the subject.

November. That gave me a bit of a start. Next month. And as far as I knew she hadn't organised anything. The station owner was looking at her, curiously now, a faint smile on his face.

'That's not long, is it?'

She shrugged as though she couldn't care less.

'You been seen to?' he asked casually.

She looked up from her tea, face flushed with embarrassment.

'What do you mean?'

'You booked into hospital and been checked over by the
doctors?'

'Not yet.' Her face was flaming now. I felt sorry for her. I
could tell she was feeling like an idiot.

The man got up and put his cup on the stump we were
using for a table. He continued mildly. 'Well, I think you
should soon.'

Michelle was looking away so he addressed me.

'You two've been doing well. Take a few days off at the
end of this week. Go to Broken Hill, book in and do
everything. We don't want anything to happen to her out
here.'

'Okay,' I said.

'She might have to stay in there for the last couple of
weeks.'

'Yeah,' I answered, surprised by the idea. I suppose I
hadn't really thought of the possibility of Michelle being
invalided in any way.

Michelle didn't say anything. She was now in a foul
mood. When he got up to organise the guns at the back of
his other truck we sat together in uneasy silence for a
while, staring into the fire. Eventually I felt compelled to
speak.

'You want to come out with us tonight, for the pigs?'

'You don't need me, do you?'

'Well . . . there'd be plenty for you to do. Jim and I will
both be up the back shooting . . .'

It was good having a third person to help but it wasn't
essential. I knew Shell hated seeing the pigs being shot
but wouldn't admit it. The first time we went she had this
terrible freaked-out white look on her face for most of the

time. The squealing of the pigs and the smell of the blood. I don't know why I was putting it on her like that. Being a bit cruel really. I guess I was trying to make her face up to reality. She was really getting big now, but I could see that as the time got closer she seemed to want to talk less and less about having the kid.

'You don't really like it much, do you?'

'What?'

'Killing pigs?'

'So?'

'So nothing. Just admit it.'

She was glowering at me. I smiled at her but she looked away angrily. I suddenly felt really spun out and relaxed with good feelings. At that moment I knew I really loved her. I felt like telling her, but I could see that now wasn't the right time. God, she made me want to laugh sometimes.

'So, November, is it?'

'Yeah.'

'I think we'd better do as he says, Shell. Don't want you to get caught out here.'

'There's at least a month to go,' she blurted out angrily.

'Okay. Okay. Still you should get checked over . . .'

She got up and walked around to the other side of the truck and carried back another log for the fire.

'Don't you reckon, Shell?' I persisted, still smiling inside myself.

'Okay!' She threw the log on the fire and stormed off into the tent.

At the end of the week, we packed up and went to Broken Hill on my bike. The station owner was using his ute so there was nothing else for it but the bike. It probably looked funny, me driving around on my bike with her on the back, pregnant and everything. Well, it worried me too. I worried that it would be uncomfortable and dangerous and kept talking about borrowing Chas's ute all the time, but she wouldn't hear of it. Fact is, she gets really dark on me even mentioning the pregnancy. Insists on ignoring the fact that it's right there in front of both our eyes. You'd think she had a rock in there or something, not a kid. The only way she ever refers to it is as an *it*. 'When *it's* over we'll go here, when I'm finished with *it*, I'll do this . . .' All the time she's getting heavier and rounder. I reckon she's got the right idea, giving it away and all, but somehow I would've thought it would mean more to her. Perhaps it does and she just doesn't want to show it. Maybe. I dunno. If that's the case then she's a bloody good actor. We talk about everything else now.

She booked into the hospital to have the baby and told them she wanted to adopt it out. Well, that caused a bit of a stir. 'Are you quite sure, dear? Have you really thought this through?' Jeez, I really had to admire her. She just stuck to her guns, refused to get emotional; said she had no room in her life for a kid and that she'd never liked kids anyway, much less babies. They were a bit dumbfounded by her at first. It was funny to watch their faces. Most girls must behave very differently to that in this situation, probably get all weepy or whatever. After it finally sank in, she had to go and see all these social workers and doctors and fill in forms by the dozen. I got sick of it after a while, went out and had a walk around the park and came back with some pies and milkshakes, only to find her still at it. After about five hours they told her that if she wanted the father's name on the birth certificate she should get his consent for the adoption. I thought, *Here goes, she'll crack now*. She hadn't contacted anyone from her home town since she'd run away. Anyway I couldn't believe it. She just said, 'Sure. Give me the form and I'll send it to him. But I'll ring him up now and tell him first.' Then she looked at her watch as though it was something she did every day.

'I reckon he'll be home now. No footy practice on Wednesdays ...'

I didn't say anything, but I suppose I was kind of shocked that she was so matter-of-fact about it all.

That was one of the weirdest phone calls! For a start, neither of us had any change. We had to scrounge around asking people to change our two-dollar coins. By the time we had it all together it was about five o'clock in the afternoon and we were in the ground-floor foyer of this big busy public hospital, standing near the phone. People coming and going, on trolleys, wheelchairs, in dressing-gowns, you name it. I was standing next to her, waiting for her to pick up the receiver but she just stood there staring at it, as though she was thinking very deeply about something.

'Come on, Squirt,' I said as kindly as I could. 'Better get it over with.'

'Yeah, I know,' she said, reaching out for the receiver and dialling. 'He won't be able to get me up here, will he?'

'Course he won't.'

We could both hear the bloody thing ringing. Her face had gone quite white and I think she was really hoping that no one would answer. The sound of it ringing was very loud for some reason. I heard the click of the phone being lifted off the hook at the other end. As soon as that happened she slammed it down hard.

'I can't, Mick. I'm scared ... I keep thinking of the shit-act I pulled on them all ... you know, running away. They're gonna hate me so much ...'

I understood what she meant. But I was also relieved that she was showing signs of ordinary feeling, if you know what I mean. For the last few hours she'd been acting like some kind of superwoman.

'You want to do this on your own?' I asked, thinking perhaps that it might be less embarrassing for her if I cleared out for a while and left her to it. But she shook her head emphatically.

'No. Stand here with me, will you? I'm going to have another go.' She picked up the receiver and began to dial again, her hand shaking a little.

When the phone was answered again, I had my face in near to her ear and I could hear every word. The sick look on her face told me that the male voice that was saying 'hello' was him. The old boyfriend.

'Kevin. It's Michelle ...' Her voice was surprisingly strong but that's all she said. She moved her mouth a couple of times as though she was about to speak but nothing else came out. There was silence from the other end for a few seconds. I tightened my grip around her shoulders when I saw her trying to gulp down her nerves.

'Where *are* you?' The guy on the other end was trying to keep his voice flat but the high pitch gave him away.

'I'm up north ... in Broken Hill ...'

'Broken Hill! What're you doing up there?' Unmistakable anger now. It wouldn't be long before he was going to let her have it.

'I've been working ...'

'Working!'

'Yeah. Out on a farm ...'

'A farm! Jeez!'

This guy was a real dumbo. I could tell by the way he was repeating what she was saying because he couldn't think of anything to say for himself. Still to be fair, I suppose he was shocked. He hadn't heard anything from her for months.

'Well, thanks *very much*, Michelle! Thanks *very very* much for phoning. Thanks very much for *everything*!'

Who was it that said sarcasm is the lowest form of wit?

'Really *great* to hear from you ... you friggin' little ...'

He sounded as if he was about to say 'slut' but he stopped himself, probably because he was afraid that she'd hang up if he got too rough. There was a bit more silence.

'So . . . er, what's news?' Michelle blurted out nervously. I couldn't help groaning. It wasn't the smartest question to ask.

'News . . . oh, you want to hear news?' He was laying the sarcasm number on with a shovel. 'What? You want to hear about your father and mother? About the way they've been sick worrying about you . . . They even spent money on some dumb private detective trying to find you . . . You want to hear about what it was like for me? You just clearing out like that? What a fool I felt in front of everyone? I've been totally affected, Michelle . . . I . . . I couldn't play football for the rest of the season . . . after you left.'

I couldn't help grinning at that last bit. He had that spoilt little boy tone in his voice. I think it gave Michelle a bit of courage too. She was probably remembering how lucky she was to be rid of him.

'Listen. I'm ringing up about something important,' she said, cutting in coldly. His voice croaked to a standstill. They both waited for a few moments.

'You ready to take in what I'm gonna say?'

'Go ahead.'

'This . . . kid I'm having.'

'What about it?' he snapped, then blurted suddenly, 'Don't think I'm gonna start paying you any money, because I'll bloody die before I do that . . . I'd give up work rather than send you any of my bloody hard-earned cash! You gotta learn Michelle, you just can't do something like this and then expect everyone just to come to the party and pick up the pieces . . . I didn't want a bloody kid! Was just trying to do the right thing by you. Only to have it pushed straight back in my face. Couldn't bloody understand why you didn't get rid of it as soon as you knew you were pregnant . . .'

'I don't want any money,' she cut in on him again. 'And I don't want a kid either . . .'

'Well, it's a bit late now, isn't it? If I remember rightly it's going to be born in a couple of months. You're going to have a kid whether you want it or not . . .'

'I know that, Kevin . . . that's what I'm . . . ringing about I . . .'

'Don't start trying to act all *reasonable* with me, Michelle! What do you want? You want something, I know that. You haven't rung to say hello.'

'I'm gonna have the kid adopted. I've given them your name. Unless *you* want the baby, could you sign these papers I'm sending down for you?'

That took the wind out of him.

'Adopted?' He said the word slowly, a bit bewildered, as though he'd never heard of it before.

'You're really going to have it . . . adopted? Give it away, like?'

'Yeah.'

'You know *who to*?'

'I can meet them if I want to. But the people here . . . you know the social workers and that. They seem pretty good. They know what they're doing. I don't think I'd know much more about it than they would . . . I think I'm gonna just get it over with as quickly as I can . . . so I can leave here and . . .'

'God, you're a selfish little bitch, Michelle, aren't ya?' he said real sharp, like a snake striking. 'Don't even want your own kid!'

'Well, do you want it?' she retorted matter-of-factly, although I could tell that his words had hit home a bit. 'You're the father. You've got the right. They told me.'

I tightened my grip around her shoulders, encouraging her, I hope, to just continue with what she wanted to say. She smiled at me and went on.

'It's yours too, Kevin. Except I'm the one who has to . . . carry it around until it's born. Want me to bring it down for you to look after . . . when it's born?'

'No need to get smart, Michelle.'

'I'm serious. It's your kid.'

'You know as well as I do that it's a whole different thing for a woman ... a normal woman. Anyway, how can I be sure it *is* my kid, Michelle? You try and pull any kind of swifty on me for money and *that's* gonna be my argument ... that you were having it off with a lot of different guys, so I'm not sure it is *my* kid. I've got mates here in this town you know. They'll say anything I tell them to in court.'

I could see her face tightening up with anger. She was trying to let his nastiness pass but ended up not being able to resist the bait.

'Oh, you're a *big* man, Kevin! Such a *tough* man.'

He knew he was offside now so he doubled his efforts to make her feel bad.

'Yeah ... about as tough as you ... moll. Hey, I can hear someone else there! Who's there with you?'

'No one, Kevin ...'

'I bet you've shacked up with someone else, have you?'

Michelle closed her eyes. 'So, Kevin, if I send these papers down ... will you sign them?'

'Do I have to pay anything?'

'No.'

'What if I don't sign them?'

'If you don't, it doesn't really matter. The adoption will go ahead. I just thought ... I thought that seeing it was your kid that you should be in on it and that ...'

'Oh, yeah,' he burst out sarcastically. 'You're so big on consideration, aren't you, Michelle?'

'I'll send the papers today? Okay?'

He didn't answer.

She put the receiver down quietly in his ear and stood there looking at it like before, dreamily as though the whole conversation hadn't happened and she was trying to decide something else quite unrelated.

'Well, what do you reckon, Shell? You've done it now.

217

Want to get something to eat?' I said softly. It was getting on for evening now. She looked tired and we were both hungry. She shuddered as though her body was trying to shake something off, then turned to me with such a smile.

'Yeah. Let's get out and buy something.'

'When do you have to come back?'

'What do you mean?'

'To the clinic. To get checked over again?'

'They say every week from now on but . . . I dunno.'

19

I managed to talk her into attending the clinic over the next three weeks for the check-ups. Although she wasn't keen she went along with it all, probably to shut me up.

It was after the third weekly check-up, as we were going through the big double doors of the hospital on our way out to the bike that I met up with a friend I thought I'd never see again. There were lots of Aboriginal people there, bringing their kids and old people in, yabbering away in their own languages. I wasn't taking much notice of anything until I noticed that Michelle had stopped to get a drink from a machine.

It was then I saw this young black guy sticking money into one of the other big drink-vending machines. Slam. Out came a can of Coke. He turned around for a couple of seconds and I saw his face. There was something . . . I was staring and he stopped and looked back at me, a serious expression in his eyes. Before it finally hit home I remember thinking 'I know him. I know that face . . .' Then the penny dropped. Buster. I gave a sort of yell of disbelief. Couldn't help it. Impossible but true! Everything I'd ever known about Buster the kid was there in this wild-looking black man, wearing a bright headband, old dirty jeans and no shoes. The eyes, the shape of the face, the tiny dent on the bridge of his nose.

'Hey, Buster,' I said. 'It's me, Mick. You remember me?'

It was his turn to look quizzical. He came closer, frowning as though the right connections weren't happening for him.

'Mick ...' he finally said slowly. 'You mean Mick Doyle from ...? He was starting to smile now with the memory. Michelle was standing there looking a bit put out as she watched us.

'Yeah. Mick Doyle from ... forever ago,' I said. We both started laughing then. He came forward and lifted me off the ground in this gigantic squeeze. Made me remember what a strong bastard he'd been, even as a kid.

'Where you been, Mick? Where you been?'

'Here and there,' I said laughing, acting cool. 'Mainly there ... and here a bit.'

'I heard you'd done time in the clanger, mate ...'

'Yeah, that's right ...'

'Well, good on ya ... happens to the best of us.'

He was a droll bastard back then too. I touched his 'We Have Survived' headband.

'What's this, mate?' I said. 'You got wild in your old age?'

'Yeah. You could say that.'

Eventually Michelle pushed us both on to the pavement outside the doors and out of everyone's way. I was elated. Out of my tree. Like, you know, nothing could go wrong.

It was all coming back to me, all that time we used to spend together as kids. The time I was living near Bourke before Mum had gone. The trees we'd climb, huts we'd build, all the mucking about. He was the best friend I'd ever had. It was a knockout to meet up with him again.

We all walked through the carpark towards the bike. Buster had invited us back to his house for a feed, so we'd decided to halt our reminiscences until we got there. But I couldn't help it.

'So what ... you married or anything, Buster?'

He grinned at me and then at Michelle's bulging stomach.

'Yep. I've got a kid. Me and me wife. He's been a bit sick. That's why I'm here ...' He pulled a bottle of medicine from his pocket. 'But nothing serious ... you know.' He winked at Michelle. 'You'll know all about it soon, eh? Your first is it?'

Michelle nodded and looked away uncomfortably. Buster turned back to me.

'Get on to that heap, mate and take your first turn left out of this joint then follow the road out about two kilometres. Anyway, follow my car.'

He waved and grinned, then headed over to a beat-up old Holden and got in. Winding down the window he yelled to Michelle as an afterthought.

'You'd be more comfortable with me in the car.'

Michelle was already sitting on the back of the bike.

'No, I'm right. Thanks.'

He roared off and we followed. Just outside the hospital grounds he stopped and wound down the window again. He shot one thin black arm out, pointing at the sky.

'Take a look at that!'

In the distance, along the horizon there was an enormous build-up of heavy grey cloud. I shook my head.

'I don't think it'll mean anything ...'

He grinned.

'What do you mean?'

'Well, we've had cloud like that for months. It hasn't amounted to anything.'

'Not cloud like that, we haven't.'

He roared off suddenly and we followed close behind. On the way out to Buster's I could see that the cloud was different and I wondered, probably for the millionth time, if those grey shapes in the sky might bring relief to the country around us.

All of the next bit was good. Seeing Buster's little kid and meeting his wife. Eating a meal with them. They were living with Buster's aunt and a few cousins in this fibro place on the outskirts of town. Not a bad little joint, surrounded by houses exactly the same as theirs. As soon as we arrived his wife, Bek, a plump woman with a wide friendly smile and much lighter, more coppery skin than Buster's, started flying around worrying about what we were going to eat. She seemed genuinely pleased to have us. But I could see that Michelle was feeling a bit embarrassed listening to all the talk about hospitals and babies. Bek was a big talker, not boring but she liked to hold the floor. Then after a while I could sense that Michelle was glad about it. Bek just took over; her constant chatter making it possible for Michelle to just sit there and listen. She didn't really have to give anything much away at all.

It turned into a real wild night. Pretty hot. We were sitting on their front verandah eating and drinking, but mainly yakking on, shouting and laughing. And people kept calling by, and busting into the conversations with yells, and slapping hands. Cousins, young blokes who worked with Buster, aunts and grandmothers. You name it. All laughing and giving each other a hard time. I don't think I've ever met so many people at one sitting. A few of the old women reckoned they could remember me as a kid up on that property near the river. I didn't recognise any of them but it made me feel real good to hear them say it.

Anyway round about the time we were finishing off the food it started to rain. It was still really hot and these heavy soft drops began splattering down, singeing our sweaty skins and sliding off into little rivulets down our backs and into joints. Very slowly at first. So slow that no one took any notice. The sun was sinking away leaving great flaring strokes of thick red and gold to seep through the heavy cloud, like paint, transforming the black sky into a great wild canvas. I was talking to Buster but part of me was watching the sky. It looked like the end of the world was just around the corner.

But all we got was a storm. Within minutes a gale had blown up and then it was on for young and old. The rain started to pelt down. And lightning. Slivers of demented electric pink and white light running off all around us. Of course everyone was beside themselves. All along the street people had come out of their houses, laughing, and walking out into it, getting soaked. It had been so long since any of us had seen any real rain that it was a novelty to feel those heavy drops stinging our skins. At that stage we had no idea if the surrounding properties were getting it or if it was only confined to the town. Everyone was hoping though. All the towns around would pick up if the cockies made a bit of money. So many of those stations were literally dying of thirst.

Eventually we all moved inside but I insisted that we keep the blinds open to watch the sky tearing itself apart.

Buster talked a lot about Aboriginal land rights and I reckon he made a lot of sense. I dunno. I suppose I hadn't thought about any of that kind of stuff before. I mean about the fact that they were here first. That the land was theirs originally. I was arguing with him a bit. Saying things about his people not knowing how to use the land, you know – making money out of it – with farming and animals and whatever. That got his back up. He got real heated, reckons that we have been wrecking the land, not using it properly. Had all this information about the spreading of the desert and the salination of huge chunks of land in Victoria and the west through overuse. I couldn't say much to that because I didn't know enough. Besides, hearing him talk made me realise that my love of the country could be traced back to that time when I was a kid with him. Buster loved the country and he had taught me to to love it too. But I couldn't see where his reasoning was leading him. I mean there's no way realistically that this country is going to go back to the old Aboriginal way of life. I mean that's bullshit talk and I told him too.

'Get real,' I said, straight out when he was raving on

about the simple life out in the bush. 'You're talking through your arse, mate.'

Well, his eyes just turned on me, the whites sort of glinting in the fading light, furious and sad, the way they used to when we were kids together. I remembered in a flash the two of us sitting up in a huge old river gum, pulling at the bark, looking at the sky above, him talking and me listening. We were both about ten. He was telling me about this long poisonous beast that had roamed through all the rivers of the land – spreading destruction and misery wherever it went. I remember my heart pounding when it was time to get down the tree and wade through the river back to the bank. I think I really believed that the snake would get me.

Anyway that night, whenever it started to get too heated, we'd both start to laugh and rubbish each other. It didn't matter somehow that we saw things differently. We'd shared too much in the past. He'd thump me on the back and say 'I remember you hiding me out under your house when things got rough down at the river' or 'what about your old man and that wild steer! The way he ran for the truck.' And we both just packed up laughing.

It was later, inside, when Michelle and me were talking about going home, that he told me the news about Beth. Of course he didn't realise that he was telling me *news* as such. He thought I knew. We were packing up the dishes and stuffing them into the sink when suddenly Buster went quiet. An odd, faraway look in his eyes made him seem as though he wasn't taking in anything that was going on in that room. Eventually Bck jokingly flipped him on the bum with a tea-towel and told him to wake up. He smiled at her and then looked at me, as though he was somehow embarrassed. And sorrowful too. The look was full of sorrow. I can't understand why but it sent a wave of panic down my backbone. At that moment I had a flash of what he was going to say. I remember thinking, he's going to tell me something bad and it's going to be about Beth. He spoke very apologetically, as though he was in some way to blame.

'Mick. We were real sorry to hear about your sister. Sorry I didn't mention it before . . .'

I stood there, unable to take the stupid smile off my face. Just stood there watching them all watching me, unable to speak. Michelle and Bek had gone quiet. Eventually I managed to mumble.

'What do you mean?'

I saw a furtive look come into his eyes, the look that said that he wanted out, didn't want to be the bearer of bad news. He was hesitating, trying to get out of talking.

'Haven't you heard?

I shook my head coldly.

'Heard what?'

Buster simply groaned, and let his upper body weight fall heavily on to his two fists on the kitchen table.

'Jeez, mate. There's no easy way to say this,' he stammered. 'She's dead. Killed in a car crash up near the Queensland border. Six . . . I reckon it would be over six months ago now. I'm real sorry. I thought you knew.'

I was immediately transported to some other space. Some cold blue place of my own, where the air was icy.

'Who was driving?' My sister didn't drive. I knew that, so there had to be some mistake.

He stood up properly then and looked at me. His mouth tight, his face kind of closed. I could tell he was thinking that he'd said enough. He wasn't going to say another word. *He knows something else about Beth, my sister, and he's going to try to get out of telling me.*

Suddenly I was furious. It was all I could do to stop myself from grabbing him by the scruff of his neck and hurling him across the room. I wanted badly to punch, to kick him in that soft flabby part just under his ribs. I clenched, then unclenched my hands. Loose, I could feel them trembling slightly and that made me even angrier. I ran the itching

225

palms down flat against the sides of my jeans and tried again.

'Tell me who was driving, will ya?' My voice was stronger this time. More certain in spite of the panic growing inside me.

Buster wasn't a friend any more. Just someone with information that belonged to me. I wouldn't have cared at that moment if he'd been bleeding to death or dying of starvation. He was nothing to me.

'Tell me what happened, Buster.'

'No, mate, you wouldn't want to know ...'

He was looking from Michelle to Bek and then back again to me. *Stupid ... dumb ... Abo.* Suddenly I lunged towards him, and pushed him up against the sink, grabbing him tightly around the neck with both hands. I pressed, as hard as I could.

'I want to know! Ya hear me! Tell me.'

His startled choking noises made the other two cry out but that was just background noise. It didn't worry me at all.

'What do you think you're doing?'

'Cut it out, Mick!'

I brushed them off me, like flies. It felt good squeezing that soft black neck, seeing the eyes starting to pop. His hands were struggling to pull mine away but they were useless. It was satisfying to know that I was stronger than he was. Much stronger. His desperate clawing made no difference at all. All the hard physical work was paying off. Even two months ago this wouldn't have been so one-sided. You've gone soft, Buster, old boy, I thought, or I've got hard. *Soft with your stories and fancy ideas. Have you forgotten those tussles we had so long ago down by the river, the tussles that would leave both of us humiliated, raw and sore? Neither of us ever won in those days. And here I am now with my hands around your throat and there's nothing you can do about it ... I could kill you with my bare hands. Just watch me.*

'I said, let go of him!'

In spite of being pretty big with the kid, Michelle managed to slip both her arms in between us so that I actually couldn't avoid looking straight at her. Her face was strange, like someone else's. White and pinched. I'd never seen her like that before.

'Let go of him, you idiot!'

That gravelly little voice caught me somewhere. Somewhere inside it had me loosening my grip. I teetered, yet my fingers hung on, pressing into the flesh, reaching deep down for something.

It was the baby's cry from the next room that brought me back to my senses. A sort of plaintive frightened cry from their little kid had me letting go and backing right away. We all must have been yelling. I dunno. I fell down on to the floor, listening to the crying of the baby getting louder. I didn't so much hear the cry as feel it, if you get my drift. And the feel of that crying hung around inside me long after Bek had left the room and comforted the kid back to sleep again. Buster was breathing heavily and I sat trembling on the floor. I half expected him to fall on me and give back some of what I'd just dished out. But instead he moved further away, around to the other side of the table, rubbing his neck.

'Your old man was driving, Mick,' was what he said.

As soon as he said the words it was as though I'd known it all along.

'Pulled out on to the highway. Didn't see the car on his left. Beth never had a chance. Your old man was hurt, but not too bad. They reckon he was so pissed he didn't feel a thing.'

'Queensland,' I said stupidly. My sister didn't live in Queensland. Nowhere near. Maybe they had the wrong girl. Beth Doyle. Elizabeth Anne Doyle. That would be a fairly common name, wouldn't it?

'How come no one told me?' My voice was strangled. I was crying but I didn't care. I could see myself, a big gaunt clumsy git, rolling up on the floor, feet and hands all over the place, staring out from a useless ugly face. Crying. I must have looked ridiculous.

'How come no one told me?' I whispered again through these boiling tears. I looked at Buster but he only shrugged.

'I dunno, mate,' he said softly. His face and voice were surprisingly gentle.

'I only found out myself well after it happened. The guy who told me said she'd been visiting your old man ... when she died.'

I picked myself up after that and made for the door.

'I'm just gonna have a bit of a walk ... okay?'

I turned around and they were all looking at me.

'Who was the guy who told you?' A tremendous curiosity suddenly hit me. Even amid all this shock and sorrow, I knew I would have to know everything – eventually. Every horrible, stupid and terrible detail.

'He was just someone up there I met. I didn't know him. He'd been out with her a few times. But hadn't been with her that night.'

'The old man still up there ... in Queensland?'

'No, mate ... last I heard he was working on a station out of Tibooburra. She's buried somewhere around there too. I'm sorry.'

After that I just stumbled out on to the street. I think I just wandered around for maybe a couple of hours in the rain, then I came back to pick up Michelle so we could go back to the van we'd booked for the night. But she wouldn't come with me. Said she was staying with Bek and Buster that night. When I said I'd see her in the morning she just shrugged, and wouldn't look at me.

'Maybe,' was all she said when I pressed her.

'Suit yourself.' Her surliness angered me. But I just didn't have the space in my head to deal with her.

I left without even saying goodbye. Part of me wanted to apologise to Buster, to thank Bek for the meal, but I didn't have the energy. I felt completely whacked. So I just went off and fell asleep in the van alone. Two hours later I was wide awake, tossing around, unable to go back to sleep. I lay there thinking, the pain ebbing and flowing inside me like poison, staring into the hot crowded dark, hour after hour, waiting for dawn to break. About then I must have fallen off to sleep again, because I remember seeing the dawn light hitting the leaves of the tree and making them go silver.

Next thing I knew, I was waking up with a start. It was after ten and I knew that I had to move on two fronts that day. Firstly I had to find out all I could about Beth's death then go and see where she was buried. After that, the big one. I had to find the old man. I couldn't put it off any longer.

It was surprisingly easy. I walked out of the Shire offices in Broken Hill with the name of the tiny northern town of Milparinka in my shaking hand after only half an hour. They'd been fantastic, really going out of their way for me. They rang the police and the public records, found the time, date, cause of the accident and where she was buried. They even had the number of her burial plot for me, in Tibooburra. She'd been killed instantly and because there had been no next of kin in any condition to decide anything, she'd been buried by a few nursing friends. So Beth had started nursing? That made me happy, just knowing she'd got away from him and started doing something she really wanted to do. I was quite calm. I knew I had to see her grave and look up the friends who'd paid for the funeral, thank them and talk to them about Beth, her last hours, the times they'd had with her, what she was wearing when she died. I'd been given the name of a girl nursing in Brisbane who had been her friend. I would ring her up later. Maybe arrange to go and see her. All that would take time but I knew I needed all the details.

I was sitting outside the town hall in the main street,

thinking all this out, not seeing anything around me. Suddenly there was a hand on my shoulder. Startled, I looked up.

'What the ...?'

'Well, the odd-bods ya meet on the street, eh?' followed by a dry cackle. It was Chas, arms full of plastic shopping bags.

'I've been stocking up. Expecting visitors to the family estate tonight.' He winked. I knew he was referring to Michelle and me.

'You're coming out, aren't ya?' he asked, handing me a can of drink from one of the bags.

'I don't think so, Chas ...'

Of course he could tell straight away that something was wrong. I didn't beat around the bush, just told him the news. Calmly I think. No dramatics. I don't think it had actually sunk in properly at that stage. Chas listened, looked through the copies of the documents in my hands but didn't say much. He took a couple of deep gulps from his can and burped. After a while he spoke.

'You want company?'

'How do you mean?'

'I'll take you up there in the ute if you like. It's a hell of a long trip. Six or seven hours.'

'Can you spare the time ...?'

'Sure.'

I was suddenly overwhelmed with gratitude. My shoulders heaved. One deep sob escaped, then I was back to normal again. I took a deep slurp of the fizzy stuff. Calm as before. It would be so much better having Chas there. And taking the ute would mean that Michelle could come too.

'That'd be bloody great, Chas.'

'No worries. I reckon we'll find him up around there too, ya know.'

'Yeah. That's what I've been thinking,' I said carefully. I had to be a bit close with Chas about my plans for the old man. Don't think he'd be so keen to help find him if he knew what I had in mind.

'Was she living with him?'

'No. That's the worst thing. She'd left. Gone nursing. In Brisbane.'

The damned rotten pity of it hit me like an upper-cut to the jaw. If it hadn't been for him Beth and I could have found each other again after all the years apart. I'd have put it on her for not writing. We'd have joked together about jail, talked and laughed. But I would never talk to my sister again. The anger inside me was perfectly controlled. I wasn't going to waste one ounce of it on anyone who didn't deserve it.

'She'd gone to see him on one of her weekends off. 'I continued. 'It'd had been his birthday or some crap. She'd gone to see him ... and he killed her.'

It was midday by the time I got around to Buster's. Bek opened the door with the baby on her hip, smiling and as friendly as ever.

'G'day, Bek. Listen, I'm sorry about last night, I ... '

She waved her hand dismissively, telling me to shut up.

'Don't worry, Mick. Come in and have a coffee if you want. Michelle left about an hour ago.'

'Left?' I stammered stupidly. 'Left where? I mean ... do you know where she went?' Trying to sound casual now but not succeeding too well. Bek was squinting a bit, looking at me hard.

'Wouldn't say much. Just that she thought she'd head towards Brisbane. Didn't seem too sure ...'

'Brisbane! What? By train?'

Bek shrugged.

'I asked her to stay. Said Buster would drive her to the train, or try to get her a ride but she didn't want to wait around.'

'Brisbane?' I repeated, shocked.

231

'Yeah.'

'Did she say anything . . . er, anything, about me?'

'Nope . . . sorry.'

Chas and I spent the next two hours driving around Broken Hill looking for her. First to the railway station. There would be no train until six that night and then it was a very indirect route to Brisbane. I suddenly couldn't imagine her waiting around for it, working out all the connections, being patient enough to do it that way. So where could she possibly be? The thought of her with that heavy belly, only a couple of weeks off dropping a kid, trying to catch rides with strangers – truck drivers and God only knew who – made me feel sick with worry. She wouldn't, would she? She'd booked in to have her baby in Broken Hill. Surely she'd know it'd be madness to head off anywhere else?

We searched the caravan parks, the city hotels, gardens, streets and cafes. You name it. She was nowhere. I couldn't work out what to *think*, much less do. Apart from being worried, I was furious. Okay, so I'd been a turkey the night before. So what? My sister was dead. Buster was *my* mate. I'd apologise. It didn't have anything to do with her . . . did it? A throbbing pain started up around my right eye. The light seem unbearably bright that day. Clear blue sky, bright cruel light. I could hardly talk. Chas would ask something and I'd just mutter 'yes' or 'no', like I was beyond everything somehow. After a while Chas and me were driving around from place to place not saying a word to each other. I don't know if he realised how I felt. He kept muttering to himself that she'd have to turn up soon. I had to believe him.

In the end Chas suggested we leave for Tibooburra as planned. I nodded. There didn't seem to be anything else to do. Chas only had a few days off.

We had to muck around a bit before we were able to leave. Get oil, fill up the water tanks and fix a headlight.

Then, on our way out of Broken Hill in Chas's ute the temperature gauge went red. There was nothing for it but to get the engine checked out at the nearest garage. I can't say I was sorry for these delays; I mean, it felt completely wrong leaving that town without Michelle. What if she was crazy enough to actually head off to Brisbane? I'd never met a female before with such a foul temper. Why the hell had I got mixed up with her?

When the ute was finally given the okay, and Chas and I were once again ready to set off, I found a few words.

'Listen, Chas. I'm ... worried about Michelle. Let's go back to Buster's to see if she's turned up.'

Chas sighed, braked the car and turned it around.

'Mick, I don't think she should come on such a long trip. I mean, she's about to have a kid. It wouldn't be right.'

'Yeah, but what the hell is she gonna do in Brisbane! I mean that's crazier, isn't it?'

Chas had to agree. By the time we'd pulled up again outside Buster's it was getting on for four. I could tell Chas was thinking that the whole operation was turning into a circus but he sat there without saying anything while I rang the front door bell. Bek came to the door, frowning.

'Michelle turned up?'

'No. Sorry, Mick.'

I shut my eyes and tried to think. What could I do? Chas could see my dilemma.

'You want to wait tonight? See if she'll turn up before you go?'

I stood still, trying to decide.

'Yeah ... I mean no, forget it! Damn.'

By that stage my head was so crook, I felt wiped out. I slammed back into the car and told Chas to keep driving out along the highway to Tibooburra. I had things to do, damn it! People to see. My whole world was crashing in but I wasn't going to admit it, even to myself. All I could do was stare out the window at the awful red dust, at the quiet shimmering heat and try to act interested in whatever Chas said.

Chas had been belting the ute out along the highway towards Tibooburra for over two hours, before we saw anything. There were hardly any other cars and after our late start we were anxious to get as many kilometres as possible covered before the dark set in. At dusk the kangaroos would be out in their droves and the trip would have to slow right down to avoid them. It had started to cool off but I left my window fully open, letting the rushing air on my face. It acted like healing balm. My eyes were closed and I was trying hard not to think of anything.

'Jeez, you'd want to be desperate!' Chas suddenly said loudly.

I blinked and spat the dust out of my mouth. Up ahead, still at least a kilometre away, a small solitary figure stood by the side of the road dwarfed by the flat, featureless plain stretching around in all directions.

'Give him a ride?' I suggested carelessly. I didn't particularly want to have to squeeze up in the front but the back of the ute held ample room.

'Yeah. Be tough trying to get a lift out here,' Chas muttered. We hurtled on, both curious now to see who we would find standing out there in the middle of nowhere. The figure retreated a bit as the ute pulled up and began to walk off. Chas and I looked at each other wonderingly then realised at exactly the same moment *who* it was. He let out a loud exclamation and immediately got out.

'Michelle!' he shouted. 'What the hell are you doing here?'

She turned to face him, without even glancing at me.

'What's it look like?' she answered coldly. 'Hitching.'

I was still in the ute. I watched Chas take a few steps towards her and then stop. His voice remained light and neutral although I could tell he was genuinely shocked.

'Where are you going?'

She didn't answer. Instead she started fiddling with a strap on her bag, pretending there was something wrong with it. I made the mistake of repeating Chas's question.

'Where are you going, Shell?'

'None of your bloody business any more, is it?' she snapped.

'We give you a ride?' Chas said pleasantly.

'Nup. Thanks.' She walked a few paces back to the road and stood there looking down the way we'd come as though she expected to see a car arriving for her any minute. All around us there was only quietness. Not even the sounds of birds in that empty darkening air.

Chas looked at me and I sighed, really confused. She was acting tough as usual. She *was* tough. But I knew she'd be scared out of her wits out there, by herself at night in that desolate country. I also knew with everything that was in me that this girl standing in front of me with her plain peaked little face, bitten nails, blue smouldering eyes, even the round belly, meant the world to me. I really didn't want to lose her. Even so, I had no idea what to say, much less what to do. Luckily Chas wasn't about to give up.

'You can't stay out here. It's gonna get really cold tonight and tomorrow will be another hot one. It's not good for that baby, y'know.'

She shrugged as though she didn't care. Chas continued firmly.

'I mean, you got any water?'

Michelle stared at him for a couple of moments before shaking her head. Chas's voice softened.

'Well, let us take you into the next town then.'

Michelle shifted uneasily where she stood. I could see her resolve was wavering a little.

'Where're you headed?'

'Tibooburra. Mick's sister is buried there and we reckon his old man will be around there too . . .' he said amiably.

She threw a stiff contemptuous look at me.

'So that's it, Mick, is it? Be clear about this. You're gonna go and find him. Then what? Knock him off? End up back where you came from?'

I didn't know what to say. Her putting it like that made the pain behind my eye worse. By this stage the idea of Beth being dead had started to really sink in and I didn't know how to cope with anything. The buzz of pain flapping around like a bat inside my head was something unreal.

'I'll come with you to the next town. That's all.'

'Squirt. Tibooburra *is* the next town,' Chas said gently. 'Just that it's about four hours away ...'

'Okay. I'll go there. Then I'll decide ... what ...' Her voice was losing its angry, confident tone but she was determined I wouldn't see. She picked up her bag, threw it into the back of the ute and began to clamber up over the tailgate herself. Chas moved over quickly to stop her.

'Waddya doing? There's no way you're riding in there. Not in your condition,' he barked.

Michelle got down and immediately reached in to take back her bag.

'Well, looks like I'm not coming with you then,' she said not looking at him.

Chas shook his head, exasperated, looking from one to the other of us.

'Will someone please tell me what the ... hell is going on here?'

We both started a bit. I'd never seen Chas really pissed off before and neither had she. I knew I was the problem. She didn't want to sit next to me. I put my hand on her bag, indicating that she didn't have to take it out.

'Leave it, Shell. I'll go in the back. Okay?' I said quietly.

'No. It's okay. I ...' She was changing her mind again. I could see by her face that she was distressed and close to tears. I watched her turn abruptly and walk to the front cabin and get in. I sighed, then got in beside her thinking that it was going to be some drive. But I was happy too. Really happy and relieved to have found her, in spite of her mood.

20

Michelle's pains started properly about two hours further up the highway towards Tibooburra. She had felt odd all day, strangely disconnected from everything that was happening, but it was only after about an hour of driving into the night, sitting between Mick and Chas in the old ute, that she admitted to herself that whatever was happening had turned into something more than just odd. Much more and much worse.

Each pain would start as an urgent rumbling uneasiness at the base of her spine, slowly climbing up her back and around to her belly, growing steadily and heavily, peaking into a dizzying pitch of intensity that lasted a few seconds before gradually ebbing away again – until the next one. While the intense pain lasted, Michelle held her breath, bit her lip and grasped the dashboard in front of her, but kept silent. She refused to accept it was really happening. After all, according to the doctor in Broken Hill, it wasn't due for at least another two weeks and this ... this thing that had overtaken her body was just too weird to admit to. Too scary by half. If she just shut up and waited, surely it would go away. After each bout she sat back, exhausted and filled with panic, clammy with sweat but still unwilling to speak about it.

The desultory conversation between Chas and Mick continued above and around her body. During the intense spasms of pain she *was* nothing but body. Simply flesh, swollen, laid open and flayed, bent on an urgent terrifying mission that didn't acknowledge anything else. Parts of herself that she'd never been aware of before became her only reality. A spot on her spine, the taut stretched skin of her stomach, the dragging pressure between her legs. Mick and Chas sounded like a couple of flies, buzzing and droning on. It was incredible that they didn't know, when she was sitting so close to both of them. Surely some of this was spilling out into the air they were all breathing.

'We passed the salt lakes yet?'

'Yeah ... sure. Half an hour back.'

'Must have dozed off ...'

'Go right ahead, mate, 'cause I'll need a rest soon.'

'Sure ...'

The headlights of the old ute beamed wide yellow light into the clear night, picking up the occasional clump of scraggy trees and making their limp foliage and bowed limbs seem ancient and majestic in the stillness. Every now and again the light would catch the shining startled eyes of a group of roos. But for most of the time it was a drive through flat rocky scrubland, where there was virtually nothing except the wide unmade road ahead and the huge round roof of bright stars above. Theirs had been the only car on this stretch of road for the past hour and a half. Every pot-hole vibrated through her aching body, intensifying the discomfort.

Chas, at the wheel of the old ute, was looking tired. Mick too, with his head slumped against the window, one arm across the back of the seat, around her. Without anything much being said, somehow just sitting there together, they'd made up. Mick asked her if she wanted a drink of juice, she'd said 'yes' and had taken the bottle with a small smile. Mick read the smile as a conciliatory sign and smiled back. And then they were laughing together at a joke Chas made about something.

Between two contractions Michelle turned to look at his

profile in the dark, bent forward and staring out into the blackness. She remembered the pain he'd been in the night before with Buster and the harsh words she'd thrown at him that afternoon. He'd looked so alone stumbling out of Buster's house, as though he didn't know who he was or where he was going. Part of her had wanted to go after him, but the big part, the more important part of her, wasn't even there. That part was hunkering down, concentrating on her own survival. She had been preoccupied all that day before, with Buster and Bek, but puzzled too because she hadn't known *what with*, exactly. It had been a warm day and she'd had strange momentary chilly flushes down her arms and legs. They gave her the feeling of being in a lull, a strange state of existing nowhere in particular. Hard to pinpoint.

But all that was so long ago now. *This* was making everything that had ever happened to her seem irrelevant. She felt the onset of a fresh bout of pain creeping into her lower back. The build-ups were getting shorter now. Suddenly it was hitting her all over and peaking for so long she thought it was going to last forever, that she was going to be sick with it. Or die. She gasped and cried out, not caring who or what heard. What did it matter about being tough or weak or embarrassing? Nothing mattered but that this was over. She gave a long, deep moan and then heard the sound – her own sound – come echoing back into her head and a small part of her wondered. Where had she heard that sound before? As a little girl of about nine, she'd once watched a cow give birth. She'd seen the slimy, black-matted, neatly folded body of the calf being pushed out on to the grass, and while it was happening the cow had made the same sound that she'd just made. Michelle threw her head back suddenly and gave a sour laugh. Here she was in exactly the same position as a cow. How long did it last? When would it finish?

'Oh, stop! Stop the car! I have to get out ... I feel ...'

Mick jolted to attention and missed the fast look that

Chas threw him across Michelle's head. Chas applied the brakes and the ute rumbled off the road to a standstill.

'What's up, Shell?'

'What's the matter . . .?'

But Michelle was in no state to answer. She followed Mick out into the cold, star-filled, empty night and squatted by the truck holding her head in her hands.

'I dunno. It's terrible. Terrible . . .'

She stood up and stumbled drunkenly off towards the beam of the headlights, one hand on the ute to steady herself.

'I'm sorry. I'm gonna be sick . . .'

She bent over and vomited. Stunned, Mick went over and held her shuddering shoulders while Chas crawled around the back of the ute looking for the old towel he kept there. He wet it with water from the water-bag strapped to the front of the vehicle and brought it over.

'Here, love . . . use this.'

Michelle squatted again, taking the towel. She ran it around her mouth then up to her sweating forehead.

'I need a drink,' she whispered. 'A drink of water . . . real bad.'

Chas brought the water-bag over and Mick knelt down beside her, holding the white pannikin for her to sip from. She took a long guzzle and was sick again.

'Did you eat something, Squirt?' he asked. There was a strong snort from Chas in the background but neither of the other two noticed.

Michelle moaned and shook her head.

'No. I think it's the . . . but it can't be 'cause it's not due for two weeks . . .'

But she couldn't finish. The heavy pain was back, tearing away at her like a wild animal. She got to her feet clutching Mick for support, pinching his fingers. He stood up, holding her steady, but was at a complete loss.

'Can I help ...? You want to walk about a bit?' Michelle didn't hear the concern in his voice as she pushed past him and stumbled off again, away from the road and into the darkness.

'This is terrible ... I'll just have to lie down somewhere and ...' she called out wildly, as though she'd been fatally struck.

Chas, who'd been looking at her thoughtfully up till now, suddenly decided to take control.

'Right. Get real both of ya,' he ordered sharply. 'It's the kid coming. Get back into the ute. It's about three hours back to Broken Hill I reckon, so we'd better get moving. We'll have to get her there ...'

He was already pulling two of the soft seat cushions out of the front cabin and throwing them in the back. Then, muttering to himself about it being a 'bloody fool idea coming on such a long trek in the first place', he hurried around to the back of the vehicle and slid up the false floor of the spare-tyre cavity and pulled out a large torch. He threw it at Mick.

'Here give me a bit of light, will ya?'

Mick switched on the torch and Chas undid the thick twine around a rolled-up piece of black rubber and spread it out on the bottom of the ute, and on top of that a weathered green tarp. Next he unzipped a thin sleeping-bag and threw that in the back along with the rest.

'Now get that blanket at the back of the front seat, will ya.'

Mick looked at him blankly. In the background they could both hear Michelle's dry retches and moans.

'What're you doing, Chas?'

'You heard her! Wants to lie down. You'll have to ride in the back with her. It'll be freezing but she should be right with these over her. If we don't make it. I mean if the kid starts actually *being born*, you'll have to bang on the roof and I'll stop.'

241

'Oh shit, Chas!' Mick went white. 'It can't be born out *here!*'

But Chas was checking the blades of his pocket knife.

'Well, this will have to do. You got any string?'

Mick went to the cabin glove-box and pulled out a small roll, handing it to Chas.

'What d'ya need it for . . .?'

Chas gave an exasperated sigh and went back to the toolbox and rummaged around again, grunting with satisfaction as he pulled out a large brown bottle of methylated spirits and a cake of dirty soap.

'Good. Now we should both wash our hands properly with this soap . . .'

'What the hell for?'

'Just do it. We might be called short. If we are, then our hands at least will be clean and we can go straight for the meths.'

Chas handed Mick the water-bag and indicated that he should pour some out onto their hands. Still bamboozled, Mick did as requested. Chas took his time to soap up properly. It reminded Mick of films he'd seen of doctors preparing for an operation. The thought sent a jab of panic into the pit of his guts. What if something happened to Michelle before they got her to hospital? He hadn't even thought about her coming on this trip like this. Why the hell hadn't either of them thought of this possibility? *Because we never talked about it, full stop.* Hands now clean, Chas calmly handed Mick the towel to dry off.

'Now just bring her over here will you and I'll help lift her into the back.'

Mick walked over to where Michelle was half lying on the grass and helped her up.

'Come on, Shell,' he said gently, trying to keep the panic out of his voice. 'We've got to get you to the hospital.'

But Michelle pushed him away angrily.

'Piss off! I can't get in that ute again. I can't! I'll have to stay here. It's too small in there. Too cramped up ... I'll stay here! You go on up to Tibooburra. You've got to find your father, so leave me here.'

Aghast, Mick looked over to Chas for help but the older man had already pushed past him. He lifted Michelle up by the shoulders and shook her a little.

'You can get in the back, love, and lie down there. Mick will be with you ... I'll get there as fast as I can.' His voice was gentle but very firm. It seemed to calm Michelle.

'You've gotta go to hospital. Ya know that, don't ya?'

She nodded, staring into his face as though she was trying to read something she didn't quite understand. She looked pale and very small in the watery moonlight, in spite of her heavy belly.

'Okay ... but ...'

'No buts ... we've got to get moving.'

One on each side, it was easy for Mick and Chas to lift Michelle into the back of the ute. Chas fitted the two seat cushions behind her head and shoulders and threw the blanket at Mick.

'Here! You settle her down under this.'

Mick gulped and nodded. He climbed into the back with Michelle, who was turning to lie on her side, and gingerly draped the blanket around her. She immediately pushed it away.

'No. No. I'm hot. Far too hot!'

How could she be hot? At nine o'clock the night was already very chilly. Mick shivered inside his old woollen jacket. Shame he hadn't brought something warmer. Underneath the jacket he only had a flimsy T-shirt. If he'd known, he could have brought something. He closed his eyes for a few moments and tried to shake off the grogginess, the sense that this was all unreal and that he'd wake up soon. *If I'd known we'd be travelling in the back like this then we wouldn't have come in the first place. Idiot!* Out in these parts, at this time of the year, the days often got stinking hot but the nights were freezing. He looked down to where Michelle was curled up on the floor of the ute. She was wearing only a shirt and a pair of shorts. As far as he could remember, Chas hadn't brought anything much more substantial either. *What if . . . what if it gets born here and . . . shit!* It didn't bear thinking about. It just simply couldn't happen. Chas was a good driver. They'd be at the hospital within a couple of hours. He sat down next to her, the blanket on his knees and rested one hand lightly on her hip. 'Tell me anything I can do, Shell . . . okay? I've got a cup here and the water-bag, and the wet towel. And tell me . . . if you get cold.'

She mumbled 'okay'. But he could tell that she hardly heard him. The engine started and the ute pulled back on to the road. Within a short time Chas had picked up speed and once more they were hurtling off into the darkness.

'You all right in the back?' he yelled, almost cheerily.

'Yep. Okay!' Mick yelled back and had a second of fury at the paucity of words in some situations. How bad did things have to be before you could say things weren't *all right*? Michelle's low moans were eating into his brain. If only he could do something for her.

She was quieter now, but still moaning, instinctively conserving her strength for what might lie ahead. Mick edged his large frame as far down next to hers as he could, his legs poking up over the top of the ute's back.

'How're you doing, Squirt?'

'Okay . . .'

'Cold?'

She shook her head then gasped and let out a loud sob, half sitting up before dropping down again with the effort of it.

'This is *terrible*, Mick . . . it's much worse than they tell you.'

He picked up the wet towel and began caressing her hot forehead again. His own hand had gone slightly stiff in the cold air.

'You want to try a bit of deep breathing again?'

She whimpered again and shook her head, letting go of his hand and twisting her body into another position that didn't seem to bring any more comfort.

'I can't . . . do anything . . .'

'It's all right, Squirt . . . all right . . . we're gonna get you there soon and they'll give you something for the pain.'

He spoke gently into her ear. In between the worst bouts his words of comfort and encouragement soothed out the frayed knots of panic that seemed to be only just holding her together. But when it got really bad she might as well have been on her own. There was only her body and the deep flow of mad agony. Each time she surfaced from one of these she was overcome with outrage. How *come* no one had ever told her it would be like this?

'It might help . . .'

Mick put one hand under her raging belly and his face into the the nape of her neck, then blew out strongly.

'Come on, Squirt! See if you can do it with me.'

The first few times, Michelle lost concentration as the pain intensified but because there really wasn't much else she *could* do, she kept trying, and, after a while she got the hang of it. They went on together for some time, breathing in and out, trying to jump over the pain together. But it was hard to keep up that level of concentration and after about half an hour Michelle began to wear out.

The ride was like a crazy nightmare. She couldn't remember the beginning, it seemed to have been going on for *so* long and she was so deeply enmeshed that she'd lost sight of it ever ending either.

'How long have we been going, Mick . . . since we stopped . . .?'

Mick looked at his watch and hesitated before answering. He wanted so much to tell her it would soon be over.

'About an hour, Squirt.'

'So when will we get there?'

'In about an hour.'

'An hour!' She was genuinely incredulous. 'It feels like at least six hours. I don't think I can ...' But she didn't finish the sentence. There was no point. It made more sense to conserve her strength.

'My feet are freezing.'

It flashed through Mick's mind then that this might mean something was changing but he didn't waste any time. He began rubbing her feet with his hands but it seemed to make no difference. In fact everything seemed to be suddenly getting worse for her. She sat up, groaning, then lay on her side. It got no better so she squatted on her haunches for a minute and when that brought no relief she pulled her feet away and lay down on her side again. Her hands sought his, she clasped them and suddenly started to shiver. She began to yell.

'Stop this! I can't take it. I hate everyone. Don't you tell my mother about this!'

'Of course I won't. You want to try a bit of the deep breathing again?' He threw the blanket on her but she chucked it off scornfully.

'I am breathing, you fucking moron! Leave me alone! Get away from me! I'm going to die!'

Then a loud scream. Loud enough for Chas in the front to hear. Sick with feeling so helpless Mick banged on the roof of the ute, but Chas had already begun to pull over. The vehicle came to an abrupt halt next to a small group of wilga pines. With the engine off the sudden silence was awesome. Above them the stars simply stared down, bright and silent and uncaring. There was nothing except stillness and Michelle's wild sobs and groans.

'Something's happened! Look!'

Mick was cradling the top half of her in one arm. She guided his other hand down between her legs and he felt the dampness under his hand. Then there was a gush of wetness, spilling over him. He could feel it oozing out onto the tarp underneath her. Was it blood? Panic ripped through him like fire. *Shit! I don't know the first thing about any of this . . .*

The front door banged and Chas was there with the torch and a gas lantern.

Mick half rose, jerking awkwardly forward and grabbed his arm.

'Look, Chas, I think she's bleeding! I reckon you ought to get back in and drive like a maniac! She reckons she's gonna die. I think she's definitely having the kid . . . but . . .'

All in a hoarse urgent whisper.

Chas silenced him with a sharp jab in the chest with the gas lantern and a box of matches.

'Well, you don't have to be Einstein to work that out. Here, make yourself useful and light this, will ya?'

He spoke mildly, very easily, as though what was happening was the most normal thing in the world. Mick calmed down a bit and began to light the lamp. Michelle's terrified short breaths became quieter.

'Now, love, I reckon your water has broken. Eh?'

'I dunno . . .'

'Well, that means it's probably coming . . .'

Chas took one look with his torch and confirmed that was the case. He picked up Michelle's hand and held it firmly in both of his.

'Listen, love . . . it looks like we're not going to make it to hospital.'

Michelle clung to him suddenly.

'There's this . . . I feel like I've got to . . . push!'

She yelled the last bit in a garbled, frantic way and Chas bent over her smiling.

'Well . . . you do what you feel like, love.'

Then very quietly he said to Mick.

'Now get the meths out of the front seat, will you? We've both got to help her deliver this kid.'

Mick opened his mouth but closed it again. He was in too much shock to speak. He went around to the cabin and brought the bottle back. Both men poured some on to their hands and felt it dry quickly in the cold night air.

'Don't you think we should keep driving, Chas? I mean . . .'

Mick shrugged helplessly, overcome with panic but trying to appear reasonable, even casual.

'This is in the middle of nowhere . . . it's bloody freezing and . . . there's no hot water . . . or anything.'

Chas handed him back the bottle.

'You want to stay in the back by yourself and deliver it while I'm driving?'

'No, but . . .'

Chas turned back to Michelle who was now lying on her back. The noises were ones of exertion now, intermingled with pain. Great puffs and grunts that filled the quiet black night with noise, and Mick, with hopeless terror. They were, the three of them, caught in a trap, a vortex spinning down into the middle of the earth. This felt like the very last day ever – or the first. And there were only the three of them left, in the whole world. A world that was spinning around faster now than ever before and there wasn't any way of jumping off. Chas put the old blanket over Michelle's stomach and upper thighs.

'Now listen, Squirt, your shorts will have to come off sooner or later. Want a hand?'

She managed to undo the buttons on the side and Chas slowly slipped them off her. He then set the gas lantern on a steel box next to Michelle's legs, and, with a hand on each spread knee, he bent down mumbling to himself.

'Now let's take a geezer here . . .'

Mick stood awkwardly to one side, aware that he should be doing something but not knowing quite what. He'd never felt so ineffectual in his whole damned life. It was stupid in the circumstances but he felt embarrassed. It was all right, he supposed, for Chas to be looking up Michelle's crotch like this, *he* seemed to know what he was doing. But Mick wasn't at all sure where his place was . . .

Chas suddenly called him over excitedly.

'Hey, Mick! Come here. It's coming . . .' Then to Michelle, quite cheerfully, as though he was cheering at a football match.

'Come on, girl. Keep it going!'

Mick hesitated for a moment. He turned to Michelle with a shy questioning look but was met only with a sweaty, gritted smile of exhaustion. She reached out for his hand in the darkness.

'Mick,' she puffed. 'I think it's coming . . .'

The puffing and panting grew stronger, more rhythmical. Mick walked around and watched the head of Michelle's baby slowly emerge from between her legs. All feelings of shyness left him, dropping away like a useless piece of clothing on a hot day. Just the top at first, a round dark patch that slowly got bigger in little bursts and squeezes around the thinly stretched skin holding it in. Then after much straining and pushing the head emerged, whole, complete with eyes, tiny nose, mouth, a head covered in black hair.

'Here she comes, love! Few more now,' Chas shouted loudly.

After the head, a shoulder, coming and going. Each time it came, a little more appeared. Chas suddenly stepped aside and began taking off his shirt.

'Go on! You move in there now,' he growled at Mick. 'When both shoulders come out you've gotta be ready to catch the rest. It'll be slippery . . .'

Mesmerised, Mick stepped into position and was suddenly calm. Everything that he'd ever done, or hoped for, settled into focus, right inside him. Like looking down a powerful lens at some exotic, brilliantly-coloured flower-petal, and seeing every detail finally picked out from what had been only a blurry mass of colour before. It was as though all his life had been leading up to this one moment, waiting at the back of a ute in the middle of a cold black night for a kid to be born. There was no way he'd foul it up. He stood there waiting, big bony hands held out to catch hold. *The same hands that have busted open cash registers, pinched money and video machines, punched people in the face, wrung rabbits' necks and sliced open pigs' throats.* They were clean now, smelling of meths. Waiting.

He called out his encouragement too, in the same way that Chas had and that he'd first thought ridiculous.

'Michelle, ya doin' really good.'

His own deep excitement must have infected her in the end because when the baby finally emerged – first one shoulder, then the other, and the rest with a thick slooshing sound, like a rubber boot drawing free from heavy mud – Michelle was half laughing between her panting sobs. The whole tiny body was there. A girl, plump and perfect, wet and steaming in the cold, with yellowy mucus stuff over most of her and speckled with blood. Right into Mick's hands. The only odd thing to him was the thick blue tube in her navel leading back into Michelle. He'd forgotten about that.

Mick stared down in astonishment. How come he'd forgotten that it was all about this? In his concern for Michelle he'd forgotten that ... *this* was what it had all been about. This small human being, squirming, new and alive in his hands.

'Is she breathing all right?' Chas didn't look at all surprised at the little body as he anxiously leant over Mick's shoulder. Right on cue the tiny creature's ancient little face suddenly screwed up. As though in protest, the mouth opened and a loud howl filled the silence around them. She stopped for a moment then and opened her eyes before giving another loud protesting cry. Chas grinned with delight as he fished in his pocket, drew out his knife and poured methylated spirits over it.

'By hell! Nothing wrong with that. Listen to it, will ya!' he yelled to Michelle over her raised knees and swiftly tied the cord in two separate places then cut it in the middle.

He then turned to Mick.

'Now wrap her up in that shirt there, will you.'

Mick picked up the shirt that Chas had earlier taken off and gingerly began wrapping the baby.

'Quick. Can't let her get cold.'

'This isn't going to be warm enough, Chas.'

'Get the blanket then.'

Of course. Mick smiled ruefully. He was so ... surprised with everything that he was thinking too slowly. Cradling the baby in the crook of one arm he plucked the blanket away from the other side of Michelle and wrapped it around the little body.

'Give her to Michelle and I'll see about this.' Chas stepped back between Michelle's legs and shifted the lamp to see better.

'Now, love, there's just the afterbirth to go.' He began pulling gently on the cut blue cord, as though he were slowly reeling in a fish.

'Give a couple of pushes now ... And after this, all my know-how comes to an end,' he chuckled. 'So don't start getting complicated.'

Mick stopped suddenly, noticing for the first time that there was blood everywhere. All over Michelle's legs and the tarp underneath.

'Okay now. A little push here now, love. Good. Another one.'

Holding the baby as carefully as he was able, Mick stepped up into the back of the ute and mutely passed it to Michelle who was up on her elbows. She lay back against the two cushions as Mick settled himself down next to her.

'Have a look at it, Shell.'

'It's a girl, is it?' Michelle's voice was flat and faint and

251

very far away as she took the bundle from him. Mick nodded.

'Did you want a girl?' he inquired shyly.

Michelle didn't answer. She stared down at the tiny face for maybe a minute, then very calmly reached over and picked up the wet towel that Chas had given her before to wipe her forehead and gently wiped the blood and gunk from the little head and face. Around the eyes and mouth and neck. She then handed the baby back to Mick.

'Could you hold it . . . I'm freezing.'

Mick took the baby tightly, in the crook of his arm, and with the other he felt around for the sleeping-bag behind Michelle. Shivering she drew it around her shoulders as Chas held up what looked like a large thick slightly odd-shaped sheep's liver.

'I'd better keep this . . . for the doctors to check.'

Michelle screwed up her face in disgust.

'Gawd it's big! . . . I don't think you need bother, Chas. I'm all right.'

But Chas had already disappeared around to the front of the car. 'There's a plastic bag here . . . I can put it in there.' Michelle and Mick looked at each other and smiled.

'Hey, Chas! Thanks for . . . everything,' Michelle called, her voice wavering a little, tentatively, as though she was about to cry. It might have been simply the physical shock of what she'd just been through. Either way Chas pretended not to notice. He called back breezily from the cabin.

'No worries, Squirt. You did well . . . We were all in luck I reckon. I wouldn't have been much good if anything'd gone wrong . . .'

'How do you feel? You tired?' A wave of tenderness for her washed over Mick. How must she be feeling? *He* felt worn thin by what had happened. Translucent. Perhaps they all were. In this chilly quietness they might all turn into birds or spiders, angels perhaps, before the night was

252

through. A part of him was hovering outside his own body, watching. It seemed quite possible that they would all soon levitate, waft up into the enormous star-studded night and be gone forever. He could see himself half lying there, tied up with invisible thread, alongside the other two – Michelle, and the baby he was holding – enclosed in the yellow light from the lamp, fixtures forever on the back of Chas's ute. She smiled then, wanly, a sad little-girl smile, as though she'd guessed what he'd been thinking.

'Yeah, I'm tired . . . and glad that it's . . . it's over.'

'I'll bet you are.'

'I feel . . . it's done now. And it's . . . she's alive and everything . . . that's the main thing.'

They shared a smile and Mick leant forward, running one bloodied hand gently over her forehead, leaving a wet red mark above her eye, like a brush stroke. He grinned as he wet his other finger with spit to wipe it off.

'I'm putting marks on you, Squirt.'

She smiled back gamely, close to tears.

'Nah. It's *my* blood, Mick. It's me putting marks on you.'

He shrugged and ran the same hand through her grimy hair.

'Mick. I need some water.'

After about an hour, and half a dozen mugs of water, Michelle wanted to clean herself down with the towel. Although a little wobbly she was quite able to stand. Shivering, she began wiping her naked thighs and but-tocks with the towel, making it red with blood within seconds.

'I reckon if this isn't an emergency, Shell, I don't know what is,' Mick joked as he brought over more water from the emergency plastic tank under the front seat to rinse the towel out. She was still bleeding of course but had nothing to stem it with, so Mick gingerly put the wrapped baby down on the back of the ute and took off his jacket and T-shirt. He passed the T-shirt wordlessly on to Michelle and she folded it the best way she could, fitting it between her legs, then put on her shorts again. By this stage her teeth were chattering loudly and she was shivering all over. Mick picked up his jacket and tried to put it around her shoulders.

'Hey, you have this too.'

'No . . . no. That's yours.'

'So's the T-shirt.' Mick grinned.

But there was no way she'd take the jacket.

Chas looked over from where he was cleaning out the back of the ute. He'd chucked the bloodied tarp out on the side of the road and was wiping down the rubber with an old rag.

'Just get her into the cabin, Mick . . . the baby too.'

'Righto.'

One arm around her shoulders, Mick helped Michelle slowly up into the warm cabin and was about to pass her the baby, still wrapped snugly in the old blanket, and breathing peacefully in the crook of his arm. But Michelle looked away.

'Mick. I don't want to hold it . . .'

He frowned, hesitating for only a moment.

'Okay,' he said softly, then grinned a little. 'I've got an idea.'

He quickly unwrapped the blanket from around the baby and tucked the infant – still swaddled in Chas's shirt – near his chest then zipped up his jacket around the little bundle. The wide elastic band along the bottom of the jacket made it a snug arrangement. She fitted there, against his bare chest with no chance of getting cold or falling out. Even so, Mick lightly supported her with one hand as he threw the extra blanket around Michelle's shoulders. Michelle snuggled into the warmth gratefully.

'There you go, Squirt. How's that?'

'That's great . . . just right. Is it . . . is she warm enough?'

Mick nodded.

Chas got in the other side of the cabin, holding a half bottle of whisky out to them and blowing on his hands.

'Here have a shot. By hell, it's a fraction chilly out there eh?'

Mick took the bottle and offered it to Michelle who had a quick nip before passing it back.

'Thanks.'

Mick took a sip and then turned to Chas with a wry look before taking another proper swig. The rough burning sensation in his throat was wonderful.

'Hey, mate. This is all right, eh?'

Chas was searching his pockets for the keys. He looked up with a grin.

'Yep. Just the trick on a cold night . . . feel like a song?'

He found the keys, turned on the ignition, then rummaged around in the glove box for a tape. The dusky tones of Patsy Cline suddenly burst into the cabin with a press of the button.

'I-fall-to-pieces . . .' The words were like dark heavy syrup, rolling out plaintively into the air. 'Each-time-someone-mentions-your-name . . .'

Mick and Michelle looked at each other and laughed.

'Give us a break, will you!'

But Chas was staring straight ahead, through the windscreen into the black night in front, singing along with the tape in a surprisingly rich, country-style bass, as though he meant every word.

'I-fall-to-pieces . . .'

It was as though he was alone, unselfconscious and proud.

Eventually that song ended and another began.

'Walk-ing after midnight . . . search-ing for you . . .'

Mick looked at his watch and let out a gasp.

'Shit, it's after twelve.'

'Yeah?' The others were equally incredulous.

'How long was it? All in all?'

'About four or five hours.'

'Jeez!'

'That bird can sing, eh?' Chas looked at the other two for confirmation and then suddenly his face cracked open into a smile.

'Well, what do you say? We get back to Broken Hill?'

Michelle lolled against Mick, her eyes half-closed. She looked as though she was nearly asleep.

'Yeah . . .'

Chas fired the engine and put one rough hand briefly on her knee.

'Get you to hospital at long last, eh, Squirt?' I reckon we did all right tonight,' Chas added and chuckled quietly.

'I reckon,' Michelle whispered. 'Imagine if I'd been on my own.'

Chas started suddenly, shocked, as though remembering something terribly important. He opened his mouth a couple of times, looking around the cabin in horrified silence, then through the back window.

'Where the friggin' hell is *it*?'

'What?' Mick asked stupidly.

'The bloody baby! *Don't* say we left it out . . .'

Mick grinned, moved forward and unzipped his jacket a little. He repositioned the baby so that its tiny round face was turned to Chas. With the black curly hair it looked as perfect as a little doll. Chas sighed and laughed in relief. Leaning forward he touched the top of its head with one finger, in wonder.

'By God! Look at her, will ya!' he murmured, as though to himself. 'Snug as a bug, eh? She breathing and everything?' Mick pulled the baby up a little and put his head down next to her face. The short, even breaths were like the delicate wings of some invisible spirit-bird touching down on the skin of his cheek.

'Yep. She's breathing.'

Chas started to laugh, a deep incredulous laugh full of

exhaustion, of pure pleasure. He thumped the steering wheel a few times.

'I reckon we did *all right*!'

'Yeah.' Michelle's eyes were closed now but she was smiling.

'Better than all right. Bloody *brilliant*. Especially me!'

Mick and Chas fired grins at each other across the top of her head then Mick let his face drop lightly on to the paper-thin softness of the baby's cheek for a moment before joining in Chas's laughter.

'You too,' he whispered into the baby's ear. 'We were all damn brilliant.'

Both Mick and Michelle were asleep when Chas eventually pulled the old ute up outside the casualty department of Broken Hill's main hospital at 3 am. Mick woke first to see the multi-storeyed building's lights twinkling at him. The place looked like some kind of menacing monolith, all eyes, taking in everything. There didn't seem to be any hideout corners around here, no dark places set aside for secret feelings or crazy plans.

So this was where their new lives would begin, he found himself thinking, now *it* was all over.

After it's born we'll head over to Lightning Ridge and have a go at the opals ... or maybe, when it's over, we should head directly north to Mt Isa ... get a job there in the mines maybe ... or Darwin.

How could he have imagined then a child asleep on his chest? Or known what a baby's fist felt like, flexing and uncurling around his finger? Who could have warned him that this little body would lie breathing, next to his skin, her tiny round face so pale and confident, so *alive* in the streaky hard streetlight? How come he thought he knew *anything* before?

Michelle yawned as she woke and Mick looked over at her with a smile.

'We're here, Shell,' he said softly, reaching for her hand.

She nodded and yawned again, stretching as best she could in the cramped cabin, and looked over at Chas's tired face.

'Thanks, Chas . . . for driving and Mick . . . for everything.'

Chas gave a laugh as he turned off the ignition and rubbed his eyes. 'Only an hour or two late!'

Mick gave a low hoot of laugher. Bloody old Chas. What would they have done without him. Michelle joined in giggling and shaking her head.

'I can't really believe . . .'

Chas turned to her.

'Listen, Squirt, you want me to go in and tell 'em you're here?'

Mick interrupted before she could reply. He could see the heavy lines of exhaustion around the old man's eyes and mouth and so immediately reached for the door handle.

'I'll go, Chas . . . you stay here with Michelle and . . .'

Michelle cut in gruffly.

'What are you talking about? Can't we *all* go in together!'

Mick and Chas were momentarily flummoxed.

'But . . .'

'But *what*?'

'Are you well enough? I mean, can you walk?'

'Mick! It's about ten yards over to that door. Of course I can walk!'

Mick shrugged and Chas grinned to himself.

'Okay.'

Mick and Chas got out either side of the ute into the freezing early morning air. Still with the old blanket around her shoulders, Michelle followed, shuffling along creakily at first, but improving gradually as she went along.

21

The two night nurses on duty were going over the intrigues of the previous night's hospital ball when the odd, dishevelled threesome shambled through the glass doors. It had been an unusually quiet night, in fact nothing much had happened in two hours. The younger nurse had been planning on having a little catnap and so sighed impatiently as she stood to check out the newcomers. The bedraggled-looking girl with the blanket looked sick enough to require a doctor and that would take at least half an hour to get one down from the third floor. Damn it. She sniffed suspiciously as they came towards her and hoped they weren't drunk. Up close she could see the girl had blood on her clothes and the old man's torn vest smelt of oil. He also had blood on his jeans. It would probably turn out to be some kind of domestic. The young man looked like a roughneck. He was probably the culprit, or involved in some way, she wouldn't mind betting. And what in heaven was he carrying under his jacket? Some weapon or ... animal? The previous day an old drunk had brought in a stray pup he'd found and wouldn't leave until everyone promised to look after it. These three looked like they'd just arrived in from World War Three.

'Good evening. What can I do for you?'

The iciness in her voice unsettled Michelle as they reached the front counter. Suddenly tongue-tied, she turned around to Mick for help. He put one hand on the counter and awkwardly indicated Michelle with his other thumb, the words stumbling out clumsily.

'Er ... we've come to ... er ... book Michelle in here.'

'What do you mean, book her in?' the nurse snapped back quickly. 'No one can be booked in until they've been seen by a doctor.' Then, feeling slightly embarrassed at her own brusqueness, she continued in a softer tone. 'Now what's the problem?'

The other nurse came busily across with forms and handed them to her colleague silently, eyes lowered. Michelle sighed and gulped. The two of them looked so crisp in their starched uniforms, their faces so attractive and bright in all that make-up. 'I've already booked in ... a few weeks ago ... to have a baby.'

Both the nurses eyes immediately became alert.

'You're in labour?'

'Well, no ... I had, the, er ...'

'How far apart are your pains.'

'I've had it.'

'What!'

'I've had the baby.'

'You've *had* the baby!' they cried in unison, unwilling to be duped.

'Where?'

'Er ... out there.' Michelle pointed haphazardly to the doors through which they'd just come. 'In the back of a truck ... well, car really.'

A few seconds went by, as both nurses stared at Michelle as though she was trying to trick them. Finally the older one took charge.

'Name please.' The freshly painted long nails hovered nervously over the keyboard, ready to poke and subdue whatever she had to.

'Michelle Brown.'

She typed the name into the computer, then a few other particulars, date of birth, address ... Medicare number.

The computer whirled a bit, then stopped. Both of them stared, frowning into the screen as though it was somehow going to spew out a secret any moment. Finally the younger one turned to Michelle accusingly.

'You're not due for another two weeks!'

Michelle felt herself reel a little. It surprised her because she was feeling quite well. A dizzy spell, like this one, would float in every now and again, making her feel a little limp and unreal, but overall, she'd have to say she felt fine. Probably it was the standing up. She could feel the blood oozing out of her and wondered how long she'd be able to keep standing here before there was a puddle of it on the floor near her thonged feet. It was making her thighs sticky. God only knew what Mick's T-shirt was like now. She'd have to buy him a new one, first chance that came up. She grasped the counter in front with both hands and decided that she most definitely didn't want to faint. It looked as though she was going to have to blow her stack.

'Well, is that so?' she suddenly hissed loudly through her teeth. The nurses stepped back, alarmed. The insignificant-looking girl in front of them had come alive suddenly. Michelle reached back to where Mick was standing, and roughly pulled the zip of his jacket down, revealing the tiny body buried there, next to his skin and still wrapped in the old shirt. The nurses' alarm deepened and they gasped in surprise.

'So what the *bloody hell* is this, then?' Michelle spat through clenched teeth. They stared back at her, shocked.

'There's no need to use ... that kind of language here.'

'You want me to put it *back* so I can take it *out* again at the right time?'

Chas snorted with laughter. The older nurse sniffed suddenly and picked up the phone.

'If you'll just wait over there on the chairs, I'll have someone down immediately.'

They all shambled over to the bright orange vinyl chairs to wait. Chas immediately lay down opposite the other two, putting both hands under his head.

'I've got to have a bit of shut-eye,' he groaned to Mick. 'Come and get me when you're ready to go.'

Mick nodded and put his arm around Michelle.

'You okay?'

She smiled wearily.

'Sure. Any discos on tonight?'

Mick grinned.

A team of four nurses arrived within a couple of minutes. For some reason their attitude was completely different to the other ground-floor nurses.

'You mean you had it in the back of a car!' one of the midwives laughed incredulously, putting a hand inside Mick's jacket to test the baby's temperature. 'Good for you! Feels fine.'

'How long all in all?'

'Much blood?'

'Who cut the cord?'

Mick and Michelle answered the questions as best they could.

When they got out of the lift at the third floor, the senior nurse turned to Michelle with a smile and touched her arm, indicating the direction she wanted her to go.

'Now, dear, if you don't mind, we'd like to examine you down this way and these nurses here will take baby off *that* way ... with her dad of course if he likes! We'll have her back to you as soon as possible.'

Michelle gulped awkwardly. So, none of these nurses knew that the baby would be going out for adoption. She looked at Mick.

'I'll tell them ... about the adopting stuff, okay?' she said quietly. 'Don't worry, I'll tell them. When they look up my proper file they'll see anyway. You can go down to Chas or anything you like ...'

He nodded. *Am I expected to pull the baby out now, from where she's sleeping against my skin, and just hand her over, like a parcel of groceries?*

'You mind if I ... er ... go with her?' Mick tapped the baby still buried under his jacket and hoped Michelle couldn't see the flush starting on his neck, or the way his hand was trembling.

'No, I don't mind ...' Michelle looked wonderingly at him as if she didn't quite understand what he'd said. 'You go ... with them if you want to.'

Mick turned away, about to walk off, but Michelle grabbed his sleeve suddenly. The nurses were standing a few feet away from them, waiting, pretending not to but watching curiously. He turned, but couldn't look at her, felt, but didn't know why, as though she was going to say something terrible to him and he was going to burst into tears.

'... *with her dad of course, if he wants!*' The well-intentioned nurse's words played back in his head, mocking him. He gulped again and forced himself to look at Michelle who was waiting to speak to him.

'Mick,' she whispered hoarsely at last. 'Let me have a last look at her, will you, I ... don't want to see her again.'

Mick undid the zip and Michelle moved in closer. When Mick indicated wordlessly that he would take the baby out for her to hold, she shook her head. Very gently, she shifted the little head around so she could see the face properly, then ran her fingers lightly over the black hair and tightly closed eyes. Then she bent over and kissed her on the tip of her nose. She turned away abruptly to the nearest nurse, her voice dry and choked.

'When does she get hungry? I mean she only cried a couple of times and she's been asleep more or less since ...'

'When was she born?' the nurse inquired.

'About ...' Michelle looked at Mick. He looked at his watch.

'Nearly three hours ago.'

'She'll be feeling like something soon,' the nurse smiled. 'Now I don't want to hurry you but it would be good if we could get you all cleaned up and . . .'

Michelle turned away suddenly as though she'd been slapped.

'Yeah. I'm ready,' she said roughly, as though the emotion she'd displayed earlier had nothing to do with her. She walked off down the corridor, ahead of the nurses.

'See ya then, Shell,' Mick called after her. But she didn't turn around.

'Yeah,' she called. 'See ya.'

Mick followed the nurses into the babies' nursery, past about a dozen steel cots, to the far end where there were tables and baths set up and all kinds of ointments and bottles lined up against the sinks. The young nurse with the bob of black shiny hair began to fill a bath, and the other one, who was older but still pretty with red hair, white skin and some kind of slight accent, got nappies, clothing and little green dishes of swabs and cotton balls ready in neat piles. They seemed to forget he was there for a while as they went about the practical business, swapping information as they did.

'Is Dr Phelan on?'

'Yes, she's coming . . . not too happy apparently.'

The red-haired nurse laughed, then turned quickly to Mick, smiling kindly.

'Not to worry . . . none of them like being woken up like this. She's the paediatrician . . . actually very nice. She'll be here soon.'

He nodded stiffly, not understanding what they were talking about.

'Your little one has to be checked over by a specialist as soon as possible.' The nurse had guessed his confusion.

'Right.'

Finally the young one held out her finely shaped olive-skinned hands.

'Now can we have your precious little bundle?' Her dark eyes were shining in the muted overhead lights, just like her hair.

Mick unzipped his jacket again and handed the baby over. Both nurses immediately began to coo and chirp at the baby as they gently took her over to the bench and began unwrapping the old shirt.

'Wonderful! Well done. You've kept her lovely and warm.'

'Isn't she lovely. Look, sleeping all the way through this.'

'She's a good weight.'

'I reckon she'd be eight pounds ... at least.'

'Pounds! Jen, where have you been for the last ten years?'

They both laughed.

'The mum wasn't big though, was she?'

'No, but Dad's tall.' They both turned thoughtfully to size Mick up and down as though he wasn't there. Only giving him a smile when they'd decided that he was indeed tall.

'You'd be around six foot wouldn't you?'

'Yeah. Around that.' *But I'm not the dad ... I'm just ...*

He watched them cheerfully throw the bloodied shirt away, recut the cord and clamp it again with a special bit of plastic, then re-sterilise the navel area with a cotton bud. He was fascinated with everything they were doing and loved the gentle confident way they handled the baby. Finally the pretty dark-haired one held out the naked, pink, curled-up baby to him.

'Would you like to bath her?'

Mick shrugged, feeling stupid as he tentatively took hold. She reminded him of a beautiful little grub. One of the ones the birds fought over in the very early morning. A tender parcel of ripe juicy flesh. Part of him wanted to come clean there and then, tell them that he had nothing to do with this baby. That even Michelle, who they'd met earlier, had nothing much to do with her either. He should tell them now that within a few days she would belong to someone else, that some childless couple neither of them knew had been notified that they were next in line for this kid. And that he and Michelle were going to be shooting off up north the first chance they got.

'I'm not sure I know how to ... I've ...'

Both the nurses were looking up at him and laughing.

'Don't worry. You'll manage. Better take off your jacket.'

Mick handed the baby back and took the jacket off. Both sets of eyes swivelled away, a little uncomfortably, pretending not to notice his bare chest and the tatts on each upper arm.

'Now, just hold her in the crook of your arm like so.'

He took the baby and held her the way they showed him, then very slowly lowered her into the warm bath water. Her eyes opened immediately, as though appraising the situation, in pleasant surprise. She then began to move her limbs a little. One clenched fist opened out slowly in the warm water, as perfect as a a pond-lily responding to the morning sun.

'Will you look at her!' the red-haired nurse whispered. Mick looked up and nodded. At that moment they were together, all three of them, staring through a window at something magical inside.

'Now here's the soap ... Your name's Mick, is it?'

'Yes.'

'Well, Mick, you just rub a little soap on your other hand ... that's right, and now just gently wash her.'

Mick did as he was told, unable to quite believe the softness of the limbs, or the little face either, looking up and around at them all knowingly. She made him think of the very old, frail Chinese woman who used to work in the kitchen with his mother on one of the farming properties. He'd been one of the kids who'd wanted her to talk to her.

Even for her to smile would have been something. He remembered watching her slowly sauntering around the side of the house and sheds in those wide black pants and the gentle slapping sound her slip-on shoes made as she walked. He'd once tried to give her some stones that he and another older boy had found in the river. They were smooth and all different colours and he was sure she'd like them. But she'd only smiled and refused to take his gift, patting his shoulder and walking away. Not unfriendly, just preoccupied with something bigger and more important. Mick had longed to know *with what* exactly. Stories about her grew wilder each year. The owner of the property vowed she'd had three husbands but someone else said four. Her seven children were either back in China, dead, or millionaires in America. In time, most of the kids either resented her or lost interest. Mick couldn't remember what category he fell into, only that she'd fascinated him and that even after so many years he still sometimes dreamt of her.

'You'd swear she could see,' he burst out, suddenly hot with embarrassment at the flood of memory that was ebbing and flowing just underneath his skin. It was as though *in there*, everything had come loose, that he suddenly contained a mini-ocean, raging back and forth against the rocks of his own bones. Bending his head, he held the child, hoping they couldn't see his face. He needn't have worried. The nurses were still looking at the baby and laughing. It was something they did every day. And they were quite used to doting awe-struck parents.

'Look at that little crease of fat on her legs.' They were leaning over the bath trailing fingers in the water, making patterns. Mick laughed a little and ran his big soapy hand along the crease on the baby's thigh.

'She's been well-nourished,' one of them said approvingly.

'You should see some of the skinned rabbits we get in here sometimes.'

'Yeah?'

'Oh, yes. Your wife . . . or, er, girlfriend . . . ate well, did she?'

'Yeah. She's pretty keen on her food.'

'I'll bet she never smoked,' said dark silky-hair, her soft high-pitched little-girl's voice full of certainty.

'No . . . she's never smoked.'

The nurses murmured approvingly and went back to looking at the baby in the crook of Mick's arm. The nearest one smiled at him and said. 'See you *are* good at it.'

He had the light, insane feeling that he'd just passed a very important exam. It made him want to laugh. He put the soap down and picked up one tiny foot, examining the five miniature toes and perfect toenails, and dunked them under the water again, up and down, making the water ripple about. Then the other one. A mad impulse told him to scoop the little body out of the water, wrap her in a clean dry towel and then pop her back inside his jacket again. But of course he couldn't do that. After a few minutes the nurses asked him if he was ready to take her out. When he said yes, one came over with a thick white towel and took her from him, over to the bench.

'Have you dressed a baby before, Mick?'

'No.'

'Well, come over and learn.'

There was laughter in her voice but it teased rather than mocked. It seemed to be saying that it was absurd *not* knowing how to do this kind of stuff. Mick awkwardly followed her over to the bench and watched as she gently dried the little body. The red-haired nurse handed him a tiny white singlet.

'Here, see if you can get this on.'

Mick shrugged ruefully, shaking his head.

'I don't know . . . I . . .'

'Of course you can.'

'You're going to have to do this a lot soon . . .'

He took the singlet and bent over the baby awkwardly.

'So what goes where . . .?'

'Will you listen to him?' The red-haired one was teasing him again.

'The head goes through that hole. Okay?'

'Okay.'

The baby looked straight at him suddenly, right *through* him and he stared back, right into her eyes. Where had he seen this little face before?

You're suffering head overload, matey. Beth's death, no sleep, the trip, the birth, and now this! Get a grip on yourself, idiot!

The last twenty-four hours rolled forward through his head like a jerky old train through a tunnel. He stared down at the little face and watched the baby's mouth loosen into a trembling smile. Mick grinned back, then up at the two watching nurses. They laughed at him good-naturedly, patted his arm and told him he was doing well.

What did he care that they called it reflexes or hunger or wind? As far as he was concerned this baby had just looked straight up at him and smiled and he didn't give a shit that she was only five hours old.

22

What would be the point of looking at her or holding her? It would only make everything harder. Mick was at me, all the time, trying to change my mind. Sometimes he'd get really dark.

'She's your kid, Michelle. Yours! Even if you *are* going to give her away then at least know what she looks like!'

Little did he know that that little face was singed on to the skin of my eyes. Every time I thought of her, my head stung inside, like a wild bee had got in there, *inside my head, trying to bite its way out.* There was no point letting him know any of that though. Why would I want to make it harder for myself?

I was pretty out of it on painkillers for the first two days. The doctor had to give me a few stitches, so my crotch hurt. And in spite of the tablets I was taking to get rid of the milk, my breasts felt like hot, overripe watermelons connected to my chest with safety pins. Whichever way I turned they were there. Hard and painful.

There wasn't much they could give me for the pain that was going on inside my head though. One of the nurses tried to get me talking one night. I told her a little bit about the way I was feeling and then, I dunno, I just clammed right up. I ended up telling her I wanted to be left alone.

Every time Mick came in he asked me if I'd seen her. I'd shake my head and he'd rave on a bit, quietly, encouraging me to re-think. Me not saying much probably made him feel even more frustrated but I couldn't help that. He'd get up and go walking around the ward like a caged lion at the zoo. He was staying in town with Buster and Bek and I knew they'd be feeding him up with how freaky I was, deciding to adopt the baby out. They were so wrapped up in their own kid, and adopting wasn't something Aboriginal people would ever do willingly. So what, I'd think to myself. *Who does it willingly anyway?* I knew what seeing her would lead to and I wasn't prepared to do it. I'd made up my mind what I thought would be best for her, and I was determined to stick to it.

When I was pregnant I'd got very good at just cutting out of anything I didn't want to think about. After the birth, somehow that ability wasn't with me any more. All the thoughts I'd swept away or pushed over into the too-hard can came flooding in on a tidal wave – my parents, brothers, friends, Kevin, and of course, the baby. Even my dreams were full of them.

I think it was the same for Mick. He looked different somehow. Every time he'd come in to see me I'd be surprised by how his face was. He looked older than I remembered him. Older and tougher. A real hunk too, I have to admit that. Compared to all the husbands of the other women in the ward, Mick was a *treat*. I spent a lot of my time there wondering how such nice women could end up with such horrible-looking men. It wasn't just their looks, more their attitude. Take Helen in the bed next to me. She was a lot older than me, about thirty-five, and had just had a hysterectomy. I couldn't see what the fuss was, I mean, she already had five kids – one my age – but I guess that wasn't the point. She was upset about it. But at the same time she was full of humour and kindness. I know that sounds corny but its true. My breasts were really sore one day. So sore I was just about crying with it and she got out of bed, came waddling over with a special cream she reckoned would help. We talked a bit after that, about nothing important, but it was nice to have someone nearby who was friendly. Anyway she had one of those husbands. I tried not to notice, but in that enclosed situation you couldn't help it. He'd come in every evening after tea with a couple of the kids and she'd try to talk to him a bit. Make some comment about the food or the weather or how she'd been getting along, and he'd just grunt back. Most of the time he'd say nothing, just flip through her magazines or stretch his neck out like a tortoise trying to watch the TV in the corner, near some other patient.

Mick would come in his jeans and T-shirt, a bit dusty from the bike, but rangy and easy looking and I'd feel something rising inside me. Pride, I suppose. Sounds a bit pathetic but I could see a few of the other women looking at him too. Okay, he wasn't Mel Gibson – not that kind of handsome – but he was worth looking at. There was no doubt that he was worth looking at. The first couple of times he came in I held my breath. A mad part of me couldn't quite believe he'd be stopping at my bed. Maybe he'd come in to see someone else. He looked like he didn't belong to anyone. I think that's what I liked most. *As though he didn't belong to anyone or anywhere.* Yet he'd be the one who'd sit there talking, and I know he really cared how I felt.

I think it was on about the third day that Mick came right out with it. He said 'You'll change your mind if you look at her.' I didn't say anything to that for quite a while because I was seething. I mean that was the whole point wasn't it? That was what I knew already! *I didn't want to change my mind.* He had no right to put this on me! I felt jealous too. I knew that he'd been hanging around with her behind my back, down in that nursery at the end of the corridor. Most nights there in the hospital I couldn't sleep, I'd be roaming around out in the corridor and I'd pass the nursery and I'd be madly tempted to go and and see if she was all right. I hated the idea of her being left to cry. I knew in my head that the nurses were good, that they wouldn't mistreat her, that they would feed her and comfort her ... but this was a feeling and I couldn't explain it away logically. I couldn't get it out of my head that she might be lonely.

One of the older nurses, who I got on pretty well with, told me that the new parents wanted to meet me but I said no to that. I figured that I wouldn't be able to suss out what kind of people they were in a short meeting, that I could very possibly get the wrong idea about them and then there would be only more to worry about. So I decided that I'd just trust the authorities to pick the right people. The social worker in charge of it was really nice. She told me their name and a little bit about them; that they were wealthy people who owned properties out the west of the state and that they were both very nice and had been wanting a child for over ten years. It tickled me a bit when she went on to tell me that as soon as they heard that they had a girl they rang up and booked her into a flash, girls-only, boarding school in Sydney for when she turned twelve. In fact I couldn't keep the grin off my face after the nurse told me that. It sounded *all right* to me! Like they were pretty organised people and I had no problem with that at all.

I can hardly bear to think about how nasty I got with Mick.

'She's not yours, so you can forget the whole friggin' idea of having anything to do with her,' I blurted out the next time he came in. I had been shaking all day. Burning with a need to hurt him, make him face up to some of the stuff that was tearing me apart. Looking back on it now I can see I was actually talking to myself too, trying to convince myself.

'I mean, face it, Mick! I'm seventeen years old. Got no family to speak of. No education ... no one likes me much and I'm not even good-looking ... and you ... what about

273

you? You're just a bloody ex-crim I met a few months ago! I don't even *know* you . . .'

I was staring at the wall opposite my bed and didn't look over to see how he was taking any of this. It had to come out some time so it might as well be now. Besides, I was coasting along on top of a wave now, half enjoying the sound of my own voice.

'You've got a job now, but after that what will happen?' I continued. 'I mean you might decide to piss off somewhere, or if things get hard . . . well, who can say? You might decide to get back into what you were doing before and land back in jail . . . I mean that would just be *great*, wouldn't it?'

I did turn around to look at him after that and I immediately felt sorry. His face had clouded over and he seemed to have shrunk right into the chair he was sitting in. He didn't even move, much less say anything for ages. Inside I started to really panic. Any moment now he'd get up and just walk out. For sure. This will have done it. It will be the end of him and me forever. My imagination started firing madly. Where would I go after I got out of hospital? What would I do? Chas probably wouldn't want to know me if Mick and I split. When it came down to it, I wasn't exactly endowed with a million friends. But he continued to sit there, frowning, not saying anything. Other things were going on in the ward, little conversations between the women, a baby crying. A couple of nurses walked past laughing. We were locked here together in our miserable silence.

'I tell you something else too, Mick,' I hissed finally, trying, but not all that hard, to keep my voice down. 'The place where I come from is full of deserted women. And most of them live up one end of town. I'm *not* going to be one of those fat frumpy chicks who wear friggin' moccasins and stretch nylon pants around all day . . . dyed hair and a fag hanging out of my mouth . . . and a different useless bloke in their bed every month. No way!'

274

It stunned me a bit actually saying this kind of stuff. I mean where had it come from? I can honestly say that I'd never really thought all this through before. But there it was, spewing right out of my own mouth. I was furious and shouting by the end. But so what? This was the reason I was doing what I was doing. This is why I was going through so much pain. Someone had to hear about it.

'And the kids with their snotty noses and no proper food 'cause the latest boyfriend has decided he needs his grog ... never knowing where their dad is ... I'm not gonna do that to my kid. No way!'

I felt exhausted. Worn-out, cheap and sad. Besides I was sick of him. Him being silent had made me say things that I'd sooner have left buried.

Finally he spoke, very quietly.

'I'm not asking you to, Squirt.'

'What?' I snapped back stupidly. 'Asking me what?'

'To be one of those women ... you hate so much.'

'I don't hate them,' I said miserably. 'I just don't want to be like that.'

'Fair enough. I don't want you to either.'

I looked at him, with a bit of smile, hoping to catch his eye, hoping I suppose, that I'd convinced him and that from now on he'd be on my side. But when he did look at me I knew it wasn't going to be that easy.

'Can't you *see*, Mick?' I pleaded as I continued to look at the wall. It was much harder to say what I had to if I was looking at him. I mean anyone with half a brain would know just by looking at him that he wasn't lying. What you saw in that face is what you got.

The silence set in again, like before. Big heavy boxes of murky silence, all tied up with steel rope and sharp corners. I lay back on the bed, completely whacked. There didn't seem to be any words left, no way at all back into those big boxes. When he eventually spoke I jumped a bit, surprised to hear his voice. I suppose I'd fallen away in my own head into this cave of despair. I really thought we'd run out of words.

'I don't want to be like my old man, Squirt,' he said suddenly, very softly. 'Leaving things in a mess for someone else to clean up.'

What in hell did that have to do with anything! I mean it was no argument at all. I was sitting up in the hospital bed. There were about six others at least in the ward. One was an old woman with cancer somewhere in her and the other was Helen with her hysterectomy. Neither of them were very well but I couldn't help raising my voice again.

'That's just what I'm not doing, Mick! I'll be giving her to people who'll love her and give her a good home. Decent things ... and ...'

'What do you know about those people?' he fired back, his voice low and angry, making me sit back a bit. 'You don't know anything except they've got a lot of money. When I was a kid I spent time in homes with plenty of money ... and it was shit ... complete shit. Because I didn't belong there. They weren't my people ...'

'Well, money's a good start, I reckon!' I said defensively. 'And this would be different to what happened to you. She'd belong to these people ... be their daughter and ...'

He shrugged scornfully and looked away. I could see that line wasn't impressing him much.

'All the time I was with those people I wished I had my own mother back. And that's the truth. I liked it better in jail because at least there, no one was pretending ...'

I thought a bit about that then turned to him.

'Seriously, Mick. What have I got to give her?'

'Give her?' he repeated, turning slowly to look at me, as though puzzled. He was giving me this *look*. Of scorn, incomprehension, of pain really, straight into my face. I backed away. To tell the truth I thought he was going to grab me, maybe shake me. Those blue eyes were blazing away, angry, like gas flame at night. I remembered him again with his hands around Buster's throat, with that same intensity in his eyes.

'You've got *me*, Michelle. You and me. We could make a life for her. You're her real mother.'

It really wrung me out hearing him say that. Because everything in me told me that he was speaking the truth. He was offering me everything he had, but it was dreamers' talk.

'Yeah, I know that, Mick, but . . .'

'I reckon we could make a go of it.'

'But what if we mess it up?' I cried. 'What if you and me don't last and she's left without a . . .'

He stood up abruptly and my heart took a dive. His face had suddenly closed off, against me. I could see he'd had enough. About to walk away, he turned back suddenly and spoke coldly as though I was a stranger.

'Do you want that kid?' he asked loudly. I was looking straight at him but around the corners of my eyes I knew those other women had looked up from whatever they were doing and turned their heads towards us, watching.

'I mean if everything was neat and dandy and you had everything you think you need. Do you want her?'

I hesitated. He was asking me a direct question. I owed him a straight answer. I shrugged. How could you give a straight answer when nothing about the whole business was straight.

'Yeah . . . I do. But it's not, is it? Nothing *is* neat and dandy. How much *say* do you reckon people like us get? Look at *our* families.'

He came back and stood at the end of my bed. My heart immediately sprang straight back into its right postion. I repeated the question as quietly as I could.

'How much say do we get, Mick? I mean . . . really?'

'You've got a say over whether you keep this baby or not,' he said quietly.

'That's right! And I'm saying I've decided! If you can't

live with that then you'd better just bloody piss off!' He looked at me in stunned silence for a moment before continuing, very quiet and cold.

'Is that right? Just piss off, eh?'

I came in fast and cruel, like I was riding a train over a cliff; I couldn't stop.

'Yeah that's right! She's not yours so you can forget the whole bloody idea of having anything to do with her! So go on, piss off! You probably will sooner or later anyway.'

I was stunned, probably just as stunned by what I'd said as he was. I watched him battling the shock and the rising anger. He leant forward into the plastic bag he'd brought in, pulled out the money that I'd asked him to bring in and threw it on the bed. His mouth opened and closed a couple of times, but no words came. I can't say how I felt as I watched him turn abruptly and walk quickly out of the ward. He didn't look back, even once.

I stayed very still for the next hour. I think I was still on some kind of furious high. I could feel it rushing through my veins at a hundred miles an hour. I knew though, at the same time, that everything inside me was crashing to bits.

The next morning I felt a lot better physically, and that made me feel more able to cope with everything. I'd had an infection which hadn't been picked up by anyone for a couple of days and that was why my crotch had hurt so much. But after twenty-four hours on the antibiotics it was on the mend. The doctors said I'd be able to leave the next day and as far as I was concerned it wouldn't be a moment too soon. This was my sixth day and I'd just about had a gutful of lying around in that joint trying to unravel my brain. Nothing was making any sense. I had this hope, I suppose, that as soon as I left everything would come clear again.

In the afternoon, two nurses came in and told me that the foster mother had arrived. The adopting parents wouldn't get to see the baby until thirty days had passed and I'd given my full permission. Up till that time I was within my rights to change my mind at any time. For the first month the baby is looked after by another woman. The nurse told me she was just down the corridor, in the nursery at that very moment, spending time with my baby before she took it home in a few days. Did I want to go down and have a talk to her? No. I acted interested when the nurse was talking to me about her, even I reckon, tried to look pleased. But when she'd left I pulled those puke-green curtains around my bed and cried my eyes out for about two hours.

Chas came to see me late that afternoon, the first time he'd been in since the night I had the baby because he'd had to go straight out bush, working his new fencing job the next day. Anyway, he came in his cowboy clothes carrying this enormous bunch of flowers, a heavy-looking plastic carry-bag, and grinning like a fox.

'By hell you look a million bucks on last time I saw ya!'

I laughed and pulled the nearby chair over for him.

'Thanks, Chas ...' I said, a bit choked up as I took the flowers from him. They weren't just flowers! Two dozen real red roses with lovely green ferny stuff all around them. I must have still been feeling raw after the terrible fight with Mick because those roses really got to me. All the other women in the ward had flowers, and although I'd tried not to mind, every time I came back from the showers or the toilet it would sort of hit me that mine was the only side-table that was bare, with no flowers. Chas slumped down into a chair.

'Where's Mick?'

I shrugged to say I didn't know. The thought of having to explain what went on the day before made me feel queasy. But Chas didn't notice.

'Did ya know Buster found Mick's old man?' he asked cheerily.

'Where?' The information chilled me for some reason.

'He's been hiding out since the girl died in some make-shift dive down by the river a few miles out of Wilcannia. No wonder we couldn't pick up on where he was. He'll be easy enough to find now though.'

'Does Mick know?'

'Yeah. Suppose. Buster didn't say actually ...' Chas turned to the smiling nurse, and handed her the flowers.

'Thanks, love. Better get these in water ...'

'Is he working?'

'Nah. Buster said his last job was in Jerilderie. Getting a bit old for it he reckons. Apparently the poor old coot has been hitting the grog pretty bad.'

'I hope Mick doesn't find him.'

Chas gave me a sharp look.

'Why not?'

I shrugged and he kept looking, a little suspiciously.

'What's with you, Squirt? You and Mick had another fight or something?'

I looked away. I didn't want to have to think about Mick going looking for his father. In truth I just wanted to start howling all over again. I couldn't believe anyone could be as dumb as I'd been. Anyway I managed to contain it.

'Hey? Come on, Squirt. Out with it.'

'He wants me to keep the kid. But listen, Chas, I'm doing the very best for my kid. I know that ...'

Chas chuckled and patted my hand as a way of saying he understood.

'So let me guess, you flew right off the handle, eh?' I nodded and he started laughing.

'It's not funny, Chas. He's pissed off on me now. And I actually told him to.'

Chas made a dismissive noise in his throat and continued to caress the hand he was holding.

'He won't go very far.'

'But you don't know what I said to him!'

Chas yawned and stretched.

'Everyone says things they don't mean when they're in a tight spot.'

I smiled a bit as I looked at this funny old leathery face sitting near me. Hoping that he was right. Praying that he'd picked up a thing or two in his fifty-odd years.

'You're doing your best, love. Mick knows that too.'

I sighed and tried to change the subject.

'Done any more on the house, Chas?'

He winked at me broadly.

'Nah. I've been out bush. I need you in there, love. You and Mick. You going to come and stay for a while when you get out of here?'

'Yeah, I reckon . . . I will anyway.'

Chas laughed cheerily as though he thought all my worries were groundless.

'Good on ya.'

Bek and Buster suddenly walked in and the mood became livelier.

'Buster . . . Bek! G'day.'

'Hey, where's Paddy?' Chas wanted to know.

'We left him with Mum,' Bek replied, smiling as she walked over to the bed and gave me a kiss on the cheek then handed over this nicely done-up present. Two in one day! After a six-day drought. I felt really high as I began to undo the ribbon. That was another thing I'd been unable to stop myself thinking as I lay awake at night in hospital. *I wish someone from home knew I was here. Maybe they'd send me a card. My mother would bring in a little present for the baby for sure. Dad was good with his hands. He could make a cradle for her. And Darren would be so good at playing with it.* Crazy stuff that made me think that my brain had turned to sludge.

'You shouldn't have,' I said jokingly. 'But I'm glad you did.'

Although they'd sent a card it was their first time to see me since I'd had the baby. And I thought perhaps they were angry for some reason. Or had given up on me.

Inside was a really nice little blue powder and soap set-up. One of those cute little things I'd never use in a pink fit, but so what.

'Hey, thanks! My favourite colour.'

Bek grinned and sat on the bed.

'We didn't come before because we wanted ... well, we reckoned you might want to be on your own,' she said softly. 'Mick told us about your decision to adopt the baby out.' I smiled as I shook a bit of the powder on to my hand to smell it, feeling the anxiety peel away like dry skin. So that was the only reason they hadn't come. And they were probably right. It was hard enough talking to Mick about all this crap. With other people around it would have been impossible. Then I saw that Buster didn't have anywhere to sit.

'You want to sit on that side, Buster.'

'Nah, I'm right.'

He was looking around the ward edgily. Probably feeling self-conscious. Their black skins looked beautiful and rich against all that hospital white, but now I could see that the other people in the ward were giving them sly little curious looks. Not hostile exactly. Just little suspicious once-overs. I was aware then how odd it was to have Aboriginal visitors here. Down in casualty you'd see groups waiting around to be seen. But you never saw them talking to whites. I mean it got to me. I caught Helen staring at them as she came back from the toilet. If it had been anyone else I would have told her to rack right off and mind her own business.

'How are ya, Chas?'

'I'm real good, Buster. How are you?'

I wished that the conversation would flow better. It was as though we didn't know each other. Chas, Buster, Bek and me. We'd got on easily before. It turned out that Bek knew Sharon from out on the station and that they – Sharon and her husband – were planning to come and see me soon. Something is missing though. *It needs Mick here. Where is he?*

282

I was conscious of the big question hanging over me and the baby but I didn't know how much Mick had discussed it with them. It wasn't as though they were judging me or anything. At least now I felt that everyone accepted my position. Funny how you sometimes just sense that kind of thing. Chas must have felt the same funny mixture of vibes because he suddenly stood up and picked up the bag at his feet, eyes twinkling.

'Hey, I was forgetting. I brought in a few little refreshments to celebrate with. Can't we go into one of those little rooms down there, Squirt, with chairs and a table? On the way in I asked the nurse and she said it was for visitors' use.'

'Yeah. Good idea. Where is it?'

'There's a few little rooms off the corridor outside.'

'Okay. Let's go.'

I climbed slowly out of bed and was surprised at how normal I felt, compared to the last couple of days anyway. There was hardly any pain at all when I walked and my breasts were back to normal, more or less.

We settled ourselves into the vinyl chairs in the boxy little room that overlooked the hospital carpark and shut the door. Chas plonked his bag on the small coffee table in the middle of the room and started hauling everything out. Paper cups, plates, bottle of beer and one of sparkling wine, packets of dry biscuits, ham, olives and cheeses. I felt starving suddenly, ready to eat a horse. Chas popped open the bottle of wine and poured some into the cups. We all started to laugh a bit as we crashed our cups together, slopping a bit of the fizzy on the table.

'Cheers, eh!'

'Yeah. All the best.'

'So what're you doing now, Buster?'

A few sips of wine and I sat back, listening to the talk around me. The others had sparked up. Somehow, being on our own like this with food and drink to concentrate on, made us all relax. This was more like it, I found myself thinking. A sense of well-being began to settle in.

Sorry, Mick. Can we start again? Remember, we were gonna head up to Lightning Ridge? Mt Isa maybe ... Pouring myself another half cup, I got up and walked over to the window to look out. Small coloured cars, parked like match-box toys, shone in the shimmering heat directly below. But further up, away past the flat town with its steel poles and multi-coloured roofs, the sky was faultless, a deep never-ending blue. Not a cloud to be seen. Same as Mick's eyes, I found myself thinking. Same as Mick's eyes on a good day. *Look at me, Veronica. See how well I'm doing. It's me. Your favourite. The one you loved. Little Michelle. I've had the kid. Gave it life just the way you wanted. I've got a great bloke. Not here but he'll be back. He's gotta come back so I can tell him it's on again. And see here ... even friends. They've all come to see me in hospital.*

Staring out into that blue then I reckon I understood what Mick was on about when he said he loved this country. I was in a silver city, plonked down on red dirt, under the never-ending blue. It would do me, no worries.

There was a tap on the door. I heard it but I didn't even turn around, I was too busy thinking. The others were talking loudly about how much rain had fallen the week before. The fall had reached many of the surrounding stations and the green tinge of grass was already visible. Still everyone was hoping for a few more points to settle the grass in. It was comforting background noise for someone as spaced out as I was at that moment. Anyway I figured if they didn't get up to answer it then perhaps I'd imagined it.

There was another tap, this time firmer. The conversation around me died. I was still looking at the sky when I heard Chas call out, 'Come in.'

A young nurse entered, smiling sweetly.

'Michelle Brown?'

284

I turned around and recognised one of the nurses who'd been working in the ward most afternoons that week.

'Yeah?'

'There's someone here to see you.'

I didn't get a chance to say 'okay' or 'who is it' or 'I'll be right out' or to even comb my hair. It did flash through my head that I couldn't think of anyone who would know I was here, *who wasn't here already*, except Mick but then he wouldn't be announcing himself like this either. Must be Sharon and ... but I didn't really get time to finish off that thought. In walked my mother. And, as if that wasn't enough, behind her, Kevin. I suppose my mouth must have fallen open because everyone in the room stopped what they were doing, looking first at me and then at them. Back and forth, they reminded me of the crowds at tennis matches you see on television.

'Hello, Michelle,' she said, her voice stringier and drier than I remembered it ever being before. Her eyes only met mine for a second before she started looking around nervously. What could I say? I was completely stunned. Both of them looked ... so much the same. Just as I remembered them, but different too. *Smaller, somehow.* They stood just in from the doorway. I wished that someone would just get up and push them out and then lock the door so they wouldn't be able to ever get in again. And that someone else would tell me that I was having a bad dream. That I hadn't seen them at all. *But hadn't I known they would find me when I rang Kevin? Could I have been waiting for this all along?*

'Hello, Mum ... Kevin,' I mumbled guardedly, hoping like hell that I didn't sound as nervous as they looked. I sat down on a chair and looked at my feet. To everyone's relief, Chas suddenly stood up and moved chairs towards them in a friendly way.

'Come on in. Here ... why don't you sit down? I'm Charlie Morris.'

Mum gave him an icy smile and perched herself suspiciously on the edge of a chair. Kevin waved Chas's offer away, indicating that he prefered to stand behind my mother. He folded his arms and, *looked exactly like a guard.* Pompous and stupid. I caught his eye and was amazed to see him look away sharply then colour up. I shuddered, remembering that I'd said I would marry him. *Imagine waking up and asking what he felt like for breakfast.* He was dressed in really daggy-looking light blue shorts and a short-sleeved light cotton shirt. And his skin looked pasty.

How come I used to think he had olive skin? And that his hair was a nice colour? That night in the front of his car, with our breath fogging up the windows. The way I'd tried to avoid his sloppy wet tongue in my mouth without seeming to, 'cause I hadn't wanted to hurt his feelings. I remembered thinking, I don't even like the smell of him.

'Well, Michelle . . . who are these . . . people?' my mother asked accusingly, the too-bright smile flittering around, first on Chas, then Bek and Buster. On everyone but me. She was trying to sound jocular and I knew *that* was usually a prelude to either tears or a heavy lecture. I shrugged. Why the hell should I introduce anyone to her? No one had asked her to come here. But before I had to think about it, Chas was doing the honours.

'This here is Bek and young Buster over there.'

They both inclined their heads seriously, wanting to be polite. She nodded back coldly at Chas and simply stared in stiff surprise at the other two, as though she'd only just seen that they were black.

'What are you doing here?' she said sharply. Just like that! As though *they* had to explain themselves.

'They're my friends, Mum,' I snarled.

'Friends?' The way she said it. The word dug in, like a tiny single tick, burrowing under my skin, getting at me. Getting into places I couldn't reach to scratch or claw. She thought I was lying. She didn't believe I had friends.

'You weren't much for friends at home, Michelle,' she snapped, still not looking at me. Then explaining to Chas confidingly, 'she's always been a loner. . .'

'And you're Michelle's mother are you . . .?' Chas queried, studiedly casual, cutting in, easy and light. For some reason, gratitude surged through me because he'd remembered my name and hadn't called me Squirt.

'Yes, that's right,' she sniffed. 'Mrs Brown. And this is her, well . . . er, her ex-fiance Kevin.'

Kevin nodded tersely to everyone present, then looked out the window.

I could see her hand shaking as it tugged the strap of her white bag. Her best bag. My mother had on a light-pink flowery dress that I remembered her making the summer before. I'd gone down the street grudgingly to buy her the reel of pink cotton. She'd cut off a snippet of material so I'd been able to get exactly the right tone. When I came back with it she'd smiled and said, 'Oh, good for you. That's exactly right.' She loved making clothes. Had wanted to make me all sorts of things but I never let her. I wasn't that kind of girl. Not that kind of daughter. I didn't like cotton prints, or summer shifts, or even shorts. I didn't like pretty blouses or jumpsuits or evening dresses. I liked wearing my brothers' old shirts with cut off jeans and stuff from the disposal store. I liked my hair tied back from my face with a pink leather bootstrap.

When she'd made that dress she'd come out to the kitchen wearing it on the pretext of looking for something. But I knew she was really wanting us to notice. Showing it off. Darren had noticed and whistled. She'd tried not to smile but had turned around a few times in the middle of the floor, letting us see her handiwork as we did our homework. 'I think it's the best thing I've done in a while.' That's what she'd said. The boys had murmured their approval and I'd said nothing. Just scowled at her and wished I was game enough to tell her she looked ridiculous. The print was too large for someone her age and the flouncy sleeves were old fashioned.

She'd dressed up for this visit. I could see it now. Her hair had been freshly set, the curls stiff as concrete around her face. I wouldn't be surprised if she'd had it done in Broken Hill that morning before heading over here to the hospital. Just the thought of her doing that sent a wave of sadness pulsating right through every part of me. Thinking of her under the dryer, reading the magazines . . . *thinking about me.*

Mum's hands were still sliding up and down the handle of her white handbag. Her lipstick was bleeding into the cracks around her pursed-up mouth, and her eyes looked sort of watery and old. I was shocked at how sorry I was to see her, *how sorry I felt for her*, even as the anger shot up and bubbled frantically inside me. She looked so out of place, so small in a way, compared to how I remembered her. *She's just a little woman.*

An uneasy silence slowly descended like heat into the almost chilly air-conditioned room. No one knew where to look. A couple of times I nearly blurted out something just to break it up a bit, but stopped myself in time. She was the first to speak, her voice wavering, unconvincing.

'You've done a dreadful thing, Michelle. We want to take you home now. For your own good.'

I looked up at her, crazy disappointment overwhelming me.

She'd come all this way . . . just to be the same.

Her hands were now tugging at the clasp on the bag, as though she was trying to break it open.

'Leaving, like that . . .' she whispered plaintively. 'Your father has aged so much.'

'Where is he?' I managed coldly.

'At home,' she snapped back. 'Where do you think! Earning his living.' She then looked around at the others and gave a little snort of contempt, as though she knew things about them that they didn't know themselves.

They looked back at her, all of them, blinking mildly at the shards of hostility that she'd thrown out in their direction. None of them understood the first thing about her. I could see that. Funny thing was I was starting to wonder if I did either. I could tell that even old Chas was out of his depth. He had this look on his face as though he was out in the middle of the playing field, quite prepared to enjoy himself, but unable to follow the rules.

'We've seen the baby ...' A loud sob escaped from the tight mouth but she very quickly pulled herself together, blinking back the tears furiously.

'Oh, yeah?' My voice grated along as though I was eating gravel. Very deliberate. I wouldn't have any part of her snivelling high-jinks. *It was the way I often treated her. Like someone to be ignored, fobbed off, not taken seriously.* Actually, I wanted to treat her very seriously. I wanted to throw the glass I was holding straight in her face and scream. What right do you have to come sneaking in here looking at *my* baby?

Chas suddenly, very deliberately, leant forward and took one of my shaking hands into his own. The warmth of his touch steadied me. Suddenly I really wasn't alone any more.

I looked at Kevin properly for the first time. But it was ages before he'd meet my eye.

'What did you come up here *for*?' I said, genuinely wanting to know. The very idea of them travelling up that enormous distance *together* suddenly seemed hard to fathom. Quite unbelievable.

'When your mother said you'd had the baby I thought I'd like to see who was going to ... adopt it.' He was going to continue but my mother interrupted. She'd always found it very hard to let anyone have the floor when she was keyed up.

'We've spoken to the couple on the phone ...' she broke in, gushing, as sweet as pie, looking at Chas for support.

'And they're *very* nice. They're very anxious to meet you, Michelle. Such nice people. I ... I wanted to see my grandchild ... and to make sure she was going to nice people. They're very nice people aren't they, Kev?' I was astonished to see real tears flowing down her face. Fumbling, she managed to get tissues out of her bag, and looking up at him like a little kid, sort of implored him to agree. *I've never seen my mother crying like this before. What does it mean?*

'Yeah, they seem all right. Really good ...' he said gruffly and put one hand on her shoulder. She gasped a little at his touch and then laid her hand on top of his briefly. This was like someone had died. I couldn't believe it. *Where does this leave me?*

'I don't know how you could bear to give away your own baby to someone you haven't even met,' she hissed sharply, somehow right back in control again in spite of the tears. 'You should meet them. All the nurses we spoke to said they *always* advised people ... like you, to meet the ones who'll take your baby.'

She was rattling on now. I remembered. She'd sulk for hours and sniff and pout and then when she'd decided to talk, you couldn't shut her up. I looked at Kevin.

'How did she know I'd had it?' I was still in a state of shock just to be in the same room as them.

'We rang the hospital. There was no problem.'

My mother had turned around to Chas now, directing it all at him.

'The lady said ... they're going to send us photos every year and if we're ever up around these parts, she's invited us to drop in and see her. She did say that they'd even think about me ... well, Dad and me, being proper grandparents. Both theirs have gone, you know. It would be so lovely being able to send her something at Christmas and ... her birthday, from Nana and Pa ...'

She stopped, overcome with emotion, tugging at tissues and the strap of her handbag.

Nana and Pa? *Oh God!* I looked around at everyone in that room and I felt *very weird* to say the least. Nana and

Pa! My mother was a grandmother. Shit. I was a mother. I was sitting there in the middle of them feeling cool. As cool and free suddenly, as a fish in the great bloody green sea. I looked around at them all. Chas with his leathery old face, the bottle of grog and the red roses alongside him, upright in their vase. Who had brought them in here? I couldn't remember asking anyone. And Buster and Bek who had hardly moved since my mother's arrival, much less said anything. Very weird. I longed for Mick to arrive in the middle of all this, in his dusty boots and grimy jeans, to just sit down in the middle of it all and ... The moment went on forever. Finally I broke it. I can honestly say that I had no warning of what was going to come out of my mouth.

'Well, I'm not meeting them,' I said, rather matter-of-factly I think. Sort of quiet and determined. Like I imagined a really nice headmistress would be to naughty children. Very kind but firm. *This is the way things are going to be from now on.*

'Because they're not having her. I've changed my mind. I'm keeping her.'

The room came alive suddenly. It was as though the walls were gasping but there was no sound. The air got thinner somehow too, like in that asthma attack, but I didn't panic, in fact I found I was breathing quite normally. A spurt of joy hit me suddenly. I had a longing to run right out of that room, down to the nursery and pick up my daughter. *My daughter.* I wanted to hold her, feed her, tell her I was sorry that it had taken me so long. I looked at Chas but he was sitting bent over, his two hands clasped together as though he was praying, staring forward out the window. He wouldn't look at me. I guess he thought it was my moment and I had to deal with it in my own way.

Bek and Buster swung around, staring at me in surprise. Delight too, I suppose, although they didn't actually say anything. Old Chas suddenly went into anxiety mode, shifting around in his chair and fiddling with his glass of beer. He didn't look unhappy, just bamboozled. He kept flashing sneaky looks at my mother and Kev from under his old, hooded toad eyes, a bit anxious, as though he was half-expecting someone to attack him any minute. My mother's face went very white. She and Kevin were both holding still, staring at me. Kevin's mouth had swung open, he looked incredibly dumb and *bland*.

'You can't do *that*, my girl,' he finally whispered hoarsely. 'You can't do that to those people, or to me.'

That really irritated me, him calling me *my girl*, but I didn't pick him up on it.

'Yes, I can.'

'You can't.'

'I can ... and I'm going to.'

Kevin stepped towards me menacingly. He stopped before he got too near though. Chas was giving off this kind of warning hum under his breath.

'It's my baby too. And I won't let you.'

'You can't stop me.'

'That would be a terrible thing to do to them ...'

'I know,' I said coldly. 'Terrible. As terrible as what I've been living through ...'

He sighed, deeply angry. I knew that because I'd seen him like it before. He was not used to being seriously crossed. The spoilt country football star was out of his depth. He suddenly pointed crudely at Chas with one slim arrogant finger.

'Don't get too smart with me, old boy! I ... we know all about you. You're a crim and that other ... lout she's picked up with is one too.'

Chas looked up with a start. He seemed taken aback by the words but not upset.

'Is that so?' he said simply.

'Yeah. It is.'

I thought Chas showed amazing restraint. He just kept

292

on sitting there in his chair. He was a gnarly old bugger. I reckon he would have been able to give Kevin a run for his money if he'd wanted to throw a punch.

I wondered where and how they would have found out about Mick's criminal record. The nurses might have found out and told them, but more likely Kevin, being who he was, would have rung up that mate of his in the police force. Yeah, all that kind of stuff would be on computer for anyone to find out. That's what would have happened.

I smiled at Chas again and he met my eyes this time. One bony hand simply grabbed my hand.

'You can't do that, Michelle,' Kevin burst out again. 'Those people have been told . . . and I don't want my kid living with a criminal.'

'I can do what I like,' I said simply. 'They know nothing is final until the baby is a month old. Unless you want her . . .'

'I *know* that I couldn't look after her! Like you *knew* the same thing about yourself, Michelle. Before now!'

It was easy to look straight back into his face. He didn't scare me. I didn't even hate him. Honestly, just looking at him, I felt bored. Besides I'd been well and truly informed about my rights by the social worker. Short of kidnapping her there was nothing they could do.

'I know that I *can* now. And I want to,' I said softly, staring at my pudgy little hand lying inside Chas's huge, dry one.

'So you decide on the spur of the moment, eh?' Kevin sneered really nastily. 'Like running away?'

'Exactly like running away,' I admitted blithely, enjoying the moment of surprise on his face as he registered my reply. 'Running away was the best decision I ever made.'

I don't know how long we would have sat there bickering, throwing insults at each other and getting nowhere. In her own crazy way my mother did us all a service by putting a stop to it all abruptly. She simply stood up slowly and then screamed, suddenly, very loudly and for a long time. All of us in the room jerked out of our chairs as rigid as broomsticks, staring at her. Probably with our mouths open. A middle-aged woman, standing there like a tin soldier, in her homemade flowery dress, her helmet of stiff blonde hair, her feet standing to attention in the sensible white slip-on sandals. She held her bag out a few inches in front of her with two hands, like a hand grenade she was about to throw any minute, and went right on screaming. The windows rattled, the whole room filled with the piercing, desperate noise. In a way it felt like we were all in church, listening. It was as solemn as a hymn.

Eventually the nurses came running – about half a dozen of them flooding into the little room with shocked harried faces, calling for calm, coaxing her out, offering cups of tea, doctors and sedatives for everyone.

She stopped as abruptly as she'd begun and allowed herself to be led away by one nurse. I tried to swallow, but my throat had swollen up and was very dry. I watched her slowly retreating back with the wild pink daisies dancing all over it. Was the print so bad after all? The colour certainly suited her eyes and ... Although she was quiet now her screams were still ricocheting around the room, bouncing off one wall and into another. We sat saying nothing, in shock I guess. I was overcome with a kind of crazy pride. It was the most sensible, daring and courageous thing I'd ever known my mother to do.

In the doorway she stopped and turned around to me. Her face was old after all that. Old and plain and worn out. The skin around her eyes and mouth was sagging into folds I'd never noticed before.

'I'm sorry, Michelle,' she whispered, as though she didn't care about anything much any more.

I suppose I could have got up then. Gone over and touched her. Let her know that what she'd done was all right with me. *You're all right with me, Mum. For better or worse I'm your daughter. You're all right.* I don't know. It's easy to regret things later and hard to know what's right at the time. I suppose there was still too much there between us. Besides we'd never been a touchy family even when we did get on. Anyway I did look at her and I think she probably saw the tears in my eyes.

'I'm sorry too, Mum,' I said, as carefully as I was able.

She nodded and disappeared.

23

Mick was heading down to get a drink from the river when he heard the sound of someone moving along the bank in the grass above him. He looked up but didn't take much notice. It was a fairly secluded spot but occasionally people could be heard walking by, tramping on the dead leaves and sticks – very occasionally the babble of voices if there was more than one. This sound was more like someone settling down somewhere on the bank; perhaps to sit and rest for a while and watch the river. But no one appeared and so he lost interest.

Only half an hour earlier he thought he heard Chas's ute, and found himself thinking with a smile that no one could mistake the particular sound of that engine, the low grind of gears and pop-pop of the damaged exhaust. Old Chas, his good friend, had come out looking for him perhaps. No problem at all with that except that there wouldn't be much to find. When it all boiled down there didn't seem to be anything much left of him at all.

There was only the wind and an occasional moan or sickly snore from the old man who was lying – half-dead it looked like – on his back outside the run-down shack near the water's edge. The silly old bugger had pissed himself – there was a long patch of wet down one leg of his thick shiny trousers, almost reaching the untied boot. Judging by the stink when he'd been up close, he'd probably dirtied himself as well. Mick wished he could erase the stench from his memory. It was awful, heavy and sickening like the dead stuff he'd smelt in the ocean when he'd gone out fishing as a kid. Except this was worse. This was his father.

From where he was standing by the water Mick looked back every now and again at the grey stubbled face where it lay, half turned towards the water as though waiting for something, perhaps expecting to be pushed in or floated away. Some kind of final end at last. The long flared nose and deep crevices running from the forehead down to the flabby chin, the bloodied mouth, showing the yellow cracked teeth, labouring through each breath. Every time he looked, he noted in wonder that the bones around the shut bruised eyelids were just as he remembered them.

Mick stood staring out across the river and wondered if his father was dying. Now that he had finally found him he realised that it didn't really matter much, either way.

Back to square one he kept thinking. Back to square one. Grief about Beth had submerged into a wilder, more intense sorrow about Michelle and the baby. What had he expected to find at her grave? Why had he thought it was important to know how she'd died? None of that curiosity was left. Where do people go when they lose everything? On his way here he'd had a vague but sure feeling he was coming to the right place, but not any more. After the first few hours the sense of destiny had left him. It had seeped away quietly, like water from a rusty tin with holes, leaving him empty. The years of waiting, of talk and build-up, ended up here on a river-bank, and it all amounted to absolutely nothing.

Place. Now that was something worth thinking about. Was this the right place for him to be at this time of his life; sitting outside a filthy old shack on the edge of a river with his father lying, maybe dying, only metres away from him. Always, from the time he was a little kid he'd wanted to be in the right place. Mostly that had meant home. Especially when he'd been sent away, he'd wanted to be home. Jail had definitely been the wrong place – three years in the wrong place. Then again that station had felt like the right kind of place, same with the shearing shed and Chas's little house, before ... things changed. Things changed without any warning. If only he'd had some kind of warning. How could he have known that the man who'd busted up his childhood, who'd evaded him all his life, wouldn't even recognise him now? How could he have possibly known he'd fall for a friggin' *baby*? It was too crazy to even think about.

The noise again. Someone was moving directly above him. He tried to see but because he was looking straight into the sun he only saw shafts of white light, then bits of red. Was it someone's shirt? Then his name was being called.

'Mick! Are you there? Mick.'

He didn't answer immediately because he didn't believe that he'd heard it. Her voice kept coming at him in this sing-song dreamy way that made him think he'd really gone mad, a voice that was echoing into and around itself.

'Mick! Mick. It's me. Michelle. Can I come down?'

Still he didn't answer. Still couldn't see anything. But he heard the scraping puffing sounds of someone scrambling through bush. Suddenly she was there, in front of him, standing maybe three metres away, wearing a red shirt he hadn't seen before, looking very different without her belly.

'Shit, Mick. Where have you been ... I ... we ...?'

Her voice faded away as she saw the figure of his father.

'Oh, Jesus! What have you done to him?'

'Nothing,' he said quietly. 'He's paralytic. Doesn't even know I'm here.'

Her eyes slowly shifted away from the prone body and came to rest on Mick. Very slowly, tentatively, she took both his hands in her own and looked into his face. Mick wanted to smile, ask questions, draw her to him but he couldn't even move much less talk. Both his hands stayed helpless like dead things inside hers.

'You were right. She's mine. I'm keeping the kid,' Michelle said softly.

He nodded, making some kind of strangled gurgle in his throat. Michelle's small peaked face broke into a cheeky grin.

'I'll make a bloody good mother, you know!'

She saw his eyes were blank with surprise.

'You pleased or ...'

He nodded again.

'That prison chaplain that you know. He's come up to stay with Chas for a while. Wants to see you ... reckons he's got some good news possibly about a job in Darwin.' She smiled.

'Maybe we'll have to forget about Lightning Ridge for a while ...'

Mick gulped and shrugged as though he didn't care. He stopped for a last long look at the old man lying by the river before allowing Michelle to lead him up the bank and back to the ute where Chas was waiting.

It took Mick ages to understand. She supposed he was in a kind of deep shock. When they reached the ute Chas wasn't there so they both sat down to wait. He sat down on a nearby log and she stood behind him, holding his back between her knees and rubbing his shoulders.

'Michelle, I thought it was finished,' he kept saying. 'I thought we were finished. I never expected ...'

She continued rubbing and could feel him unlocking, de-freezing under her touch and voice. After a while she began to laugh, in the low mad chuckling way he loved and he turned around and grabbed her around the legs and kissed both knees and hands.

'Don't ya want to come back and see her?' He'd doubted he'd ever heard anyone sound so happy.

'Where is she?

'In the hospital. I've started learning everything about feeding and ... everything. They promised to look after her while I . . . we set out after you.'

He stood up to face her then. More or less the old Mick. The bright blue warmth back in his eyes.

'I've never had anyone come after me before, Shell,' he said simply.

She grinned and pointed to Chas who was now slowly walking towards them, a few hundred yards up the river, hands in his pockets and whistling.

'There's a first time for everything, ya dag!'

24

Mick and Michelle set off for Darwin on the bike at about quarter to five in the morning, two weeks after the day they'd originally planned to head over to Lightning Ridge to dig for opals.

The prison chaplain, Brian, had called in to see Chas, detouring on his way home from visiting his sister in Sydney. One of his brothers in Darwin was manager in charge of building a new entertainment complex there, overlooking the water and costing millions of dollars. They would be hiring a lot of men over the next few weeks. Did Mick want to think about heading up there for a job? Mick's eyes lit up. A year's work on good pay was just what they needed. Even Chas, the great optimist, was unsure of when things were going to even out. The last bit of rain had helped things but there were all the other factors: markets, prices that no one was sure about. Everyone was saying it was a matter of things getting worse before they got better.

Elizabeth, now over two months old, and already smiling and playing with her hands when awake, didn't even stir when Michelle lifted her from the makeshift cradle that Chas had made out of a wooden gun crate and popped her into the closed sidecar that Mick had bought and cleaned up the week before, along with the rest of their things. A bag of clothes for each of them at the baby's head and feet, food supplies tucked in here and there, and as much of the infant paraphernalia as they could fit anywhere. Bottles and jumpsuits, wash cloths and nappies. Under the mattress lay the seven frilly hand-made baby dresses that Michelle's mother had sent, just about one a week for the last seven weeks since leaving the hospital. They were all too big, as yet, and too, well … *ornate* to be actually useful, at least as far as Michelle was concerned. But beautiful. Each one of them was beautiful and different, smocked and stitched and gathered in fine materials. Lawn and Viyella, polished cotton and fine wool. Baby tartan and delicate flower-prints, appliques, lace and ribbon. Michelle couldn't begin to think about how long it would have taken her mother to make each one. She fitted the coverlet snugly over the baby, packed in a few other bits and pieces, and allowed herself a wry smile as she put on her helmet and looked around. The engine was already turning over but Mick was going over some last-minute information with Chas inside the house, their muffled voices the only sounds in that, clear morning air, apart from the bike. Well, she'd been wrong before. Maybe Elizabeth would love those frills as she got older. Maybe she'd grow up loathing the way her own mother looked in the faded trousers and men's work shirts. Maybe Elizabeth and her grandmother would join forces to try to get Michelle to change style, become more like other mothers. Michelle laughed aloud just thinking about the odd twists and turns life could take.

Mick and Chas came through the back door, ambling slowly towards her, still talking. She turned from them and took a moment to watch, maybe for the last time, the burnt gold of the sunrise, creeping steadily over Chas's rambling backyard, making the washing line, really only a limp piece of wire tied between two wooden posts, sparkle suddenly into something heavy and precious. It hung there haphazardly, firing with gold where the sun hit it, as though it was some exotic animal harness in a royal garden. Later would be just another hot day, with the high sun burning its dry relentless heat, but now, at this time in the morning, with the dew still shining on the grass and the quivering pattern of golden light filtering through the leaves of the peppermint-gum on to the side of the half-fallen-away back shed, the place was rich and sweet with perfection.

Michelle felt something rush up from her feet and burst apart inside her chest as she hugged Chas one last time. The suddenness of it caught her by surprise. She wondered for the hundredth time if they were mad to be leaving.

'Don't forget to come up and see us, eh?' she said loudly into the rough twill of his shirt. One thick hand held the back of her head tightly for a few seconds then pushed her away.

'I will, Squirt. I will.'

He meant it but she turned abruptly and fitted herself behind Mick. Chas had also said, the week before, that the distance would probably be too much for him – not to mention the ute – and that the new job he had going out the west of the state would tie him up for at least another six months. Last night he'd told them that his heart wasn't as good as it should be and that he wasn't planning on doing anything about it either. They'd both laughed. Now it didn't seem so funny.

'And listen, Squirt ... both of you, look after that little one, eh?'

They smiled and nodded. All three of them looked down and watched the baby open one sleepy eye in surprise as the bike moved a few inches, then close it again in absolute confidence that everything was in order in her world.

'Well, we're off, mate.'

'Yeah. Get as many miles under your belt before the heat.'

'Thanks for everything, Chas.'

'No worries, mate. Good luck with the job.'

'Thanks.'

'We'll write.'

'Sure. Me too.'

Chas bent over suddenly and touched the baby's head in

a final gesture, his old gnarled face loose somehow, suffused with a succession of fleeting expressions that Michelle found hard to pinpoint but found unbearably moving. Was it happiness that made his mouth twist like that, or was it a sense of loss or regret that made his eyes shine so deeply?

They took off, with a flamboyant yell from Mick. Michelle watched Chas step back on to the verandah. She knew that there was love in the tilt of that old head as he saw them away, and the angle of the wave too. For sure. Chas had loved Elizabeth over those last few weeks, as unequivocally as if she'd been his own grandchild. As the old face finally faded from view, Michelle leant into Mick's back and grinned to herself. There would be no way that Chas could resist seeing Elizabeth again. He was an inquisitive old codger. He'd want to see that Elizabeth was doing all right. She'd bet on that. He'd be up to see them within the year.

The Norton, newly serviced and upgraded for the long trip ahead, roared through the the early morning stillness of the sleeping town. Michelle took her right arm away from where it had been clinging around Mick's waist and made a mad little sign of the cross, over her heart. 'For the future,' she said aloud. Mick hadn't heard her, so she yelled it again.

'For the future.'

'What you say, Shell?' He half turned as they slowed down to approach the intersection that would take them on to the main highway.

'Nothing. Just crossing my heart for the future,' she yelled above the pulsating roar of the bike. 'Veronica used to say to make the sign of the cross any time I was unsure or scared . . .'

She saw him nod, but because of the helmet, couldn't see the expression on his face. Was that a grin or was he taking her cross seriously? The bike throbbed, stationary for a few moments as Mick checked first left and then right before slowly turning on to the highway that would take them north. There wasn't another vehicle in sight, only the

304

golden morning, pristine and silent, fading away slowly in front of them. They both relaxed and settled in for the long ride.

MORE TEENAGE FICTION FROM PENGUIN

☆☆☆☆☆☆☆☆☆☆☆☆☆☆☆☆☆☆☆☆☆☆☆☆☆☆☆☆☆☆☆

Ganglands   Maureen McCarthy

The dramatic story of the summer when Kelly leaves school – when she will be faced with the toughest decisions of her life. Set in the cultural melting-pot of inner-city Melbourne, from the author of the *In Between* series.

The In Between TV Tie-in Series   Maureen McCarthy

Four novels which look at the interconnected lives of four teenagers growing up in tough, multicultural Australia.

Alex

Alex is eighteen, streetwise and unemployed – and in love with Angie.

Angie

Angie's tough – or so she likes to think. But being pregnant is not something she or Alex bargained for.

Fatima

Fatima wants to live her own life. Her Turkish father has other ideas.

Saret

Saret's Cambodia no longer exists – his new friends are all he's got when he's on the run.